Slay Ride

Lauren Biel

Library of Congress Cataloging-in-Publication Data

Slay Ride/Lauren Biel 1st ed.

Cover Design: Qamber Designs

Editing: Sugar Free Editing

Interior Design: Sugar Free Editing

For more information on this book and the author, visit: www. LaurenBiel.com

Please visit LaurenBiel.com for a full list of content warnings.

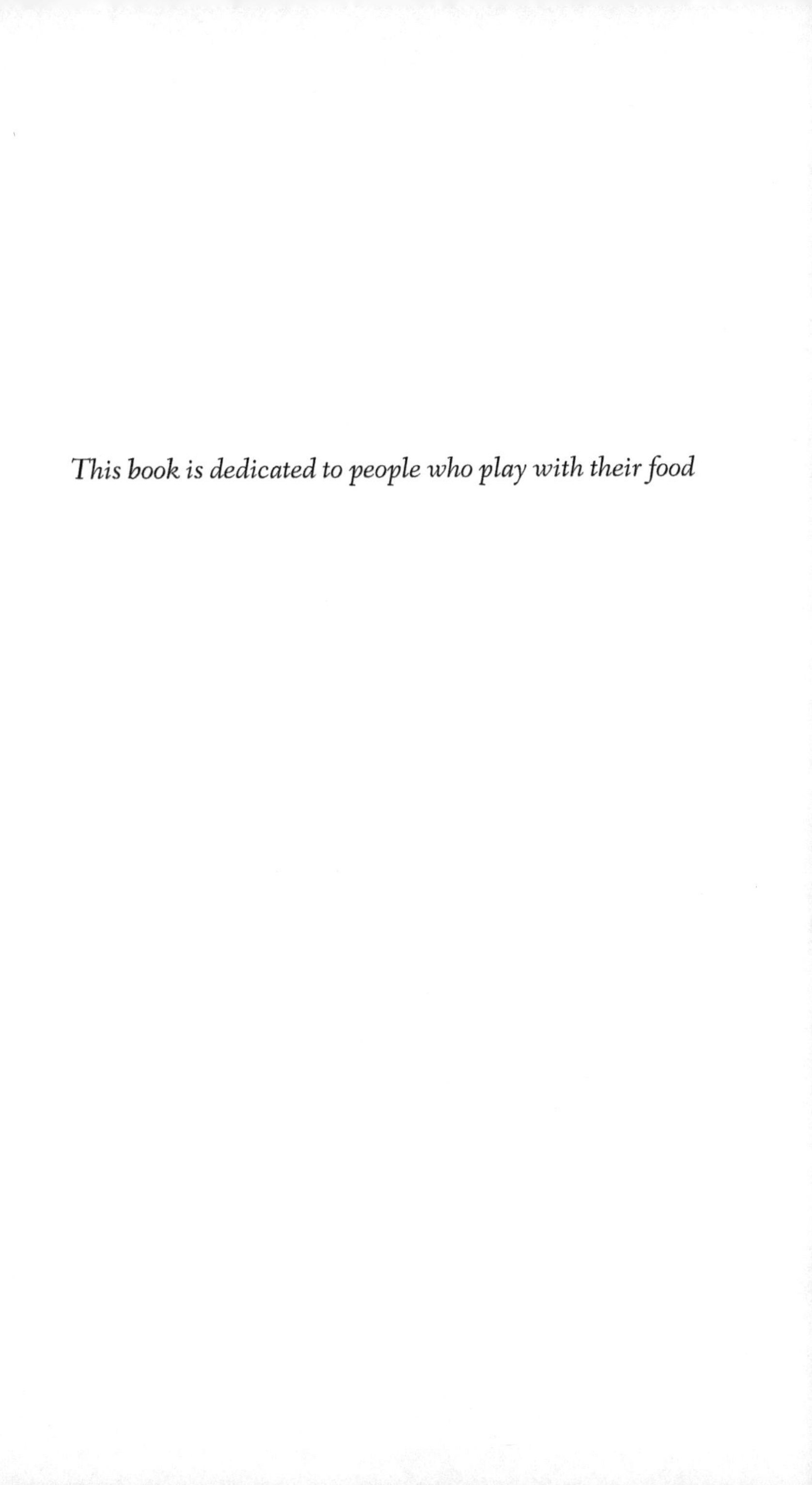

This book is dedicated to people who play with their food

Chapter One

Cat

Snow rushes past the living room window that overlooks the backyard. I don't want to see snow right now, though. It's a reminder that I'll probably miss the winter retreat next week, which means I'll also miss another chance to get my first kill.

I rip the curtains closed, and the silver hooks squeal across the black metal rod. Kindra looks at me with dark, narrowed eyes that relax when she sees the cup of coffee in my hand. I hand it to her, and she drags her judgmental gaze back to her laptop screen.

"You aren't on the clock, Cat. You can chill for once," she says.

"I can't *chill*. I'm waiting for an important email."

Kindra turns to look at me, her black waves bouncing around her face. "The audition?"

"Not just any audition. It's for a supporting role in a local production of *Cats*. This could be my big chance, Kindra. I might finally break out."

Kindra licks her lips and closes the laptop. "Isn't that a musical? I didn't know you could sing."

"We'll find out if I can as soon as I get that email."

Kindra looks at me with a stony gaze that I've grown to love. "You don't know if you're good at singing? That's like jumping into the ocean when you aren't sure you know how to swim."

She has a point, but I'm not exactly tone deaf. I also have a dance background, so that should win some brownie points . . . as long as they don't fact-check and realize I took a class once when I was five, then never returned.

I begin to pace the living room. Nervous energy pulses through my body, and I need some way to relieve it. My heels tap on the worn hardwood floor with each step. Kindra hates incessant noise, so it's not a surprise when she spins around and bites my head off.

"Can you stop making that sound?"

"Walking?"

"Yes, walking. Go take off your shoes if you're going to tap dance all over your fucking house."

Her abrasive tone should damage my fragile feelings, and a few months ago, it might have. Now I know her, though. Her fuse is short, and she's a bit grumpy a lot of the time, but she's my best friend and I love her, regardless of her poor attitude.

Not everyone can pretend to be happy all the time.

Kindra takes a deep breath and sheds the coil of metal surrounding her persona. "I'm sorry. I didn't mean to snap at you. I'm struggling with an impossible story for work, plus the prep for the winter retreat, and I'm over it. Listen, it will all work out how it's supposed to."

"And if it doesn't?"

"We deal with it, Cat. Just like we deal with everything else."

I hate that she's right, but she is. The part is either mine or it's not, and pacing incessantly won't change the casting director's decision.

Maybe it's best if I'm not on that list. Rehearsal schedules might interfere with work, and I have bills to pay. Or maybe I'm just not cut out for acting. Like everything else in life, maybe this is just another thing Cat Novak can't do.

As I sit on the sagging couch, my phone buzzes. I nearly drop it as I maneuver it out of my pocket. An alert stares up at me. One new email.

And it's from the production team.

My thumb drops on the banner, and I'm taken to a lengthy email that details the practice schedule and call times for each cast member. I skim through the list, but I can't find my name. I wasn't even considered for the ensemble cast. Not even as an alternate.

"I didn't get it," I say, my voice unusually meek. I fight back burning tears. Kindra may be my best friend, but she's also my longtime idol, the Heartbreak Killer, and I hate crying in front of her.

"Oh, fuck. I'm so sorry." Kindra comes and sits beside me. She isn't the touchy-feely type, but she knows I am, so she wraps an awkward arm around my shoulder. "They don't know what they're missing out on. But hey, look on the bright side. Now you can come to the winter retreat!"

I appreciate Kindra trying to make me feel better, even though comforting others isn't her strong suit. Missing the retreat was the one downside to potentially being cast in the play, so at least I still have something to look forward to.

"Bennett for sure isn't coming, right?" I ask. If he

changed plans and wants to attend, I'll just stay home with my cat.

"He's still in Florida. Ezra talked to him yesterday, and he said he'd rather drink a cyanide cocktail than step foot in snow."

"I hope he forgets his helmet while he's riding around on his motorcycle."

"Cat! Bennett is obnoxious, but no one wants him to die."

She can speak for herself. "He fed me his fruity girlfriend, Kindra. It's still too soon."

"Fair," Kindra says with a laugh.

And her laugh makes me laugh. The temptation to cry fades away as I remember that as long as I have my friends—and the opportunity to commit a justified murder—then I'll be okay. There will be other auditions . . . if I can find the will to subject myself to more defeat.

"Can I bring Shorty to the retreat?" I ask.

The sound of shredding fabric reaches our ears, and we turn our attention to the massive black cat climbing up the curtain. With his ears pressed back and his eyes wide, he looks like a tweaking meth-head.

He lets out a languid yowl as I stand and try to pull him from my ripped curtains. He flails and writhes in my arms, scratching my skin.

"He's just so friendly," I say.

Kindra is staring at me, so I pretend he wants love so that she won't realize he's an absolute terror sometimes. I bring the clawing psycho up to my shoulders to hug him, and his needle nails puncture my shirt and drive under my skin.

Instead of screaming, I smile at Kindra, which probably looks more like I'm gritting my teeth. Because I am.

"Put the damn thing down, Cat."

There is no putting a cat like this down without getting clawed to shit, so I pull him away from me and drop him from waist level. Like a shadow demon, he zips along the edge of the room and tucks himself beneath the couch.

"Why did you call the biggest fucking cat I've ever seen Shorty? That thing came from something part dog."

"I named him after Elizabeth Short, the Black Dahlia."

"Of course you did."

"I didn't know Kindra Amato then or I'd have named him after you."

"How are the things that come out of your mouth equal parts weird and sweet?"

"So can I bring him?"

A black ball of lightning shoots across the floor, pauses, then launches itself at the curtains again. Shorty isn't doing himself any favors. He's actually a very sweet cat when he isn't primed for destruction, but of course Kindra is here to see this side of him.

She takes a deep breath and shakes her head. "Since Bennett isn't going, I don't see why not. I'd be concerned he might 'lose' your cat in the Alaskan wilderness. If Shorty rips up curtains at the cabin—or anything else, for that matter—you're on the hook for it, though. Just remember that."

That's a fair trade, so I nod.

"Hey, are you sure you're okay about the audition?" Kindra asks. "It's okay to not be okay."

"I know, but I'm fine. What's one more for the growing pile of rejections?" I force a laugh and flop onto the couch again. "Besides, I didn't want to miss this retreat, and now I don't have to. If I'm not meant to be an actress, maybe I'm meant to be a prolific killer."

What I don't say is that I've had doubts about that as well. Bennett blocked my kills at every turn on the island, but even if he hadn't, I'm not sure I'd have gone through with it. The last thing I want is for Kindra to think I'm a failure at literally everything, but that's a real possibility if I choke again.

"Hey, quit biting your nails and get over here and look at wallpaper swatches with me," Kindra says. "I have to leave for the flight soon, and I need to pick up the supplies as soon as I land in Alaska."

"You're heading up early?"

She nods and turns the laptop toward me. "I've left Ezra to his own devices for two weeks, and I'm worried he's bungled it. Want me to go ahead and book your flight? I'll give you the window seat."

For the first time since getting that shitty email, I smile. "I'd love that."

I can worry about auditions and how my life is a mess when I get back from the trip. For the next week, I have only two missions: get my first kill and kiss Maverick Eaton.

Chapter Two

Bennett

Doc Whitlow sent the email less than an hour ago, but I still feel a growing sense of urgency as my motorcycle picks up speed. He said she's talking, but we never know how long these spells will last.

A slight chill slides through my shirt and kisses my skin as I make a left and cut down a road that runs beside the beach. South Florida is the perfect place to hunker down for the winter and ride my bike. The poor girl has been in storage too often lately.

On two tires, I eat up the open road. Though many people overwinter here, most have grown bored with the beach, so traffic is light. A group of women turn to look and giggle as I rumble past. If I weren't headed somewhere, I'd be inclined to stop and take one for a ride.

But I have somewhere to be, so I turn onto the main road that winds through the beach town's center. My destination lies ahead, tucked deep inside an oasis of palm trees, koi ponds, and an antiseptic smell that spoils the illusion of paradise.

During the summer months, the shops and restaurants on this strip bustle with activity. It's a great place to people watch, if you're into that sort of thing, but not today. Aside from a group of elderly gentlemen hobbling into a small cafe for brunch, the sidewalks are unoccupied.

Past the main drag, the sign for Sanctuary comes into view, but only if you know where to look. Despite the amount of money these people hoard from their clients, they've allowed the foliage to overtake the entrance signage. Philodendrons and Petra plants crowd everything.

As I turn down the paved path, I feel crowded too.

It isn't that I don't want to visit her. I just wish she didn't have to be here.

The foliage breaks apart, and white marble columns file into view. If a stranger happened upon this place, they'd think it was a mansion tucked inside a tiny jungle. The director did an excellent job of making this look like anything other than what it is.

Which is a place where people go to waste away.

I suppose there are worse places to spend your final years. The staff keeps everything clean, and the residents are well looked after. No one is cruel. Well, the nurses, doctors, and other staff aren't. The residents can be a different beast altogether.

After easing my bike into a parking spot in the under-ground garage, I head toward the elevator that will deposit me inside the facility. Next up, the security check. The residents are housed under lock and key for their safety. If it weren't for the meticulously crafted Michelin-worthy meals and the stunning grounds and accommodations, I'd call this a prison.

As the elevator doors ease open with a *ding*, a security desk comes into view. The guard behind the desk smiles and holds a red badge toward me.

"Doc is waiting in his office," the man says. As I step closer, I'm wrapped in a cloud of garlic, onions, and olives. There's no food in sight, so the pizza this man had for lunch is seeping through his pores.

I take the badge without breathing through my nose. "Thanks."

He nods and buzzes me through the first airlock, and I take a deep breath as soon as the doors close behind me.

I enter a long hallway with windows lining one wall. Now that I'm inside the mansion, the facade falls away and I can see this place for what it really is. Gleaming white floors and windowed hallways are a hospital staple.

My mother sits in the courtyard just outside. A row of boxwood hedges stands just behind her chair, casting a shadow over her frail body. Beside her, on a small wrought-iron table, sits a dainty saucer and teacup. My mother always did love her afternoon tea.

But if she's taking her afternoon tea, that may mean I'm too late. When she's lucid, she won't say things she shouldn't.

I feel slightly guilty for looking forward to her bad days, but only slightly. When she received her diagnosis, it was her decision to be placed into immediate care, and I chose Sanctuary. Considering how much I pay this place every six months, the least I can do is get something out of it. I only wish my mother could get something out of it too.

But there is no cure. She'll never leave this place, especially since the bad days have become more frequent.

I hurry past the windows and make a beeline for Doc's office on the second floor. He requested I see him before speaking with my mother, and I already know why. I slide my hand into my pocket and finger the slip of paper.

My knuckles rap against the solid oak door, and a thready voice says I may enter. The doctor sits behind a massive mahogany desk, frantically clicking something on his computer as I take a seat in front of him. Soft moans dribble from the speakers, and I've never seen a man's cheeks turn so red.

"Press alt and F4 at the same time," I say. "That'll close the active window."

Doc searches for the keys, presses them, and the moans cease.

"Probably best not to sneak in a meat-beating sesh when you have a scheduled meeting, no?" I smirk and slide the cashier's check across the desk. "I'm guessing this is why you wanted to see me?"

He clears his throat, straightens his white jacket, and grabs the piece of paper worth a sickening sum of cash. After studying the numbers, he looks at me for the first time since I entered the room. "Yes, this covers your past-due balance, plus the next six months."

"Six months? That should cover the next fucking year!"

"Inflation has hit all of us especially hard, Mr. Carter. I can refer your mother to one of our less-expensive facilities, but you've chosen to house her at our premier location, and that comes with premier pricing."

I shake my head. It's bad enough that I have to keep my mom in one of these places. If she has to be looked after, I only want the best.

"You'll need to come up with the remainder before the end of next week," he adds. "Based on your lapse in payment, we won't be able to handle a different arrangement."

I grip the chair's leather armrests for no other reason than to keep myself from launching across this desk and using his stupid blue tie as a garrote. Having nothing more to say to the piece of shit, I stand and turn for the door.

"Next week, Mr. Carter. Don't forget."

I turn to face him before I leave the room. "Alt and F4, Doctor Whitlow. Don't *you* forget. I never will." I give him a parting wink.

As I travel back downstairs, I work to keep my breathing level. No matter what state my mother is in when I see her, I don't want to bring any negative energy. She worked her ass off to raise me on her own, and she never brought any of her stress to the dinner table each night. Now I strive to keep *my* stress away from *her*.

She's still seated in the chair by the boxwoods when I step into the Florida sunshine. Beyond the hedges, a few patients totter around the edge of the koi pond. A fence prevents them from falling in, but I've seen my fair share of gown-wearing deviants hop it in one leap to go for a swim.

My mother hasn't noticed me yet, but I'll know her mental state as soon as she does. Her eyes tell me everything. Despite her diagnosis, the dementia only rears its head on rare occasions. The doc says that will change. Her illness will progress as her brain deteriorates.

It feels wrong to hope that she's having a bad day, but it's the only way I can learn more about any siblings we may have. Before her mind started to go, she'd begun delving into my father's past. She wanted to destroy him for no other reason than leaving me fatherless. She never made it far enough to uncover proof of his many misdeeds, but she did uncover siblings.

Plural.

She hears my footsteps on the cobblestones. As she

turns toward me, the distant, foggy look in her eyes is unmistakable. The neurons aren't firing as they should.

"Could you be a dear and fetch a cup of tea for my friend here?" she asks me. She thinks I'm an orderly, and I won't correct her. The medical team taught me it's best for her if I don't confuse her.

"Sure, Mrs. Tierney. Do you mind if I sit with you for just a bit first? It's mighty warm today, and my legs are tired."

She offers a sly smile. "I won't tell if you won't, but it's Miss Tierney, I'm afraid. I never married."

Again, guilt eats away a little more of my soul. I've learned that calling her Mrs. instead of Miss will grant an opening, so I use it to my advantage. I'm not perfect.

"A pretty thing like you? I'm shocked no one scooped you up." I study the two chairs beside the table. I want to sit, but I'm not sure which chair holds her imagined friend.

She motions to the chair closest to her. "You can sit there, beside Ronnie. She doesn't bite."

Ronnie. That was my mother's sister—an aunt I never met because she drowned at the tender age of nineteen, three years before I was born.

I turn to the empty chair and nod. "Nice to meet you, Ronnie. It isn't often that I meet a redhead."

"Don't try flirting with her," my mother says with a chuckle. "She's wise to the ways of men." Her voice lowers to a scandalous whisper. "You don't have the right equipment, if you catch my meaning."

I learn all sorts of things on her bad days.

My mother stretches her hand across the table, reaching out for someone I can't see. "Take care, Ronnie. I'll see you as soon as I'm back from vacation."

Her eyes follow the departing apparition, then turn to me. These interactions aren't my favorite. It's easier when I can eavesdrop on a conversation rather than participate.

"No need for the tea, I guess," she says. "You and I can have a little chat, though. As long as the boss doesn't come around."

"I'm due for a break, so they won't mind." I force a smile. "I'm still shocked you never married. Surely someone stole your heart at some point."

She turns her teacup and shakes her head. "Stole is certainly a good word for it. The man was a cad. I wouldn't be surprised if he left a woman with child in all fifty states, and that's just America."

"How many children does he have?"

"I only know of three for sure. My son, Bennett—such a good boy—Ezra, a boy in the UK, and Luisa, a girl in Texas."

I've searched for a Luisa Carter in Texas, but she doesn't exist. My mother and Ezra's mother gave us our father's last name, but I'm not surprised that the third woman chose to leave off the asshole's claim to her daughter.

"Do they all share the last name?" I've asked this question twice before, and both times I received a knowing look, like she was just a tad too lucid to spill those beans. She might be far enough gone to tip the cup now.

"The boys do," she says. "I guess the British woman and I were a little too fond of the fellow who cut us so deeply. The woman from Texas passed down her maiden name."

I sit on the edge of my seat. This is the closest I've come, and I'm mere seconds from getting enough information to find our sister.

My mother places her dainty fingers to her forehead.

"Oh goodness. What was it? It wasn't Gonzalez, but it started with a G and was Hispanic in origin."

"Garcia?"

"No."

"Gomez?"

"No, no. I can't remember. Would you like some tea, young man?"

She's already forgotten I'm supposed to be an orderly. But it doesn't matter. She's given me enough for today, and I don't want to push her any further.

"I'm not very thirsty right now, but I'd love to sit and visit with you for a bit."

She smiles. "I'd like that."

For the next hour, I talk to her about other things and steer clear of the topics surrounding my father. I listen to her tell the same stories I've heard a million times, and I smile and nod in all the right places. For her.

I'm a bit of a mama's boy. Fucking sue me.

Then her eyes begin to fog a bit more, and the ugly side of her disease rears its head. She shifts from confusion to rage in the span of minutes, moving so gradually between each phase that it's hard to realize what's happening. Especially for her son.

"Leave me alone. I'm tired," she finally says. "This shirt is uncomfortable."

Before I can stop her, she begins ripping off her clothes. I call for one of the nurses. I'd drape my jacket over her shoulders to preserve her dignity if I thought it would help, but she'll just fight me. Dementia is an asshole like that.

The orderlies arrive in their white outfits, and, after a bit of gentle prodding, they convince her to retreat to her room where she might be more comfortable. She'll be safe with them.

Once they disappear inside, I head back toward my bike. When I get home, I need to get in touch with Ezra. If anyone can figure out who this elusive Luisa G. is, it's him.

Chapter Three

Cat

The plane touches down in Alaska in the early morning. You wouldn't know it was morning, though. It's still so dark outside. During this time of year, the area only sees a few hours of sunlight each day.

Kindra and Ezra thought of that, though. They made Jim install lighting to every event area so that we can see what the fuck we're doing. The mansion windows have also been fitted with screens that come down and mimic daytime. It's supposed to help with seasonal depression.

Who the fuck could get depressed on vacation? Not me, that's for sure.

Shorty lets out a yowl as I pull his carrier from beneath my seat. Everyone on the plane thought his little protests were cute at first. Now, more than a few pairs of eyes shift toward me with an angry glare.

"At least it isn't a crying baby," I say with a smile.

"I'd have preferred a wailing newborn to the incessant yowling," a man grumbles.

"Then go fucking make one," Kindra says.

I'm so glad she's my friend.

And to be fair, it's not as embarrassing as Kindra's plane ride a few months ago. My toys stayed quiet for their flight to Alaska.

We make our way out of the airport, and Shorty begins to lose his mind. With the way he's flailing around in his carrier, I must look like Clark Griswold when he's holding the box containing Aunt Bethany's unfortunate cat. He screams and claws the sides, and fur flies from the air holes.

"Is he always so pissed off?" Kindra asks as we slide into the limo Jim ordered for us.

I place the carrier on the seat, and the yowling kicks off again. "He probably needs to use the bathroom. He's been in that thing for hours. You'd be pissed off if we crammed you into a tiny box."

Shorty goes quiet, and moments later, a foul stench fills the limo.

Kindra gags and rolls down her window, but she quickly rolls it up again as an icy blast enters the car. "I changed my mind. I'll take the yowling over that smell any day."

I peer into the carrier, and Shorty hisses at me. Great. Now he's pissed off and his back feet have little poo shoes. Shit smears paint the floor with each angry step he takes.

"I'm so sorry, Shorty," I whisper into the air holes.

"You're apologizing to the *cat*? How about the humans that have to smell that for the next hour?" Kindra pinches her nose and breathes through her mouth.

I place the carrier between us on the seat. "We just have to smell it. Poor Shorty has to wear it like a shameful badge, and now I'll have to bathe him. He hates water."

Kindra already stocked my room with the cat supplies I requested, but I didn't put cat-safe shampoo on the list. This is Shorty's first trip, and I didn't realize he'd be so upset. I probably should have put him in a cargo carrier with a litter box, but I was too worried the airline would lose him.

This isn't the best start to the winter retreat, but it can only go up from here.

I hope.

At least Bennett won't be there, which already makes this trip better than the one we took this summer. We'll all breathe a little easier without his incessant fuckboy energy hanging over us like a dark cloud. Well, we'll breathe a little easier once we're out of this car.

In his place, we have Maverick, and that's a major upgrade. He's tall, tan, and his green eyes could convince a woman to strip in two seconds flat.

As much as I hate to admit it, Bennett is attractive too. His dark hair, bright blue eyes, and tattoos are incredibly easy on the eyes, but his personality is more akin to a honey badger—angry, volatile, and unforgiving. That's where Maverick really shines. He's so sweet.

"Stop daydreaming about Maverick," Kindra says beside me, though she sounds like she's talking through a cold because she's still pinching her nose.

"What makes you think I'm daydreaming about him?"

Kindra lets out an exaggerated, feminine sigh. "You do that shit . . . that pathetic little sigh. That's how I know."

Everyone seems to think I'm tossing my line into empty waters, but Maverick hasn't said he isn't interested. I mean, he hasn't said he *is* interested, but that's beside the point. By the end of the retreat, I'll gather the courage to make my move and get my answer.

"How'd he get his name, anyway?" I ask. "I can't find anything online about why he's called the Midnight Masochist."

"Jesus, are you stalking him?"

Maybe.

"No. I was just curious," I say.

Kindra laughs and looks out the window. "He was originally the New England Nightstalker, but he hated getting lumped with Ramirez, so he wrote to the papers—my paper, to be exact—and requested the name change upon threat of a spree. Understanding how personal a name can be, I changed it to what he requested, and it stuck."

"I can't picture him as an actual masochist, though. Can you?"

Kindra gags. "God no. I don't want to yuck someone's yum, but the thought of being the dominant one in the bedroom makes my skin crawl, and if Maverick is a masochist, that means he'd be the sub."

I don't know if I could pull it off myself, but I'm willing to try.

The road gets rougher as we bump along. Snow drapes everything in winter's finest, and even the towering trees are dressed for the season. I pull out my phone to check the weather app, but my cell signal is abysmal already, and we aren't even on the back roads yet.

The lack of connection can be a bit annoying at times, but I enjoy the unplugged experience Jim's locales provide. Sometimes it's nice to disconnect from the world and just experience things.

"I hope we bought enough booze," Kindra says as she stares out the window. "On the island, Jim could have the pilot fly into town for supplies if we needed them, but out here, we're on our own. We have someone to relay important messages each day, but we're too far from fucking Walmart if we need anything in a timely manner."

I pat her jean-clad thigh. "Relax. Since this is the inaugural winter retreat, there are bound to be hiccups, but I bet you'll discover that you're more prepared than you think."

She stops gripping her nose so that she can give my hand a squeeze. "Thanks for the vote of confidence."

"Anytime."

Unlike Kindra, I've had my fair share of friendships throughout my life, but this friendship is unlike any other. She feels more like family than a friend.

A while later, the limo pulls to a stop beside a very large shed. A patch of dirt serves as a small parking lot, though it's mostly covered in snow. Earthy bits peek out here and there.

The driver opens our doors, and we step into the icy air. I hold in a fart for fear it might freeze my asshole if I let it out. I've never experienced such temperatures.

Kindra hands a pink ski mask to me, then pulls a purple mask over her face. "We'll take one of the snowmobiles to the mansion. I didn't want to ask the coachman to pull the horses out just for us. I hope that's okay."

"Whatever gets me to the nearest roaring fireplace is fine by me. Let's do this." I pull the mask down and inwardly recoil at the way it presses my hair to my neck.

I have some pretty hardcore sensory issues, but I try to keep them hidden. I learned to mask my little idiosyncrasies when I was in school. The girls at the lunch table only had to make fun of my sockless feet one time before I learned it was better to be uncomfortable than to be bullied.

Now that I'm an adult, I still work to keep my non-normal behaviors in check. Instead of asking Kindra to wait while I move my hair so that it doesn't annoy me, I swallow the discomfort and try not to think about it. Or about the way the tag in the jacket keeps making a really annoying crinkle sound. Or about the fact that the mask fabric feels like steel wool on my skin.

It's not that I can't trust Kindra with this secret. I don't fear she'd make fun of me. But sometimes, people change once they know. They try to handle me with kid gloves, constantly checking to be sure I'm comfortable. I don't want to put that burden on my friends.

Kindra pulls one of her bags from the trunk of the limo, and I do the same. It's our winter gear. We hurry inside the shed to dress, and though the gray metal walls block the wind, they do little to dispel the bone-chilling cold. My nipples get so hard that it hurts, and I won't be shocked if they pierce the lacy bra and put my eyes out.

"Put your gear on over your clothes," Kindra says. "It will help with the cold."

I pull out my ensemble—bought on clearance because I'm poor and New York is expensive. "I hope Maverick doesn't see me in this," I say as I place one leg into the fluffy pants. "By the time I get all this on, I'll look like the Michelin Man."

"Better than having your skin turn black from frostbite."

"Good point."

I hurry and finish dressing, then squeeze into my winter coat. Now that we're protected from the elements, complete with hideous goggles, we only have to ease the snowmobile out of the building and onto the trail. Unfortunately, my arms are pinned in a position that makes me look like the letter T.

We toddle out of the shed and stop. Our luggage—and the wallpaper Kindra ordered—huddles in a little pile where the limo once stood. I look from the snowmobiles to the pile, then at Kindra.

Kindra huffs. "The driver could have at least brought

our things into the shed before taking off. Help me get the bags safely into the building so that Ezra can come back for them in a bit."

The driver probably had to hurry back to the airport. Most everyone arrives in a few days for the opening ceremonies and the New Year's Eve bash, but Maverick planned to fly out soon after our flight departed. He should arrive tonight.

I can't wait.

In all the excitement, I forgot about Shorty and his poop predicament. I hurry to the pile of bags, expecting to find one very disgruntled and cold cat, but his carrier is nowhere to be seen.

My heart drops to my asshole.

"Kindra, did you happen to grab Shorty's carrier from the back seat?"

She lowers the two bags she's just picked up. "Please don't tell me he's still in the limo."

"Okay, I won't." I pause. "But I think that's what happened."

Kindra rips off her gloves and wrestles with her pockets until she finds her phone. As she brings it up to her face, she closes her eyes and releases a deep sigh. "I have no way to contact him. He couldn't have waited five minutes?"

Tears fill my goggle-covered eyes, and my shoulders quiver with a sob. "I'm the worst cat mom ever. I forgot my child in the car. The government will probably take him away from me now."

"Don't be so melodramatic. CPS doesn't stand for Cat Protective Services. And besides, the actual CPS fails children on a daily basis, so it's not like you have that much to worry about."

It doesn't change the facts. I forgot my child—my shitshoed child—in the back of a limo that is now who knows how far away. As if that wasn't bad enough, now Shorty will be forced to sit with the stink.

And so will Maverick, once the driver picks him up.

I want to crawl into a deep hole, bury myself, and hibernate for the rest of winter. Maybe life will be less bleak when I emerge.

"Cat, there's nothing we can do about it here. Let's get up to the mansion and figure it out someplace warm."

Kindra eases the snowmobile out of the shed, and we clear the parking lot of our things in record time. Despite knowing Shorty is speeding away down the road, I still feel another twinge of disappointment when we reach the bottom of the pile and find no cat.

I'm just about to give up hope when we hear the crunch of snow under tires. We both turn as the driver steps out of the limo.

He opens the back door and shoves the cat carrier into my waiting arms. "I'm charging a hefty cleaning fee, just so you know. I do this job as a favor to Jim, but I draw the line at that smell."

Before I can apologize for the tenth time in three seconds, he's slamming the driver's side door and peeling away.

I breathe a sigh of shit-tainted relief and hurry back into the shed to transfer Shorty to his backpack for the ride in. Kindra follows me, though I'm not sure of her emotions right now, since a purple ski mask covers her features. I'm willing to bet she's three-parts as relieved as I am and one-part annoyed that I'm slowing things down.

The little space-pod backpack sits at the bottom of the pile. I dig it out and remove my gloves so that I can transfer Shorty from one container to the next. Using a nightshirt from my bag, I clean off his paws so that the smell won't transfer with him.

To say that he's angry would be an understatement. His dark pupils demolish his gold irises, leaving a raging black hole in each eye socket. I've scruffed him, yet that doesn't stop his claws from swiping ever closer to my face.

Once he's mostly clean, I stuff him into the space pod and loosen the straps so that it will fit on my back over all these layers. This will keep the cold wind away from him.

Outside, we hop onto the snowmobile and start into the woods. The treads grind over the trail. It's not a very smooth ride, but Jim couldn't secure a team to build a road on such short notice. By next year, we'll have a cobblestone path that will make this ride much more enjoyable.

Though we might need to adjust the time of year. The sun is just beginning to rise, and it's almost eleven in the morning. Just before three in the afternoon, it will set again.

At least the trees have been cleared. The path is fairly wide, though I suppose it needed to be to accommodate the horses and carriage. That was my idea, and while it took some begging and pleading, Jim agreed to it in the end.

After a few minutes, the trees break apart and the mansion looms before us. It was built to look like a quaint cabin in the woods, but I've never seen a three-story log cabin with a fountain out front.

Ezra stands on the wraparound porch. He gives us a wave as we bring the snowmobile to a stop. With the grace only an Englishman possesses, he descends the stairs and welcomes us to the Alaskan wilderness.

The winter retreat has officially begun.

Chapter Four

Bennett

The microwave beeps to let me know my two-dollar TV dinner has reached an edible temperature. I'd better get used to eating these. For what Doctor Beats-His-Meat wants to charge to care for my mother, I'd better get used to a lot of things.

Loud, playful music blares from the apartment above mine. Seconds later, little feet begin pounding overhead. This is a daily occurrence. When the mother with five kids needs to unwind in her bedroom, she pops a loud-ass kiddie program onto the television and retreats to safety.

A bit of plaster crumbles from the light fixture after an exceptionally excited stomp, and I've just about had it.

I grab my sad meal and go to the tiny bathroom. If I eat on the toilet, I'm furthest from the noise. I'm also kept in good company, what with the little family of mice that have taken up residence within the crumbling walls. I drop a noodle into the corner between the tub and the toilet as a treat for them.

Most people would set out traps, but I can't bring myself to do it. They're just trying to make their way in life, same as anyone else.

At least they aren't cockroaches.

I'm halfway through my depressing tray of what's supposed to be shrimp scampi when my doorbell rings. On my way to the door, I deposit the remainder of the "meal" in the trash, where it belongs.

Through the peephole, I spot two youngish men in pressed white shirts, dark ties, and dress pants. Fucking Mormons.

I open the door to two of the brightest smiles I've ever seen, which immediately remind me of Catarina Novak. And now I want to punch them both in the face even more for making me think of that vapid bitch.

"Good afternoon, sir," the taller one says. "Could we possibly leave some literature with you?"

"It's gonna be pretty hard to read it in the dark, so you'd best keep moving," I say.

The taller one looks at the shorter one. "Your lights seem to be working okay. Why would you have to read in the dark?"

I step forward, encroaching on their space. Which is actually *my* space because I pay to live in this rundown shit hole. "Because your little asshole is too tight to let in any light, and that's where your pamphlet will end up if you don't get it out of my face."

My phone rings in my pocket, blasting some hard metal music, and the men take their leave. Smart decision. I wasn't kidding about shoving that pamphlet up his ass.

I pull out my phone and answer it, even though I don't want to. It's probably Ezra, and I'm not in the mood to hear him wax on forever about how great this retreat will be and how much he wants me there. Ain't happening.

But it isn't Ezra. It's Maverick.

"Afternoon," he says through the speaker.

I set the phone on the coffee table and plop onto the threadbare couch I found on the side of the road when I first started renting this place a year ago. "Did you find anything out?"

"Not yet, but could you take me to the airport? I've already missed my flight due to car trouble, and I'm bound to miss the next one too."

"I'm in Florida. You're in New York. How will that work?"

Maverick pauses for a moment, then rushes ahead. "I was here for a job."

I'm not sure why that was so difficult for him to say, but okay. "If you don't mind riding bitch on my bike, yeah, I can take you. But I don't know where you'll put your luggage."

"I fit everything into a backpack."

I wait, giving him a moment to elaborate, but he doesn't. "Maverick . . . you're headed to one of the coldest places on this planet. Winter gear is a must. How did you fit everything into one backpack?"

"Oh, I sent some things ahead with Ezra when he flew down a couple of weeks ago. I had to finish up some work for—"

"Wait, back up to that. You're still getting work? I thought the well had run dry. I haven't been contracted since the last gig."

"About that . . ."

"Go on. What do you know that I don't?"

Maverick lets out a sigh, then drops the bad news. "You

aren't likely to get a call anytime soon. After that last job, they—"

"They sent me on a suicide mission, and I still got shit done."

"He was a celebrity, Bennett. They didn't want his death to look like anything other than a suicide."

"It could have been a suicide."

"I don't know of any cases where the person disembowels themself after dying of hanging."

"The hanging was so boring, though. It needed a little color."

"Regardless, upper management has bumped you so far down the roster that you aren't likely to get a job for a while. It might be time to look elsewhere until this blows over."

Oh, yeah. I'll just grab the hitman classifieds and start cold-calling people. Cue the infamous Bennett eye roll.

"I'll worry about that later," I say. "But first, tell me what you plan to do now that Cat will be at the retreat."

"My flight leaves in two hours, so I kind of need to call a ride service if—"

"You aren't getting out of this conversation. Why don't you tell her you aren't interested?"

"I don't want to hurt her feelings. She's a sweet girl, and beautiful too, but I'm not in a place to date right now. I'm too busy climbing the ladder at work."

Yeah, and the rung he just stepped on sits right above my head.

"I'd be happy to let her down for you," I say with a laugh.

He laughs too, because we both know I wouldn't let her down gently. I'd drop her ass from the Empire State Building, then race down to see the carnage at the bottom.

"Just pick me up and take me to the airport. If you'll do

this for me, I'll see if I can put in a good word for you with the higher-ups."

Ouch. That hurts. It wasn't so long ago that a green-eyed youngster came to me to get into the game. I was the one putting in the good word. Now . . . I'm finished.

I tell Maverick I'll be by his hotel to pick him up shortly. He gives me the address, and I end the call and head toward the door.

But then an idea strikes me as I'm reaching for the door handle. I'll already be at the airport, so maybe I should pack a bag and catch a flight myself. Since I don't have any work lined up, I have plenty of free time. Silver linings and shit.

I hear Texas is nice this time of year.

Well, parts of Texas are still warm. If I'm forced to go north, there could be some cold and snow. I'll pack some light winter gear, just in case. I'm chaotic, but I'm never underprepared.

After tossing a few things into my suitcase, I shut down the apartment, turning off lights and unplugging appliances. Now that I know why the work river has stopped flowing my way, I'll need to be more careful with my already strained finances. My mother's care comes first, though. I'll live in a box and scrub car windows with newspaper before I make her do without anything.

I don't know how long I'll be out of town, so I call a ride service. I won't leave my bike in a parking garage. Maverick can pay for the ride since he'd have paid for one if I hadn't agreed to take him. It's the transitive property or some shit.

With a plan in place, I take my suitcase downstairs and wait for the driver to pull up. In a few short hours, I'll be up in the air and miles away from my problems. Maybe this is just what I need.

Or maybe what I need is in Alaska after all.

Without a real lead on Luisa G., our infamous missing sister, it seems pointless to waste a plane ticket to Texas. I'll also end up spending a lot of money while I'm there. If I go northwest, however, Ezra will cover the plane ticket, and there are no lodging expenses for insiders like me.

Not to mention the havoc I can wreak. I know how excited Cat must be to get her first kill, but I'm even more excited at the prospect of preventing that from happening. The look on her face when I arrive will be enough to soothe my broken soul.

As the car pulls against the curb, I've made up my mind. I lean into the window and say, "I need five minutes. I've forgotten my winter finest."

And just like that, I'm Alaska bound.

Chapter Five

Cat

The mansion is a hub of activity today. I had no clue just how much went on behind the scenes at one of these retreats, but I've learned a lot since arriving. Kindra and I were plastering wallpaper to the bathroom walls until nearly three in the morning.

Now I'm in the kitchen with Chef Maurice. Since I took his class at the summer retreat, Kindra thought I'd be the best fit to help him. She seems to have forgotten how much he hates me after I refused his brain puffs.

He certainly hasn't forgotten. As he spins around the stainless-steel kitchen, he pins me with an icy glare every few turns. His eyes are a bit hard to see below the thick red caterpillars hovering above them, but I get the message loud and clear.

"I've cut the chicken, Chef," I say. "Did you need help with anything else?"

He glowers at the massive pot before him. "It shouldn't be chicken. It should be a finer delicacy than this."

"Maybe we can talk Kindra and Ezra into letting you serve human during the cooking classes. We have enough Cattle stored in the basement. There should be a few we can pull for that."

Chef Maurice scoffs before stirring the sauce inside the pot. "Yes, well, if you can make that happen, I might be a little kinder to you. Go and see what you can do."

I remove the filthy apron and wash my hands before leaving the chef and his small team to handle the rest. Kindra shouldn't have an issue with my suggestion, especially since it's not like she has to eat it. She hates cooking.

I find her in the front hall. She and Ezra are locked in a heated discussion with one of the grooms. Stepping closer, I learn that one of the coachmen slaughtered the other, so now we're down to a single driver.

"I might be able to help," I say. "My family had horses, so I have some experience."

Kindra looks from me to the groom. I understand her trepidation. Most of the workers are former convicts who survived the hunt on the final day of Jim's summer retreat. Since I haven't even killed anyone yet, she's worried about my safety.

"I'll be fine," I whisper to her. "Jim doesn't let the sex offenders survive, even if they make it through the hunt. Most of these men and women are wanted for financial or drug crimes, not violent crimes."

"Except that a coachman just killed a coachman over a disagreement about a horse's coat color," Kindra fires back. "I just don't think it's a good idea."

"Let her try, pet," Ezra says. "The men need the help, and you and I don't know the first thing about driving horses."

Kindra looks between us, then relents with a drop of her

shoulders. "Okay, but you have to take my knife." She slides the massive bowie knife into my hand. "You'll help them get the horses into the traces. You can ride to pick up the first load of guests too, if you want."

A few months ago, I would have squealed like a schoolgirl when the Heartbreak Killer placed her murder weapon into my hands. Now, I just slide it onto my belt and carry on.

I'm squealing on the inside, though, just so we're clear.

I follow the groom to the large barn at the back of the property. Many feet have cut a path through the pile of snow, clear down to the earth beneath it. Grass squeaks under each step I take, occasionally followed by the satisfying crunch of snow when I make a misstep.

The sweet scents of hay and horse manure rush up to greet me as the doors swing open. It's the bittersweet scent of home—sweet because it reminds me of the good times, but bitter because there were bad times too.

Maybe not bad so much as sad, but either way, I push those thoughts out of my mind. I lock them in a bedroom we don't open anymore.

As we step further into the barn, another scent hits me. This one is more metallic, and I recognize it.

It's blood.

The body lies in an empty stall. Well, the body parts lie in the stall, and I can't identify most of them. The man has been so finely diced that he covers the straw in shades of red, pink, and yellow. If I didn't know he was a man by the groom's account, I'd know by the penis nailed to the wall.

"Maybe we should put the coachman to work in the kitchen," I say as I study the carnage. "His knifework is impeccable."

"Thanks," the groom says with a smirk. "I was actually

the one who killed the guy, but I didn't want to get into trouble, so I lied."

As an uneasy feeling creeps over me, I close the stall door and look for the horses, but the barn is nearly empty. There should be six horses here—four to pull the sleigh and two to swap out if any get tired or injured—but I only see two.

Speaking of the sleigh, it's MIA as well.

"Where's the other coachman?" I ask. "And the horses and sleigh, for that matter."

The knife weighs down my right hip with an insurance policy. If he tries anything stupid, I'm not afraid to go for it.

"He left to pick up the first set of guests over an hour ago. That's when I killed the other guy. And now, I'm going to kill *you*." He takes a step toward me, but I step back to keep some distance between us.

"Why me? What the fuck did I do to you?" I ask.

"I wanted the other one. The boss lady. But any of you elite pieces of shit will do. You think you're better than us, but you aren't. You're one of us, and yet you walk around free as a fucking bird."

I take another step back and ease my hand to my right hip. "Isn't this better than prison, though?"

"Why don't we swap places and find out?"

As he takes another step forward, I begin to backpedal with a quickness, but I never take my eyes away from him. Kindra taught me that. No matter what happens, keep your eyes on your target.

Unfortunately, that advice sends me backing into the wheelbarrow containing god knows how much horse shit. I topple into it, and I'm soon covered in a lumpy brown blanket.

Which also means I can't get to the fucking knife.

I ram my hand into a few feet of horse crap and dig around for the filigree handle as I scoot backward. My fingers find the sheath attached to my belt, but the knife has fallen out. I have no weapon.

Unable to defend myself, I reach for the only nearby option. I grab handfuls of horse shit and fling them at the skinny little son of a bitch stepping toward me like an emaciated panther. Most of it's too dry to do any damage, but some of the harder clumps connect with his head and knock him off balance.

"Oh, you filthy little bitch," he says through clenched teeth. "I'm not a rapist, but I might make an exception for you."

As he's making his limp-dicked threat, I spot the knife. The gleaming tip pokes from a nearby clod of manure, and I reach for it. The psycho lunges for me at the same time, and I narrowly escape his strike as I roll across a carpet of shit and clutch the knife to my chest.

And this is it. It's really happening. I'm about to get my first kill, and even though it's morally justified in the most legal sense, it still counts.

I spin the blade in my hand like I've practiced so many times in my bedroom mirror. Even smeared in horse droppings, I bet I look cool as fuck. "Be careful. Wouldn't want you to get *scratched*."

He pauses, and his eyebrows pull together. "Is that . . . is that your tag line? Wouldn't want you to get scratched?"

"Is it bad?"

He shrugs his shoulders. "I mean, it's not the worst, I guess. It could be better, though."

"Okay, wait. I have another I could try."

He folds his arms over his chest and nods for me to go on.

I clear my throat and spin the blade again, followed by a dramatic pause. "Be careful. This kitten has *claws*."

He licks his lips and blinks at me.

I lower the knife. "That was worse, wasn't it?"

"Yes, way worse."

I groan. "I got nothing else."

"What's your killer name? Maybe I can think of—"

Before he can say anything else, a gunshot rings out and the side of his head bursts open in a spray of red. I'm too stunned to do more than gawk as brain matter paints the stall.

Then, as his body drops to the ground, I spot Maverick behind him.

He saved me? My crush, the man who hung the moon, this glorious god of a man, saved *me*?

I take a step toward him, then halt almost immediately. Standing a few feet behind him and to the side, tucked away in the shadows, is Bennett Carter.

And he's holding the smoking gun.

Chapter Six

Bennett

When we reach the mansion, Cat rushes straight to Ezra and Kindra to tell them what happened, but she's got part of it very wrong.

"No, that is *not* what happened," I say. "I didn't save your stupid life. I prevented you from getting your first kill. There's a difference."

Maverick steps forward and puts his arm around my shoulder. "I was there, and you definitely saved her life."

"Bull fucking shit. That guy weighed maybe a buck. A buck ten if he needed to take a healthy shit." I shake my head and laugh. "If he'd charged her, she could have stopped him with her pinky finger."

"Bennett, my hero," she says as she bats her long lashes over her bright blue eyes. She's only doing it to annoy me for kill-blocking her.

"Fuck all of you." I grab my bags from the pristine marble floor and head toward my room. If they want to live in a fantasy land where I saved Cat as a good deed, they can. I'm firmly planted in reality, and goodness never factored into the equation.

As I stroll through a mansion hallway drenched in fine art and fresh flowers—in fucking Alaska, mind you—I'm slightly taken aback by the level of grandiosity my brother has risen to. This rich-people shit ain't us.

Our father, the illustrious Desmond Carter the third, has plenty of money. He probably wipes his ass with the stuff. His children, however, never see a penny. Or a birthday card.

Not that any of that shit matters to me. My mother taught me that you have to work hard for what you want in life, and she gives me a birthday card every year without fail, though I'm pretty sure one of the nurses helped out with the last one. She was going through one of her bad spells.

I find my room toward the end of a hallway. A large four-post bed dominates the back wall. A shimmering silver fabric creates a canopy over the top. It looks like something out of a period drama, and I hate period dramas.

A massive wooden dresser stands beside the bed. I pull some pants from my suitcase and open a drawer to put them away. That's when I spot the small ceramic pineapple tucked inside, along with a note and a little hand towel.

YOUR ROOM IS RIGHT BESIDE CAT'S. IF YOU PLAN TO FUCK ANY FRUIT, PLEASE FOLD THIS TOWEL AND PLACE IT BETWEEN THE DRESSER AND THE WALL SO SHE DOESN'T HAVE TO HEAR IT. UNFORTUNATELY, I DIDN'T SPOT ANY PINEAPPLE ON THE SHOPPING LIST, BUT I'M SURE YOU'LL FIND SOMETHING THAT WILL BE JUST AS APPEALING

EZRA

This bitch.

I crumple the note and toss it on the floor. I love how everyone acts like they don't have a weird fetish when I know for a fact they all do. If anyone ever creates an organization for the ethical treatment of fruit, I'll reconsider my ways. Until then, I'll fuck whatever I damn well please.

The tiny pineapple joins the note on the floor, and I busy myself with stuffing clothes into drawers. Ezra likes to hang his things, but not me. If the wrinkles in my dress shirts bother anyone, they don't have to look at me. I'd prefer it that way.

An event schedule stands on the nightstand. It's a step up from the pamphlets they offer at the summer excursion, and it actually looks like it was designed in this millennium. Then again, the odd 70s vibe is what made the summer retreat so unique. What does this winter shindig have to offer?

Snow, sub-zero temperatures, and Cat, that's what. And I hate all of it.

None of that matters, though, because making that blonde's trip the worst it can be will make up for the discomfort and misery. That's what I kept telling myself on the freezing sleigh ride in.

After flopping down on the bed, I grab the event list from the nightstand. Just out of curiosity. I won't be choosing which events I participate in because I'll be the one tagging along this time. Wherever Cat goes, I'll be hot on her heels to ensure she doesn't get that first kill.

Just like the summer retreat, the events look innocent enough on paper. We've got a skiing lesson, cooking demonstrations, snowboarding, and curling, among other activities. What the paper doesn't say is that most of these events will involve killing or maiming the Cattle.

There's also the mandatory dinner on the first and last night, with the last night holding a black-tie requirement. God, I hate wearing a monkey suit. I'm a t-shirt-and-jeans kind of guy.

I check my watch. Several hours stand between me and a gourmet meal. I could take a nap to pass the time, but that won't help the mild jet lag from a four-hour time difference. Which means I'll need to find something to do.

The first day at the retreat is meant to orient the guests with their surroundings, so I'll start with the mansion's interior first and see how I feel. If I decide I need to venture into the winter wonderland—my version of hell—I'll pop back to my room to change.

I step outside my bedroom and glance around. Cat's door glares at me. I squash the urge to snoop around in her personal space, though I'll probably cave eventually. If I find a flagpole, I'm not above running her skimpy drawers to the top of it. I never said I was mature.

Instead, I head down the grand double staircase. How ridiculous and utterly pointless. I hope I'm never rich enough to feel the need for two sets of stairs that lead to the same damn place.

"Need someone to show you around?" Maverick asks as I reach the bottom of the stairs. He's standing beside my arch-nemesis as she stares up at him like he was the one who saved her fucking life. Not that I did. "Cat just gave me a quick tour, and she's a great guide."

"Sounds like a good time," I say with a smile. "Why don't you show me around, *kitten?*"

"Please fucking die," she says. "And don't ever call me kitten again."

She flicks her blonde hair over her shoulder, then turns back to Maverick as if I'm not standing here.

"I was serious about that tour," I say. "I don't know where anything is, and you seem to know everything, per usual."

"Do you hear something?" Cat says to Maverick. "Sounds sort of like an annoying fly buzzing around a decimated pineapple."

"Or an angry fly buzzing around a turd with some blonde hair poking from the top," I say.

Maverick shifts his weight between his feet. "I think I'll head to my room now. I . . . uh, need a nap before dinner."

As Cat's body deflates, I realize why they say someone looks like the wind has been sucked out of their sails. The girl shrinks before my eyes, her shoulders dropping and her smile fading. She watches him until he disappears at the top of the stairs.

"No worries, *kitten*. Now you're free to give me the tour."

Remembering I'm here, her face shifts from dejected to disgusted. The feeling is mutual.

"I'll give you the tour on one condition," she says. "Promise you'll stop calling me that."

I grin at her because she's made this entirely too easy for me. "I absolutely promise to stop calling you that if you promise to show me around like a good little girl. And no sass."

She takes a deep breath, and I try to keep my eyes away from her full tits as they rise and fall with the inhale and exhale. It's like my brain and my dick are on two different wavelengths.

"Okay," she finally says, "but you'd better not break that promise."

"I don't break promises."

She thinks of a retort—I see the cunning in her eyes, the

excitement at the prospect of a really good zinger—but her lips snap shut and she just says, "Follow me."

Oh, this is going to be fun.

I'll keep setting her up, and she'll remain unable to knock anything down because she fears being called kitten. Why wasn't *this* activity listed on the brochure? I'd participate every day.

She takes me to the kitchen first. Again, no expense was spared, as is evidenced by the gleam of silver no matter which direction I turn. Rich aromas greet my nose—lemon, dill, and braised meat. And judging by the scent, it isn't human meat.

Chef Maurice stands by the stove, yelling at his subordinates for turning a stew into a soup. I didn't know there was a difference.

"Let's move on," Cat says.

From there, she leads me to a library. "There's a secret passageway in here," Cat says as she takes a turn about the room. Her fingers light on a few book spines as she trails past. "I won't tell you where, though."

"Where does it lead?" I ask.

"Ask your brother if you want to know that badly," she says. She gives me a sweet smile, then heads toward the door.

I stick out my lower lip in a faux pout. "Aw, come on. I've been nice so far. Can't you show me which candlestick to pull to get the big hole to open up?"

There is so much content there, and she can't use any of it. She can't tell me to yank my own candlestick and see what happens. She can't say the big hole is already open, and she'd love it if it closed. She can't say any of it! All she can do is shake with the knowledge that her powers are useless here.

So she says nothing, turns with a huff, and hurries to the next room.

"This is the indoor pool." She pushes a glass door and guides us into what may be the warmest room in the building—the natatorium. It's like a sauna in here.

As I look around, I understand why. Tropical plants stretch toward artificial lighting, and I recognize those massive hibiscus leaves from the island. I guess Jim wanted a little bit of home here.

The large pool takes up most of the space, but a couple of hot tubs burble against a wall of windows that overlooks the snowy landscape. They likely add to the heat in the room. A bright purple light glows in each roiling tub.

"No sacrificial slab, huh?" I ask.

Cat shakes her head. "Not that I've seen."

"While we're here, why don't we go for a dip?" I take off my shirt and drop it onto a small glass tabletop as her eyes widen.

She licks her lips and turns away. "I don't have my swimsuit on, and . . ."

Her voice trails off because she can't say what she wants.

"And? And you'd rather die than swim with me?" I prod. "You'd sooner drown yourself on dry land than share any body of water with the dirty *fruit fucker*?"

"I take it you found Ezra's note?" She tries to hide her smirk and does a horrible job. "He told me about it when you went to your room."

I step closer to her, if for no other reason than to make her as uncomfortable as possible. I'm near enough that she should feel the heat radiating from my Florida-tanned skin.

"Oh, I found the note. Thank you for asking."

When she turns and realizes we're nearly touching, her

features shift. She looks almost . . . scared. Her fingers quiver as she swipes a bead of sweat from her forehead.

"Personal space," she whispers, but she doesn't sound very sure of herself.

I step closer, and her fingers brush my chest. She lowers her hand and recoils as if she's just jammed her fist into a roaring fireplace. Before she can dart away, I lean closer and brush away the hair that's fallen over her forehead.

"My god, Cat," I say as I lick my lips. "I never realized just how . . ."

She licks her lips, mimicking my action as she waits for me to finish the sentence.

I clear my throat. "I never realized how easy it would be to get under your thin skin."

With a gravelly groan that is one-part scream, she swats my hand away and storms toward the door.

"Ah, ah, ah!" I call after her. "Remember our deal?"

She flings the door wide, then turns back to look at me. "Fuck the deal. You can call me whatever the fuck you want because for the rest of the trip, I'm staying as far from you as possible."

The door slams behind her, and I have to applaud Ezra and Jim for choosing a good glass company. A lesser door would have shattered.

"Good luck with that, kitten," I say with a smile. For the rest of this trip, my goal is to do the exact opposite. The more I'm around her, the more I can annoy her. Maybe I can even get her to leave early again.

With a spring in my step, I head back to my room to get ready for dinner. Let the games begin.

Chapter Seven

Cat

Bennett Carter is officially the most horrible man I've ever met in my life. He is cruel, annoying, and downright insufferable. He's also incredibly attractive, and he fucking knows it. That's why he took off his shirt and stepped into me. He thought his masculine aura and sinful tattoos would send me into a tizzy.

And it worked.

I drop face-first onto my bed and scream into the luxurious comforter, but no amount of expensive fabric can muffle the anguish I feel at letting him get the upper hand. He got to me, and he knows he got to me.

I roll onto my back. "Recognizing that Bennett is attractive is not the same thing as *finding* him attractive," I tell myself.

Yes, I noticed his mountains of muscles, but that doesn't mean I want to climb Mount Bennett and plant my flag. But I also can't pretend that the experience left me entirely unaffected, either. The moment of unwanted closeness created a twinge between my legs, and now it's grown into an ache.

I glance at my phone. With only a couple of hours between now and dinner, I don't have much time to get ready, but I really need to take care of this misplaced arousal. Because that's what it is. It has nothing to do with Bennett and everything to do with that tall, blond, perfect man named Maverick.

My gaze drops to the small nightstand. I tucked my sex toys away in that drawer for easy access. The entire collection has grown too large to carry along, so I chose only my favorites for the trip. I reach into the drawer and fish out my old standby—the Hitachi Magic Wand. This device should be in every woman's repertoire.

After plugging it in so that it's ready when I need it, I lie back on the bed and slide my hand up my shirt. I close my eyes and imagine it's Maverick's hand stroking my breasts and tweaking my nipples.

I picture his mouth dipping over my stomach, licking and nipping his way lower. My fingers walk the same path, providing the physical touch to match fantasy Maverick's mouth. God, he's good.

As I imagine his mouth moving over my pussy, I grab the toy, turn it on, and press it between my legs. I come almost immediately, but I'm careful to swallow all sound. I don't want Bennett to hear me next door.

With my eyes still closed and my fantasy still rolling through my mind like a movie, I come down from my orgasm and look between my legs to thank Maverick for pleasing me. But when he lifts his head, it isn't Maverick.

It's fucking Bennett!

My eyes snap open in reality, and I throw the Magic Wand away from me with a scream. The toy threatens to drill its way to China, so I reach down and cut it off before it damages the floorboards.

A light sweat slicks my brow. I lick my lips and take a deep breath as I try to push images of Bennett's head between my legs out of my mind. That wasn't a fantasy. That was a fucking nightmare.

Someone knocks on my door, and I scramble off the bed. Panic slowly builds because I'm undressed from the waist down and my sex toy is still lying out in the open. I shove it into a drawer as the visitor knocks again.

"Everything okay in there? I thought I heard a scream." It's a deep female voice I don't recognize, but at least it isn't Bennett. There were some new names on the list for this retreat, so maybe it's a new friend.

I throw on a pair of panties and go to the door. "Sorry about that. I—"

"Gotcha," Bennett says in his best falsetto. He grins at me and pushes into my room before I know what's happening. "Did you see your reflection in the mirror or something?"

"No. As a matter of fact, I dozed off and had a nightmare about your stupid face. That's why I screamed. Now, if you'll kindly fuck off, I need to get ready for dinner."

Bennett glances at his watch. "You'll need more than an hour to make yourself presentable. You might as well give up."

"Please leave."

He looks past my shoulder, and his face lights up. "What's all this about?"

My stomach climbs out of my throat as he heads straight for the nightstand. I shoved the toy into the drawer, but I forgot to unplug it first. The cord still dangles from the drawer to the wall. By that gleam in his eyes, I know he knows exactly what waits inside.

I can't stop him. I'm forced to stand here and watch in slow motion as his fingers wrap around the golden knob. The panic and disbelief freeze me so fully that I can't even utter a cohesive argument when the drawer begins to slide open.

"Jesus fucking Christ, I didn't know masturbation could be considered a hobby," he says. "Do you claim this shit on your taxes? There must be at least a grand worth of toys in here. At least tell me your collection is insured."

He plucks a rope of anal beads from the drawer and holds them up to the light. I want to die.

"You must have a tight little asshole if that's the biggest you can fit in there," he says with a laugh. "All that ass and can't do a damn thing with it. What a shame."

My senses return, and I snatch the beads from his hand and shove them into the drawer. "My room isn't part of the tour, and the size of my asshole isn't any of your concern. Please keep your STD magnets away from things I put in my body."

I push the drawer closed and point to the door, but he just laughs and shakes his stupid head.

"Get out of my room," I say, hoping a verbal rendition of the order will get him moving.

He leans closer. "Make me."

I place my hands on his chest and push, but he's like a brick wall. Completely immovable. I push harder, but that just makes him laugh.

"Harder, kitten. You're turning me on."

An idea strikes me. If I want to win this game, maybe I need to play by his rules.

"Actually, you can stay right there," I say. "Make yourself comfortable if you like, but I have a dinner to get ready for."

I reach for the hem of my shirt and pull it off, leaving me in nothing more than a bra and a lacy set of underwear. I'm turning up the pressure, just like he did to me in the natatorium.

He seems completely unfazed, however. He takes my suggestion and sits on the edge of my bed as if I'm not nearly naked here.

That's fine. I can keep going.

I reach behind me and unfasten my bra, then toss it to the floor to join my shirt, but this doesn't seem to affect him either. If stripping until the other person gets uncomfortable were a sport, I'd be losing. I need to take this up a notch and make him so miserable that he has no choice but to admit defeat and leave.

"Scoot over. That's my side of the bed." I motion for him to move, and he does. Shit.

He's already seen the sex-toy collection, so I rip open the drawer and pull out the Magic Wand again. It's still plugged in and ready to go. I place it between my legs, rubbing the silent head right on top of my panties.

This does nothing for me, and I'm not even remotely turned on, but I let out a soft moan and pretend it feels amazing. I even throw in a subtle roll of my hips.

To my horror, Bennett rubs the swelling crotch of his pants and releases a low growl deep in his chest. Surely he doesn't plan to compete?

I spread my legs and turn the device to its lower setting. "Mmm, Maverick, that feels so good."

Bennett follows suit, lowering his pants and stroking a mass that leaves me blushing. I've seen it soft, and it was impressive, but holy shit. Do big dicks just run in the family? Kindra regaled me with tales of Ezra's cock, and I always thought she was exaggerating. I'm sorry for ever doubting her.

My gaze snags on the vertical bolt of silver piercing his cock, just below the head. I shouldn't stare, but then I see his balls. Two more piercings run horizontally through his sack. I've never seen anything like it in real life. Only in porn.

But it isn't Bennett's cock I should be thinking about, so I force myself to look away. I count to ten so that he doesn't think I'm feeling some kind of way about him, and then I let out a louder moan.

The bed begins to shake as Bennett speeds up his strokes. He makes sounds to match mine, but they're much more masculine. Groans, growls, and grunts rush from his parted lips instead of moans and whimpers.

If he's trying to match everything I do, I'll just have to up the volume. Nothing is more ridiculous than a man screeching like a woman, so he'll be forced to reach my heights or admit defeat, and I get a laugh either way.

"Oh, god!" I yell. "I'm going to come! I'm so fucking close! Don't stop, baby!"

"Yeah, you little slut!" Bennett yells, matching my volume. "I'm gonna come too! I'm gonna fill that little pussy!"

I'm nowhere close to coming, but the vibrator must be working some magic because Bennett's words give my pussy a little love tap. I've never tried degradation—I'm ashamed to admit I haven't tried much at all—but this man might have unlocked a new kink.

To be explored fully with Maverick, of course.

"Fuck, fuck, fuck!" I scream.

I dare to look over at Bennett, and I can tell he's faking

his enthusiasm just as much as I am. Hell, he's going over the top at this point. His hand moves so fast that I'm beginning to suspect he's part Sonic the fucking Hedgehog, and if he keeps this up much longer, he's going to get a nasty friction burn or start a small fire.

I can't have that. I have to win.

Getting onto my hands and knees, I click the switch and put the vibrator on its highest setting. I buck my hips and fake the best orgasm of my life, complete with cries of ecstasy and bed-shaking theatrics.

And that's when the door to my bedroom flies open.

Chapter Eight

Bennett

I don't know how I expected this to play out when I tried calling her bluff, but Ezra and Kindra were never a factor. Yet here they stand, eyes wide and jaws hitting the floor as Cat and I fall off opposite sides of the bed.

"Kindra! Oh my god, look away!" Cat squeals. Judging by the shuffle of fabric and the way the comforter disappears to the other side of the bed, she's pulled it down to cover herself.

I tuck my stiff dick into my pants and debate standing up. Despite faking my enthusiasm, the erection was real, and it doesn't want to go down, even in spite of this horrifying outcome.

Peeking over the side of the mattress, I spot Ezra and Kindra in the doorway with their backs to us.

"We thought someone was being murdered in here," Ezra says. "I'm glad you two are getting along so famously now, but maybe tone it down a bit."

Cat has used the comforter to conceal her front, but her ass faces me in all of its glory as she rises to stand. I might despise the girl, but her perfectly full cheeks scream well-done BBL. She claims she's all natural, but no one gets these dimensions without a lot of work, and I've never seen her in the gym.

"It isn't what you think," she says.

Kindra dares to turn around. "We walked in to both of you pleasuring yourselves and screaming out in the throes of passion. What else are we supposed to think?"

"She told me she wanted to pay me back for saving her life, didn't you, kitten?" I say as I stand. The boner has retreated, though looking at Cat's ass didn't help things along.

"Don't call me kitten! And you didn't save my life, remember?"

"Either way, you started it," I say.

"And I'm finishing it." Ezra turns around. "Dinner begins in exactly thirty minutes, and if you aren't in the dining hall at precisely that time, you will go hungry. I have worked too hard to orchestrate this retreat for the two of you to make a dog's dinner of it. Understood?"

Cat and I nod in unison. Ezra doesn't put on his serious face often, but when he does, I've learned to pretend I'm listening. Nothing—not even my brother's stern looks—will deter me from making Cat miserable.

"Guess I'd better throw something on and get to the dining hall," I say as I walk across the room, fully clothed.

That earns a frustrated grumble from Cat. Her hair is a mess, she's still nearly naked, and she doesn't have enough time to shower before dinner. She'll have to sit beside Maverick while looking like a woman who's just woken up on the wrong side of the bed.

Everything worked in my favor.

Per usual.

I slip past Ezra and Kindra and head for my room, which is only a few feet away. My brother's eyes burn a hole in my back as I make my retreat.

I don't know why he's so goddamned butthurt about this. Even after Cat announced her plans to attend, he invited me to this retreat. Hell, he practically begged me to come. Did he expect me to leave her alone? Does my brother know me at all?

I go to the dresser in my room and pull a wrinkled t-shirt and some jeans from a drawer. Unlike Cat, I have no desire to impress anyone here. Or elsewhere, for that matter. When a woman falls in love with me, it's usually when the clothes are off anyway.

After washing my hands in the bathroom—I'm not a total slob—I head to the stupid double staircase and spot Maverick on the landing. He's standing with Ice Pick.

I give the men a wave, and they wave back, but I don't head over to join their discussion. If I want to make sure I'm seated beside Cat, I need to hurry to the dining room and check the name cards. While forcing her to sit beside her crush while she looks like a bedraggled sea monster is tempting, I've decided it will be more enjoyable to witness her misery from a closer vantage point.

Unlike the dining room on the island, this place lacks the single massive table that runs the length of the room. Instead, it's set up more like an event space, with several round tables dotted about.

I travel through the tables and search for my name. My designated place waits between Ice Pick and Grim. That won't do. I pluck my card from the snowflake table setting and hurry to find Maverick's card. That's who Kindra has put beside Cat. I'd bet my bike on it.

Sure enough, I find the two cards side by side. I feel a little guilty for moving Maverick to a different table, since he's like family to Ezra and me, but his conversation with Ice Pick seemed amicable enough, so I don't feel too terrible about what I'm doing. By the time I swap the cards and take my seat, the guilt has already subsided.

Minutes later, the guests begin filing in. Maudlin Rose and Grim enter together, followed by a handful of people I don't recognize. Maverick and Ice Pick aren't far behind, closely followed by Jim, Ezra, and Kindra. Those three are at my table.

Well, the table I've commandeered.

"Bennett, how have you been?" Jim approaches and brings me into an awkward hug. "Your brother has worked wonders with this retreat, has he not?"

"Kindra gets most of the credit," Ezra says as he takes his seat. "For someone who thinks home decorating is an elitist hobby, she certainly took to it like a duck to water."

"More like a chicken in water," Kindra says. "You sort of shoved me in, so I had to sink or swim."

"Where's our little blonde friend this evening?" Jim looks around the dining room. "I so enjoy seeing her ensembles. Such a fine figure, too."

Poor Jim. He's overcompensating again.

Not quite ready to come out of the closet, he tries to pile on covers so we won't see who he truly is. I am not a compassionate man, but even *my* steel-lined heart breaks for him. None of us gives a flying shit about his sexuality, and we've all known his preferences for years. But we also understand that he has to make the choice to reveal this to us in his own time, so we just play along.

"Too bad she doesn't have the brain to match," I say with a laugh, but no one joins in. I clear my throat. "Kindra, you were with her earlier. Will she be joining us for dinner?"

"Actually, no. She was feeling a bit tired, so she's going to stay in her room for the evening. I'll have Chef send something up for her."

Another plan ruined. I sink in my seat and try to find a reason to exist that doesn't involve torturing Cat.

But then, an idea strikes me.

When Cat ate the fruit salad at the summer retreat, she thought I'd dished up the same pineapple I'd dicked down. I never corrected her because I was too ashamed that I hadn't thought of it first. Now I have a chance to make her eat something I've shoved my dick into.

I excuse myself from the table to a round of suspicious looks. They know I'm up to something, but they can't prove it. Thanks to Cat's brief tour earlier today, I know exactly where I'm going, so I don't even need to ask for directions. As far as they're concerned, I'm just making a trip to the bathroom.

When I'm certain no one is looking, I slip through the door to the kitchen. Pure chaos echoes off the walls of stainless steel—that's the only way to describe it.

"No, no, *no!*" Chef Maurice shouts as he tosses a pot of scalding soup at one of the kitchen staff.

Boiling liquid melts the man's skin, and the worker collapses in a writhing, screaming heap. I consider myself a pretty hardened killer, but I think I just found my hard limit. Having your skin seared off is a pretty shit way to go.

"Don't just stand there!" Chef shouts at another worker. "Take him to the freezer! I have no use for a man who over-seasons my food. I said a *sprinkle* of salt, not a pinch!"

A woman in a white apron grabs the man's feet and begins dragging him toward the walk-in freezer. Thankfully, the hot liquid didn't reach that part of his body, so his skin doesn't slide off. Unfortunately, it did land on his face, which is now scraping the floor and leaving a pretty gruesome trail.

"You just can't find good help these days," I say with a shake of my head.

Chef Maurice agrees with a curt nod.

Now that I have him on my side, it's time to lay it on a little thicker. Nothing gets through to this man quicker than a compliment, even if it's a lie.

"Say, Chef, you wouldn't happen to have something I can take to a guest's room, would you? She's not feeling well, but we want to make sure she gets to enjoy your incredible food."

"Oh, of course! I can prepare a quick-service plate. No soup and salad, but she can have the entrée, which is roasted pheasant with a lemon-dill sauce, mashed potatoes, asparagus spears, and scones."

"She's going to love it," I say with a devilish smirk.

Chef totters off to prepare the plate, and within minutes, I'm weaving through the backstage corridors with a cloche-covered dish in my hands and a bounce in every step.

Before I head to her room, I go to mine first. Mashed potatoes are a favorite of Cat's, but they appear to be missing something. I know just the thing to make them taste even better.

I place the dish on an ottoman in the corner of the room and remove the cloche. Fragrant steam rushes up to greet me. Now I'm almost sad I'll miss dinner, but the results will be more satisfying than any meal.

But there's another problem. I just planned to stick my dick into the potatoes a few times and serve them to her, but now that I feel the heat rising from the plate, I'm worried about third-degree burns. As soon as the heat travels into my king's crown piercing, I'll also scream like a girl.

I fan the food with my hand and blow on it, but it's not working fast enough. Does this plate hold in heat or something? I pull off my shirt and use that to create more air movement than I can with my mouth. Her dinner won't be piping hot, but that's fine. I'm sure she'll still dig right in.

After unzipping my jeans, I look down at the plate with a smirk. "Come to daddy."

I've just driven my dick into the mashed potatoes when I hear a knock at my door. For fuck's sake. I haven't been gone long enough for anyone to come looking for me, and besides that, I don't need a fucking babysitter.

I use my finger to repair the large dent in the potatoes, and then I tuck my dick away and head for the door. What I find on the other side isn't what I expect.

"I heard you come back from dinner pretty early," she says. I don't miss the way her eyes flit to my exposed chest before rising back to my face. "What are you planning? Haven't you done enough damage for today?"

My mind scrambles for an excuse. "I was just about to bring you a plate. Kindra said you weren't feeling well."

"But you had to come to your room first?" Her eyebrow rises, and before I can stop her, the little cockroach drops beneath my arm and wiggles into my room.

It doesn't take her long to spot the plate on the ottoman. With the way the artificial sunlight streams in and lands right on it, it's practically in a spotlight. She looks from the ottoman to me.

"You really are sick," she says. "Is it the smell of the food that compels you to fuck it, or is it something about the way it looks?"

"I wasn't going to fuck anything. The cloche must have fallen off when I set it down so I could change into something more comfortable."

"More comfortable than a t-shirt and jeans?"

"Take the food or don't, but get the fuck out of my room."

I step toward her and reach out to grab her arm, but she ducks beneath my grasp.

"Your pants are unzipped and you're shirtless," she says. "You've probably already violated that poor pheasant, and there's no way in hell I'm eating it now. I'd rather starve."

"Suit yourself, then." I shrug and walk toward the ottoman.

"What are you doing?"

"If you aren't going to eat it, I'm not going to waste it. I've already missed dinner, so I might as well make the most of the food you don't want because you're paranoid." I sit on the edge of the bed and wave the plate beneath my nose. "Man, this smells amazing."

"So it *is* the smell," she says with a curl of her lip. "Give me that."

I pretend to tug the plate out of her grasp as she reaches for it, but I only do enough to make her believe I don't want her to have it. Because that makes her want it more. She plucks the plate from my hands and starts for her room. It's a shame I won't get to witness the moment she puts the potatoes into her mouth, but I can always fantasize. Besides, I need to plan for tomorrow.

Once the door closes behind her, I grab the event sheet and look at what's on offer for the first official day. It's hard to decide what to plan for when I don't know what Cat will be doing, though. Then a note about tomorrow evening's festivities catches my eye.

Tomorrow is New Year's Eve, and there will be a party to celebrate. The brochure promises dancing and drinks and masked fun in the ballroom following dinner. After that, we'll go to the natatorium to watch fireworks through the wall of windows while we remain in a heated room. I don't know how we'll all fit in there unless some of us are in the pool, though.

I guess I'll find out tomorrow night. The party is mandatory, and I wouldn't miss it for the world. If Cat thinks she's going to kiss Maverick at midnight, she's only setting herself up for disappointment. For now, I'll just have to be content with knowing the girl is in the next room with my dick in her mouth.

Chapter Nine

Cat

It's almost nine in the morning, so I'd better get a move on. The carriage for the ski lift leaves in fifteen minutes, and I'm wearing little more than panties and a full face of makeup.

Shorty jumps onto the bed and headbutts my elbow, which bumps my arm and sends a glob of black eyeliner racing up to my temple. I'm fine. This is fine. Just one more log to add to the growing pile—which will soon combust.

"Go play with your toys," I say as I pull him close for a cuddle. "Mommy has to get ready for a snowboarding lesson." I gently place him on the floor.

He trots a few steps before flopping onto his side with an annoyed flick of his ebony tail. I set back to work, repairing the errant eyeliner and applying some mascara. Maverick won't even see my eyes through the goggles, but it gives me confidence.

After brushing the cat hair from my pink snow gear, I dress as quickly as I can. Layers matter in this climate, so I even toss on a hideous pair of long johns underneath everything else. It's not like anyone will see them, and if I don't focus on them, I can almost ignore the way they're scratching my skin. At least the puff of blonde hair peeking from the bottom of my pink toboggan looks cute.

"Be good," I say to Shorty as I head for the door, but he only flicks his tail and squints his eyes.

I totter down the stairs, barely able to bend my legs under the weight of all these clothes. How do snow bunnies look so cute for winter sports? I feel like a monster in a black-and-white horror flick as I approach Grim, Ice Pick, and Maverick near the front door.

"Are we the only ones going snowboarding?" I can't contain my excitement at the prospect of an entire event with Maverick . . . without Bennett anywhere in sight.

Maverick glances up the stairs. "It appears that way."

He looks like a snowy dream. Unlike me, he moves so fluidly in his winter gear. I wish I could ride *him* to the bottom of the mountain. A snowboard will have to suffice, though.

"Rosie planned to join us," Grim says. "I will just pop up to her room and check on her. If I have not returned in ten minutes, you can count us out."

Ice Pick peeks past the curtain covering one of the narrow windows on either side of the door. "The carriage isn't here yet, so you have time."

Grim just smiles, nods, and heads-up the stairs. Something tells me they won't be joining us.

"What about Ezra and Kindra?" I ask. I leave off Bennett's name for fear of calling forth the demon.

"They're busy setting up for tonight's New Year's bash," Maverick says. "It was supposed to be a masquerade ball, but the masks never arrived. Kindra's trying to whip something up with what we have around here."

A good friend would help her with that. Hell, a good friend would have known she needed help to begin with.

"Guess I should skip the snowboarding, then," I say as I reach up to pull the toboggan from my head.

Maverick shakes his head and places his hand over mine. "No, I have strict instructions to make sure you go snowboarding and that you get your first kill."

I don't have to ask who issued those instructions. Kindra is really winning at this friend thing.

But now my nerves are acting up. This is really happening. With no sign of Bennett, I'm guaranteed to get a kill. My stomach rolls into my chest.

"Maybe I should go help her anyway," I say. "After all she's done for me, I kind of owe it to her."

"Kindra thought you might say that. I'm supposed to respond by saying that if you don't go snowboarding, you're welcome to help Bennett with the mask making."

So that's how she's kept him away from me this morning. She went to a lot of trouble, and now I can't let her down.

"That's what I thought," Maverick says with a laugh. "Looks like you're stuck with us."

He wraps his arm around my shoulder, and I want to climb inside his coat and feel each rippling muscle. I snuggle a little closer, then look up into his face. But it's not his face. It's fucking Ice Pick.

"We'll take real good care of you, sweetheart," he says, and I can smell the onions from whatever he had for breakfast.

I take a step away and pat his hand. He's a harmless flirt, but I'll puke if another oniony breath blows into my face.

To be honest, I feel kind of bad for the guy. He wants so badly to fit in that he often goes a little too hard. We all treat him kindly enough, but we don't exactly go above and beyond to include him in things. I wish I could, but I'm afraid he'd take it as flirtation instead of friendship.

"Wait!" a female voice calls from the second floor. "Don't leave without me!"

A tall figure rushes down the stairs. When she reaches the group, she bends at the waist, puts her hands on her thighs, and struggles to catch her breath.

"My flight was delayed last night, so I didn't even arrive until dinner was nearly over, and then I overslept this morning," she says. Thick box braids drape from either side of her head, the ends tapping against her heavy designer coat with each breath she sucks in.

As she stands, I get a better look at her face. Her high cheekbones accentuate her dark eyes, and her umber complexion is flawless. I don't even think she's wearing any makeup.

She's stunning.

And Maverick hasn't taken his eyes off her since she joined us.

"Guys, I'd like to introduce you to a new friend of mine," he says as he steps closer and brings her into a hug that never seems to end. By the time they separate, my body temperature has risen at least ten degrees. "This is Eve, also known as the Alimony Killer."

"Only among those in the know," she says with a smile. "I'm a contract killer. When wives are dissatisfied with their current arrangement and wish to try something new, I help them keep the benefits of their current marriage while disposing of the liabilities."

I'm not sure how I feel about that. The reason I hold

Kindra, Ezra, Maverick—and yes, even Bennett—in high esteem is because they kill with purpose. Eve doesn't appear to have the same morals, and that makes me uncomfortable.

"We met at dinner last night," Maverick adds. "Imagine my shock when I learned she loves snowboarding in her free time."

"When I'm not modeling or pursuing a target," she says with a laugh that sounds like music.

Of course she's a model who loves snowboarding and murder. And they met at the dinner I skipped because of Bennett. I didn't even get to eat last night because of him! When I discovered his devious little short and curly beside the mashed potatoes, I realized how close I'd come to eating more of Bennett's sexual conquests.

"I guess that's everyone," Maverick says. "Shall we head to the sleigh?"

We nod, and the four of us head out into the dark. Someone was kind enough to shovel and salt the walk, though, so at least I don't have to worry about slipping on ice and making more of a fool of myself.

Who am I kidding? I've done nothing but make a fool of myself since I arrived, and it's only getting worse. Now I'm about to fall down a large, snowy hill, and when I reach the bottom of the slope, I'll probably chicken out of the kill. Then this braided goddess will swoop right in and take it without batting her perfectly applied lashes.

As we climb into the sleigh, my heart sinks again when Maverick sits beside Eve. Ice Pick seizes his opportunity and snuggles up to me, bringing an onion-scented cloud with him.

There go my hopes and dreams for the party tonight. When the clock strikes midnight, Maverick would be stupid to kiss me instead of her.

The coachman clicks his tongue and gives the reins a gentle snap, and the horses start forward. Old-world lamp-posts line the path on either side, casting a soft glow to guide the sleigh. A light snowfall patters down, each flake melting as soon as it touches skin.

"Might be a good idea to put on any face coverings now," Maverick says over the sound of the rails cutting through snow. "Your face might ice up, and that's not particularly comfortable."

I pull a pink ski mask from my pocket and ease it over my face. The itchy wool makes me want to rip it off immediately, but the thought of literally freezing my face off stays my hand.

Eve pulls her mask on as well, though it's much thinner and looks infinitely more comfortable and stylish than what I'm wearing. It covers the bottom half of her face, and instead of looking like a colorful bank robber, she still looks like a fucking model.

"Goodness, I don't know how you can stand that wool," Eve says.

"I just wanted to make sure my face stays warm," I say through a forced smile.

Eve reaches into her pocket and pulls out a second thin mask. "I brought two in case someone forgot theirs. It's just as warm as wool, but it's more comfortable."

Great. She's beautiful, confident, *and* kind.

I take the mask from her and slip it over my head. She was right. Despite the thin material, it's just as warm as the wool and much softer against my skin.

"Wouldn't want your pretty face to end up with a rash," Eve says with a wink. "You can keep it."

I can't tell if that was a backhanded compliment or

something more genuine, but then Maverick brings things into striking clarity for me.

"Eve, Cat's into guys, so you're barking up the wrong tree," he says with a pat of her thigh.

"So you like girls *and* guys?" Ice Pick says to Eve, and I can already see him imagining her head between my legs.

"You wish," Eve says, and the corner of her mask lifts as she smirks. "I'm into women exclusively, and no, you can't watch."

And like a beacon in the night, hope shines eternal. Maybe I'll get that New Year's Eve kiss after all. I just have to get through this snowboarding kill first.

I don't know why I can't be honest with everyone. When I first started documenting Kindra, I was merely finding a place to turn my interests into something tangible. The fascination wasn't with the killings, though. It was about the psychology behind the slayings. Unfortunately, I didn't realize this until after Kindra agreed to take me under her wing.

Now I'm too chicken to admit that I don't think I can do it.

As the clearing for the ski lift comes into view, I'm running out of time to come up with an excuse to get out of this. I don't even have Kindra here for support. The horses stop, and everyone exits the sleigh, but I'm stuck sitting here. I don't know if I can do this. I don't know if I *want* to do this.

Then Maverick's face pops up beside my knee, and he offers his hand to me. "You ready to do this?"

My brain screams a resounding *no*, but I slide my hand into his, and he helps me down from the sleigh. Prepared or not, if I want Maverick to see me as one of them, I have no choice but to make the kill when I reach the bottom. With my resolve set, I take a deep breath and smile.

"Ready as I'll ever be."

Eve steps closer and places a light hand on my shoulder. "This is going to be so much fun, Cat. You just wait. I'll have you snowboarding like a pro by the end of this trip!"

The snowboarding isn't what I'm concerned about.

"The lift is on!" Ice Pick calls from a nearby building.

A large motor grumbles to life, and the seats begin to move on the track. With my eyes, I follow the long wire forging a skyward path up the mountain. More seats dangle at regular intervals, all of them coming and going much faster than I anticipated.

"We have to get on while it's moving?" I blink at the chairs, which seem to be speeding up.

Eve bends so that her mouth is beside my ear. "It's easier than it looks," she whispers. "Ask Maverick to help you."

With a subtle shove, she pushes me toward him. I feel bad for disliking her at first. She's a real girl's girl after all.

"Need some help?" Maverick asks, and I can only nod.

He takes my hand and guides me closer to the chairs rotating around a large cylinder. I struggle to get on an escalator without stumbling, so I don't know how I'll pull this off.

"First, watch how Ice Pick does it," he says.

Ice Pick comes out of the building and heads toward the chairs. He waits for one to pass, then steps onto the platform and walks forward until his feet meet a bright yellow line. As the chair nears him, he sits, but instead of being lifted into the wild blue yonder, the coupling attaching the chair to the cable releases, and down comes the chair, Ice Pick and all.

"Okay, maybe don't use him as an example." Maverick rushes forward and moves the chair out of the way before the next one swings through. "Didn't Jim have this shit inspected?"

Ice Pick shrugs. "No clue, but at least it let go here at the station."

"Is there a chance it could let go while we're in the fucking air?" I ask.

"There's always a chance," Eve says as she steps up. "Is the risk worth taking?"

A chair swings by, and she sits. We all hold our breath as we wait for the coupling to release, but it holds this time.

"I always take the risk!" she yells back as she floats higher.

"Me too," Ice Pick says, and he drops his ass into the next chair that swings by. This one holds too.

Maverick turns to me. "What about you? Will you take the risk?"

Fate has given me an out. I could say the lift debacle has frightened me. I could hop into the sleigh and catch a ride back to the mansion. I could avoid the embarrassment of getting to the bottom of this hill and admitting I'm not a killer.

But then the chair bumps against my ass, and off I go, rising into the air and heading toward my fate.

Whatever that may be.

Chapter Ten

Cat

Snowboarding has been more difficult than I first imagined. I thought it was all about balance, but it takes a ridiculous amount of core strength, which I don't have. My thighs, abs, and back will be sore for the foreseeable future, and God bless my ass. I've lost count of how many times I've landed on it.

And these were just the practice runs.

Watching Maverick in his element has been a soothing balm, though. In his yellow winter coat, he moves like a brightly colored panther on that board, switching his direction with a subtle swivel of his hips. He hasn't fallen a single time.

Neither has Eve. She's also been helpful, encouraging me to keep trying each time I fall. I can't imagine her killing someone, yet that's exactly what she plans to do when she takes her turn down the big mountain.

"Will the weapons be down at the bottom too?" I ask as we grab our gear and head toward the final slope.

Maverick nods. He's walking a few steps ahead of us, clearing a path with snowshoes to make it easier for the rest of us.

"There's an equipment shed at the top and bottom," he says. "That's where we store the gear and weapons. There's also a cabin somewhere nearby in case we ever get stranded out here."

"Won't be of any use if we don't know where it is," Ice Pick says behind us. He's struggling to keep up, so we all slow our pace.

"That's a good point," Maverick says. "I probably should have gotten the coordinates from Ezra, but I don't think it will be an issue today. The weather's holding, and the snow stopped."

"I think I'll need a long nap when we get back to the mansion," Eve says. "If I don't show up for lunch, don't wake me."

"Same," I say. "Though I can't skip lunch. I already missed last night's dinner."

Huffing and puffing, we reach the top of the slope. The path cuts a wide gash through the forest, and visions of Sonny Bono and Michael Kennedy play like a gory newsreel in my head. Better than a tree literally going through my head, I guess, though that's a real possibility.

Snowmobile engines buzz somewhere in the distance. I can only assume it's the staff bringing the Cattle from the mansion basement. By the time one of us reaches the bottom, they'll have the kill set up. Then it's up to us to dispatch them.

"I'll go first," Ice Pick says. He sits in the snow, and Maverick helps him slot his feet into the bindings.

I don't move. I keep staring toward the bottom of the

mountain as anxiety takes hold of my heart and gives it a squeeze.

Eve steps in front of me and looks into my face. "Hey, you okay? You look a bit pale."

She pulls off her glove, and her warm fingers brush over the little strip of forehead peeking above my goggles. Her fingers come away damp.

"Honey, you'll catch a chill if you keep sweating like this. If you're scared, we can go down together."

I'm grateful she's keeping her voice to a whisper. I'd be mortified if Maverick saw me freaking out. He's almost finished strapping Ice Pick into the boots on the board, so I'm running out of time to compose myself.

"I am a little nervous," I admit, "but it's not only about snowboarding. I've . . . I've never killed anyone before."

Before she can ask anything else, Ice Pick gets to his feet and shuffles the board to the start of the slope. A look passes between Eve and me, and we communicate so much in our silence.

I don't want to talk about this in front of anyone else, my eyes say, and she replies with an affirmative nod.

Ice Pick lowers his goggles and aims the nose of the board downhill. With all the confidence of an X Games athlete, he pushes off and starts to move forward. And with all the grace of a landslide, down he goes, right onto his ass.

Maverick sighs and shakes his head. "I should probably go with him."

A few hours ago, this might have upset me, but now I see it as an opportunity.

"I have a better idea," I say. "Why don't you help him get down the mountain, and then Eve can go down alone so that she can enjoy herself? I'll head back to the lift via the path we took from the practice area. You all can head back to the mansion in the sleigh. Have the workers ride with you, and I'll take the snowmobile back. Kindra taught me how to drive one on the day we arrived."

Maverick looks between me and Ice Pick, who is now struggling to get to his feet again. "Are you sure? This was going to be your first kill, and I'd hate for another one to get fucked up."

"She said what she said, Maverick," Eve says. "No need to babysit a full-grown woman."

"But what if Kindra—"

"If Kindra says anything to you," I say, "just tell her I demanded it be this way. She knows how I am. When I'm set on something, there isn't much you can do to stop me. Plus, I feel like I need a little more practice before I go tumbling through a mess of trees and rocks."

He blows out a breath and lowers his goggles. "Okay, but if my ass gets chewed for this . . ."

With a shake of his head, he calls for Ice Pick to stop rolling around in the snow so that he can get on his board and help him. Moments later, Maverick starts toward him, leaving Eve alone with me.

"Thanks for that," I tell her when the men disappear around a bend in the slope.

She waves me off. "Don't mention it. But are you sure you're okay to get back to the path on your own? If you want, I can wait for you at the bottom. Once you get there, you can decide if you want to get your first kill. If not, I'll help you come up with a reason why you didn't."

I flop onto my ass—intentionally, this time. "I appreciate the gesture, but I think I just want to use the fear of smashing into a tree as an excuse. Do you mind keeping this just between us?"

She smiles down at me and shakes her head. "Not a bit.

But you know . . . you may not be a killer, and that's okay. Not everyone is cut out for this hobby."

Eve wields these words as if they're flowers, not realizing the rose stems still bear thorns that pierce my heart. Knowing her intentions come from a place of kindness doesn't soften the blow.

Because I've heard these words before.

It's okay if you aren't good at sports, Cat.

It's okay if you aren't good at dancing, Cat.

It's okay if you never get a callback from an audition, Cat.

But it's not okay. None of it has ever been okay. When will I finally discover something I'm good at? When will I finally belong?

"No," I say. "I want to do this, but I want it to be on my terms. I think it'll be easier if I can make my first kill on my own. Could you make sure everyone is gone by the time I get down the mountain?"

"Sure thing, honey." She kicks a clump of snow with the toe of her boot. "So . . . are you sure you're only into men?"

"Unfortunately, I am as straight as a board, but if I wasn't, I'd eat a hole straight through you."

"Fuck, don't tease me like that," she says with a moan.

"I'm serious. You're the full package. I was jealous of you at first because I thought you had eyes for Maverick, and I knew I didn't stand a chance."

"I don't think any woman stands a chance with him."

"Why do you say that?"

Eve places her hands at the small of her back and stares down the mountain. "When I sat with him at dinner, he mostly talked about work. We're in the same field, so there was plenty to talk about, but he never steered the topics toward anything else. He gives the vibe that he's emotionally unavailable."

"Kindra's mentioned something similar," I say. "So has Ezra, come to think of it. I guess it would be silly of me to try to kiss him at midnight, huh?"

"I wouldn't say *silly*." Eve sits beside me and begins strapping her feet to the snowboard. "He's a very attractive man, as far as men go. He gives off golden-retriever energy, too, and bitches love that."

I sigh. "Yeah, bitches do."

She stops fastening the ankle straps and looks at me. "You're a golden retriever too, though."

"Me?"

"Yeah, *you*." Her fingers set back to work again, and then she stands. "You're like a little ball of happiness, spreading joy wherever you go. You don't even have to try."

"Thanks, Eve."

"Don't mention it." She gathers her braids, tucks them into her hood, then lowers her goggles. "I'll see you at the party tonight, yeah?"

"You can count on it. If I chicken out with Maverick, you can be my kiss at midnight."

"Don't do that unless you're prepared to question your sexuality."

And with that, she disappears down the mountain, leaving me alone with about a mile to walk. At least the sun is up now.

I pull my mask into place and lower the goggles over my eyes. The latter serves a dual purpose, protecting my eyes from the freezing winds and dimming the glare on the snow as well.

Once I'm in the woods again, the animals come to life.

Dark squirrels with bushy tails leap across the branches above me. A hare in its white winter coat darts across the path in front of me, there one second and gone the next. If it weren't for the little footprints he left behind, I'd think I imagined him.

After wandering for a half hour and fearing I've lost my way, the familiar practice area comes into view. There's the log I smacked my leg on. And the pile of snow I fell on that was actually a snow-covered rock.

The whir of the lift buzzes nearby, and I head in that direction after depositing the snowboard and other gear in the equipment shed. I board the lift, just like Maverick taught me, and I'm proud when I don't slip and fall to my death on the first try.

A blanket of white expands below me. As I pass near a stretch of trees, a caribou runs to the shadows for safety, its clunky feet pushing it silently along. It would be a magical moment if I wasn't heading straight for doom.

"You can do this, Cat," I whisper to myself. "Just get there and make the kill."

I hope the Cattle's mouth has been glued shut. If they plead for their life, I don't know that I'll have the strength to go through with it, regardless of what they've done. Maybe asking to make a kill without an audience was a bad idea. Peer pressure has its benefits. I wouldn't have tried anal without it, and I love anal.

Unable to focus on the natural beauty in every direction, I turn inward and try to hype myself up. I just need to cut through the thick moral fiber that tethers me so firmly to righteousness.

Kindra says killing makes the world a little brighter because she's ridding it of darkness. When she's the one wielding the knife and doing the stabbing, I can see the rightness of her actions. Why can't I feel that same sense of purpose when the knife is in my hands?

Maybe a knife is the wrong weapon?

Most killers have a preferred methodology. Not only do they prefer a certain victim, but they also prefer a certain way of getting the job done. There's something to that, I think. I have my victim pool, so maybe I'm just missing the right weapon.

Exhilaration runs through me. I've just had an epiphany, and my determination to make this kill is renewed. Maverick said there's a weapon shed at the bottom, which means I'll have pick of the litter. With no audience to make me nervous, I can take as long as I need to find which weapon feels right for me.

As the lift nears the station, red splotches on the snow come into view. Three bodies lie in a pile nearby, though I'm still too far away to discern how they were killed. A fourth figure kneels in the snow, and as the chair moves closer, I can see that the figure is shivering. It's a man in a red snowsuit. He lacks any type of face covering, and his hands are tied behind his back. Since he isn't making any noise, I can only assume his mouth is glued shut.

I step off the lift like I know what I'm doing, then hurry to the narrow path tucked behind the small building. This is the only path in the area, so I can only assume the weapons are this way. After a few minutes of walking, I find what I'm looking for.

The tin shed stands right off the path. It's much smaller than the shed where we keep our gear at the top of the mountain, so I'm worried I won't have much to choose from. I won't know until I take a look, though, so I hurry to the door, whip it open, and step inside.

Sunlight struggles to filter through the doorway, so I reach out and feel for the lights. A single bulb dangles above my head. I pull the cord attached to it, and the bulb flickers to life.

This space looks more like a tool shed than a weapon cache. A bloody hammer lies on a wooden table, so I guess someone took out a lot of anger with their kill. Wrenches, saws, and extension cords hang on the far wall.

I take a few timid steps toward the extension cord and pull it from the hooks holding it in place. The weight feels good in my hands, but I doubt I have the strength to strangle someone. Kindra says it takes a lot longer to accomplish than what they show in the movies. I could always give it a try. If it doesn't work, I can move on to something else.

Then again, if it takes too long, I might change my mind. I need something more final.

A case for a chainsaw catches my eye. That would certainly be quick, but then I remember what happened at the summer retreat. I need to make sure it actually works before I haul it all the way back to the kill site.

I step over a jackhammer and nearly break my neck as the extension cord tangles around my feet. *Thank goodness for all this padding.* That's all I can think as I go down. I may not look cute, but at least I didn't break anything. Instead of getting to my feet, I shuffle on hands and knees to the chainsaw case and open it.

It's empty.

I guess someone else had the same idea, but they could have put it back where it belongs when they finished with it. Now what am I supposed to do?

Gripping the nearby wooden table for support, I try to pull myself to my feet. I'm no longer grateful for all this padding as I struggle to stand. And that's when I notice the silence.

Instead of the distant whir of the ski lift, I hear only my heartbeat and each squeaky breath that whistles out of my nose. What a terrible time to get a nose whistle. If the Cattle somehow managed to get to his feet, he only needs to listen for each noisy breath I take.

But if I'm to be pitted against a killer again, I won't let Bennett steal my thunder this time. I'll take out this piece of shit all by myself.

My gaze flies around the room, landing on everything and coming up with an immediate reason why nothing will work. Most of these items require close combat. I need distance.

As I pull myself upright with a final heave, my panic only increases because the silence has been eaten up by the angry growl of a revving chainsaw. To make matters worse, the piece of shit knows which way I went. It won't be difficult to follow my footsteps straight to me.

Shit, shit, shit. I have to get out of here.

I reach to the right and grab the first thing I see: a long flathead screwdriver. It isn't much, but it's better than nothing. With a steeling breath, I head for the door.

The sun is about as bright as it's going to get today, which means it's already lunchtime. Staying to the right of the path, I cut through the woods and head toward the sound. If nothing else, I can hop on the snowmobile and zoom to safety before the sicko notices me.

No cute woodland creatures scatter before me this time. It's as if they're just as terrified as I am. They know that evil walks the woods right now, and I'm heading straight toward it.

Shadows give way to light, and the silent lift appears further ahead. The chairs hang from the cable, and not even the wind causes them to wiggle. It looks like a picture.

The chainsaw noise cuts off abruptly, and I creep forward until I can see the bodies and the blood on the snow. Just as I feared, my Cattle no longer kneels where I left him. A dent in the snow provides the only proof that he was there to begin with.

A flash of red catches my eye, and I turn my head. I blink, unable to understand what I'm seeing. My quarry shuffles toward me, then falls face first onto the cold white ground. His hands are still tied behind his back, so how did he turn on the chainsaw?

He raises his face from the icy earth and opens his mouth to scream, but the skin on his lips only stretches to impossible lengths without releasing any sound. As I hoped, his lips are glued shut. But that also means he can't explain anything to me.

I tighten my grip on the screwdriver and step from the cover of bushes and tree trunks. He doesn't have a weapon, so I have nothing to fear now.

"Looks like you're *screwed*, buddy," I say as I step toward him. I twist the screwdriver in my hand, glad no one was around to hear that one. It was worse than any of the others I've tried.

The man wiggles until he's on his back, and this is somehow worse. I can see his eyes, and they're currently pleading for me to help him.

I take a step back and close my eyes. How does Kindra do this? How can she kill someone who so badly wants to live?

Then I see red, and I don't mean figuratively. In my

mind, I picture his jumpsuit. It tells me how Kindra does this. She does this because this man has hurt people, and now it's his turn to hurt.

With my eyes still closed, I take a deep breath, step forward, and raise the screwdriver. That's when the chainsaw whirs to life once more, and it's right behind me.

Chapter Eleven

Bennett

This couldn't have gone more perfectly if I'd planned it. Not only am I going to steal her kill, but I get to terrify her in the process. My only regret is that I won't see the fear on her face when she wheels around and sees this masked figure with a chainsaw in his hands, then raises that pitiful screwdriver with a scream.

I step toward her, and she takes off into the woods. She doesn't even look back to see if I'm chasing her, which means she's in a blind panic.

Shit. Even if I'd had a plan, this wouldn't have been part of it.

"Sorry we don't have time to play," I tell the man on the ground. "I need to go save the wildlife from Sleeping Booty over there. I'm sure you understand."

The man starts wildly shaking his head, but then the shake turns to a spin as the growling treads melt through his neck. The head flies off behind his body, landing with a dull thud. His legs make a few weak movements that get weaker by the second, and then he stills.

I drop the chainsaw beside his body. While I'd love to leave Cat to freeze to death in the woods, Kindra wouldn't like it if I let anything happen to her little pet. That's why she kept me locked inside all morning. I'm not stupid.

And if Kindra isn't happy, no one will be happy.

Cat's footsteps are easy to follow. Even when the clouds begin to drop fat snowflakes on my head and the light begins to wane, I'm able to track her. She needs a few lessons in evasion if she ever wants to make something of herself.

The distance between each divot in the snow begins to shrink after a half hour, which means she's getting winded. She's slowing to a walk now. But then she surprises me. As the sun continues to dip, her path is harder to trace, and the increasing cold isn't helping matters. Eventually, the foot-prints disappear altogether.

As I wrestle a small flashlight from my pocket, I realize just how frozen my toes and fingertips are. They've gone from cold to painful to numb, which means frostnip isn't far off. If I'm in this shape, there's no telling how bad off Cat is. I've been tracking her at a steady speed walk, but the girl has alternated between a full run and a jog, which means she's likely doused herself in sweat.

That's bad. That's *really* bad.

"Hey!" I yell into the shadows. "If you can hear me, we need to head back!"

I stand still and hold my breath, listening for movement or any sort of reply. I hear nothing.

If the sun is going down, that means it's past two o'clock, and that means I've been chasing this bitch for nearly two hours. That's about an hour and forty-five minutes longer than I thought I'd have to chase her.

It's time to face facts. She's outsmarted me, but she's doomed herself.

She won't survive out here all night, especially if she's collapsed somewhere. If I can't find her, all that sweat will ensure she's a blonde icicle by morning. I can't stand the little twerp, but I don't want her to die.

Who will I torment if she's gone?

I stop walking and pull down the half-mask that covers the lower half of my face. "I'm not a killer, so you can come out now!" I shout. "Well, I am a killer, but I'm not going to kill *you*. This cold won't be so kind, though, kitten!"

"Bennett?"

Her small voice comes from behind me, and I turn and find her a mere five feet away. All this time, I thought I'd lost her trail, but that was only because *she's* been trailing *me*.

"How long have you been following me?" I ask.

Instead of a snappy comeback, she stumbles a step and catches herself on a tree trunk. With her face. Down she goes in a heap of pink and white.

"Fuck," I grumble as I rush forward and drop to my knees beside her. I didn't want to kill her, but I didn't want to take care of her, either. I should have just stayed at the mansion.

A long scrape runs through the goggles covering her eyes, so I can only hope they took the brunt of the impact. If the girl loses any more brain cells, she'll be in a real mess.

I smack her cheek a lot softer than I want to. "Hey, get up. If you can make it back to the snowmobile, I'll drive us out of here."

Her eyelashes flutter behind the scuffed plastic, but she

doesn't speak. I only hear her breathing, and it's a little too quick and shallow for my liking.

Snow begins to fall again. Rebellious white flakes squeeze through the canopy and land on her pink jacket. Staying here isn't an option anymore. Since she can't walk under her own power, I guess I'll have to carry her.

I get to my feet and bend down to scoop her up. If I only had to carry the girl, I'd be fine, but her snow gear makes doing everything more difficult. Typical Cat. She can't even make her rescue simple.

Stumbling forward with an unwanted package in my arms, I do my best to retrace my steps through the snow. That would be a lot easier if I didn't have so many factors working against me, such as fresh snowfall and another set of footprints to untangle from mine. Inevitably, we end up back where we started, and I don't mean the ski lift.

Cat's breathing hasn't improved, and other than asking about her cat when I nearly tripped over a hidden log, she's been silent. She's likely suffering from hypothermia coupled with dehydration. She needs to get warm, first and foremost, and then I can melt snow to give her something to drink.

I stand still and look around. Yes, we're definitely back at the tree where Cat popped out behind me. The piece of bark her goggles chipped from a towering pine is evidence of that.

The wood here is too wet for a fire. Even if I had time to craft a feather stick and some kindling, the humidity is just too high. Without a Ferro Rod, a friction fire is my only option, and that ain't happening in these conditions.

Cat stirs in my arms and tilts her head to the side with a groan. "The cabin," she whispers, and I almost don't hear her.

"Yeah, there's one out here, but I don't know where it is. If I'm honest, I don't even know where we are anymore."

"That way." Her hand drifts to the side, and she points to the spot where she came out of the woods behind me earlier.

Without another question, I pick up my aching legs and head in that direction. I'm glad my arms are numb, though. If I could feel them, they'd be screaming at me.

It's not that she's heavy, but the awkward shape of her bundled body makes her difficult to carry. She does her best to hang on, now that some of her strength has returned, but I don't know how much longer I can keep this up.

I've gone about twenty yards and am about ready to give in when the woods break open and a small cabin comes into view. Compared to the mansion, it's an outhouse, but compared to the cold, frozen wasteland we're in right now, it's a mansion.

The narrow wooden porch groans as I step up and disturb the snow. I place Cat on her feet beside the door, and she crumples in a shivering heap. As I reach up to try the doorknob, I find it locked.

"Who the fuck are they keeping out? Is there a goddamn squirrel cartel out in this hellscape?" I step over Cat and try the window, but it's also locked. Can nothing in my life come easily?

I grab Cat's arms and drag her away from the door. Judging by the absolute deadweight, she's either passed out again or has finally succumbed. I'm running out of time.

As I run off the porch, turn around, and barrel toward that wooden rectangle, I'm not thinking about the fact that Jim spares no expense. I'm not considering that this is probably a solid door made from some genetically engineered tree that's so dense that it must be cut with a special laser. It doesn't even cross my mind that the latches and hinges are made of Kevlar and titanium.

No, I don't think of any of those things until my shoulder collides with the door and I bounce back like a rubber ball.

"The window," Cat whispers.

I rub my shoulder and roll my eyes. "I already tried it. It's locked."

She struggles to stand, then goes down in a heap again. When she tries to speak, I can't understand her. I move closer and bend down so that my ear is right beside her mouth.

"The glass, you moron," she whispers. "Break it."

"I was just about to do that before you interrupted me, O wise one."

In my panic, I actually hadn't thought of that, but I won't say so out loud.

I stand and send my elbow through the window, though I'm shocked Jim didn't outfit the cabin with bulletproof glass. The thin pane shatters and falls in clear shards on the floor inside.

I reach in through the hole and unlock the door, then rush to Cat and pick her up with a grunt. "You need to lay off the potatoes," I say. "If you expect men to carry you through the forest, you might want to watch your waistline."

"At least I eat them instead of fucking them," she whispers, and that's when I know she'll be okay. When she wasn't being mean, I was really concerned.

"So you discovered my little trick and didn't eat them?" I ask as I hurry into the cabin and kick the door shut behind us. "You're breaking my heart, kitten."

"Stop . . . calling . . ."

"Stop calling you kitten?" I drop her onto the couch in

front of the empty fireplace. "I'll consider it if you promise you won't die on me."

I wait for the snappy retort, but it doesn't come. She's out again. It's for the best. Saving her is a lot harder to do when she's reminding me of all the reasons why I should let her freeze to death.

Now that we're out of the elements, we still aren't out of danger. The wooden walls block the wind, but it's still below zero in here. A few split logs have been stacked by the fireplace. It's a good start, but I don't know how long we'll be here. If we're stuck here overnight, that stash won't last.

Regardless, it's what I have for now, so I set to work.

Seeing nothing with which to start the fire, I pull out my pitiful keychain flashlight and take another look around. A couch and coffee table stand in front of the fireplace, but that's all the furniture to be seen. On the other side of the room, a wood-burning stove crouches amid towering cabinets, counters, and more cabinets. It appears there's no power, nor running water.

I head for the cabinets and begin rifling through everything. Non-perishables and MREs line the shelves of one cabinet, but I see nothing combustible. In the next, I find only medical supplies and cans of purified water that are surely frozen solid.

Then, in the last cabinet, I strike gold.

Inside, I find several boxes of starter logs and stacks upon stacks of newspaper. Now all I need to do is build the fire.

After setting the starter log in the fireplace, I pile some of the logs around it, then cram newspaper into the gaps. I leave a hole in the center so that I can push the fire onto the starter log. I crumple and twist some newspaper into a long wick, then stand there like a dumbass.

I'd planned to use the stove to light the wick, but it's a wood-burning stove.

At least Cat isn't awake to make fun of me.

Speaking of Cat, I'm not sure how she's doing while I play Where's Waldo with a fucking source of fire. Too scared to check on her, I head for the drawers beneath one of the wooden counters. Inside the first one, I find a lighter.

I rush back to the fireplace. After lighting the wick, I hold the growing flame to the starter log. The flame catches, and a pitiful burp of warmth puffs toward me.

"I will feed you so that you grow big and strong," I say to the flames as I toss in a few more newspaper balls.

I still need to find more wood on the property, but now that we have heat, we need to get dry. That has to be the next priority. Our gear is great for keeping out the cold, but the sweat inside is what gets you.

By the time I've stripped down to my boxers, the temperature has already risen to a near-tolerable level. The stones that make up the fireplace absorb the warmth and distribute it further, helping evenly heat the small space.

I turn my attention to Cat. I don't enjoy the idea of undressing her, but I don't exactly have a choice, so I set to work.

Now that some feeling has returned to my fingers, I can tell just how damp her clothes are. I pull off her gloves first. Her fingers have become slender ice blocks. They're freezing. And pale.

"Frostnip is setting in, kitten. We have to get you warmed up. I have to take off your clothes, but I'm enjoying this about as much as getting a lobotomy, so don't worry."

I don't wait for her objection, which is fine because

she doesn't even budge. When I remove her goggles and the mask from her face, I see why. She's knocked the fuck out.

Her feet didn't fare much better than her hands, but at least she was smart enough to wear two pairs of thick wool socks. That might be the only thing that saves her red-tipped toes.

This next part is usually the moment I enjoy most. Pulling off a woman's clothes is like unwrapping a present. You usually love the gift inside, but this time, I hope it came with a gift receipt.

But as I peel away the layers—which include not one, but two pairs of sweatpants, three sweaters, and a long-sleeved Henley—I discover that Cat isn't a gift at all. She's a box of Cracker Jack's, complete with a surprise inside.

"Were these your dad's long johns? Jesus Christ, they're hideous."

Cat stays silent, and that annoys me more than when she speaks. It's frustrating to have all this content and no one to riff off of.

I can't tell if the full-body underwear is cold or damp, so I err on the side of caution and decide to remove everything. Unfortunately, I learn the hard way that removing what is essentially a onesie from an unconscious adult is easier said than done.

I'll have to cut it off.

When I was scrounging around for a lighter, I saw a pair of scissors in the drawer. I go back to the kitchen—which is only about twenty feet from the couch—and retrieve the shears.

Starting at the ankles, I cut the fabric away. This delicate act hums with an undertone of violence. I've used scissors in much different ways before. Maybe that's why I'm getting hard from this. Or maybe it's because, despite my reluctance to acknowledge it, the girl is gorgeous.

The fire's glow kisses her pale skin, casting her in a light I've never viewed her in before. I don't have much feeling in my fingertips, yet her softness reaches through. It's like brushing my hand over warm velvet.

I run the scissors through the fabric covering her left thigh, but I place my free hand on her skin, providing a barrier to protect her from each snip of the blades. As I reach the top of her leg, my fingertips brush against a lacy warmth.

My fingertips recoil.

Well, they recoiled in my mind. In reality, I'm fighting off the urge to feel what's under that lace.

I drop the scissors, and they clatter to the wooden floorboards. They're the problem. That has to be it. It's misplaced arousal from a past kill and nothing more. I am *not* horny for *Caterina* goddamn *Novak*.

"Down, killer," I whisper to my dick as I grasp the scissors and get back to work.

I cut the material straight up the middle from the crotch, and I don't make the mistake of putting my hand on her this time. If I slice her from slit to tit, oh fucking well.

Once I've wrestled off the scraps of hideous long johns and her skimpy undergarments, I snatch a thick quilt from the back of the couch and drape it over her naked body.

Out of sight, out of mind.

I've done all I can for her right now, so all that's left is to hang our clothes to dry and hope that Kindra and Ezra show up before Cat wakes up. If we have to spend an entire night together, the cold won't be the only concern. We're likely to kill each other.

Once my clothes are dry enough, I'll dress and chop

some wood. Just in case. In the meantime, I'll start looking around for something to do until help arrives. If no one shows up by morning—and if we survive the night—I'll trek back to the snowmobile and get Cat some assistance at first light.

I look at my watch. It's nearly dinner time now, so we just have to make it through the next twelve hours.

God help us.

Chapter Twelve

Cat

I've died and gone to hell. That's the first thing I think when I wake up naked beneath a scratchy quilt as the bane of my existence stands before a roaring fire in nothing but his boxer briefs. His back is to me, and the fire provides the only light. Bright oranges and yellows catch and cling to his outline, hugging the round curves of his shoulder muscles and dripping down to his thick forearms.

My pussy clenches, and I want to scream.

"Come away from the fire, Beelzebub," I croak. "You're blocking all the heat with your massive head."

As he turns to face me, he seems to breathe a sigh of relief, but it's probably just the way the light dances over his very full, very sculpted chest.

Why am I looking at his *chest?*

I clear my throat and try to sit up, but a sharp pain thuds in my head and keeps time with my heartbeat. "Fuck, my brain hurts."

"You'd have to have a brain for it to hurt." He goes

behind the couch and returns with a warm mug, which he places in my hands and doesn't release until he's sure I've got it.

I tip the mug toward my face and inhale. Steam rises into my nostrils, but I can't discern the scent.

"It's chicken broth. You had two mugs about an hour ago, though you were pretty out of it."

"Is it drugged?" I ask with a curl of my lip. I still haven't forgotten that. "And there aren't any . . . special ingredients?"

I haven't forgotten *that*, either.

"No, *kitten*. Now drink your broth like a good little girl. If you finish all of it, I might even make something for you to eat."

"Shorty . . ." I say, remembering my beloved pet when he calls me kitten. "I have to feed him. His bowl has probably been empty for hours, and his blood sugar could drop."

"I've seen your cat. He can stand to step away from the table tonight."

"He's fluffy."

Bennett's eyebrows rise. "If you say so."

"This. This is why we can't get along. You don't have a feeling bone in your body."

He scoffs and heads behind the couch again. "Says the woman whose life I saved. Twice."

I'm about to close my mouth and admit defeat when I remember that we wouldn't be in this predicament to begin with if it weren't for him.

"I'm not the one who decided to play Alaska Chainsaw Massacre," I quip, though I'm not sure if he heard me. My voice sounds like I gave sloppy toppy to a fucking Dalek. "You're the villain in this story, not me."

Something clangs behind me. "No, please don't cast me in my favorite role," he pleads.

I roll my eyes and tip the mug to my lips. If I want to get out of here, I'll need my strength, drugs and demon seed be damned.

When I lower the mug, that's when I notice the red fabric lying on the floor beside the couch. I reach down to pick it up, and the cotton is enough to make my fingers ache. I let out a yelp and drop the scrap of fabric before I can figure out what it is.

"The frostnip on your hands was pretty bad," Bennett says as he sits beside me. "Buy better gloves next year. And scoot over. You've hogged the couch for hours."

I set the mug on the coffee table in front of the couch. More of that red fabric lies scattered around the floor, and it looks so familiar. I just can't—

"Bennett! You ripped off my fucking *clothes*? My sweaters? Everything?" I wrap the scratchy quilt tighter against my skin and wish I sounded more threatening. No one takes you seriously when you sound like Bobcat Goldthwait.

"No, I only cut the ugly long johns, but even if I had destroyed your precious sweaters, you were soaking wet! Would you have preferred that I let you freeze to death? I was busy saving you, remember?"

"Wait, you didn't save us. I did!"

He tips his head back and laughs. "Ha! Like hell you did. You just lay there and moaned. That's probably how you are in the sack, too. A fucking dead-fish lay."

"If the women you fuck aren't very enthusiastic, look inward, jackass. And yes, I saved us. You walked by the trail to the cabin three times. I only spoke up because I was trying to help you."

"And then you collapsed immediately after and made me carry you through the woods. Yeah, such a *big* fucking help."

I've had about all I can stand. On shaking legs, I get to my feet and look for a place to go, but this appears to be the only room.

The kitchen area takes up the cabin's back wall. The fireplace, dwindling firewood, and stacks of green Army cots take up the front wall. To the right is the exit, and to the left, there are two doors. One appears to lead outside, and I can only hope the other leads to a bathroom.

"Nowhere to run to this time," Bennett says. "Better settle in and accept your fate."

Our clothes lie on the hearth. If I can at least cover my breasts and stubbly pussy, I'll feel a little better. I didn't shave this morning because I didn't think anyone would be looking between my legs today. Let this be a lesson in preparedness.

"I'm getting dressed and going for the snowmobile in the morning," Bennett says. "You should relax for right now. There's nothing to be done."

I snatch up my bra and panties and put on some armor before I turn to face him. "Why wait until morning? The sun won't be up until after ten, and I won't survive until then."

"I'll chop some more firewood so we won't freeze."

"I wasn't worried about freezing." I snatch up my sweater and groan when I think about going back into that cold.

Bennett stands up and joins me in front of the fireplace. He grabs his pants in a huff and begins putting them on. "Fine. If you must be a nagging *bitch* about it, I'll go right now."

He zips up his pants, stuffs his hands into the pockets, and . . . his eyes widen. His hands move to his rear pockets, and I don't know how it's possible, but his eyes widen even further. If he endures much more shock, I fear they'll fall out of his head.

"Don't tell me you lost the fucking keys to the snowmobile." I drop the sweater back to the hearth, but I don't take my eyes away from Bennett.

He shakes his head and starts removing his pants again. "No, the pants are still damp. They need to dry a little more before I set out. Besides, you need to eat. I'm surprised you can even stand up right now."

As he tosses the pants back to the hearth, I hear a reassuring jingle when they land on the stones. What isn't reassuring is the sudden wave of dizziness that sweeps over my brain like a fog.

I step toward the couch, and the darkness gives way to a fuzzy white light. Sound fades away, and I can't tell if I'm standing or falling. No, I'm definitely falling. That's the floor, and it's getting closer.

Arms wrap around me before I strike the ground. Bennett lifts me into his arms as if I'm made of paper. I *feel* like I'm made of paper. He could fold me up so small that I would just disappear.

He places me on the couch and covers me with the horrid quilt again, though I can hardly feel it. It's more like a faraway memory.

"You have to rest," he says, and there isn't a mean bite to his tone now. His voice is like honey. It glides over my skin, warm and smooth, seeping into secret places like a balm. "Just stay here and let me make something for you to eat. You need some calories."

I hate that he's right, but he is. I didn't eat anything for dinner, breakfast, or lunch. On top of the dehydration and hypothermia, I've seriously put my body through some shit today.

"Maybe Kindra and Ezra will come for us tonight," I say as I settle into the quilt. The dizziness has finally passed, but I still feel hazy.

Another pot clangs.

I wince. "What are you cooking, anyway? I can't imagine there's much here."

"Just sit there and sip your broth like a good girl."

God, he's the worst.

"Is there any alcohol?" I ask as I stare into the almost empty mug. "A spot of something strong would be good right now."

"There's a surprising amount of alcohol in these cabinets, but you're too dehydrated to drink any of it right now."

"Since when do you care if I give myself the worst hangover known to man?" I peer at him over the back of the couch when he doesn't answer. "Aw, does Bennett have a wittle crush on Cat?" I say. The goal is to annoy him to the point that he plays waiter and brings me the booze. "Are you doing a big protect with your alpha-dog energy?"

"You know what? Fuck you." Bennett slams the wooden spoon onto the counter, rips open a cabinet (literally), and grabs the neck of a glass bottle. Then he stomps over and holds it toward me. "If you want to make yourself sick, be my guest, but when the sun comes up tomorrow, I'm leaving. With or without you."

If he thinks I'm opening this myself, he has lost his mind. I look up at him and wait.

Bennett jiggles the bottle and raises his eyebrows. "Cat, do you want the booze or do you not want the booze?"

I bat my eyelashes and form the perfect pout with my lips.

"How many times has that actually worked for you?" He sets the bottle on the coffee table and walks away.

With a huff, I lean forward and grab the frigid glass. I guess I can't win all the time. But as I try to peel the plastic from the bottle's neck, a fiery pain rockets through my fingertips when they touch the icy glass. The bottle slides from my hands and clatters to the floor. I let out a yelp when I flex my fingers. It feels as if they're splitting open.

Before I can register what's happening, Bennett is beside me. He takes my hands in his and begins checking them over.

"Can you come closer to the fire?" he asks. "I can't see over here."

I nod, and he helps me up. At first, I'm worried he's just pretending to be nice so that he can push me into the fire. He'll tell everyone I tripped and that he did what he could to save me. But then he says something I don't expect.

"You aren't pretending to be hurt so you can push me into the fire, are you?"

I cough to cover the laugh that tries to escape my chest. "No. If I wanted to attack you, the bottle would have been better than trying to push your big head into the fire. You'd just clog the chimney."

The hearth is too warm to sit on comfortably, so we kneel together in front of the fireplace. He turns my fingers toward the flames, and even the minimal heat feels like I'm fingering Satan's asshole.

"Ow," I whisper as I pull away.

"Was that too hot?"

I nod. "Yeah, but only on the fingertips."

He lets out a deep sigh. "You've done some damage, but

you'll heal fine with rest. Get back on the couch. I'll open the fucking bottle."

I wish this felt more like a win. Instead, I shuffle back to the couch feeling . . . strange. Even as I settle in and Bennett shoves the open bottle into my hands, I still can't process what just happened. He was so kind. And gentle. He heard my whimper, and he rushed to find the snake that bit me.

He wanted to protect me.

If Maverick has golden retriever energy, then Bennett is a purebred German shepherd.

Careful to keep my fingertips away from anything and everything, I tip the bottle against my lips and take a small swig. Since I don't often drink, I can't place the type of liquor, but it burns like fire on the way down.

"Is there any more broth?" I rasp.

"No, but I have some warm water."

I pop a thumbs-up over the side of the couch and dare to take another swig from the bottle of doom. Fire races through my insides. As does all that broth I had earlier. Jesus, when did my bladder start taking percussion lessons?

"Hey, Benny Bear? I gotta piss."

He chuckles to himself before he says, "Sucks to be you, *kitten*. The outhouse is about twenty feet away from the cabin, and you ain't making that walk in your prissy panties."

"An outhouse? Ugh." I take another swig for strength. "What the fuck am I supposed to do?"

"Lay down some of those newspapers in the corner and let her rip."

"I'm not a fucking puppy, asshole. I need an appropriate place to go."

Bennett places his hands on the counter and looks at the ceiling. His lips are moving. Is he . . . counting?

"Just worry about the food. I'll figure this out." I stand and look around, and a cramp seizes my bladder.

I yank my clothes from the hearth and begin putting them on as quickly as I can. Each time my fingertips hit an extra-warm spot, I'm forced to power through an intense pain. But no matter what, I will not piss on the floor like a dog. Nope. No way.

Peering through the tiny window in the door, I can just make out the outhouse in the moonlight. I turn toward Bennett. "I'll be right back!" I yell in my scratchy voice as I rush through the back door and head into the darkness.

Chapter Thirteen

Bennett

Eleven minutes. That's how long she's been gone. I know, because I set a timer on my watch as soon as the door closed behind her. I told myself I'd give her fifteen minutes, but I'm already dressed. I might as well make sure she's okay while the clothes are still warm.

I take the food off the stove. Despite my best attempts, I can't get the pot of beans any warmer than cold. Cold is better than freezing, though. If Cat wants to complain, she can give it a fucking shot.

After pulling my gloves from the hearth, I slide my fingers into the slots and revel in the warmth. That will soon pass. The cold has a way of sucking every degree of warmth from anything it touches, and in Alaska, it touches whatever it wants.

Headlamps wait in the pantry, so I fetch one before I head out the door. If Cat hadn't rushed outside on legs made of lightning, I'd have given her one.

I stop walking toward the outhouse. What the fuck am I

doing? This sudden protective streak needs to stop. First I go running at the first sign of her discomfort, and now I'm trudging through the snow . . . for what? To make sure she didn't get her ass stuck to the toilet seat? To help her *again?*

And yet I'm walking forward once more, heading straight for that outhouse with the hope that she'll just tell me to fuck off. That she's okay and I'm a dirty pervert for trying to catch a peek of her with her pants down.

That's not what I hear from behind the outhouse door, though. There are no words, just muffled thuds and thumps over the sounds of crunching snow beneath my feet.

"Cat?"

"Bennett! The door is stuck!"

I reach forward and give the handle a tug. It holds fast. "The door won't open from my side, either."

"No shit? You figured that out all on your own? Well, gosh, I guess the scarecrow has a brain after all!"

After a few more bumps and bangs, something clicks from her side of the door, and then it opens. Cat stumbles into the snow. Her eyes look straight ahead, and she walks with a faux arrogance to her posture.

"Locked yourself in, huh?" I say.

She squints into the headlamp light and tries to screech her rage, but a pitiful and hoarse wheeze putters out of her throat. "You know what? You're right. I did. I guess that makes *me* the scarecrow."

"Aw, then who will I be?"

"You're the fucking tin man, remember? No feelings." She stomps toward the cabin, not needing my light to guide her. There's a slight tilt to her walk, but it has more to do with drinking hard liquor on an empty stomach than lack of light.

I follow her into the cabin, and we strip down to our

underwear again. It doesn't even strike me as odd until I grab the cold beans—that are now colder beans—and set them on the coffee table beside the bottle of whiskey.

"Why are we both in our underwear?" I sit beside Cat and hand her a spoon.

"I'm not sure. For me, it's habit. You want some of this?" She takes another swig from the bottle, then holds it toward me.

"Why not?" I grab the bottle from her and take a long pull. I'll regret this tomorrow, but that's a problem for later. Then the whiskey nearly goes down the wrong pipe when my brain registers what she just said. "Wait, habit? You habitually walk around in your underwear?"

She laughs and takes the bottle from me. "What? No!"

"Okay, because I was about to say—"

"I habitually walk around naked."

"That's . . . Naked? Really? I knew Rosie and Grim were part of the Bare It All club, but you too?"

After she swallows another mouthful of whiskey—and these swallows are getting bigger by the minute—she nods her head. "Yeah. I have an aversion to certain textures on my skin. It gives me the serious ick. When I'm home, I just stay naked as much as possible."

"Do you lock yourself inside the bathroom at home, or is that only for vacations?"

"Do you fuck food at home, or is that—"

I dip my hand into the pot of baked beans, curl my fingers around a fat clump, and ram it into her mouth before she can finish her sentence. Huge mistake.

Her mouth is so fucking warm, and as her soft tongue pushes against my fingertips to get me out of this sacred space, I nearly come in my pants. When I don't move my fingers, the push becomes more exploratory.

I'm about three seconds into a rapid-release boner when her teeth clamp down.

"Ah, fuck!" I yell. "Okay, let go, let go!"

She releases her death grip and commences to chewing the mouthful of cold beans like she didn't just try to take off my fingers at the first knuckle. This bitch is savage.

Closing her eyes, she lets out a moan. "Mmm, cold baked beans and filthy fingers. What a combo."

Fuck her. I grab the bottle and gulp down more whiskey as she pulls the pot onto her lap and digs in. This is going to be a long fucking night.

I lean back and watch the fire as Cat plays the part of a starving animal that's just been given a meal. The alcohol must really be doing its thing now. I've never seen someone so satisfied by a pot of cold beans. But with the way she's chowing down, there won't be any left for me.

That's okay. I can just make something else.

After gathering the courage to venture back into the freezing pantry, I shuffle into the tiny room and use a headlamp to light the labels. A few jars of honey snag my attention. That would probably be good for Cat's voice.

My hand moves toward the jar, but as I pull it closer, I realize I'm doing it again. I came in here to find something *I* could eat, yet I was about to walk out of here with something to help *her*. Am I sick? Am I dying?

I keep my grip on the honey and look for something to pair it with. The stovetop is big enough to warm up more than one thing at a time. Canned chicken might be okay. It's already cooked, so I don't have to worry about foodborne illness. My bigger problem will be heating the honey enough to break down the crystals that have formed in these freezing temps.

I take the honey to the hearth and set the jar near the

fire. "You mind turning this every few minutes? It needs to warm up if I want to cook with it."

"You're cooking more food?" She wraps the quilt around her shoulders and shuffles to the fire. "I always get so hungry when I drink. That's why I wanted the alcohol. My appetite is pretty shit."

She settles down beside the hearth and touches the jar, then pulls her fingers back with a wince.

"It's the temperature fluctuation," I say. "Your fingertips will be more sensitive for a while. Maybe forever."

Her gaze moves to her hands. "I won't lose my fingers, will I?"

"It's possible." I step away from the fireplace and head toward the kitchen again. Her fingers won't fall off, but life is more fun if she thinks they will.

"Why aren't your hands as bad off as mine? You're touching everything, and you don't have any pain."

I shrug. "I had good gear. Yours looks like you picked it out of a bargain bin."

"I did."

That wasn't what I expected her to say, and I don't like this game. Instead of lobbing the ball back to me, she aimed it right at my chest.

"I, uh, I need to cut more wood for the stove. Will you be okay in here for a few minutes?"

She tips the whiskey bottle against her lips and turns the jar a few inches, but she doesn't answer me.

"If you need the company, I can bring the logs inside and cut them," I say. "I might put some gouges in the floor, but Jim can replace the boards with his pocket change."

She still doesn't say anything, which is enough of an answer for me. Her pride won't let her speak her truth. She doesn't want to be alone.

If I'm just running out to grab the logs and the ax, there's no need to put on all my gear. Hell, I could probably make the run to the woodshed in my boots and underwear. I pull my warm socks from the hearth and put them on, then slide my feet into my boots. The thought of the winter wind hitting my chest gives me pause, but I won't be out there for longer than a minute.

Still, I take another pull from the whiskey bottle to give me a little extra warmth. I have a mild buzz going, which also helps with the poor decision making.

"I'll be right back," I say. "Don't forget to keep turning the bottle."

She gives me a drunken salute, then returns her focus to the honey.

After fastening the headlamp on my head once more, I grip the doorknob, take a deep breath, and race into the cold.

Chapter Fourteen

Cat

Locking him outside in the cold would be mean, especially after all he's done for me, but I'm fighting the urge to do just that. Even if it's only for a few seconds, seeing his terrified, freezing face filling that tiny window would be hilarious.

I clutch the quilt around my shoulders and hurry to the door, though the hurry is more of a stumble as the ground sways. I should probably cut back on the alcohol. Probably should . . . but probably won't. It's the only thing getting me through this time with Bennett.

Standing on my tiptoes, I can just see outside. His headlamp light bobs in the distance, but it's coming closer. He's already headed back to the house. And he appears to be running.

With a giggle, I lower myself to flat feet and lock the door. I can't wait to tell Kindra about this. She'll regret that she wasn't here to witness it.

The quilt scrapes my back as I lean against the door and

wait for the knob to jiggle. A premature laugh creeps out of me at the thought of his frantic knocking. Payback is a bitch, Bennett Carter.

But the knocks don't come. Neither do the footsteps on the stairs or the jingling of the doorknob. I stand on my tiptoes again and peer out the window, but I don't see him. His light has disappeared.

Oh, shit. What if he fell? What if he landed on the ax and now he's lying in the snow, bleeding out?

I hurry to the hearth and nearly topple over as I stuff my feet into the warm socks. I reach over and give the honey a quick turn, not wanting to shirk my duty while in rescue mode. My brain hasn't even begun formulating a plan for what I'll do if I find him injured.

The front door flies open as I'm punching my arms into what I'm pretty sure is not my sweater, and Bennett charges into the room.

"I thought you were hurt!" I croak as I lower the sweater and drop to the floor. The adrenaline has worn off, and not even the alcohol can mask the weakness now.

Bennett releases the wood and an ax to the floor, then hurries over to the fire. "I saw your stupid head in the back door's window. Figured you locked it, so I headed for the front."

"I wouldn't have left you out there for too long."

"So you locked it, huh?"

"Maybe."

He shakes his head land smiles. "I can't blame you. I would have done the same thing. I even considered leaving you in that outhouse for a bit, but you found your way out."

"Yeah, but you would have missed having someone to torment, so that's why you came to my rescue."

"How'd you know that?"

"Because I was thinking the same thing. Oh, shit, the honey." I scoot forward and turn it. The crystals have dissolved, and the stiff liquid has taken on a more fluid consistency. "Fuck, this looks good enough to eat. Do you think it's safe?"

"Honey has antibacterial properties, so you don't have to worry about it spoiling. This jar will be safe to eat for years." He picks it up and turns it in front of the fire. "I'd say this is almost ready to cook with."

He places the jar on the hearth, and as he retreats to the stove again, I take a moment to watch him walk away. He's still wearing nothing more than underwear, his boots, and that ridiculous headlamp, yet there's something annoyingly sexy about him right now.

I look at the bottle of whiskey and take one more healthy swallow before swearing it off for the night. If I'm having thoughts like that about Bennett, I'm well on my way to oblivion.

Drawers fly open behind me, and a few curses spring from Bennett's lips. "I want to know which genius forgot to order a can opener when they bought all this canned food."

Another drawer opens, and he shuts up, so I can only assume he found what he needed. Moments later, more fucks and shits follow.

"Do you need my help?" I ask.

He scoffs. "The day I need your help is the day I need to forget how to breathe."

I look at the bottle of whiskey and fight the urge to guzzle it. "I have an idea. Why don't we try to get along for the rest of our time here? Kindra and Ezra are probably on their way with the cavalry as we speak, so it shouldn't be more than a few hours."

"About that . . ."

"Before you say whatever you're about to say, should I take another shot to steel myself?"

"You might want the whole bottle. I sure do."

Fuck this. He hasn't even told me yet, and I already want to down what remains.

He dumps a frozen block of chicken meat into a pan, then joins me in front of the fireplace, where he wiggles his fingers for his turn with our new mediator, Jack Daniel's.

After guzzling a hearty amount, he sighs. "I don't have the key to the snowmobile at the lift."

My stomach sinks, but it could be worse. "That won't stop Kindra. She'll take the sleigh to the shed at the start of the property and use one of the snowmobiles to get to us. I'm sure they have a spare key."

"They might have a spare key for the snowmobiles, but they don't have a spare key for the shed." He pulls a jangling keyring from his pants pocket on the hearth, and I recognize it. It's the same set of keys Kindra used on the day we arrived.

I grab the bottle from him and knock it back. I need it more than he does.

"They'll probably come in the sleigh tomorrow morning," he says, "so we just have to make it through tonight."

"Why wouldn't they come tonight? I have plans!"

Bennett looks at his watch. "If you want to kiss Maverick at midnight, you'd better start walking. It's eleven forty-five."

"Just my fucking luck." I groan and drop my head into my hands. "Why did this have to happen tonight?"

"Maybe it's for the best. You're here with me, so there's no chance of you getting embarrassed after you try to maul the poor guy and then get shut down in front of everyone."

"Listen, I'm getting really sick of everyone telling me I

don't have a chance with Maverick. Wouldn't he have told me himself if he wasn't interested? I mean, my signals are pretty obvious."

Bennett takes a deep breath, then opens and closes his mouth a few times.

"Just say it," I groan.

"He's not into you like that, Cat. He's afraid to tell you because he doesn't want to hurt your feelings." He runs his hands through his hair and looks at the floor like he's the one who just received heart-crushing news.

I scoff and pretend my soul isn't disintegrating. "Why do *you* look so sad? It wasn't as if you were the one pining after someone who's too nice to tell you off."

"I just thought it would feel better to burst your bubble. It kind of sucks, if I'm being honest."

"So the tin man does have a heart," I whisper to the dying flames.

"Only when I drink," he says with a laugh as he tips the bottle to his lips again. "Guess I'd better get to chopping some wood, huh?"

He stands and places his hands on his lower back, then leans back to stretch. The alcohol is doing funny things to my emotions too, because the heartache isn't lingering, and I'm seriously considering what it would be like to lick Bennett's abs.

I lick my lips and look at the half-empty bottle on the hearth. "Hey, can you let me know when it's eleven fifty-nine?"

Bennett looks at his watch, then lifts the ax. "It's eleven fifty-eight, so count to sixty *really* slow and you should be about there. You can count to sixty, can't you?"

Rolling my eyes, I drink a bit more and start counting in

my head. I need some liquid courage. What I'm about to do might get me killed.

One . . . two . . .

As I count, I watch his muscles tense and relax as he brings the ax down in an arc, over and over. He only misses every few swings, but the way he purses his lips and brings the ax down with more determination on the next swing is kind of sexy.

I don't even realize I'm biting my lip until it starts to hurt.

Twenty-three . . . twenty-four . . .

A bead of sweat snakes down his forehead and clings to his stubble. The firelight dances within it, reminding me of the honey in the jar. I reach forward and pull it away from the heat. It's going to evaporate if I leave it there.

And it's not the only thing at risk of overheating.

Forty-seven . . .

Is this really a good idea?

Forty-eight . . .

I grip the quilt around my shoulders, stand on shaking legs, and step toward Bennett. He stops chopping and turns to face me as he wipes his forehead with his forearm.

"Get too warm by the fire?" he asks.

I shake my head. *Fifty-four . . .*

"Well, I can't keep cutting wood if you're standing in the way. Can you move?"

Sixty.

I drop the quilt and step into him. Fighting off the shock that he hasn't bolted in the other direction, I take a deep breath and get on my tiptoes and . . . I kiss Bennett on the mouth.

For a brief moment in time, we forget our feud. We're

just two people lost in a frigid hell, clinging to each other for a New Year's kiss.

But then Bennett remembers who I am, and his hands go to my hips. He shoves me away and wipes his mouth. "What the fuck are you doing?"

I can't even answer him. I especially can't explain why I liked it. Or why I want to do it again.

Then he's stepping toward me, his eyebrows drawn down and a fiery look in his blue eyes. And I have nowhere to run.

Chapter Fifteen

Bennett

I look down at my watch. "*Now*, it's midnight," I say as I take her into my arms and kiss her again.

She pulls her mouth from mine. "I was never good at math," she says in a breathless whisper.

I can't explain what's happening as I press my lips to hers again. It's as if all the hatred I have for this woman has crammed itself into my dick, and I want nothing more than to fill her with every inch of disdain.

And why wouldn't I want to fuck her senseless? She's beautiful, witty, and despite all my teasing, she's not actually stupid. I thought she was at first, but after knowing her for months, I see that the ingenue act is just that. An act.

There isn't a bed here, and the cots and couch are too narrow for what I want to do to her, so I settle for the quilt. I pull myself away from her and hurry to position the aged square of fabric in front of the heat.

As I lie down and pat the empty space beside me, I spy

a moment of hesitation. She's just as confused about this as I am. We both look at the bottle of whiskey.

"We can blame it on Jack," I say as I pat the quilt again.

She hurries over and sits beside me. "Or we could just keep it between us."

I lower her left bra strap and kiss her pale shoulder. "We certainly could."

"A moment of weakness," she says. "That's all, right?"

"So weak." I press her shoulders so that she lies down beside me. "That's all it is."

She pulls her arm out of the bra strap, and I lower the lacy cup until her pink nipple pops into my mouth. A soft moan leaves her lips, and her hands race through my hair, pulling my head closer.

This woman has no right being this soft or smelling this nice. I thought a night of passion with her would be more like a night of misery, but fuck, she's delicious.

"Take them off," I say. "I want to see all of you at once."

Her hands fly to the straps, then pause. There's that hesitation again. "Maybe this is a bad idea."

"Oh, it's definitely a bad idea, but we're doing it anyway." My hand moves toward her panties, but she grips my wrist.

"Wait. If we do this, I want you to promise that it won't be used against me later. No jokes about my O face, got it?"

I hadn't even thought about the chance to stock ammo for later. This is what I mean when I say she's smarter than we give her credit for. She's often thinking two steps ahead.

"I promise if you promise," I say.

She closes her eyes, bites her lip, and nods. "Okay, we promise that no one will ever know about this, and we won't use anything that happens as torture tools. Deal?"

Sober Bennett would never agree to this, but Buzzed-

and-Horny Bennett can't make the promise fast enough. "Deal."

She releases my hand, but instead of letting me take off her remaining clothes, she scrambles onto her knees and does it herself, lying back to kick off the panties once the bra is off. Not wanting her to be the only naked participant, I stand and kick off my boots, then lower my boxers. Cat has taken great pains to avoid looking at my dick in the past, but now she gazes at it like it owes her something.

"I forgot how big it is," she says with a gulp.

"Don't worry. I'll work you up to it." I get down to her level and cover her body with mine. "I'm not the type of guy who just sticks it in. You have to beg me for it first."

I lower my mouth to her neck, and her full breasts press against my chest as her back arches. Her hands move to my shoulders, and her fingers map every muscle they find. This featherlight touch sends a shiver up my spine.

"I've never been with a man who's pierced," she whispers in my ear. "Go easy on me."

"Never." I nip her skin and move lower. "A soft, gentle lover won't get you where you need to go. But I can."

My lips move over her breast. As I whisper each word, goosebumps rise. Another moan eases out of her as I take turns caressing and sucking her sensitive skin. Now that I've had her tits in my hands—and mouth—I'll have to stop calling them fake. She's just genetically blessed.

"I want your mouth on me," she whispers. "Please . . ."

I kiss a little lower, moving down to her stomach.

"Don't tease me," she says as her hands try to push my head closer to her pussy.

"You want me down here?" I smirk against her left thigh and give it a nip. "Or maybe over here?" I take the meat of her right thigh into my mouth and suck.

"Less talk, more pussy eating," she groans.

I grip her thighs and pull her against my mouth. She sucks in a breath and reaches for her tits.

"Yes, right there," she whispers. Then she freezes. "Shit. I forgot that I didn't shave this morning. Maybe you shouldn't—"

"Exfoliate my face." I bat her hands away as she tries to move my head. "Let me taste you. Come on, kitten."

The pushes become weaker, and she lets out another whimper when my tongue dips into her warmth. "Not gonna lie. That nickname is doing something to me now."

I smirk against her pussy, then tease her clit with my tongue. The nickname has always done something to her. That's why she hated it.

My full focus returns to devouring her. I don't just want to get her off. I want to give her an out-of-body experience like she's never known. As wet as she is, that won't be too hard to do.

With two fingers, I tease and stroke the sensitive skin just outside her opening as I swirl her clit with the tip of my tongue. Her hips rise, begging for more of my mouth. As I slide my fingers inside her, I take her clit into my mouth and suck.

"I'm so close," she whispers. "I want you inside me when I come."

I shake my head, moving my lips over her sensitive areas. "You'll come in my mouth, then on my cock. You're going to come in whatever position I command."

Her head pops up. "Bennett, I can't! I can only come once, and then I'm spent."

"You've been with the wrong men."

I lower my face to her pussy again. I always get what I want, and she won't be the first to defy me.

Within seconds, she grips my hair as her thighs slam against the sides of my head. I want to look up and witness this O face she's so scared for me to see, but if I break the rhythm now, I'll fuck up everything. Instead, I keep my nose to the stubbled grindstone and don't stop for air until she's relaxed again.

"Fuck, that was amazing," she breathes. "I can't remember the last time I got off without my toys."

I kiss my way up to her chest. "Better catch your breath. We aren't done yet."

"I think I'm ready for you now."

"Not yet."

Her eyebrows rush together as I lean to the side and pull the jar of honey from the hearth. "What are you doing with that?"

I unscrew the lid and dip my finger inside to ensure the temp is just right. The texture certainly is. The golden liquid moves like viscous water.

Then I sit on the couch, lower the jar, and push my dick inside.

Cat's eyebrows abandon pulling together and instead shoot toward her hairline. "I figured you would want to fuck me, but I forgot about your food fetish. I can't compete with honey."

"It's a very sexual food, I agree, but you have it wrong. Honey can't compete with *you*." I pull my dick from the honey and place the jar on the coffee table. "Now get over here and clean me off."

Cat scrambles to her knees and rushes over. Her eager attitude toward oral is a major turn on, not gonna lie. She grips the base of my cock and tries to avoid touching the sticky substance with her fingers as she runs her tongue up the shaft.

The warm honey transfers to her tongue, and she moans as she swallows it. Her courage grows, and she dares to get a little dirty as she fists my cock and strokes over the sweet, sticky, golden lube.

Then she does something I don't expect. She cups my balls with her hand and, while continuing to stroke my cock, she begins sucking and licking the skin of my inner thighs. I see why chicks like this shit. It's sending zaps and tingles all the way down to my fucking toes.

Especially when her fingertips graze my two hafada piercings. If she keeps this up, I'm going to embarrass myself and nut before I can fuck her.

"Clean it off," I say as I sit forward. "I need to be inside you now."

She looks up at me with a bite of her lip. "You aren't the one in charge right now, so I suggest you shut up and appreciate what I'm doing for you."

Her fingertips press against my chest, and I allow her to push me back until I'm resting against the couch again. I'm not the type to let a woman boss me around, but for her, I'll be an obedient boy.

For now.

She renews her grip on my junk, then lowers her tongue to the silver ball just through the ridge on the upper side of my dick. White heat swirls in my mind to the tempo of her mouth flicking over the piercing. Just when it starts to feel uncomfortably sensitive, she takes me fully, pushing me into her throat.

Her very open, very welcoming, very warm throat.

I can't tear my eyes from the perfect curve of her back as she kneels in front of me, and I need to if I want to last. But there's nowhere else to look. Everything about her seems perfect right now.

So I tip back my head and let it happen.

With a groan, I fill her throat, and she takes every drop. Not only does she catch all of it and keep sucking, but she manages to swallow without gagging. When she stops, she sits back and looks at me.

I'm pretty sure we have the same look on our faces. It's probably the same look anyone has when they try something forbidden and realize they like it too much to stop.

"Fuck, what have we done?" Cat whispers.

"Made a mess, for starters," I say as I drop my hand into a sticky spot on the couch.

"No, I mean . . . this. What we just did. If Kindra finds out—"

"She won't find out. Neither will Ezra. We aren't telling anyone about this, remember?"

She takes a deep breath and climbs onto the couch. "Right, but things will be different. You don't think they'll notice?"

"So I wasn't the only one who wants to do this again?"

When she doesn't answer, I look at her. I don't know how I'll recover my bruised ego if she doesn't feel the same.

Cat groans and buries her face in her hands. "I don't know how I feel. I thought it was just the alcohol, but now I'm not sure."

"We could always try it again when we're more sober," I suggest. "You know, for science."

She thinks this over, then nods. "I guess as long as no one knows. Not because I'm embarrassed, of course. I've always thought you were attractive."

"Right, same."

Wow, this is really fucking awkward. We need to get back to fucking around. That seems to be the sort of communication we can come together on . . . no pun intended.

But then she snuggles into me, and the awkward feelings intensify. Am I supposed to put my arm around her? Pull her closer? This romantic shit is new territory. In the heat of a sexual moment, it comes easily enough. It's the price men must pay to offload into warm waters. But outside of sex? I don't cuddle.

"You can hold me," Cat says. "I won't bite. This time."

It's not like my arm will rot off if I placate her a little, so I do it. I put my arm around her and pull her closer, and as she rests her head against my chest and sighs, I remind myself that she's probably right. This won't be our new normal. It was all the alcohol, and when we sober up in a few hours, we'll be right back to clawing each other's throats out.

There's only one way to find out, so I close my eyes and let sleep take me.

Chapter Sixteen

Cat

When I woke up, I was curled underneath Bennett's arm like I belonged there. The memories of seeing his ball-bag piercings seemed like a distant dream. Or a nightmare. I haven't decided yet.

He was still fast asleep, sitting up with his head dropped back as I hurried to dress. As I looked at his mouth, I remembered where it had been.

I set to work immediately, busying myself in the dark so that I didn't have to think about it. After building a fresh fire so that we wouldn't freeze to death, I braved the cold and dumped the still-frozen chicken into the snow outside.

That's where I am now. In the dark, outside, with no clue how I'm going to come back from this.

Or if I even want to.

All the teasing and mean-spiritedness between us feels more like foreplay now. That's how it seems to *Sober Cat*, at least. I don't know how Sober Bennett feels, and I'm too afraid to wake him up and ask him.

I kick some snow over the chicken and hope a bear doesn't sniff it out before we've been rescued. That's the last thing I need right now. When the choice is between the bear and the man, can't I pick neither? Maybe Eve is onto something.

The door opens behind me, and a squinty-eyed Bennett shivers in the doorway. "What the fuck are you doing out here? Get back inside. It's only four in the morning. Too early to risk walking back to the mansion."

"Is that what we'll have to do?" I ask. My voice still hasn't gone back to normal, but at least I don't sound like Joan Rivers anymore.

"I doubt it," he says. "Just get inside before you get sick."

I wait for the hammer to fall, for him to follow up his concern with a low blow, but it doesn't come. He just stands there and waits for me to get back inside the cabin.

"Now take off those fucking clothes," he adds when the door closes behind me. "We have a theory to test, remember?"

"Right," I say, though I wish he wasn't treating this like a science fair project. Maybe we aren't on the same wavelength after all.

As I strip away the layers, I try to recall what gave me such a massive change of heart in the first place. I mean, we're talking about Bennett here. Yeah, he's hot and protective and about as alpha male as alpha male gets, but he's also as mean as a one-eyed dog with a bone. Now that he's back to the gruff-asshole persona, I don't know if I feel the same as I did when I had liquor to numb the bite of his words.

I reach for the bottle of whiskey, but he pulls it away.

"We're doing this sober. If we want to know how we really feel, we have to have our full faculties."

I lick my lips and look up at him. I don't know if I *can* do this without Jack's help. It's just so fucking weird.

"Unless you're rethinking this?" He steps closer and tilts my chin so that I'm forced to look into his eyes. "I know I'm a prick, but I'll never force you to do anything you don't want to. If this isn't what you want, we can stop right now."

Oh fuck, now he's talking sweet again. I'm Ado Annie, being seduced by the peddler's words. If he tells me I'm like a Persian kitten with a soft, round tail, I'll melt.

"Kitten, what do you want?"

Close enough.

I rip off the last remaining fabric between us and step into him. "I want to know how I really feel about you. Let's fucking do this."

He pulls me into his body as we stand before the fire. My rational mind screams for me to stop, but I can't. I'm careering down a hill at full speed, and I don't care what I crash into.

His hands fall to my hips, squeezing my flesh and pulling me closer. My hand moves to his rock-hard dick and comes away sticky.

"Oh, shit. We've got to clean this honey off before we fuck," I say, though I'm not sure how we'll manage it. Heating snow will take ages on that shitty stove.

Bennett smirks at me, then leans down. When he stands again, he holds the jar of honey toward me. "I set it by the fire so it would get warm again. Instead of cleaning up, I say we make more of a mess."

Before I can argue that this is unsanitary and liable to give me a yeast infection, he pours warm honey over my breasts, then lowers his head to lick it off.

Okay, maybe this isn't so bad after all. Monistat has come a long way, after all.

"Lie on the quilt," he says.

My legs can't move fast enough, even though my brain says I shouldn't look so eager. But what do I care? This is a secret. He wants everyone to know what we're up to just as much as I do, which is not at all.

As I lower myself to the quilt, Bennett is right behind me. He drops to his knees between my legs and tilts the jar over my stomach. Golden warmth blankets my abdomen and cuts a lazy trail down my side.

We'll have to burn this quilt. It's evidence now.

Bennett leans down so that his mouth is beside my ear. "Turn over," he whispers. "I want you covered in this before I demolish you."

Being destroyed has never sounded so good.

I flip onto my stomach, and warmth coats my back. His tongue follows the trail. From between my shoulder blades to the crack of my ass, he doesn't miss a drop. His arm slides beneath my pelvis, and he raises my ass in the air before drizzling honey into my ass crack. I don't have time to object, and then his mouth is on my asshole.

This is a first for me. I've done a fair bit of anal, but ass-to-mouth is new. And kind of hot. As long as he doesn't expect me to return the favor, that is. Even with honey to sweeten the task, I don't think I can lick a butthole.

There's no hesitation from Bennett, however. His tongue swirls through the honey and knocks at the back door. My eyes roll into my head and I moan.

"You're fucking filthy, and I love it," Bennett groans before diving between my cheeks again.

I push into him, wanting more. "Not sure why you're calling me filthy when you're the one eating ass," I moan.

He slides two fingers into my pussy, stroking me inside while he continues licking me. "Oh, I'm filthy. I'm fucking *disgusting*, and you're about to let me inside you."

More honey coats my back. Instead of licking it away, he rubs it in with his hands, massaging sweet warmth into my sore muscles. Maybe this food kink isn't so bad after all.

I'm just about to tell him to fuck me, but a distant sound pushes my lips together. Was that a voice?

"Bennett?" I whisper.

He keeps eating my ass.

I turn to look at him, and his eyes are closed. I never knew a butt buffet could bring such bliss, but there's no time to think about it now. Someone is definitely outside.

"Bennett, stop!" I whisper-shout. "Someone is outside! We can't let them find us like this!"

He freezes and listens, and sure enough, someone is shouting our names nearby.

"Why would they come for us at"—he looks at his watch—"nearly five in the morning?"

I turn onto my side, and the quilt sticks to me everywhere. "Oh, shit, shit, shit! The evidence!"

I scramble to my feet and snatch the quilt from under him. He turns to the side and tries to grab the jar of honey before it topples over, but he isn't quick enough. It rolls into the stone hearth, bursts into fine shards, and coats the hardwood in its golden blood.

No use crying over spilled honey. I toss the quilt into the fireplace and hurry to get dressed.

It's hard to see what I'm grabbing in the dark, but it doesn't fucking matter. Once we get our big coats on, no one will be the wiser. I cram my head into the armhole of a sweater, then find the neck on my next try. Dressing by firelight should be an Olympic sport.

Bennett is just pulling on his coat as the door flies open. I drop to the couch and try to pretend I've been sitting here all along. If I can stop breathing like I just ran a marathon, I might even pull it off.

"Cat? Cat, are you alive? He didn't kill you, did he?" Kindra rushes toward me.

Ezra stops in the doorway and sniffs the air. "What is that smell?"

"Honey?" Bennett says as he looks at me.

What the fuck is he doing? He'll blow our cover right here and now if he uses sweet pet names in front of them!

"We, uh, got in a fight over the honey jar," Bennett says when I don't speak. "I dropped the jar, and it made a mess. That's probably what you smell."

Oh. He meant that.

"Yeah," I say. "I'm a real butterfingers. We had to burn the quilt because I dropped it right on top of it."

"I thought Bennett dropped it," Ezra says.

"Uh, he did," I say.

"But then she dropped it again when she picked it up, and that's how it got all over the quilt." Bennett pokes the fire, and a few logs collapse inward. "This should burn out on its own. Why don't we head back now?"

He hurries to the door, leaving Kindra and Ezra to look at me like I've lost my mind.

After what they almost walked in on, maybe I have.

Chapter Seventeen

Bennett

As it turns out, we were closer to the ski lift than we realized. Not that it would have done us any good, considering I lost the key to the only snowmobile not currently trapped inside the shed at the start of the property.

Ezra is pissed. They had to cancel the New Year's Eve party because of "my shenanigans," as he put it. Psh. It wouldn't have been a very good party without me there, anyway.

Kindra, Cat, and I load into the sleigh, and Ezra uses the spare key to drive the snowmobile back to the mansion. I can't wait to get back to my room so that I can wash all this honey off my body.

The sleigh lurches forward, and I look over at Cat. Lights along the path catch on her face every now and again, but I can't see her expression through the mask pulled over her lips. She leans over to Kindra every now and then, and the two of them whisper and giggle.

If she knows what's good for her, she'll keep her mouth shut. The last thing I need is for my brother and his fiancée to catch wind of what transpired. If this gets out, the pineapple fiasco will pale in comparison.

I wouldn't care if they made fun of us for fucking each other, but knowing them, it would be the opposite. Not only would they crow about how right they were about us, but they'd get love hearts in their eyes too. If they try barking up that tree, I'll just have to chop it down. Fucking Cat and wanting to date Cat are two very different things. I'm not certain we'll fuck again, but I can say with great conviction that dating is firmly off the table.

After a long drive through the dark woods, the sleigh pulls to a stop outside the barn. "Can't bother taking us all the way to the front door?" I ask as I climb down.

"One of the sleigh's rails broke on the return trip with Maverick, Eve, and Ice Pick," Kindra says. "We rigged it for the rescue run to save you two, but I told the coachman to stop at the barn. I don't want to do more damage."

That explains why the rescue took so long. And why they had to cancel the party.

I turn to help Cat, then remember that I'm still supposed to hate her. And I do. I hate her. Can't stand her. I definitely haven't thought about the cute way she snores.

I trudge toward the mansion and step into a blast of warmth. Ezra stands just inside the front door, so I try to skirt him, but he reaches out and grabs my hood before I can scurry away.

"We need to have a chat," he says as he pulls me toward the study.

I try to dig in my heels, but he just keeps pulling. "Can't we talk later? I've been in the cold for twelve hours, and I kind of want to shower."

He stops in the hall, just outside the study door. As he sets his jaw and shakes his head, he looks the picture of my principal in sixth grade when I pulled the fire alarm so I could skip English class.

"Do you realize what could have happened?" he finally says. "And for what? So you could tease Cat? You're thirty-three years old. It's time to grow up, Bennett."

I shrug my shoulders. "What could have happened didn't happen, though. Hop down from your high horse before you get a nosebleed."

"Your actions didn't just affect you and Cat, though. Kindra put a lot of time and effort into that party, and you ruined it. Are you pleased with yourself?"

"Are you just going to keep tossing things at me until something sticks? Ruining the party wasn't the goal," I say, and it wasn't. I feel bad for ruining her party. I'm not completely devoid of all emotions. Just most of them.

"Then what was the goal, hmm? To get Cat so lost in the wilderness that she ends up dead? To be a complete bellend because you're miserable and you think everyone else needs some misery too? Well, old boy, I've got some news for you. Some of us enjoy being happy."

"I'm not miserable."

"You're not?" He rocks back on his heels and laughs. "Could have fooled me. Everyone knows you lost some business after that last hit, and have you forgotten that I'm the emergency contact for your mother when you can't be reached? You're struggling to pay for her care. Your life is a shambles, man. Wake up."

"Fuck you." I turn to walk away.

Ezra keeps pace beside me as I trudge toward the stairs. "Life doesn't have to be this way," he says. "People change all the time. It's never too late to let go of your pride and accept some help."

I stop at the top of the landing and turn to face him. My right fist balls at my side, but I won't punch him. Despite the venom he's hurling my way, he's still my brother. "I'm not an addict or a drowning victim, Ezra. I don't need to reach out for *help*. I fucked up, and I'll apologize to Kindra, but as for the rest of it, it will all sort itself out."

"You've been iced out. I received word yesterday morning, but I wanted to wait to tell you once we were back in New York."

"Yeah, okay." I scoff. "There's no cell signal or internet access here, but you magically got word?"

"We have a contact in town who works much like the pilot on the island. Emergent news is delivered when necessary, and your former agency has been busy in the last twenty-four hours."

As I study his face, I find no pleasure there. He isn't enjoying this, which means this isn't some phony wake-up call or prank. This is real.

If I've been iced out, that means I'm no longer a contract killer. I'm just a killer. The contract is the important part, though, because it pays. Killing just satisfies an urge.

"I'll just find a job when I get back from this shit-ass trip," I say.

"Doing what? You have no experience in any field that would pay enough to support your mother's care. Nothing legal, anyway."

"Then I'll do something illegal. Problem solved. Can I go shower now?"

Ezra sighs and shakes his head. "Yeah, go shower and get some sleep."

When I start to walk away, he clears his throat. I grit my teeth and turn to face him.

"Bennett . . . just . . ." He shakes his head again. "Never mind."

"No more bad-news bombs to drop on my head?"

"Just be kinder to Cat, okay? She's going through some stuff too."

I was kind enough to give her an orgasm last night, I think as I roll my eyes and head for my room. Ezra can clear his throat again if he wants, but I won't turn around. I'm done talking.

The door creaks open on hinges that shouldn't be squeaky but are. I'll have to ask Kindra for some WD40. I click on the light and begin undressing. A hot shower will put everything right. I can wash off the memory of what I did with Cat, and I can start formulating a plan to get back in my agency's good graces. This isn't the first time they've blacklisted me in the industry.

Unfortunately, unlike last time, I have obligations to consider now. Scraping by is well and good for me, but it won't do for my mother. She spent years without basic necessities so that I could have what I needed, and I'll be damned if I have to take her away from the luxury accommodations she deserves.

I toss my sticky clothes onto the floor and head for the bathroom. A dull headache looms behind my forehead. That's what I get for drinking booze without adequately hydrating.

Thinking about the whiskey brings my mind around to Cat again. We were interrupted before carrying out our plan, so does that mean we still need to do it? It would be easier to forget the entire thing ever happened. Going back to hating each other is probably for the best. I don't even know what she wants. We didn't exactly have time to discuss what happens next.

Instead of embarrassing myself, I should just let it go. She'd probably laugh in my face if I suggested we go through with it.

But my dick can't seem to let it go. The honey releases its hold on my skin as I scrub away the remnants of Cat, but my brain clings to the memory of her body pressed against mine. When I close my eyes, I can almost hear her soft moans.

As I wrap my hand around my stiffening cock, the moans become a gag. That definitely wasn't part of my fantasy. With a retreating boner, I press my ear to the shower wall, and there it is again. A low moan, followed by a gag.

My bathroom must be up against Cat's. Since our rooms are side by side, it would make sense. What doesn't make sense is that god-awful sound she keeps making. It sounds like she's in the throes of anguish instead of pleasure.

I hurry and rinse away the soap, then dry myself with a towel. Everyone in the mansion is probably fast asleep by now, so it should be safe to check on her. If she greets me with a sour attitude, I'll know where we stand.

After shoving my legs into some sport shorts, I free-ball over to Cat's door. The hall is dark, quiet, and empty. From here, I can't even hear her in her bathroom anymore. I raise my fist and tap my knuckles against the door.

A few seconds of silence pass before the door opens just enough for Cat to poke her head through. Her hair is a mess, and red rings rim her puffy eyes. Tears cling to her long lashes, binding them together in clumps.

"Now isn't a good time," she whispers, then sniffles. "Allergies."

She didn't bite my head off, but she didn't welcome me in. Providing comfort isn't exactly my bailiwick, however. Maybe she knows how uncomfortable I'd be if she started wailing and rending her clothes in front of me.

So why do I feel the disgusting urge to pull her into me and ask who hurt her?

"Who is it, Cat?" someone says behind her.

I lean to the right and spot Kindra sitting on the edge of the bed. Jesus fuck. Shouldn't she be screwing my brother right about now?

"I can't sleep with her making all that racket in the bathroom," I say. "I just popped by to ask her to shut the fuck up."

Cat winces. "Fucking tin man."

The door slams in my face, and I'm left in the hall with more questions than answers. Tomorrow, I'll need to find time to get Cat alone. First I need to explain that what I said was only to throw Kindra off our trail. After that, I want to know why she was crying. Ezra mentioned that she was having a tough time too.

It has nothing to do with caring about her, either. That fleeting urge to comfort and protect her has passed. I'm just being nosy now.

Most importantly, though, when I talk to Cat tomorrow, I need to know if she's still down to fuck around and find out. She's consuming my thoughts, and fucking her is the best way to clear both heads at once. After that, I can finally put this whole shit show behind me.

Chapter Eighteen

Cat

Shorty purrs and stretches his claw-tipped toe beans toward my face. With closed eyes and a deep sigh, he's the picture of contentment this morning. I wish I felt the same.

I look at the faux sunshine streaming through the window. Technology has come a long way, but that realistic image lacks something. It makes me think of Bennett. He's just like that rectangle of pixels. He can fake the sweetness until you almost believe it, but when you get too close, you realize what's missing.

The warmth.

I turn onto my side and slam my fist into the pillow. Shorty stops purring as he assesses the situation, but his rumbling resumes when I cease throwing a tantrum. But why shouldn't I pitch a fit? Especially after the bomb Kindra dropped last night.

While my audition lineup isn't exactly what anyone

would consider emergent, Kindra was kind enough to have my messages forwarded to the service we use for our retreats. All the cast lists I've been waiting on were released in a clump together, and I wasn't on any of them.

I even applied for a commercial for wart cream. *Wart cream!*

I knew breaking into this business was supposed to be tough, but I never expected it to be impossible. The rejections were par for the course, as was the mounting disappointment. Now that disappointment has piled so high that I can't see the other side.

Before the hopelessness can swallow me whole, I roll out of bed and drag myself to the bathroom to wash my face. I don't know why I bother. Maverick is no longer on my radar after what Eve and Bennett had to say.

And I sure as shit don't want to impress Bennett.

Like an idiot, I was actually disappointed when Kindra and Ezra interrupted us at that tiny cabin, but now I think it was for the best. After the way he acted when he came to my door and saw me crying, I'm happy to go back to being mortal enemies.

Someone knocks on my door just as I've applied the cleanser to my face, so I hurry to rinse it off. A bit of soap squeaks past my clenched lids and infiltrates my left eyeball with the fire of one thousand suns.

"Shit, shit, shit," I whisper as I waterboard myself.

The knocking intensifies.

"Just a second!" I scream.

I look for a hand towel with my good eye, then pat my face dry before going to the door. Eve stands outside, holding a plate in her hand and wearing a smile on her face.

"Brought you some muffins," she says as she holds the

plate toward me. "We were all so worried about you last night."

I take the muffins and motion for her to come in. "I was worried for a bit, too. I've never minded the cold, but these temperatures are something else."

"Most people can't understand it until they've experienced it." Eve sits on my bed and looks around. "Where's the cat? Kindra said you brought one."

The spot where Shorty was curled on my pillow lies vacant. I place the muffins on the bedside table, then drop to my hands and knees and peer into the darkness beneath the bed. Two yellow eyes stare back at me.

"He's under there," I say as I get to my feet. "He hates strangers. Kindra's the only one he doesn't run from besides me."

"I'm more of a dog person, myself," Eve says.

I won't hold it against her.

As I dress in a pair of jeans and a snug sweater, she fills me in on the change in plans for the day. The outdoor activities have been canceled due to a coming snowstorm, so we're all gathering in the rec room for a little fun and games.

"Just keep Bennett far away from me," I say as I step into a new pair of knee-high leather boots. I really should have broken these in before the trip.

"Is he that fuckboy with piercing blue eyes and the badass tattoos?" she asks, and I nod. "He actually tried to bring the muffins to you, but Ezra plucked the plate from his hands and placed it in mine."

Now that I know they're safe, I grab a muffin and shove it into my mouth. "Figures," I say through a mouthful of warm blueberry goodness. "Fuck, these are good."

"That chef is pretty talented."

"He is, but mind the meat. He likes to cook with people."

Eve grimaces. "Thanks for the heads-up."

She stands and makes her goodbyes, then tells me to be in the rec room around ten. When the door closes behind her, Shorty slinks out from the shadows.

"You aren't very good at playing welcoming committee," I say.

He blinks up at me.

I hurry to the bathroom mirror and slap on some makeup after I scarf down another muffin. When Bennett sees me, I want him to regret every mean thing he's ever said or plans to say to me.

That's going to be hard when one of my eyes looks like it has a contagious infection. How do I even have skin left on my face if my cleanser is this strong?

I scrounge through my toiletry bag, searching for a bottle of Systane. My fingers fumble through a graveyard of expired Dramamine, faded packets of Advil, and the crushed Tums tablets that escaped their container. The eye drops are AWOL.

Maybe no one will notice the highway of inflamed capillaries sprawling across my sclera. I stroke my mascara wand over my lashes a few more times and hope for the best.

"Guard the palace while I'm gone," I say to Shorty, though I know he'll probably just spend most of the morning cleaning his asshole and clawing the curtains. I'm surprised Kindra didn't notice his artwork last night.

Fate is not my friend as I step into the hall. As soon as my door closes behind me, Bennett's door flies open. He steps out of his room and nearly knocks me over.

His hand wraps around my arm as I try to hurry past him. "Hey, you got a second?"

"Maybe," I say as I turn to face him. I should have snatched my arm away and kept walking. My brain searches for something mean to say, but I can only think of the way his hands felt on my naked body.

At least the lights are dim. He shouldn't notice my bloodshot eye under these weakly glowing sconces.

"Look, I just wanted to apologize for last night," he says.

"If you want me to apologize for keeping you awake, you'll be waiting for a while. I'm not sorry at all."

Bennett looks around. "Drop the act. No one's here."

"It's not an act. The night in the cabin changed nothing. In fact, I—"

He steps into me and walks me backward until my ass hits the wall. Judging by the fire in his eyes, he's about to silence me. Permanently. Then his mouth falls on mine, and before I realize what's happening, I'm kissing him back.

My stomach dips and rolls. A whimper slides out of me. I can feel how much he wants me through my jeans, and if he could feel my panties, he'd know how badly I want him, too.

"I thought we weren't doing this anymore," I say when I pull away.

"Because of what I said at your door?"

I nod.

"Kindra was sitting right behind you. I couldn't exactly ask what was wrong without drawing suspicion." He leans down and nips my neck. "But either way, I'm not exactly a nice guy, kitten. Not even your incredible pussy can make me into something I'm not."

He speaks the truth, but his tongue is useful for so much more than hurting feelings. Like right now, it's making me feel pretty fucking good as it drives circles over my pulse point.

"So?" he asks. "Are we doing this or not?"

"I don't know if this is a good idea anymore."

His hands drop to my hips and squeeze. "I'll be honest. I can't stop thinking about fucking you, and it's driving me insane."

"And what, you think you'll get over this new infatuation if you fuck me?"

"That's the hope."

"And what if it doesn't work? What if we both realize the alcohol wasn't the issue?"

He smirks. "So you can't stop thinking about it either, huh?"

Fuck him and his sneaky ways. I swat his chest and scoot away from him before he can kiss me and scramble my brain again.

"I need some time to think about this," I say.

He shrugs and steps toward me again. "Tell you what, I'll fake a headache after the activity. If you're game, my door will be unlocked. You can consider the issue dropped if you don't show, and we can go back to what we've always been."

I bite my lip and look down the hall as Grim and Rose appear from the same door. Hearing the door click shut behind them, Bennett clears his throat and walks away as if we weren't just having a conversation.

Those two have it all figured out. They meet at the retreat, have a wonderful five days of fucking, then part ways until the next event. Maybe I should corner Rose and ask her to reveal her secrets. If she could speak, that would be a great idea, but she scurries away unless we ask yes or no questions.

I lean against the wall with a groan. Bennett's plan sounds great on paper, but as he disappears down the stairs, something nibbles at my mind. The one little issue he hasn't considered.

What do we do if we can't go back to the way things were?

Chapter Nineteen

Bennett

The rec room is tucked away in the sprawling basement, along with a metric fuck ton of other amenities. Jim built more below ground than above, it seems. I stroll past a small theater, a narrow kitchenette, a gym, and a mini spa before I reach the large double mahogany doors at the end of the hall.

Pushing them open, I step into a massive room lined with more of those fake windows they have upstairs, only larger. An entire wall showcases a winter scene, complete with the occasional squirrel or deer visitor.

If I look at the windows for too long, it makes me feel sick. It's not the sweet sentimentality of the scenery, either. It's the fact that my brain knows I'm underground while my eyes believe I could step through the windows into that scene.

Maybe that's why the situation with Cat makes me feel sick too, only my dick is the one who can't seem to sync up with my brain.

Ice Pick waddles through the door and gives me a wave before he heads toward a few arcade games against another wall. With a scratch of his hairy stomach, he settles on Galaga. Excellent choice.

Grim and Rose aren't far behind him, but instead of heading toward the billiards tables or the arcade games, they choose to have a seat in the chairs that have been arranged in a semicircle in the center of the room. I go and join them.

"What exactly are we doing in here?" I ask Grim as I sit in the chair beside him.

Grim pulls off his glasses and begins wiping the smudged lenses. "*Unwissenheit ist ein Segen.*"

"My apologies, but I seem to have left my German translator at home."

"It simply means sometimes it is best to know nothing."

I don't know why I expected more from him. He loves speaking in cryptic phrases.

With no help to be found, I look around and try to find something to clue me in, but this room isn't giving me much to go on. This is clearly a killing field, judging by the rolls of tarp covering the precious carpet underneath the chairs, but how will we kill? Do they expect us to beat our victims over the head with pool sticks until something falls out like some macabre piñata?

I mean, I'm game.

Cat enters the room next, accompanied by Kindra and an unfamiliar woman with long, thick braids and cheekbones that could cut glass. I try to keep my eyes on anything else, but my attention keeps returning to Cat. Those tall black boots hug her calves, and I'd like to see her in them without the rest of her outfit.

Her gaze meets mine, but she quickly looks away. Now I wish I'd forced her to give me an answer in the hallway.

The anticipation is killing me, and she isn't giving me any hints.

The three women take a seat on the opposite end of the semicircle, meaning I'll be facing Cat for this little circle jerk. We're both on the very ends. Kindra sits between the women. As she engages the taller woman in conversation, I wait for Cat to look at me. When she doesn't, a flare of rage fires off in my gut.

She really isn't thinking about me. This bitch.

The doors open behind us, and the rest of the merry crew saunters in amidst a flurry of loud conversation. Ezra, Jim, and Maverick walk together at the rear, each of them holding a large bowl in their arms. Once they've placed the bowls on a nearby table, they join everyone else and take a seat.

Kindra clears her throat and addresses the group. "I just want to thank everyone who chose to join us for this inaugural venture into winter retreat territory. I planned to make this speech last night at the party, but someone fucked that up for everyone."

She levels me with a pointed stare, and I smile and wave. Her death-dagger glare might work on Ezra, but it's powerless against me.

Undeterred by my arrogance, she continues. "It seems that Mother Nature also wanted to fuck with us. We had originally planned to host the Winter Olympics outside, but a sudden storm forced us below ground."

"But we still get to kill someone, right?" a male voice says from the center of the group.

Kindra takes a deep breath, probably to stop herself from calling the guy a fucking moron, as is her way. "That's the entire point of the retreat, and we haven't lost sight of that. As for the masquerade New Year's Eve party, that will be held on the last night."

I groan internally. The last thing I want to do is cram myself into a tux and attend what is essentially a winter formal. Missing that stupid party was the singular consolation prize for getting lost in Alaska and discovering a latent attraction to the bane of my existence.

Though, I guess I have to stop calling her that, now that I've had her asshole in my mouth. I mean, you don't exactly do that for someone you hate.

"Since we had to bring the games indoors, we also had to do a bit of last-minute brainstorming," Ezra says from his chair. "If the games are rubbish, I take sole responsibility."

"I'll share the blame," the unfamiliar woman beside Kindra says. "I'm Eve, by the way, for those of you who haven't met me yet." She gives a small wave, then pulls her braids over one shoulder.

She's a stunning creature, but something tells me I'm not her type. The small scissor tattoo hiding behind her ear probably doesn't represent being president of the quilting club.

"For our first game, you'll be competing in pairs," Kindra says. "We'll each draw a number from a bowl, and the two matching numbers will go head-to-head."

Ezra must have forgotten his cue, because he leaps out of his seat like a man possessed when Kindra glares at him. He runs for one of the bowls on the table, then weaves through the chairs, letting everyone pull a number from inside. He and Kindra pull last.

The room becomes a vacuum of mutters and mumbles as everyone tries to figure out who they're up against. As luck would have it, I'm up against Cat. I hear her telling Eve her number.

Before last night, I would have seen this as an opportunity to kill-block her once again. Now I see this as a major problem. If I lose to her, I'll look like a fucking chump, but if I beat her—and that's almost a guarantee—she'll get pissed off, and there goes any chance that she'll wind up in my room after this.

I lean closer to Grim. "Any chance you'd want to swap numbers?" I say.

"No swapping!" Kindra shouts.

Flopping back in my seat, I try not to pout. Either I kill-block Cat and shoot myself in the foot or I lose to Cat and shoot myself in the ego.

"It wouldn't be the retreat Olympics without another twist." Kindra grabs a second bowl and begins pulling large paper bags from inside. "Now you'll choose your weapon, then figure out a way to kill your victim first to win!"

As if on cue, part of a wall slides away and two lackeys wheel in a couple of Cattle in wheelchairs.

"Who's up first?" Ezra says with a clap of his hands.

I feel like I'm on the set of some fucked-up game show. This is when the crowd would cheer and the theme music would blast through the television screen as someone races to the killing field.

Ice Pick and Eve raise their hands, and Kindra motions for them to choose a bag.

"But no cheating," Kindra adds. "You can't lift the bag until you choose it, and once you touch it, it's yours."

Eve chooses a bag quickly, then opens it. From the brown paper, she produces one of those elves that parents destroy the house with.

What shit luck.

Ice Pick goes next, and luck isn't on his side, either.

While Eve tries to murder her victim with a toy, Ice Pick gets to do it with a roll of gift-wrapping tape.

Eve and Ice Pick each stand behind their chosen wheelchair as their victims squirm and scream through their noses. The Cattle's hands have been bound behind their backs to prevent injury to participants, and their mouths are glued shut so we don't have to hear their bitching. Kindra and Ezra were even smart enough to shackle their shaking legs down so they can't kick.

"Oh, this is so exciting!" Jim says as he settles in his seat. "I wish my dear friend Ronaldo was here to see this, but he's overwintering in the Maldives this year."

I don't know about exciting, but what we're about to witness will surely be interesting.

"On my word," Kindra says as she raises a stopwatch. "Go!"

Eve sets to work right away. With slender fingers, she slices through the seal on her Cattle's lips, then shoves the tiny doll's head into the man's mouth before he can scream. Wearing a smirk, she then grips the two tiny cloth hands and crams them into the man's nostrils.

Ice Pick has a similar idea, also choosing suffocation as the Cattle's vehicle to hell. Instead of ripping open the mouth, however, he just starts winding the clear, sticky-sided cellophane around his victim's head.

"This will take ages," Grim mutters beside me, and Maudlin Rose nods in agreement.

Eve seems to realize this as well as she watches her Cattle squirm in his chair, his eyes bulging. But what other option does she have? It's a fucking child's toy. Companies take extra pains to avoid maiming and murdering their clientele these days, and those safety regulations are working against her.

Eve looks at Kindra and raises her finger. "Question . . . May I alter the item in any way, or do I have to commit the murder with the item as-is?"

"As long as you kill them with the item, I don't fucking care," Kindra says. "I'm a journalist, not a fucking event planner."

"Thanks, hon," Eve says as she plucks the elf from the man's mouth. She turns it over in her hands, looking for a way to turn it into a lethal weapon as her victim sobs incoherent words.

To her right, Ice Pick's victim has managed to open his mouth by stretching his jaw until the glue lost its grip on his skin. Actually, considering the blood, the skin lost its grip on his lips. Yikes.

"Please let me go!" Ice Pick's Cattle screams. "I promise I—"

Ice Pick winds the tape around his mouth. "Whoops! Don't want you getting any air."

The man's muffled screams grow weaker, and he eventually pisses himself and goes limp.

Meanwhile, Eve is still trying to find a way to turn this around, but it doesn't look good. Jim is already approaching Ice Pick's Cattle to search for a pulse. She tosses the toy to the floor and takes a seat when Jim nods.

"We have a winner for round one," Jim declares.

"Oh, thank God," Eve's Cattle whispers. "I've been spared. I'll never hurt anyone again as long as I live. I swear it."

Jim steps closer to the man and smiles down into his face. "Are you ready to meet him?"

"Who?"

Jim presses something against the base of the man's skull. "Why, God, my dear boy."

Blam!

Everyone jolts and someone—probably Cat—lets out a squeal as brain matter and blood splash across the center of the semicircle. No one told me there was a designated splash zone, and now I'm sad I didn't sit in the center.

Jim lowers the gun and pats the man's shoulder, and what's left of the man's head slumps to the side. "Who's in group two?"

Chapter Twenty

Bennett

There's only one pair ahead of us now, and it's Maudlin Rose versus the Heartbreak Killer. It figures that Cat and I would be the last to compete in this event.

Ezra struggled in the last round, and now I'm getting nervous. He pulled a short candlestick and chose to beat his victim to death after first trying to shove the stick through the man's eye. The flared design made it pretty impossible to hit the brain.

Jim ended up besting him, though only by a few seconds. The son of a bitch lucked out and pulled a carving knife from his chosen bag. If he hadn't opted to grace us with a Shakespearean soliloquy before plunging the knife into the woman's abdomen, he'd have won by more than a few seconds.

I'll never understand theater people.

Before them, a slew of randoms and unknowns took their turns, and most of it was pretty boring to watch.

Amateurs, all of them. Now, only four bags remain on the table, and I'm nervous to see what Cat and I will pull. So far, we've seen the many uses of a tree topper, a nutcracker, a pair of scissors, and a DVD of the gripping 1994 film *The Santa Clause.*

As Kindra and Rose head toward the remaining bags, I steal another glance at Cat. She hasn't looked at me a single time since that first time we locked eyes, and it's driving me insane. She's turning this into a dangerous game. I'm used to getting what I want, and where women are concerned, I'm not accustomed to hearing the word no.

Kindra and Rose step to the front of the class, and I'm forced to look away from Cat. If her best friend notices I'm staring, she's liable to confront one or both of us about it. That's one complication I don't need.

"Looks like I get to use an ornament hook," Kindra says as she holds up the tiny sprig of metal.

Maudlin Rose turns a piece of paper in her fingers, then holds it toward Kindra.

"Oh, you got the ax," Kindra says. "It was too large to fit in the bag, so we just wrote it down."

Ezra appears beside her with the ax and holds it toward Rose, who accepts it with a gleam in her eye. Then she turns and studies her Cattle with a frown. She prefers to kill men, and her victim is a woman.

"Do you want to switch?" Kindra asks, and Rose nods.

That's the sort of kindness I'll never understand. Kindra is already against the ropes, and forcing Rose to kill a woman could have given her an advantage. She basically handed her the win.

The women get behind their victims, but before Kindra can give the word to begin, Cat raises her hand.

"What are you, twelve?" I say. "You aren't in school, Miss Novak. If you have something to say, just say it."

When she scowls at me, I remember that I'm supposed to keep my mouth shut. She makes that difficult when she does dumb shit like raising her hand, though.

"You can alter the item, right?" Cat asks Kindra. When Kindra confirms, Cat stands and hands something to her, then whispers, "Good luck."

Swallowing the urge to call the pair of hens a couple of cheaters is like choking on glass, but I manage.

When Kindra says they can begin, I expect Rose to start wielding the ax like a madman, but she doesn't. She strolls around her victim, caressing his cheek with the blunt side of the ax head.

Meanwhile, Kindra is busy jacking off the world's smallest dick behind her wheelchair. That's what it looks like, at least. Whatever Cat handed her, she's making use of it now, though I don't think it'll be of much help. When she raises the hook to her eyes and studies it, it still looks the same to me.

As Kindra bends over the woman's neck and begins performing some weird sort of pseudo-surgery, Rose finally swings the ax overhead and brings it down between the man's legs. Everyone with testicles immediately recoils.

Blood flows through the wheelchair's thick canvas seat and patters on the tarp, forming a fresh puddle. The man shakes and jerks so violently from the pain that the chair topples backward. Despite the carpet beneath the tarp, his head makes a loud *thunk* as it strikes the floor.

Rose walks around her writhing victim and raises the ax as she looks down into his eyes. The man looks back at her, sucking air through his nostrils with such force that they keep slamming shut. He shakes his head, yelling, "No! No!"

through those flaring nostrils. Tiny little Rosie just laughs her silent laugh and pretends to bring the ax down on his head, always halting the arc just before impact.

We've all stopped focusing on Kindra, so it comes as a shock when she requests that Jim check her Cattle's pulse. The woman's head lolls to the side, and she certainly looks dead, though I can't see how Kindra killed her. Then I spot the red freshet burbling from the woman's neck. The blood has slowed to a languid trickle, but that's only because most of what was in her body now covers the tarp beneath her wheelchair.

Jim tips the woman's head to the side, revealing a slim gash in the thin skin of her neck. After checking for a pulse in three places, he declares Kindra the winner. As he raises her hand in the air, Rose chooses that moment to hoist the ax and separate her Cattle's head from its body.

With an elegant sidestep, Jim saves his precious Italian leather shoes from the encroaching red river. It's a wonder no one has slipped by this point.

"Maybe we should swap out the tarp," Cat says, almost as if she was thinking the same thing.

Or maybe she's stalling . . .

She licks her lips and looks around, then resumes picking at the side of her thumb like she's been doing for the last twenty minutes. Either she has one hell of a hangnail, or she's about to shit herself with nerves.

"Thanks for the assist," Kindra says as she tosses a nail file to Cat. "I never would have been able to get that blunt tip through her skin otherwise."

"Only one pair left to do battle." Jim steps over the red smears and puddles as he heads for his seat. "Just mind the blood and you'll be fine."

As the lackeys wheel the dead bodies away, I stand

and head toward the two bags on the table behind the chairs. Cat hurries to join me, probably to be sure I don't cheat by peeking in the bags. She knows me so well already.

She steps in front of me, and I catch a whiff of that fruity shampoo she uses. I close my eyes and allow myself a few milliseconds to enjoy the scent. Any longer and someone might notice.

"I like those boots," I whisper near her ear. "Make sure you wear them when you come to my room."

"I never said I was coming to your room," she whispers back.

"Any chance we could hurry this along?" Kindra says. "Lunch will be ready in twenty minutes, and some of us need to change clothes."

I pluck up a bag when she takes too long to decide, which earns me a huff from her pouty lips. She should have been quicker. Once she grabs the remaining bag, we walk to the front of the room, where two fresh Cattle have already been positioned.

Kindra rolls her hand through the air. "Let's get this shit show on the road. Go!"

Opening my bag, I find a glass reindeer statue the size of my hand. Unless a gun waits within that brown paper in her hands, this couldn't be any easier for me. I lower the reindeer to the floor, then step on it while holding one of the antlers. Crystal crunches under my shoe, and I come away with a sharp, pointy spear about the size of my finger, complete with a smooth antler grip.

"I know Christmas was a couple of weeks ago, but I'm feeling quite festive." I turn to my prey and drag the sharp end down the man's cheek. Blood beads along the cut.

Giggles erupt from the peanut gallery, and I'm feeling

quite pleased with my joke. Until I realize they aren't laughing at me. They're laughing at Cat.

Since everyone is looking at her, I feel safe enough to take a peek, but when I see what she's doing, I don't find it funny at all. With the grace of Mia Khalifa, she's deep-throating a jumbo peppermint stick.

"You're supposed to use it as a weapon, not suck it off," I say. "You'll be here all day at this rate, so I guess I can take my time with my kill."

She rolls her blue eyes and keeps sucking.

I turn my attention back to the squirming man in front of me before Cat's erotic impression of a Dyson gives me a gnarly case of blue balls. It'll take her at least ten minutes to shape that thing into a tip that's pointy enough to do damage. I should know. I used to make peppermint shanks every Christmas.

This actually presents a good opportunity to let her win, though. While I pretend to lose myself to torturing this asshole in front of me, she'll have time to sharpen that point and make her first kill. Then I can act all mad before I rush to my room and strip down to my boxers so she can put her mouth skills to better use.

But time ticks by, and Cat still doesn't make a move. My victim is an artwork of bloody lattice etchings; hers is still entirely intact. He doesn't even look concerned anymore.

Cat pulls the peppermint stick from her mouth and takes a look. The end is sharp enough, but she inserts it into her mouth again and keeps sucking.

"Oh, for fuck's sake," I mutter under my breath.

She's nervous, and I don't think she has the balls to make the kill. Kindra and I might be the only people who know her well enough to spot the panicked glint in her eyes, but it will become obvious to everyone if I don't do something.

I step over to her, snatch the red-and-white rod from her mouth, and plunge it into her Cattle's throat. Repeatedly. The pointed tip holds its shape until the fourth downward swing, when it breaks off inside the man's neck.

Cat stands behind her gurgling victim, her mouth gaping and her eyes wide. I can't tell if she's relieved or pissed.

"Bennett, you have about three seconds to get out of range before I start swinging," she says.

Pissed. She's definitely pissed.

"Okay, I think that's enough for one day." Kindra stands and hurries to get between us before Cat can rush forward and claw out my eyes. "Everyone, take fifteen to clean up, and we'll all meet in the dining hall for lunch."

She wraps an arm around her blonde friend's shoulder and begins leading her out of the room. Eve joins them, though she takes extra pains to turn and scowl at me. I raise my middle finger in salute before the door shuts behind them.

"Boy, you've really put your foot in it this time," Ezra says with a shake of his head as he helps Maverick begin gathering the bloody tarps. "You couldn't just let her get the kill? She was so close."

People are filing out of the room, but there are still too many ears present for me to tell Ezra the truth, which is that I wasn't trying to be a dick for once. I was trying to help her.

So I shrug and say what is expected of me. "She was taking too long, and I was sick of waiting."

"Then why not kill your target, hmm? Why go for hers?"

"To make it more interesting, I guess," I say. "I don't know."

Ezra drops his corner of the tarp, sending a slosh of red onto the carpet. Jim sucks in a breath and kneels to examine the stains as Ezra steps into me.

"You have to stop with this childish shit, and soon. Kindra and I put a lot of work into—"

"Yeah, yeah, I got it. You worked so hard, blah, blah. I'm going to my room. I have a headache."

I storm out before he can say anything else, and I wasn't lying. I'm starting to get a real nasty tension headache. My intentions weren't nefarious for once, and yet I'm still labeled the villain. They won't make me feel guilty for doing what I could to save Cat from embarrassment.

Now I just have to hope Cat understands.

Maybe I was wrong. Maybe she would have made the kill. That glint in her eyes could have been anticipation instead of panic.

When I reach the foot of the stairs to the second floor, Kindra materializes from the nearby shadows and yells for me to wait. She's out of breath, so she must have run the whole way here.

"Ezra already bitched at me," I say. "Whatever you need to say, I've already heard it."

She shakes her head and grips the polished banister as she gulps air. "No, that's not it." Her hand goes to her chest, and she looks around before she leans closer and says, "Cat told me everything."

Cat

The door to my room bursts open, and in waltzes Bennett without so much as a knock. I file this away as a lesson learned: lock the door.

"I didn't go to your room for a reason." I try to step into his path and push him out of the room, but he sidesteps me. "That's called a fucking hint, Bennett."

With the casual grace of an invited guest, he makes himself right at home and flops onto my bed with a contented sigh. He doesn't even bother to take off his filthy boots as he drags his legs onto the bed and crosses them at the ankles.

"You almost fucked up big time," he says.

"I didn't know what to do. I choked." I pull the earrings from my ears and toss them onto the small silver trinket tray atop the dresser. "The candy cane was sharp enough, I know that, but I just couldn't force my hand to do what it needed to do."

Bennett laughs and shakes his head. "No, I'm not talking about the way you froze like a nun at an orgy. I'm talking about the fact that Kindra caught up with me and said you told her everything. Naturally, I thought she meant the fucking around."

"You told Kindra we *fucked around?*" My mouth goes dry, and my legs nearly crumple beneath me.

"Jesus fucking Christ!" Bennett shouts, and I turn in time to see Shorty scurry under the bed. "I forgot you had a cat in here. I wasn't expecting him to sneak up and start kneading my fucking scalp with his claws."

"I'm surprised he came out at all. He hates strangers."

He rubs his head where Shorty must have clawed him. "Yeah, well, keep the filthy shit away from me. I hate the things. They stink and they don't do anything useful."

I kneel by the bed and attempt to coax Shorty from the shadows so that I can make sure he's okay, but his yellow eyes just stare at me with unbridled contempt and complete distrust.

"You've traumatized him," I tell Bennett as I pull myself to my feet. "He doesn't usually greet strangers, and now he probably never will."

"That's why cats make shitty pets. They're too temperamental."

"You told Kindra we screwed around, *and* you're shitting on cats?" I shout at him. "Do you have a death wish?"

"What the fuck are you talking about?"

"Maybe I lack motivation." I pluck a decorative snow globe from the dresser and test its weight in my hand. "With the right motivation, I could make the kill. I know that because I'm feeling *very* homicidal right now."

Bennett hardly has time to move out of the way as I launch the hefty glass globe at his head. It clunks against the headboard, and we're both shocked when it doesn't break. It just rolls off the mattress and thuds to a stop on the carpet.

He smirks and rolls back to his spot—which is actually *my* spot, because I prefer the side of the bed closest to the door. "Cats fucking suck, and I won't back down on that, but I didn't tell her we fucked. That's only because she plowed ahead with her concerns about you before I could, though."

"Concerns? She didn't seem too concerned to me. Scoot over."

To my surprise, he does.

I pull off my boots because I'm not a complete caveman, and then I stretch out on the bed. "What was she worried about?"

"Mainly, she's worried you'll take off like you did at the summer retreat. She doesn't want you to feel pressured to kill if you aren't ready, but she wants you here because she cares or some shit."

"And why would she feel the need to bring any of this to your attention?"

He shrugs. "I don't know. I wasn't really listening. I zoned out when I realized she didn't know you've had my dick in your mouth."

Thank god for small favors.

"So why'd you do it?" he asks.

"Do what?"

"Why'd you tell Kindra that you choked?"

I roll onto my side and face away from him, unable to admit my reasoning for coming clean to her. Well, coming clean to her about *that*, at least. As much as I love and trust Kindra, I may never grow courageous enough to tell her what I've done with Bennett.

And what I've decided I won't be doing again.

"Hey, can we talk?" I ask, and I hate the way my voice sounds. It's like I'm speaking through a wad of cotton. I clear my throat and try again. "Seriously talk, I mean. Let's call a truce to the snark for five minutes."

"Look, I've gotten tested religiously ever since I contracted something on that godforsaken trip. If you've got some weird infection or disease, it didn't come from me, I can fucking assure you."

"What the actual fuck? No! I want to talk about . . . us."

"Aw, kitten, I didn't know we were an item." He scoots closer and tries to wrap his arm around me, but I sit up and push his grabby hands away.

"Snark truce, remember? I'm being serious. I think we need to just . . . cancel the whole thing. We don't need to know if the sex is good."

His face remains a mask of indifference, but I don't miss the brief flicker of disappointment that slips through. He wanted this as much as I did. As much as I still do. If we didn't have to hide it, it wouldn't be so bad, but I hate this sneaky shit.

Plus, there are other complications.

He clears his throat and does his best attempt at sounding unbothered. "Yeah, I mean, if that's what you want. Am I allowed to ask what changed your mind?"

I can't answer that honestly without tipping my hand, so I scramble for a lie. My lips part and my brain reverses everything in my head so that I can say the exact opposite of how I truly feel. "There's really no chemistry, if I'm being honest."

"No chemistry, huh?" He rolls onto his side and trails his fingertips along my thigh. "You sure could have fooled me. Seems like we have *too much* chemistry."

Fuck, I hate it when he sees through my charade.

Because he's right. The draw to look at him and be near him and tell him things . . . it's overpowering my thoughts and freaking me out.

Maybe honesty is the best policy here. Bennett sees my refusal as a challenge, and he loves to overcome a challenge. But if I tell him the truth, that I'm getting attached and wanting more, he's liable to back off. If Bennett is Superman, then even a whiff of something resembling commitment will be his kryptonite.

"I told Kindra about freezing up because I didn't want anyone to be upset with you," I blurt. "I knew what you did for me, saving me from looking like an idiot, and I wanted someone to know the truth. That I was appreciative of what you did for me, not upset."

"What does that have to do with fucking me?"

"Don't you see what's happening? You stole that kill to save *my* ass, and I fessed up to Kindra to save *your* ass. The dynamic has shifted, which can only mean we're in danger of developing feelings."

"Do you always over analyze things, or is this a new problem?"

I don't know why I expected him to understand.

His hand travels higher, his fingertips nearly brushing against the denim over my pussy. And I want them to. Fuck, I want him to rip off my clothes and touch me harder. What is wrong with me?

I place my hand over his to stop his tempting teasing. "Please don't make me weak. I need to be strong right now."

He sits up and breathes against my neck as I grip his hand in mine. His lips move over my skin, speaking words I can't hear, gentle whispers meant only for that hidden part of me I keep locked away.

But that part of me doesn't want to remain hidden. It

rattles inside its confines, begging to break free. Begging for his fingers, his mouth, his pierced cock.

His fingers snake out of my half-assed hold, and he squeezes my flesh as he gives my neck a gentle nip. "Tell me what you want me to do. Just say the word and I'll leave this room. I promise. But if you want me, tell me now." He sucks my skin and squeezes my thigh in his powerful hand. "Tell me, kitten. Tell me what you want."

I can't think with his mouth writing a sonnet on my skin. My brain shuts down so that I can only feel, and my body screams out for his touch. For more. For everything.

"Fuck me, Bennett," I say on a moan. I push him down and straddle his waist in one movement. "Let's do it. Let's fuck. And if you get attached, you'll just have to deal with it."

He grips the hem of my sweater and raises it as far as he can, but he isn't fast enough. I need to be naked *right now,* before I can change my mind. I hop off his lap and strip off my clothes as he hurries to remove his shirt.

"What if you're the one who falls?" he asks as he takes in my naked body with unrestrained lust in his blue eyes. "What do we do when you can't get enough of me?"

I climb onto his lap again, grinding my bare pussy over his jeans. "You don't have to worry about that. You're too chaotic for me."

He pulls me down and sucks my left nipple into his mouth. Pleasure pulses through my pussy as he nibbles the sensitive nub.

"You don't have to worry either," he whispers against my breast before pulling me down and blindly pawing with his hands. "You're too high maintenance for me."

"You're too immature," I moan as he squeezes my breast and sucks my nipple until pain wells to the surface.

I pull away from his mouth and slide down his abs, licking each ridge on my way to his waistband.

Bennett groans and places his hand on the crown of my head. "And you're fucking obnoxious."

With a smile, I nip his skin, and his body jerks. "You're arrogant as fuck."

"Your *ingenue* act pisses me off."

I unzip his pants, then lower them and his boxers, revealing his thick cock. When I get to his feet, his boots stop my progress. "You have no manners."

He sits up and struggles to unlace his boots. The thin laces tangle and knot together. With a grunt, he wrenches them off, nearly taking his feet with them. The pants and boxers follow, and he tosses everything to the floor.

"You're the antithesis of suave," I say.

"Hey, it was my turn." He grips my shoulders and pushes my back onto the bed, putting himself back in control. "You're too fucking pretty."

"That's not a burn. That's a compliment." I shiver as he situates himself between my legs and looks down at me.

"Are you sure you want to do this?"

I nod because I can't bring myself to say yes. This is a terrible idea, and I still have time to change my mind, but my pussy is a wanton, thirsty bitch, and his cock is a tall, fat drink of water.

Drown me.

"Oh, I almost forgot!" He climbs off the bed and goes for his pants. As he digs around in the pockets, I hear the crinkle of plastic. He brought a fucking condom, which means he *knew* I'd give it up. Am I really so predictable?

But as he approaches the bed again, I see that it isn't a condom at all. It's another giant peppermint stick like the one I deep-throated down in the rec room.

I'm not really one who finds that sex and food make a good pairing, but the honey situation was pretty fucking hot. Maybe if I can take off my Judgmental Janice glasses for a moment, I can try something new.

He slides his hips between my legs again, then lowers the long red-and-white stick toward my face. "I want to see you suck it again."

That . . . wasn't where I thought this was going, but okay.

I part my lips and look up at him as he slides the peppermint stick onto my tongue. He pushes it in and out of my mouth, gently guiding it over my tastebuds. With each inward breath, a cool, minty rush coats my lungs.

Then I feel it. His cock. Rubbing against my slit.

I close my eyes and moan around a mouthful of peppermint. This is so wrong, but fuck, I can't stop myself. I want this. I want *him*.

He pulls the girthy stick from my mouth and leans back so he can drag it through my slit. "Fuck, your pussy looks good enough to eat."

I spread my legs.

"Oh, is that what you want, *kitten?*"

I bite my lip and nod, anticipating the sweet heat of his tongue on my clit, but as he pulls the peppermint candy away, I question if I answered correctly. Bennett isn't exactly known for giving me what I want. I probably should have said no so that he would see it as a challenge.

But the man continues to be full of surprises. He drops to his stomach and drags his tongue up the length of my pussy. I shudder and let out a whimper in response.

"You're so wet, and I've hardly gotten started." He dives between my legs again, lapping and licking and teasing me until I ache.

"Please make me come," I beg.

"I will, but I'm not done with you just yet."

Something unyielding presses against my opening, and I don't need to look down to see what he's planning to slide inside me. It's that peppermint stick, and he's about to turn my insides into a winter wonderland.

I tilt my hips, essentially giving him permission. Because that's what his hesitation feels like. A question. *Is this okay? Are* you *okay?* It's so unlike him, and it makes me feel . . . special.

With his answer secured, he slips the peppermint stick into my pussy as he lowers his hungry mouth to my clit. While easing the stick in and out to slicken the candy, he sucks and licks me until my thighs begin to quiver. The peppermint creates a simultaneous cooling and warming sensation inside me, and I'm right on the verge of an amazing orgasm.

"Hey, Cat? Are you coming to lunch?" Kindra says . . . just outside my fucking door.

I freeze.

Bennett freezes.

Even my orgasm hovers at the edge and waits for what will happen next.

"Can I come in?" she adds.

"Just a second!" I shout. "I'm . . . uh, I'm in the middle of something."

I look down at Bennett, and he shakes his head, which is still situated between my legs. His chin scruff brushes over my pussy lips and sends a pleasurable sensation crawling along my spine.

"N-no! No! Don't come in! I'm . . . masturbating."

"Oh . . . okay, well, come to lunch when you're finished, I guess. But remember to wash your hands!"

"Okay, I'll be down soon!"

Bennett and I look at each other before we both relax and breathe a sigh of relief as the sound of her footsteps fades down the hall. I go to sit up, figuring the moment is ruined, but he grips my thighs and holds me in place.

"We aren't leaving this room until we fuck and get this out of our systems," he says. "No more interruptions. No more excuses. You'll go to lunch with my come inside you, and that's that, understood?"

I look down at his face between my thighs. This isn't like moments ago when he asked a question. This is a demand, and my answer has no weight.

But I answer with a nod anyway.

"Good girl," he growls before creating a vacuum seal between his mouth and my clit.

My head tips back, and I see stars. Sensation rushes between my legs again, as if we weren't just put on hold. He drives the peppermint stick into me in time with his suction, and I'm about to come.

Hard.

He senses this and growls against my mound, creating a pleasurable vibration that rockets me over the edge. I grip the pillows behind my head and grit my teeth so that I don't cry out. Jim spared no expense on the mansion, but the walls are paper thin. If I open my mouth and sing Bennett's praises for the Lord's work he's doing between my legs, everyone in the dining hall will hear me.

I swallow each moan until I'm filled with pleasure. When I can't possibly take another gulp, I push his head away.

"Fuck, you really are an ace at that," I moan. I can't remember the last time I felt this relaxed.

He pulls the peppermint stick out of me, and I've never been so empty. But I don't feel that way for very long, because something else just as hard and unyielding and *thick* presses against me now.

I brace myself as he enters me, expecting him to just barrel inside me without any care, but he's surprisingly gentle. A little too gentle, actually. The piercing in the head of his cock brushes in and out of me, but he isn't really going for it like I thought he would.

Then I learn why.

We're still in the foreplay stage.

He climbs up my body, positioning his knees just below my armpits. He grips the headboard to steady himself, then lowers his dick toward my mouth. "Open up. Let me fuck your pretty face."

Looking up at him, I part my lips and guard my teeth as he enters my mouth. Tears spring to my eyes almost immediately as he pushes his cock to the back of my throat and holds it there.

At least it tastes like peppermint.

I hold off a gag for as long as I can, but my body eventually retches and tries to force the massive object from my throat.

Bennett swipes the tears from my cheeks and looks down into my eyes. "That's it, kitten. Choke on me. I want you to gag. I want your tears."

Once again, Bennett is introducing me to things I've always thought were gross and now am second-guessing. I'm not quite ready to scream out and say, *Hurt me, daddy,* but I'm close.

"Can I take you now?" he asks, his voice a gravelly whisper as he shallowly thrusts to the back of my throat.

"Can I use your body selfishly? Can I fuck you with only my pleasure in mind?"

He pulls his cock from my throat to allow me the air to answer.

And like the horny bitch I am, I say yes to all of it.

Chapter Twenty-Two

Bennett

The moment my cock slid onto her tongue, I knew I was in trouble. I almost came right then. All my grand plans of skull-fucking the shit out of her went right out the window.

I don't want to be known as a two-pump chump. In certain circles, I'm known for my stamina, and I can't have this temptress running back to New York with tales of my failure. But something about this girl puts my balls into overdrive.

"Turn over and raise that ass in the air," I say. Watching her tits bouncing around as I rail her won't exactly help me with my problem. If she's facing away from me, I can close my eyes and think of other shit without offending her.

She rolls over and stuffs a few pillows under her stomach before looking at me over her shoulder. "Don't go easy on me," she says. "Fuck me like you hate me, Bennett."

"That won't be hard to do," I say as I get behind her and wrap her hair around my tightening fist. "I do hate you."

I snatch back her head, and her spine arches beautifully. Her slender fingers curl around the sheets, gripping, tearing, rending them as sweet pain sizzles through her scalp. With my free hand, I aim my cock at her glistening entrance and force my way inside.

"How are you so fucking *tight?*" I ask through gritted teeth.

She sucks in a breath as I push forward, stretching her around my girth. Her hand whips to the side, and she grabs another pillow from the other side of the bed, which she takes between her teeth. Then she backs into me, taking the last few inches without my assistance.

I'm in trouble.

Her hips bounce as she rocks on my cock, trying to chase the pleasure I can't give her without coming too quickly. I knew being inside her would be amazing, but I didn't anticipate or appreciate the full effect of her body. All of it.

She releases the pillow from her mouth and peers at me over her shoulder. "Little help?"

I snatch her hair, turning her face toward the headboard again. If she wants me to fuck the shit out of her, so be it.

After transferring my grip from her body to the headboard, I push inside her and bring a whimper from her throat. But I don't stop. I don't ask if she's okay or if she needs me to be gentle. She asked that I fuck her like I hate her, so that's what she's going to get for a total of fifteen seconds.

I close my eyes—the visuals are too much—and plow into her with every ounce of hatred I can muster. Each time I ram my hips forward and curl them slightly, I'm rewarded with a muffled scream. I can't tell if she's crying out in pleasure or pain, and I don't care anymore.

But those sounds are another problem entirely. Each whimper squeezes my cock to the beat of her spasming pussy walls. Not even visions of a naked Grim can chase away my orgasm now. I release the headboard and grip her hips, pulling her ass against me as I fill her.

"Are you coming inside me?" she squeals in a whisper. "Bennett! What the fuck?"

She tries to scramble away, but I keep her ass tucked against my pelvis, right where it belongs. By the time I release her, I've left red marks on her hips that will be bruises within the hour.

With a frustrated squeal, she dips her hand between her legs and tries to hurry to the bathroom. I grab her arm and yank her against me before she can get more than a few steps away.

"Hey, I said you have to keep my come between your legs while you eat lunch. You aren't leaving this room any other way."

"Bennett, honey . . ." She laughs. She actually fucking laughs as she plucks my hand from her arm. "I had sex with you to answer a burning question in my mind. The question is answered, and unless I want burning questions in my vagina, I'm going to clean up."

This bitch.

I follow her into the bathroom, pushing through the opening before she can shut the door in my face. "Is this because I came too fast? Look, it's been a while since I've had sex, and you're insanely hot."

She grabs a rag from the rack by the sink and begins running it under the warm tap. In the mirror, I see the way she tries to hide her laughter by pressing her lips together.

"Give me another shot," I say. "I'll fucking show you. I'll come prepared."

"I don't know . . ."

"Come on. You've been keeping me worked up for days now. Next time, I'll be ready."

She waves the rag in my face, trying to shoo me out of the room. "Can I wash my pussy in peace, please? I don't want to miss another meal!"

With a sigh, I turn for the door. "Okay, but this isn't over."

And it's not. The first moment I have alone with Cat, I'll make up for this.

Chapter Twenty-Three

Cat

As I step into the dining room, I feel like everyone's eyes are on me. I feel like everyone knows that I fucked Bennett.

And liked it.

He was so terrified that getting off so quickly would be a huge turnoff, but I've never felt more confident and desired. Nothing can make a woman feel taller than when she's just pulled a man's soul from his body using only her pussy.

While he wasn't inside me for very long, I'm already thinking about next time. I'll have to pretend I'm not, though. If he knows how badly I want him to fuck me stupid, he'll lose interest. And that's a very real fear. It's also part of the reason why this situation grows more terrifying with each sexual encounter. Instead of getting it out of my system, I'm creating a very unhealthy addiction.

"I saved you a seat!" Eve calls from a table near the wall. She's seated beside Kindra and Ezra.

I make my way to their table, careful to walk like I didn't

just have a massive, pierced cock between my legs. Lunch has already been served, and judging by the nearly empty plates in front of each diner, I'm running out of time before dessert arrives.

"What's on the menu today?" I ask as I take a seat.

Kindra leans past Eve and gives me a wave. "Lamb lollipops, and they are amazing. Much better than the literal human rump roast he served at the summer retreat."

We still have two days to go, so she shouldn't get too complacent. If she doesn't want Chef Maurice to slide in some sneaky cuts of meat, then she'll have to stay on top of him.

Bennett enters the dining room as I'm demolishing the second of three lamb lollipops. He's changed into a forest-green Henley and pushed the sleeves up, exposing his thick forearms. As I remember how those powerful arms held me in place when he filled me, a low moan leaves my lips.

"They can't be that good," he says as he takes a seat beside me. "Where the fuck is my plate?"

Ezra leans forward and clears his throat. "If you want to have lunch, you should be in the dining room when lunch begins."

"Why the fuck does Cat get food and I don't? She wasn't here, either!" He folds his arms over his chest and pouts, then realizes his misstep. How did he know I wasn't at lunch unless he was with me? "I heard her door shut a few minutes before I came down, so I know I wasn't that far behind her."

I relax again, and he has a point. It does seem a little unfair. I'd give him the rest of my food if the act of kindness wouldn't look so suspicious. Then again, he did help me out at the activity . . .

I slide the plate in front of him. "You can have the rest of mine."

Everyone at our table stops eating. Their eyes fall on me as their mouths close in unison. It's like the world's weirdest flash mob.

Noticing everyone's shock—and my inability to voice my reasoning for showing the cretin some kindness—Bennett saves the day once again. He pushes the plate in front of me and shakes his head. "I'm just fucking around. I'm not that hungry, anyway."

His stomach burbles beside me, but I pretend I don't hear it. Surely they'll at least give him dessert.

Satisfied, everyone resumes their conversations. The attention shifts away from us, and I return to munching on the food.

"You won't miss the party on the last night, will you?" Eve whispers as she leans closer. "I've been doing a little reconnaissance, and I think Maverick might be up for that kiss after all."

The third lollipop becomes a glob of flavorless lead in my mouth. If she'd said this to me only twenty-four hours ago, I'd have been a bouncing ball of uncontainable excitement and questions. Now?

Now I'm just fucking confused.

"I thought he wasn't interested," I whisper once I've wrestled the damned wad of meat past my gullet. I wash it down with a gulp of water.

Bennett clears his throat and leans over me. "I want in on the secret sharing, ladies. What are we talking about?"

"*We* are discussing something private." Eve motions between me and her. "*You* can fuck off."

"Where's the fun in that?" He gives her his devilish smile. The same one that used to make me want to punch him in his smug face. Now I just want to clear the table and *sit* on his smug face.

"There's a partner activity after lunch," Eve says, ignoring Bennett. "Any chance you'd want to team up?"

Kindra leans forward. "I'm partnered with Ezra, so I won't be jealous," she says with a wink.

I'm about to open my mouth and say yes, absolutely, but Bennett speaks before I can.

"She's partnering with me."

So much for trying to keep this thing quiet.

I turn and look at him, telepathically willing him to take it back. If anyone gets the slightest whiff of what we've done—what we're still fucking doing—I don't think I will ever live it down. This wouldn't open a can of worms. This would lay each worm on a table with a diagram pointing to and describing each segment.

They'll know.

"Remember the bet you lost in the cabin?" He looks at me and winks. "You said you'd agree to do whatever I want for the rest of this trip if you lost."

I made no such bet. I know I made no such bet. Bennett knows I made no such bet.

But the others don't know that.

"Oh, right," I say as I try to look disappointed. "Darn that . . . lost bet. Hey, Kindra, are you gonna eat your last lamb lollipop?"

Kindra pulls her plate away as I reach for food to shove into the hole that doesn't know how to work without Bennett's dick inside it. "Wait, you didn't tell me about a bet. How'd you lose so horribly that you'd end up Bennett's pet?"

Her word choice brings up visions of me with a collar

around my neck as Bennett cracks a whip across my ass for pissing on the rug.

I'm sick. I have a problem.

"Go ahead," Bennett says with a wide grin. "Tell them the story."

"You're the one who made the stupid bet, so I think you should tell it." I level him with an equally wide grin.

Bennett raises his scarred eyebrow, silently questioning me. *Are you sure you want me to come up with the story?* that look seems to say.

I'm not sure. Not at all. But what choice do I have? Everyone at the table is focused on us again, and I seem to put my foot in my mouth every time I open it.

"Okay," he finally says. "She bet she could stay in the cold longer than I could. Naked, too. She thought she had it in the bag, seeing how I hate the cold and all that, but I beat her by a solid three minutes."

"Yeah, but almost ten minutes in subzero temps is nothing to sniff at," I say, piling on the lie.

"How about a rematch?" Eve says with a laugh. "The challenge today is similar."

"How similar?" Bennett and I ask in unison. I surmise we both have the same fear, which is that we're about to be outed for our fibs. Neither of us can stand the cold for more than a few seconds, let alone minutes at a time.

"It's a twist on the polar bear plunge," Maverick says as the waiters begin to remove our plates. I didn't even realize he was seated at our table. "I came up with the idea, and Jim and Ezra ran with it. The storm wasn't as severe as expected, so we'll be headed to—"

Ezra dabs his mouth with a napkin. "Don't tell them everything. I want some of it to be a surprise, especially if we're up against two people who suddenly have a penchant for cold weather."

Bennett's hand finds mine under the table and gives my fingers a reassuring squeeze. Or maybe it's supposed to be a punishing squeeze, because he's really bearing down.

"Sounds fun," he says with the most forced smile I've ever seen. "Oh, look! Cream pie for dessert. Isn't that your favorite, Cat?"

I snatch my hand from his and end up bumping it on the table. With tears brimming in my eyes as I swallow the pain, I manage to say, "How should we dress for this . . . event?"

"Dress however you'd like for the ride in, but wear a swimsuit underneath everything," Maverick says.

A swimsuit. In this weather?

I should have let myself choke on the lamb.

Chapter Twenty-Four

Bennett

As I pull a pair of jeans over my swim trunks, I hear a gentle knock at my door. It's too timid to be anyone other than Cat. Fastening the button, I walk to the door and open it to find her looking up at me like a wild animal caught in a trap. She glances down the hall, then pushes past me and hurries to close the door.

"This was a terrible idea," she says as she begins pacing. "The whole time I was getting dressed, that's all I could think. This is the worst thing we could do."

"Then we'd better do it quickly before anyone comes looking for us." I move closer to her, but her hands spring upward and land on my bare chest.

"No, not the fucking, though that's horrible too. I mean partnering up."

"I don't think we have enough time to fuck, anyway." I dip my head and run circles on her neck with my tongue.

"You only needed fifteen seconds last time," she says on a breathy moan. "Do you really think this is a good idea?"

"Fucking you is always a bad idea, but I want to do it anyway."

"No, not that!" She swats my chest and glares up at me. "You seriously have a one-track mind. Focus! I mean us partnering up on this activity. What if you slip up and call me kitten?"

I smirk against her skin. "Then you'd better cover for me and pretend to be angry instead of turned on."

Her body relaxes for a split second before she stiffens and steps away from me. "I'm being serious, asshole. Stop trying to overpower my anxiety with your cock."

"Was it working?"

She huffs and looks down at her feet. "Yes."

I chuckle and go to the closet to retrieve the rest of my ensemble. The Henley was too thin for whatever hell they're about to put us through, so I pull a thick sweater from the depths. I also grab both coats I brought.

"Here, put this on," I say as I toss the better of the two to her.

She catches it, then studies it like it's a bomb. "Why? I have a coat."

"A cheap coat that won't do shit to bring up your body temp once you need to warm up again. Just wear the coat I offered and say thank you."

"Not all of us can afford name brand, jerk." She tears herself out of her fluffy pink coat and slides into the earth tones that will actually keep her comfortable. "This is pretty warm, though. Thanks."

What she said strikes a nerve. My brother and his fiancée have enough money between them, but I'm currently struggling to rub two pennies together, thanks to my employers icing me out. It's a problem I'm trying to forget while I'm at this retreat.

"I'm not rolling in cash, if that's what you think," I say. "I took the coat you're wearing off a dead guy last winter. Figured he wouldn't need it in hell."

She recoils and looks down at the coat like she might die in it next.

"Don't worry," I say, "I scrubbed the blood out."

She studies her hands as I pull on my boots. "My pink gloves are going to look fucking stupid with this color combo. Did you happen to pull a spare set of those off a dead guy too?"

I return to the closet and pull my gloves from my bag. "These should match enough, though I'm sorry to say they aren't off a dead guy."

"What will you wear?"

I shrug. "I used to make snowmen with nothing more than socks on my hands, so I think I'll be okay."

She shoves the gloves into my hands and shakes her head. "You take them. I can wear the pink ones."

"Suit yourself." I cram the gloves into my pocket, and we start toward the door.

As we step into the hallway, voices from down below reach our ears. Cat freezes and grips my arm, forcing me to do the same. Her eyes widen as she looks at me for a solution.

"Let me go down first," I whisper. "They won't mind waiting on you if you're running late."

"You're right," she says with a nod. "They'd just leave you behind."

I roll my eyes and leave her in the dark hallway as I descend the stairs.

Ezra, Kindra, Grim, and Maudlin Rose stand near the entryway. Grim looks over and gives me a wave as I reach the bottom of the staircase.

"Are you excited to test your physical limitations today?" he says as I step closer. It's the sort of thing you'd expect to be said with a smile, but Grim doesn't do that very often.

"In Bennett's mind, he has no physical limitations," Ezra says. "Isn't that right?"

"I'm not *that* arrogant." I turn to Rose and give her a nod. "Morning, Rosie. Have you been enjoying this weather?"

She purses her lips and shakes her head.

"Me neither," I mutter.

"Where's Cat?" Kindra asks. "We've already sent everyone else ahead, and we need to get moving as soon as the sleigh shows up again."

I shrug. "I don't know, and I don't care. She's probably up there playing with her pussy."

"She has been masturbating an awful lot on this trip," Kindra says as she peers up the staircase. "Unless you meant Shorty, her actual cat. Maybe I should hurry her along." She takes a step forward, but I step into her path.

"No! I mean, I'm sure she'll be down *any minute*."

I put extra emphasis on the last two words and hope Cat hears me. I can't hold Kindra here forever, and the last thing we need to explain is why Cat is standing around in the upper hallway's shadows. Thankfully, she materializes seconds later.

"Sorry, I couldn't decide which coat to wear," she says as she shuffles down the stairs. "Then I decided on this one and couldn't find the matching gloves."

"Isn't that Bennett's coat?" Ezra says.

Shit.

"No, it's definitely mine," Cat says with a little too much confidence for someone who's wearing a coat with the name CARTER embroidered across the right front pocket.

I gave her the wrong fucking coat.

"You sneaky little bitch!" I rush forward and grip the coat's collar in my hand so that I can pull her ear a little closer to my mouth. "Play along," I whisper, but her idea of playing along is to look up at me with wide, terrified eyes.

I'm on my own.

"It's another bet we made," I say. "I told her if she could sneak into my room and steal something, she could have it. At least she has good taste."

She licks her lips as her brain catches up with the fake scenario I've conjured. "Right! I thought I was being slick by taking his only coat, but he brought two."

"Cat, why are you playing his stupid games?" Kindra asks as she steps closer. "This isn't like you. You've always said the quickest way to get him to go away is to ignore him."

"Oh really?" I look down at her.

"Yeah, well, it wasn't working, so I thought I'd try a different tactic." Cat snatches her shoulder to the side and wrenches out of my grip. "Turns out, he's the human version of herpes and will never go away."

"Herpes, huh?" I whisper. "That isn't what you said earlier."

Cat ignores me and steps toward the door with a bright smile on her face. "Well, now that that's settled, let's get going!"

Everyone gives me one more reproachful glare before turning and filing out of the mansion. I'm getting a bit sick and tired of being the butt of every joke. I understand why Cat wants to keep this quiet, and I agree with her, but something has to change. The closer I get to Cat, the further I get from everyone else. If things keep going as they are, I'll be banished to Jupiter by the end of the trip.

After we finish this activity, Cat and I need to have a long talk. She might not like some of the questions I'll ask, and I might not like some of her answers, but things can't keep going as they are.

Chapter Twenty-Five

Cat

Bennett stays quiet for the ride to the site. He's seated across from me, with his arms folded over his chest and a sour look on his face as he stares into the dimly lit woods. Lost in thought, he doesn't even notice when I try to play footsie when no one is looking.

Or maybe he's ignoring me. What shifted in him between our time in his bedroom and boarding the sleigh?

The rails bump over a rock, and I'm sent into Kindra's shoulder. We both let out a yelp from the impact. I glance at Bennett to see if he noticed, but he doesn't so much as look at me.

"Are you okay, pet?" Ezra asks Kindra. He feels her shoulder and looks into her eyes. He gives a shit, which is more than I can say for Bennett.

This shouldn't bother me. After all, I'm the one who's put so much emphasis on keeping our arrangement well below anyone's radar. He's probably just being extra cautious.

Right?

Moments later, the sleigh comes to a stop in front of a pure white blanket of snow. The trees have been removed from the space, creating a wide rectangular clearing. The retreat guests mill about near the center, many of them occasionally looking at the ground.

"You brought us to an empty field?" I ask.

"Stand up and look again," Ezra says with a smirk.

As I stand, the angle shifts, and I can see what he means. The people in the field aren't looking at the ground. They're looking at a narrow strip of water.

"Maybe I'll just sit this one out," Bennett says.

Ezra grabs his arm and hoists him to a standing position. "No can do, I'm afraid. This is a partner activity, and you claimed a partner at lunch. You aren't ruining the fun for Cat."

"She can partner with that smoke show who offered earlier." He tries to wiggle out of his brother's hold, but Ezra maintains his grip. "This isn't my idea of fun, dude. Let me go!"

Ezra does as he asks and releases his coat, and Bennett tumbles out of the sleigh. We hurry to follow him so that he can't weasel his way back to safety.

As we step fully into the clearing, I'm able to see more of the interior surroundings. A few log buildings dot the perimeter. Some are narrow, and some are more squat and fat. Steam rises from vents in the roofs of the fatter buildings.

"What's all this?" I ask Kindra.

She looks as bewildered as I do as she glances around. "I haven't a clue. Ezra and the guys ran with this one."

"Yet I wasn't included in the planning," Bennett grumbles.

"Yes, well, if you hadn't been so busy chasing skirts in Florida, we might have included you a bit more." Ezra levels him with a glare that shuts his mouth.

Those little jabs at his expense usually give me a twinge of joy, but not this time. Can no one else see the glimmer of hurt in his eyes? Perhaps this glimmer is something new, something brought on by our little affair. Maybe I've softened him.

Or maybe that glimmer of pain has been there all along, and we've all been too self-absorbed to see it.

I tuck this little tidbit away for later. If I bring it up now, he'll get defensive and I'll get nowhere. In fact, I'll get the opposite of nowhere. I'll go backward. His walls are already up for some reason I have yet to discern, and the last thing I need is for his alarm system to start wailing.

"Everyone, gather around over here," Ezra calls to the people wandering the edges of the narrow strip of water.

But as we step closer, I realize there isn't only one lane. There are several, each of them set at an equal distance from the next. The lanes aren't terribly long, but from this distance, I can't tell how deep they run.

Eve appears from the group heading our way. She sidles up to me and puts her arm through mine, then pulls me closer. "Glad you made it," she says.

"Do you know what we're doing?" I ask.

She shakes her head, and her braids rub against the inner lining of her hood. "Not a clue. I tried to get more info out of Maverick, but he said Ezra would break his fingers if he leaked the details."

"Speaking of Maverick . . ."

"Oh! Right!" She starts to pull me away from the group, but Ezra stops her.

"Ladies?" he says after clearing his throat. "If you don't mind, I was about to explain the activity."

We offer him matching smiles of equal sheepishness, then move back to the group.

As Ezra runs down the rules for the event, I try to pay attention, but my mind keeps wandering to Bennett and Maverick. Eve can answer any questions I have about the latter, but she can't tell me why I don't care anymore.

Maverick has been my obsession since I met him after the summer retreat. He's easy on the eyes, and he's sweet enough to give a toothless grandmother a cavity. Kindra and Ezra encouraged it at first, but somewhere along the line, they changed their minds and subtly hinted I should put my efforts into someone else. I'm not desperate enough to continually throw myself at someone who doesn't want to catch me, but I also wasn't ready to relinquish my crush. Hoping he'd eventually develop feelings if given enough exposure, I inserted myself into situations just to be near him.

It's not an easy thing to admit, but the obsession I had with Maverick was borderline unhealthy.

And that's what's so puzzling to me.

The obsession I *had* with Maverick.

"Earth to Cat?" Bennett's fingers snap in front of my face. "Did you hear anything he said?"

I look around. Eve is no longer beside me, and everyone has split off into their pairings. Bennett and I are the only two still standing away from the lanes.

"Sorry, I was lost in thought," I say.

Bennett scoffs. "Your brain isn't big enough to hold more than one empty box, so you couldn't have gotten that lost."

"In case you haven't noticed, we're the only people over here. You can drop the asshole act."

"It's not an act. I'm an asshole, remember?"

Yeah, something is definitely different.

"Bennett, what's wrong? You're acting strange."

"Maybe I'm just realizing some things, that's all."

"What sort of things?"

"Let's get this show on the road!" Kindra yells from one of the lanes. "We can't start stripping until you two line up!"

I turn to Bennett. "Are we up first?"

"No, we all go at the same time." He grabs my arm and starts hauling me toward the first lane.

"But I don't know what we're doing," I whisper as I try to keep pace with his long strides. "Can you go first?"

"Nope." He brings me to a stop at the head of the lane. "Take off your clothes, swim to the end of the lane, and drown the Cattle at the end. If you get too cold, tag out and I'll jump in."

"Tag out? How do I tag out?"

He rolls his eyes and starts unbuttoning my coat when I don't move. "Just yell my name, and I'll jump in and save the fucking day. Like I usually do."

With a glare, he rips off my coat and gets to work on my pants.

"Won't we die of hypothermia?" I ask.

He shrugs. "That's why you're going first. So I can decide if I even want to torture myself."

I peer down to the end of the lane—which looks impossibly long, now that I know I have to swim in it—as the workers position Cattle at the end of each rectangle. The Cattle's hands are bound behind their backs, and their feet are wrapped in a heavy chain that trails into the water.

"Are we supposed to pull them in?" I ask. "I don't have the upper-body strength for that."

"Figure it out, *kitten*."

The pet name is no longer doused in longing and lust. Now it's dripping with condescension and hate. Something is definitely wrong.

"Hey, maybe we should talk before we have to rely on each other in this game, you know?" I say.

He finishes unlacing my boots and looks up at me. "Pull your fucking feet out of the boots."

I do as he says, and he pulls them off.

"How has your day been, Cat?" he asks.

"This wasn't the sort of conver—"

"Mine was great too. Now take off your clothes. You're holding everyone up."

I look down the line, and he's right. A bunch of nearly naked people stare back at me, each of them shivering and looking miserable.

Shit, shit, shit.

I shed the rest of my clothes, and Bennett does the same. Now that we're all down to our swimsuits, the games can begin. The games that I don't know the rules for.

"On your marks!" Ezra yells.

I look back at Bennett, mentally pleading with him to give me a hint.

"Get set!"

Bennett smirks.

"Go!"

I jump into the water, expecting the freezing depths to bury me up to my head, but my feet collide with the ground when I'm only chest deep. With a squeal, I shuffle through the water and try to remember to breathe. My lungs don't want to work at these temps.

But as I shuffle along, I realize the water isn't as cold as the air outside. In fact, it's almost bearable in the center of the lane, which makes me think there's some sort of temperature control at work here.

It's still miserable, though. The cold penetrates my skin like needles, and each breath comes in too quickly. I grit my teeth and shuffle forward a few steps, and the freezing water rises past my shoulders.

"It-it's an in-in-incline!" I call back to Bennett.

"No shit?" he calls back, and I can hear his eyes roll in his head.

The water not only gets deeper as I move from the center. It's much colder as well. Whatever warms the frigid depths near the middle can't reach this far, it seems. And now I have to start swimming because the bottom ceases to be.

As I bob toward the end of the lane, I try to peer over the edge to see what others are doing. Maybe if I see how everyone else gets their Cattle into the water, I can just follow suit. But no matter how much upward thrust I apply to each kick of my legs, I see only snow and black water.

I can't stay in these temps much longer. The prickly needles have become swords sawing at my bones. I swim back toward the middle and look to Bennett for help.

"Wrong fucking way!" he yells as he rubs his arms. "Swim toward the Cattle!"

"You have to do it!" I yell back. "I'm not strong enough!"

As I make my way back to the beginning, splashes come from the other lanes. Bennett holds his hand toward me as I draw closer, and I reach up and grab it. He hoists me out of the water as if I weigh nothing, then hops into the frigid ice bath.

"Fuck!" he roars as he rushes down the lane. "Shit! God damn this snowy hell!"

A warm blanket drops over my shoulders, and I look back and see Maverick. "You'll freeze," he says. "Your partner was supposed to have it waiting for you."

"Where did it come from?" I ask. "And how is it so warm?"

Maverick nods toward the squat building I noticed earlier. "Those are steam rooms. We can warm up in them when the event is over, but the blankets are meant to keep us from freezing to death in the interim."

"Couldn't we have done this activity in the heated pool?"

As soon as the words leave my mouth, a loud splash comes from the end of my lane. Bennett managed to wrestle the Cattle into the deep end, and now he's glaring at me.

"Your turn!" he calls as he starts making his way back.

"Looks like my partner needs a little help too." Maverick looks at his lane, where Ice Pick's bald head bobs like a cork in rough waters. He's struggling to keep his victim's head below the surface.

As Maverick jogs away to save the day, I drop the blanket and mentally prepare myself to go back into the water. The sooner I can drown the fucker at the end, the sooner I can get warm.

And that's Bennett's plan, apparently. He easily could have done the drowning and ended this thing for us, but he wants to make me look like a fool.

"Thanks for the warm blanket," I mutter as I step to the edge to pull him out.

He smiles up at me. "Don't mention it."

I release his hand, and he falls back into the water. "Whoops! My hand slipped."

His hand wraps around my ankle, and down I go, right into the water with him.

"Looks like your feet slipped too," he says as I sputter to the surface.

Body heat comes off of him in waves, giving me an idea.

"Did Ezra say we couldn't be in the water at the same time?" I ask.

Bennett catches my meaning and grins for the first time since climbing in that sleigh. "He sure didn't. Climb on."

I hop onto his back, and he turns and takes us toward the Cattle at the end of our lane. Our combined body weight makes it easier for Bennett to press the man's shoulders and keep him underwater, and we're able to last longer in the lower temps because we're sharing our body heat.

"No cheating!" Kindra calls from her lane.

"Go ahead," Bennett grunts so that only I can hear him. He shifts his grip on the man beneath him. "Tell them it was my idea. In fact, let go before someone sees you touching me."

"Is that what this is about?" I ask through clenched teeth. It's all I can do to keep them from chattering. "Are you upset that I want to keep this a secret?"

"Lean forward a bit. Help me drown this piece of shit." He shifts his grip again, and I realize why he's struggling. The Cattle has kicked the chains free, and now he's using his lower body to power upward.

I lean forward, but it doesn't do much good. The man is able to lift his nostrils above the waterline and get a breath.

"You'll have to get off my back and help me end this," Bennett finally says. "Swim down for that chain. I'll wrap it around his neck and finish this a little quicker."

"Answer the question. Are you upset that I want to keep this a secret?"

Bennett releases a guttural groan and pushes the man's head below the surface again. "If you will just help me kill this sorry motherfucker, I will answer any question you have. Now swim!"

I slide off his back and immediately regret it. A wall of cold pushes through my body and steals my breath. In fact, taking a deep breath so that I can dive seems a near impossibility at this point. But I try. I suck in what air I can, and down I go.

The cold is almost more bearable when I'm fully submerged. Maybe that's why so many people drown in cold water. The thought of piercing the surface and feeling that frigid air once more is almost more than I can bear once my hand wraps around the chain's tail. But up I go, ready to deliver the weapon that will end this battle.

Careful to avoid the man's untethered feet, I rise and push the chain into Bennett's hand before trying to climb onto his back again. I want his warmth, but more than that, I want to feel close to him.

Now that I know the weird attitude wasn't part of my imagination, now that I know something is truly bothering him, the rift between us causes me more discomfort than I thought it would.

An obsession still worms its way inside me, but it no longer focuses on Maverick. Like it or not, I have a new problem on my hands.

I have a crush on Bennett.

Chapter Twenty-Six

Bennett

The entirety of my rage transfers to the chain in my hands. I wind the thick metal links around his neck, tighter and tighter, pulling until I can't tell where the chain ends and my hands begin. Water moves over his face and distorts his gaped mouth and widening eyes.

"Is he almost dead?" Cat asks against my ear, and I hate that her warm breath makes me shiver.

"Almost," I say.

I renew my grip on the chain and shove his body lower, ensuring he can't rise for air again. In his death throes, he drives upward one last time before he finally goes limp. Seconds later, bubbles rise to the surface.

"He's done. Let's get the fuck out of here." I release the chain, and the man stays put.

Cat grips me tighter as I turn and head for the exit. "But his mouth . . . his mouth was still moving."

"Agonal breathing." My feet meet with the ground, but

I don't tell her to get off my back. "The body doesn't know when to quit."

And neither does the heart.

I shouldn't revel in the way her breasts press against my back. I shouldn't want to help her overcome her fear of killing. She shouldn't be any concern of mine, because I'm just her dirty fucking secret.

Yet I can't turn it off.

"Can we get a check?" I yell down the lanes, but I don't wait around to see if we came in first. With Cat still firmly attached to my back, I haul us out of the water and start for the steam huts.

"You read my mind," Cat says against my ear, and I'm sure she felt the shiver that time. I'll just pretend it's from the cold.

I can't feel my feet by the time I wrench open the heavy door and deposit Cat on a wooden bench inside the hut. Before anyone can interrupt us, I turn and lock the door.

Cat's eyes widen as she pulls a robe from a hook and slides her arms into it. "I think these huts are supposed to be for everyone, not just us."

"Yeah, well, there's more than one. They can crowd into those. You wanted to talk, so let's talk." I rifle through the robes until I find one that will fit. Then I take a seat beside her on the bench, drop the back of my head against the cedar wall, and sigh through the intense shivering. Warmth from the stones and fire in the center of the room sends prickles of pain into my wakening limbs.

"What if people ask questions?" Cat says.

I close my eyes. "Then you answer them."

"I mean about us. What lie can I come up with this time? Why have we locked ourselves in this hut, alone?"

"Tell them the truth."

"I can't. And neither can you."

"You're free to leave, then," I say, motioning toward the door. "I'm not keeping you here. The lock only works on people who aren't in here."

"I know how locks work, Bennett."

"Says the girl who panicked after locking herself in an outhouse."

No, she doesn't understand how locks work at all. If she did, she wouldn't have let me past her defenses in the first place. Now we're both fucked.

"Why does this have to stay a secret?" I ask.

She fumbles with her words before finally saying, "You know why."

"Is it because you're embarrassed? You say that isn't the reason, but I think it is."

She grips the edge of the bench and sits forward, looking into the small fire in the center of the room. "I guess I am embarrassed, in a way. It's just . . . I don't want to justify my decisions to everyone who knows us."

Someone knocks on the door, followed by Ezra's voice. "Everything okay in there?"

"We're fine!" Cat says, loud enough for him to hear her. Hell, the Cattle in the mansion's basement probably heard her. "We're . . . talking."

"Talking?" Kindra says through the crack in the door. "Why on earth would you two try to do something like that? And without a mediator, too?"

Cat motions to the door and gives me a look that says, *See?*

"She said we're fine, now fuck off!" I say, and that's enough to get them away from the door. I can tell because the light filters from underneath once they walk away. "We all tease each other," I whisper. "The jokes wouldn't be anything new."

She shakes her head. "It's more than that. I'll have to field questions, and you'll get it even worse than me. *Don't hurt her, Bennett. Don't cheat on her, Bennett.*" She scoffs and runs her toe through the dirt. "Is that really what we want to deal with?"

Some things are worth it.

That's what I want to say, but my lips won't form the words. I can only watch the way the flames cast a glow over her pale skin.

"Then what do you want to do?" I ask instead.

"I don't know. This would be so much easier if we were back in New York. We're under a microscope here."

Another knock comes at the door. This time, it's Ice Pick. "Hey, any chance I can squeeze in there? The other sweat rooms are pretty packed."

"The constant interruptions certainly don't help," I say to Cat. "Let's pick this up back at the mansion. We'll have a few hours before dinner."

Cat nods as I stand to unlock the door.

"An hour after we're back, let's meet in the natatorium," I say. "I doubt anyone will want to go near water for a while after this."

I walk to the control panel in the natatorium and turn off those horrible screens. All that fake sun disappears, replaced by reality. And reality is dark, snowy, and cold. The overhead lights work off the same panel, so I dim those as well. The less attention I can draw to this room, the better.

Everyone was pretty tired after the disaster event, so we should be safe. Cat and I completed the only successful drowning. All the other Cattle died from hypothermia while the participants warmed themselves in the steam huts. Everyone should be in their rooms right now, sleeping off the cold and dreaming of the late dinner Kindra orchestrated to give everyone time to nap and warm up.

Not Cat, though. If she's sticking to our plan, she should be coming through those glass doors at any minute.

I adjust the champagne and slender glass flutes at the edge of one of the hot tubs, which is tucked away in an alcove behind a few tall plants. It's the only spot in the room that offers any privacy from prying eyes.

And that's the thing. It's not that I dislike the secrecy surrounding our exploits. It adds an element of fun, if anything. But I'd be lying if I said I was okay with the reasoning behind it.

Or that it will be hidden forever.

The fact that I'm thinking in timelines doesn't exactly bode well for me, either. Relationships and commitment and feelings have never been a consideration. If I fucked a girl one day and my buddy fucked her the next, it was never a problem. Hell, sometimes we'd both fuck the same girl at the same time. I didn't care.

Until now.

I knew this was more than I initially bargained for when I looked up and saw Maverick wrapping a warm towel around Cat's shoulders at the event. Because that's when the white-hot needles of jealousy plunged into my chest.

He sees her as a sister, and I've heard Ezra say he's told him as much too, but the way he looked down at her as he draped the warm material over her exposed skin . . . Let's just say it was a very incestuous glare if he considers her his sister. If I ever have the chance to meet my illusive sister, my gaze won't form a fucking airlock on her nipples.

The door to the humid room swishes open. Cat enters and hurries over to the pool as if someone's right behind her. Before I can call her name, she jumps into the water and disappears below the surface. Clothes and all.

"What the fuck?" I whisper as I continue watching.

She silently dog paddles to the side of the pool facing the door, then grips the edge so that she can peer over. And there she waits, watching the wall of frosted windows until a dark figure happens past.

Ice Pick toddles to the door, which isn't frosted, and peers inside. Cat lowers her head beneath the water as Ice Pick continues searching for her in the shadowy room. Satisfied that his quarry isn't here, he continues on.

"The coast is clear, Ariel," I say when she resurfaces.

She squeals and nearly drowns herself as she spins to see where the voice came from.

I give her a wave and raise the champagne bottle. "Figured a little alcohol might help."

"I need something stronger than champagne," she says as she hauls her dripping body out of the pool. The pink sweatshirt clinging to her curves threatens to send her back into the water, so I hurry to help her.

Once she's secure on dry land, I help her out of her clothes and lead her to the hot tub. She studies the romantic setup with wary eyes.

"What's all this?"

"Me first," I say. "Why were you running from Ice Pick?"

She steps into the roiling water, then lowers herself with

a sigh until only her head pokes above the surface. "He saw me come down the stairs and started heading toward me. Figuring he wanted to try out flirting again, I nearly broke my neck trying to get away from him before he could catch up."

"Aw, does my kitten have an admirer?" I say with a smirk. I slide into the water and nearly send it into a full boil with what she says next.

"Apparently, he isn't the only one. Eve mentioned that Maverick might not be so against something between us after all."

I swallow the possessive words creeping up my throat and do my best to seem indifferent. "That so? What do you plan to do with this information?"

Her slender shoulders lift in a shrug that barely clears the waterline. "I don't know. But that isn't why we're here. You said you wanted to talk, so talk."

What I planned to say—that I'm falling for her and I think we should consider what that means—doesn't seem so wise now. If I'm sick of being the butt of everyone's jokes, I have to stop setting myself up so easily. She'll just laugh if I tell her how I truly feel. Especially now that her obsession is within reach.

So I stare into the water and say nothing.

"Wow, something really is bugging you," she says, and there's no condescension in her voice.

"It's nothing. Just a me problem."

She slides a little closer and places a hand on my thigh, then almost immediately pulls her arm away, instead choosing to pat my back. The second action isn't any less awkward than the first.

"We aren't very good at this," she says with a small smile.

"What? Comforting each other? We could be."

"How so?"

I wrap my arm around her waist and pull her onto my lap. An action I almost regret, because the feel of her slippery skin against my thighs is enough to stiffen my dick. If she notices, she's too polite to say anything.

Brushing her hair away from her face, I look into her eyes. If I want this—and it's becoming clear that I do—I'll have to put in a little more effort. She likes Maverick because he's an open book, so maybe I just need to crack open my cover and at least give her a peek at *something*.

But not the feelings I have for her. I'm not ready for her to read that part of my story yet. Those words may stay buried in a chapter I have to close at the end of the retreat.

"My mom . . ." The words jumble in my throat, choking me with their truth. It's one thing to lie to Ezra about my mother's condition. It's another when I lie to myself about it. Telling someone the truth makes it real. "My mom is dying."

The words tumble out before I realize I've said them, and the situation almost cheapens them. In a way, I'm spilling my guts to manipulate Cat into liking me more than Maverick. But in a way, I'm telling her these things because she's the person who can put me back together when I break, even if she doesn't realize it.

Cat leans down, enveloping me in her arms and resting her head on my shoulder. "Bennett, I'm so sorry. We all knew she was in a care home, but Ezra hasn't mentioned her condition."

"Because he doesn't know."

"No wonder you walk around with a chip on your shoulder and a glare in your eyes."

"Everyone eventually dies. I don't know why this is affecting me like this, but it is."

"No, I don't mean your mother's situation." Her fingers trace lazy circles on my back beneath the water. "You're a man alone on an island. You depend on yourself for everything."

"Isn't that what men are supposed to do?"

"No, jackass." She giggles against my neck, and that taunt becomes a term of endearment as it falls from her lips. "No one should be expected to get through a shitstorm alone. It's okay to let other people care about you."

"I'm not stopping anyone from caring about me."

"But you are."

"How?" I tilt my neck so I can look down at her.

"If you don't tell people when you're hurting, how can they care?"

I scoff. "You're talking about pity. I don't want anyone to pity me."

"Well, for what it's worth, I don't pity you. I care about you."

She snuggles into me as her words dig barbed hooks into my heart. The girl is making herself right at home there.

If only she'd stay.

Chapter Twenty-Seven

Cat

Warm water burbles over my skin as Bennett holds me in his arms. I'm scared to move, afraid I'll shatter the illusion he's created if I animate more than my lips to offer a reply. Even the words I speak feel packed with trip wires. One misstep, and he'll raise the defenses and blast me away so that I can't get close to him.

"It's a form of dementia," he says after a long silence. "Her brain is essentially shrinking, and there isn't much time now. I try to adjust to the rapid changes in her personality, but it's like meeting a different person every time I visit. I rarely see my mother anymore. I mean, physically she looks the same, but . . ."

"I understand what you mean," I say when he doesn't continue.

"Do you?"

His walls are rising again, and I need to find a way to stop them. If I want a ceasefire, I'll have to agree to the terms of this war, and that means I'll need to lower my walls as well.

I'll have to explain how I understand what he's going through.

"I wasn't always an only child," I say. "I had an older brother."

"With dementia?"

"No, cerebral palsy. It was pretty severe. He never walked or talked, and he spent most of his life in a wheelchair, but he was my brother and I loved him."

His shoulders deflate a bit, and he pulls me even closer, wrapping his arms around me so that I can fully relax in his hold. "Tell me about him."

The way Bennett holds me and wants to know more about my brother has undone some tight thing inside me. It uncoils and loosens until the knot in my throat dissolves.

"His name was Seth. He had blond hair and blue eyes, just like me, but his eyelashes were way fuller than mine."

"Eyelashes, huh? I bet he got all the ladies."

I chuckle against his neck. "Oh, the nurses loved him, that's for sure. He couldn't express himself with words or actions, but his eyes held so much life. It might sound crazy, but he *could* communicate. When I would play around his chair or place a toy into his hand or lap, there was joy. When Dad fell through the ceiling while trying to remodel the upstairs bathroom, there was concern. He spoke through his eyes."

"How'd you deal with his loss?"

I take a deep breath and try to find the right words. Nothing seems to convey the anguish my family felt—and continues to feel—in my brother's absence.

"I don't think we ever really dealt with it," I say. "Not in a healthy way, at least. Mom locked up his room and sold all of his medical equipment to recoup some of the costs. She and Dad kind of act like I never had a brother at all, which is hard for me because I *did*."

"I never knew you had a brother," he says. "I don't think Kindra knows, either. She's said you're an only child on several occasions."

"It's not something I tell many people."

"Including your best friend?" His fingers land beneath my chin and raise my face so that I'm looking into his blue eyes. "Kitten, it seems I'm not the only one on an island."

"Well, maybe I was partly wrong. Maybe islands aren't so bad if you let people visit every now and again."

"Is that all we're doing?" he asks. "Just visiting? Because I'm not so sure anymore."

His words register in my mind, but I don't have time to respond as Bennett moves us to the other side of the hot tub. I spin in his arms and sit on the seat, facing him as he cages me between his biceps and hovers above me, his mouth so close to mine. I close my eyes, and he kisses me.

And this kiss is unlike any we've shared before.

The vulnerability transfers to the intimacy, and the kiss sparks something inside me. It's wild, unbridled, and brimming with warm passion. It's honey and peppermint. It's devoid of familiar hatred and rife with something foreign.

It's dangerous.

I push him away and gulp air. When he kisses me like that, so completely, I can't breathe or think. He reduces me to a mindless blob of need.

"Bennett, what are you saying?" I ask.

He closes his eyes and presses his forehead to mine, but the words require more vulnerability than he can muster, it seems. Instead of angering me, his silence reassures me.

Despite the consequences, we are very much on the same page.

"Me too," I whisper.

Bennett groans and releases me so that he can drop down beside me. "We really can't be anything, can we?" he asks as he stares at the drooping monstera blocking his view of the door.

"I don't see how we could," I whisper, and here come the tears again. I clamp down on the inside of my cheek to give myself another painful sensation to focus on so that I can forget about the way my chest aches.

"I hate keeping it a secret, but if that's the only way, then—"

"If I'm being honest, I don't like keeping it a secret, either. What's the point of having mind-blowing sex if you can't brag about it to your girlfriends?"

Bennett smirks. "Mind-blowing, huh?"

"Don't start."

"Come on, kitten. A little praise never hurt anyone."

"Your ego is the last thing that needs stroked."

"Is my cock the first thing?"

I groan and smack his arm. "Are you genuinely incapable of serious conversation? I'm beginning to get concerned."

"Okay, okay." He sighs and falls silent, but a question nags him until he's forced to ask it. "So . . . are you gonna go for Maverick since we can't be anything?"

I shrug. "I don't know. I mean, what's happened between us kind of . . . changed some things in my head."

"Right."

More silence fills the spaces between our words, and an uneasiness settles over us. We have no trouble with the hot-and-heavy moments, but the quiet times that pass so easily between lovers create an obstacle course I'm not sure we can get through.

Bennett's hands grip my waist, and he pulls me onto his lap so that I'm straddling him.

"What are you doing?" I ask as I try to pull away, but he doesn't let me go.

His grip tightens as he looks into my eyes, and I'm almost afraid. There's a fire there I don't recognize. And it's aimed at me.

"Look me in the eye and tell me you don't want me, Cat. Can you do that?" His hips pulse upward, pressing his hard cock against my bikini bottoms. "Can you tell me you don't think about me when I'm not around? Can you say you don't look for me when I'm in a room?"

I do all of those things and so much more, but that doesn't mean anything. It doesn't mean that outing ourselves to everyone is the answer.

"What if it doesn't work out?" I say. "What then? We'll be forced to split our friend group, and that's after enduring their questions and commentary for God knows how long."

"And what if it does work out?"

I close my eyes and bite back a moan as he rolls his hips again.

"So tell me the truth," he demands. "Answer my questions. Tell me it wouldn't rip your heart out to go a day without me now."

His girth brushes against me again, and my eyes nearly cross. This isn't fair. He knows I'll say whatever he wants to hear when he's dangling an orgasm in front of me.

Well, two can play that game.

I grip his shoulders and grind my hips. "Do you think of *me*, Bennett? Is that why you want to know if I think of you?"

His hands grip my hips, trying to stall my movements. "What are you doing, kitten? Don't be disobedient."

"Oh, I'm *very* disobedient." I pick up speed and grind a little faster. Water and heat slosh between us. "Now tell me, what sort of things do *you* think about? Dirty things? Or are they sweet?"

He grits his teeth as a moan spills from my lips. I can't help it. The friction feels amazing.

"Do you look for *me* in a room?" I bite his neck and hump him like my life depends on it. "Fuck, you do, don't you?"

I do whatever it takes to keep from answering those questions myself, because the answers terrify me almost as much as that heat in his gaze.

"You're going to make me come if you keep that up," he says.

I smirk and keep moving against him. Again, this is incredible for my confidence. I don't think I've ever made a guy come in his pants.

"Kitten, if you make me come like this, I'll have to punish you later for embarrassing me."

"You gonna strip me down and bend me over your knee?" I whisper in his ear. "Tell me how you'll do it. Tell me how you'll punish me."

His hand slips between us, and he squeezes my breast. "The spanking is just the start. You're in need of a lesson, and I want to make sure you don't forget it."

I grind on him harder, and he sucks in a breath.

"I'm serious, Cat. Cut it out," he says.

My hips roll and rock as he grips me tighter. His cock is a steel rod, and my skin is electric. The water conducts our spark, heightening the sensations until I fear I'll come too.

He buries his face between my breasts, holding me

against his firm body until I can barely move my hips. His cock jerks, pulsing like a faint heartbeat as he grunts against my skin and comes. Seconds later, he releases me and swipes the hair away from my face.

"Oh, kitten." He takes a deep breath and lets it out. "You're in trouble."

Chapter Twenty-Eight

Bennett

I try not to slip as I hoist Cat over my shoulder and carry her into the hall. The things I need to do to this woman require a little more room and a lot more privacy than this hot tub can provide.

"My clothes!" Cat says with a giggle. "They're still on the floor. What if someone finds them?"

"I'll tell them I suspected you were the Wicked Witch of the West, so I doused you with water and proved my theory correct." I smack her ass, and it jiggles beside my head. I can't wait to bite it.

Male voices reach my ears as we near the main hall, and I'm tempted to walk right out in the open with my prize draped over my shoulder like a championship belt. But I feel Cat tense against me, and I can't do it. I can't betray her trust. I lower her to her feet, and she chews her lip and looks up at me.

"Let's just keep it quiet until we figure out what . . . this is, okay?" she whispers.

"And what is this?" I ask.

She motions between us, then toward the upstairs rooms. "You know . . . We're fucking, I guess, but I still don't know if there's more to it."

I hate that she thinks the ball is entirely in her court. Like I'm some lovesick puppy she can play with when she feels like it. That's the *real* problem here.

After taking a few steps forward, I peer around the corner and spy Maverick and Jim by the staircase. She might have snuck off with me had it been anyone else, but the moment she sees Maverick, I'll be forgotten, despite what she said in the hot tub.

"Who is it?" Cat whispers.

I sigh and motion for her to see for herself.

She tiptoes closer and peers around the corner. As soon as she spots Maverick, her body tenses and she nearly leaps backward.

"Shit," she says. "There's no way we can walk out together without drawing attention. We're both in swimsuits, so that looks suspicious enough."

I try not to wince as her words strike a soft spot inside me.

"Yeah, you go on ahead," I say. "Leave your door unlocked and I'll slip in once the coast is clear."

I don't like the moment of indecision that flickers through her eyes before she nods her head. She might have said she was undecided about Maverick, but it seems like she's more undecided about me.

I swallow my emotions as I watch her steel herself to round the corner. It's difficult to admit that I want her more with every passing second, but I do. Not just her body, but everything about her.

When she told me about her brother, that's when I knew. Hearing the hurt in her voice made me hurt for her. Something inside me longed to ease her pain and ensure she never hurts again. Empathy isn't a foreign emotion for me, but it is where love interests are concerned. As terrifying as it is, though, I find myself wanting to explore this more than she does, and that's more frightening than anything else.

Her musical voice reaches my ears as she greets the two men, and I grit my teeth as I cower in the shadows like vermin. She lets out a soft laugh, and I want to punch a hole in the nearest wall. Whatever Maverick just said couldn't have been *that* fucking funny.

I step a little closer to the corner so that I can listen in, but they're too far away. Their voices reach my ears, but the words are a series of muffled mumbles and mutterings. Goddamn all this wood and its sound-absorbing properties. If I want to hear what they're talking about, I'll need to get closer.

I round the corner like I have somewhere to be, careful that my gaze doesn't linger on Cat for too long. It's a feat, really, because she's still in that tiny bikini. Maverick is too focused on her glistening tits to see me coming, though, so that's a bonus.

Jim gives me a small wave as I start up the stairs. I wave back and keep going, but he calls my name before I reach the top landing, and now I'm stuck. I wait at the top as he grips the railing and makes his way to me.

"Dinner's been cancelled, I'm afraid," Jim says. "Well, not cancelled, but there won't be a formal call to dinner. Chef has agreed to accommodate a limited room-service menu for the evening."

"Is everything okay?"

"Well, yes, for the most part. A few of the guests felt a little under the weather after the event, so Ezra and I thought it best to give everyone the night off to do whatever they'd like. It was that or cancel the excursions in the morning."

I cock my head and look at him. "Excursions?"

"Oh, yes, we've packed the final two days full of fun. We're doing a hunt in the morning, though it won't be nearly as grand as what we do on the island."

"A hunt in the dark? Are you sure that's wise?" I glance down the staircase, and my eyes fall on Cat. "We have more women than usual, and I'd hate to see one of them get hurt."

Jim chuckles and shakes his head. "We all know how sad you'd be if Miss Novak fell victim to the Cattle, but safety measures have been put in place, I assure you. The entire hunting ground has been rigged with cameras, which will be monitored during the event to ensure the safety of all guests. We don't want another problem like we had at the summer retreat."

He's being sarcastic, but I'm genuinely concerned about Cat's wellbeing. The hunts can get crazy.

"After getting lost in the woods, I doubt Cat wants to go on another trek through the frozen forest." I offer a small laugh. "She'll probably sit this one out anyway."

Jim shakes his head and looks down the staircase. "No, I think she has every intention of attending. That's what she was just discussing with Maverick. He's offered to take her out to the range to practice with a bow."

Anger runs through my veins like molten lava. My skin heats, and a light sweat rises on my brow. We took Maverick under our wing when he came to us a few years ago, and now he's not only taken my job away from me, but he's about to take the girl too.

"Yeah, we'll see about that," I say under my breath.

"Beg pardon?"

I look at Jim and smile. "Oh, nothing. Nothing at all." I give him a parting wave, then head to my room. "See ya, Jimbo."

"That's *Jim*," he says to my retreating back. "You know I *hate* being called Jimbo. It's so . . . unrefined."

I ignore him and keep walking. I don't even spare a glance down the stairs as I stride past the two chatty love-birds at the bottom, but I feel Cat's gaze bore into me as I pass. She can lie to herself all she wants, but I know the truth. What I feel isn't a one-sided infatuation. This obsession goes both ways, and I'll make her admit it to me by the end of this retreat.

Hell, I'll make her admit it to everyone.

But before I can do any of that, I need to wrench her away from Maverick's claws.

The door clicks shut behind me once I enter my room. I hurry to the closet, nearly tripping as I rush to step out of my swim trunks. Cat still needs to dress, and she'll probably want time to paint her face, since she'll be with Maverick, but that's why I'm in a rush. If I want to know why Maverick's had a change of heart about the girl, I need to talk to him when she's not around.

Especially if I want to properly sabotage things and ensure she chooses me.

As I'm pulling on my coat, I hear the door to her bedroom click shut. Moments later, the pipes hum in the walls as she starts the shower.

"Good girl," I say under my breath as I tie my shoes. "Give me all the time I need to make you mine."

And she will be mine. I've made up my mind on that matter. It has taken me too long to find a woman I'm unwilling to share, and now that I have, I refuse to let her go. If I have to chain her to the bed and make her come until she's insane enough to love me, I'll do that.

I'll do whatever it takes. And it starts today.

Chapter Twenty-Nine

Bennett

He's difficult to track down, but I eventually find Maverick in the barn. Instead of setting up the sleigh, however, he's busy fiddling with one of the snowmobiles, which is great. The snowmobile is far less romantic.

"Little dark for a drive through the woods, huh?" I say as I step closer.

Maverick looks up and smiles, and I want to punch his white teeth until they aren't so straight anymore. "I'm taking Cat out to practice with the bow. You're welcome to join."

"You sure you didn't want it to be just the two of you?" I raise an eyebrow and wait for his answer.

"No. Why would I want that?" He eases the snowmobile out of the barn until the treads meet the snow. "I know she has a thing for me, but I see her as a—"

"Little sister. Right."

"Yeah." He turns to face me. "But if I saw her as something else, would that be a problem?"

I don't much care for the tone of voice he's using with me, and I don't even know where this sudden hostility is coming from. I fold my arms over my chest and posture to remind him that he's the pup here.

"No, it wouldn't be a problem," I say with a shake of my head. "But if it was a problem, would that be a problem?"

"Would it be a problem if it was a problem that it was a problem?"

I blink. "Okay, enough cryptic shit. Are you making a move on Cat or what?"

"Bennett . . ." Maverick sighs and nudges a clump of snow with the toe of his boot. "Look, I'm just trying to be nice to her because you're giving her such a hard time. Everyone's getting sick of running interference between you two. It's a full-time job at this point."

My eyes widen, and I can't believe what the fuck I'm hearing. Interference? Giving her a hard time? Cat and I have been worried people will realize we're fucking, but we're so good at hiding it that they think we're more volatile than ever.

"Wait, so you're taking her on a pity date?" I ask as my brain registers what else he said. "You're going to make her think you like her when you don't? Isn't that kind of fucked up?"

"That's what I said, but everyone else seems to think this is a great idea."

"Everyone else? Are you guys having fucking *meetings* about us? What the fuck?"

Maverick runs his hands through his hair. "I agree. Everything about this is fucked. But Kindra's really worried about her, and I am too. She's been so depressed since the uptick in audition rejections she's received."

Depressed? She hasn't seemed so very depressed. Hell,

she hasn't even mentioned the failed auditions to me. Why does Maverick know about them when I don't?

More jealousy fills the growing pit in my gut.

"So what happens when you have to destroy her after raising her hopes?" I ask. "Seems like this plan will do more harm than good."

"Again, that's what I said."

"So don't do it," I say. "Don't take her out. Let me do it."

Maverick starts shaking his head before I can even finish my sentence. "Definitely not. Ezra and Kindra gave everyone strict orders to keep you two away from each other, and I'm not risking Kindra's wrath. Have you seen her when she's pissed?"

I shudder, because yes, I have.

But I have to do *something*. If Maverick puts the moves on Cat, she'll cave, and if she kisses him, I'll have to kill him. He's pissing me off right now, but Ezra and I see him as an unofficial little brother, and I really don't want to kill him.

"Don't do this, Maverick. I'll deal with Kindra and Ezra."

"Eve, Grim, and Ice Pick too? And you can't forget Jim."

I scoff, realizing how deep this goes. Cat's concerns that everyone will hound us to death don't seem so fabricated now. "What about Rosie? Is she in on this too?"

Maverick shoves his hands into his pockets. "Surprisingly, no. She shook her head the entire time, but she refuses to say why she disagrees with the plan to keep you two away from each other."

"Refuses to . . . Maverick, she can't talk."

"She can, but only Grim understands her. He says she won't talk about it with him, either."

"So everyone hates me," I say. "Is that what you're telling me?"

Maverick rocks on his heels and looks at the snowy ground. "Hate is a very strong word."

I nod and turn my head to spit the bitter taste of loneliness out of my mouth. Maybe Cat wasn't so far off when she said I'm a man on an island. She's wrong about how I got here, though. I didn't choose to be alone. The people in my life made that choice for me.

As I turn and walk away, Maverick calls after me. I don't stop. What's the point? He's set on being their lackey and fooling Cat into thinking he's falling for her. *They* want to hurt her. Not me. Yet I'm the one she needs protection from?

White-hot rage blinds me as I make my way back to the mansion. I have to stop her before she gets hurt. With all those hearts in her eyes, she won't be able to see what's going on.

By the time I reach the front door, I still haven't seen her. I know I didn't miss her because there's only one path to the barn. That means she's probably still in her room, preparing for her little date.

I have to stop her, but how? If I tell her the truth, that Maverick is pretending to be interested out of pity, it will crush her. For the first time since I met her, I don't want that. I want her to be happy.

With me, of course.

I power walk through the empty front hall, then take the stairs two at a time. If I can't convince her to stay behind with me, I could always hold her hostage. I imagine what she'd look like tied up on the bed. Beautiful perfection. But that won't win any brownie points with everyone else, so I scratch that idea.

As I pass her door, I give the handle a jiggle and find it unlocked. Despite her plans to spend the evening with the golden boy, it seems she hasn't forgotten about the orchestrated rendezvous with her tarnished lover—me.

Stepping into her room, I spy an outfit sprawled across the bed, but Cat must be in the bathroom, because I don't see her. A clatter and a curse word come from behind the closed door, confirming my suspicions. Seconds later, a blow-dryer fires up.

Since she's occupied, I take a look around the room, trying to find a way to sabotage her and ensure she stays here. Talking would be so much easier, but again, I can't bear the thought of seeing the pain in her eyes. I also don't want to be the consolation prize. If I tell her the truth, it all but guarantees she'll run right into my waiting arms, but that isn't how I want to win.

I want to be chosen.

The bra-and-panty set on the bed catches my attention, and I step closer. I lift the tiny pink thong and run the patch of lace through my fingers. The hard-on is immediate.

I glance back at the bathroom door, wondering if I have enough time to beat my dick and force her to wear come-soaked panties on her little date, but then the cat jumps onto the bed, and I have a better idea.

No, I'm not about to beat off on the cat. I'm not *that* deranged.

"Hey, Shorty," I whisper as I step closer. "You're about to help me make nice with your mommy."

The humongous black cat just looks at me and flicks his tail. He takes a seat—right on Cat's pink bra—and begins grooming his paw. His rough tongue flicks out, swipes his paw pads a few times, and darts back into his mouth. When that doesn't quite satisfy him, he takes to gnawing at whatever is there.

"Something bugging you, buddy?" I sit beside him on

the bed and take his paw into my hand. The largest pad is warmer than the rest, and a splinter pokes from the center. "Damn, that looks uncomfortable. Let me help you."

I pull the cat into my lap, and he purrs as I pluck the splinter from his paw. Despite how disgusting and vile I find these animals, Cat loves them—this one in particular—so I kind of have to help him. Once the sliver of wood has been removed, I can't even tell it was there in the first place.

"You're a tough little asshole, hmm?" I scratch under his chin as the blow-dryer cuts off in the bathroom. "Looks like we need to make a move."

Tucking the cat under my sweater, I hurry back to my room before Cat sees me in hers. Once she realizes he's missing, she'll cancel her plans with Maverick so that she can look for Shorty, but only if she doesn't see me catnapping him. That's when I'll swoop in and save the day by "finding" him myself.

It's one hell of a plan. What could possibly go wrong?

Chapter Thirty

Cat

Looking into the mirror, I drag vanilla-scented lip gloss over my mouth as I try to think of a way out of this. I can't go with Maverick this evening. I want to spend more time with Bennett. We were finally getting somewhere, and now this happens.

But I can't say no. It's no secret that I had a major crush on Maverick, and as far as everyone else is concerned, I'm still hung up on him. Staying behind when he's asked me to an activity would be suspicious as fuck.

I step out of the bathroom and head to the bed to dress. I'd hoped to find Bennett sitting on my bed by the time I finished getting ready, but I guess he changed his mind. Not that I blame him.

He probably sees this situation as me choosing Maverick over him, but that couldn't be further from the truth. Bennett is the man I want. He just can't know how badly. He can't learn how much I miss him when he's not around. It's like I've lived my entire life with a piece missing from me, and now that I know how well he fits in that gaping hole, I want to be filled all the time—double entendre intended.

I just need more time, that's all. Telling Kindra about this will be one of the most difficult conversations I'll ever have, and Bennett's side of things won't be any easier. The difference is that he doesn't care what everyone thinks.

But I do.

Black fur clings to my pale pink bra as I lift it from the bed. I give it a good shake, but it doesn't matter anyway. No one will see me in this. Maverick might make a move, but I'll have to play coy. Because my heart belongs to someone else now.

"Shorty, come give your mama a cuddle," I say as I dress. "I need it."

By the time I finish piling on clothes—including Bennett's coat, which still smells of his cologne—Shorty hasn't emerged. Even when I get on my hands and knees and reach for the ever reliable *pspsps*, he doesn't show his adorable little face.

"You might be able to resist my charms, but you'll never say no to treaties!" I say in a sing-song voice.

I hurry to the dresser and pull the little tube of stinky cat treats from the middle drawer. After giving them a good shake, I turn, expecting to hear heavy little paws padding toward me.

But he doesn't appear.

My heart beats a little faster in my chest, but I hold the panic at bay. Shorty can be a bit difficult sometimes, but he's still in my room. He has to be. It's not as if he grew opposable thumbs and opened the fucking door.

I grab my phone from the nightstand and use the flashlight to look under the bed, dresser, and inside the closet, but my poor cat is nowhere in sight. I hurry to the bathroom next. It isn't his favorite room, what with all the water, but he sometimes sneaks in when I'm getting ready.

He isn't in there, either. The bathroom is just as empty as I left it.

Despite my best attempts to remain rational, panic creeps in. What if he got out of my room? Worse, what if he got out of the mansion? My poor baby isn't cut out for cold weather, and the expensive mansion furnishings aren't cut out for cat piss. He's litter-box trained, but the only litter box is in this room, where he isn't.

I hurry into the hall and knock on Bennett's door. He takes too long to answer, but I'm too flustered to complain when he finally appears.

Tears brim in my eyes. "Shorty is missing. I think I lost my cat."

"Hey, hey, don't panic. I'm sure he's around here some-where." Bennett steps into the hall and wraps his arm around my shoulder as he closes his door behind him. "Let's go to your room and find him."

Relief washes over me the moment he says he'll help me, and we head into my room. Bennett begins searching all the obvious places I've already looked. Under the bed and dresser. In the closet and bathroom. He has the same luck I had. Shorty isn't in here.

I can't hold the tears back anymore, especially once Bennett wraps his arms around me. I weep against his chest, not caring that I'm getting snot all over his shirt.

"I suck at acting. I suck at being a personal assistant. I suck at being a friend because I can't even talk to my bestie about the guy I'm fucking." I take a deep breath in. "And now I can't even take care of a fucking cat. A *cat*, Bennett. I chose this species because it's the most difficult to fuck up, and yet I still managed."

Bennett guides me to the bed and sits beside me, but he doesn't hold me and let me cry. He grips my chin in his hand and forces me to look at him.

"You don't suck at acting," he says. "In fact, you're so good at it, you have everyone at the retreat thinking you hate me more than ever. So what if a few casting directors can't see your worth? I see it. Fuck all the rejections."

While his words are sweet, they bring forth a question. "How did you know about the rejections? I never mentioned them to you."

Bennett shrugs and closes his eyes. "I may have talked to Maverick, and he might have mentioned them."

"You talked to Maverick?" I almost shout the words at him. "What the fuck were you *thinking*, Bennett?"

He sets his jaw as he looks at me. "Are you afraid your little crush might catch on? Afraid he might not want you once he finds out Bennett's had his dirty dick inside you?"

"I don't have time for this," I say as I head toward the door. "I have to find my cat."

I almost run into Maverick as I fling the door open. He's standing in the hallway, his fist raised to knock. I leap back into my room and slam the door before he can get a good look inside.

"Hide!" I whisper-shout toward Bennett.

Like a crazed cartoon character, he runs from one side of the room to the other before diving between the bed and the wall. He bumps the nightstand on his way down, and the lamp teeters before coming to rest at the edge.

I take a deep breath before opening the door.

"Everything okay in there?" Maverick asks as I peep through the small crack.

I smile up at him. "Oh, yeah. Everything's great. I just . . . I can't go because my cat is missing."

"Want me to help you find him? He couldn't have gone far." Maverick pushes his way into my room. I've dreamed of this moment for so long, but it's playing out like a nightmare now.

"He's probably just sleeping somewhere," I say as I hurry to get in front of him before he can check the other side of the bed. Or under it. "I'm sure he'll turn up soon."

Maverick stops in the center of the room, his left eyebrow raised as he studies me. "So you aren't concerned, but you're too concerned to attend shooting practice?" He fingers the hem of my coat. "You're already dressed and everything."

"I got dressed before I realized the cat was missing. Now I can't go. You understand, don't you?" I blink up at him, silently pleading for him to let it go.

But instead of leaving, he grabs my hand and guides me toward the bed. Again, the moment I've dreamed of is now cast in a nightmarish light. The man I want is now cowering behind the bed, where the man I no longer want is leading me.

And I don't know how to stop this train from derailing around the next bend.

"You know what?" I say. "Maybe you could give me, like, thirty minutes. Just let me find my cat, and I'll meet you down at the barn."

Maverick stops. "Is someone under your bed?"

My eyes widen, and I freeze. "No. Why would you think that?"

I turn to see if he's spotted a boot or some dark hair, but I don't see any sign of Bennett. Then, I hear it. The slight creak of the bed at regular intervals . . . like when someone breathes.

"Well, that's probably Shorty. Mystery solved!" I push Maverick toward the door. "I'll be down to the barn soon. Thanks for your help."

He braces himself in the doorway, and I'm nowhere near strong enough to push him through. As he spins and rushes past me, I nearly fall into the hallway. I can only stand and watch as he rounds the side of the bed and stops, his eyes wide, but when he reaches down, I'm forced to act.

"Don't hurt him!" I shout as I rush toward the bed.

But as he stands upright again, he isn't gripping Bennett's shirt collar in his hand. He's holding the lamp cord and shaking his head.

"You have to be more careful. This could have started a fire." He holds up the cord. Copper wire peeks through the places where Shorty has chewed.

I smile and bite my bottom lip to hold back the scream. "Well, now that you've saved us from a fiery death, I'll see you down at the barn."

As he goes to turn, I spot Bennett's boot peeking from under the bed. Maverick will trip on it as soon as he turns around, so I halt his progress.

"On second thought, have you seen how comfy my bed is?" I yank him forward, and he falls onto the mattress. "Really soft, huh?"

He tries to stand, but I pull him down again.

"No, you really have to lie on it to get the full effect. Come on." I coax him onto the bed, and he reluctantly agrees. "Man, they really spent a lot on these luxury mattresses, didn't they?"

He lies back and folds his hands over his chest, like he's

in a coffin. Meanwhile, I wish for death more with each passing second.

"Yeah . . . the bed is great." He sits up. "Who were you worried about me hurting?"

"Huh?"

"When I went to the side of the bed, you said, 'Don't hurt him.' Who were you worried I would hurt?"

"Oh, the . . . the cat. I was worried you'd want to hurt him once you noticed that cord."

"Do I strike you as the kind of guy who would hurt a defenseless animal?"

I shake my head. "Nope."

He holds out his hands, silently asking the question.

Then why?

I don't have a convincing answer.

"Cat, everyone's really worried about you. Could you just tell me what's going on? Maybe if we understood, we could help you."

"Why is everyone worried? I'm fine."

"For starters, you've spent most of your time here holed up in your room. We understand why, since Bennett is always sniffing around, but we're trying to keep him away."

"Is that what tonight was about?" I ask, realizing how deep this conspiracy goes. "Are you trying to cheer me up by taking me on a pity date?"

Maverick drops back and sighs. "Don't be pissed. Rosie and I thought it was a bad idea. And for once, Bennett was looking out for you, too."

"Bennett knew about it?"

He nods his head and covers his face. "It was so stupid. I never should have gone along with it."

Part of me is angry about this betrayal, but the other part of me is still worried about Maverick discovering

Bennett under my bed. That side wins out. I can forget about the turmoil surrounding this pity date if he'll just leave my room.

"You shouldn't have gone along with it, you're right about that," I say, "but the reasoning behind it was sweet. If it helps you out, just tell Kindra that I said you and I make better friends than lovers."

"I didn't want to hurt you, Cat."

I laugh because this is too funny. I *should* be hurt right now. Tears should be streaming from my eyes, and I should be embarrassed that I chased this man who didn't want to be caught. Now I've caught a man who didn't want to be chased.

"I'll be okay with time," I tell Maverick through the most somber face I can muster. "Just go to your room and think about what you've done."

He eyes me, and I don't blame him. My blasé reaction isn't quite right. "Are you sure you're okay? I can still take you bow hunting, and I want to stay friends."

Before I can answer, a horrible smell drifts toward us. The fetid stench of ass singes my nose hairs, and I'll have to thank Bennett later for this perfectly timed fart.

"Look, the real reason I don't want to go is because my stomach is . . . Well, you smell it." I offer a sheepish smile and run my hand through the fart cloud that refuses to dissipate. If anything, the smell is stronger.

Maverick's nose wrinkles, and I'm pretty sure I see him battle a gag. "That's you? Are you sure we don't need to call a doctor? Cat . . . it smells like you're dying inside."

"Yeah, I should probably use the bathroom."

"Smells like you might have already done that," he says as he goes to get off the bed on Bennett's side.

"No!" I shout. "Come this way."

I slide off the bed and hold my hand toward him as an audible fart rumbles the floorboards.

"Is your asshole into ventriloquism, because that sounded like it came from . . ." He gets off the bed, bends over, and peers underneath.

And just like that, my tryst with Bennett is no longer a secret.

Chapter Thirty-One

Bennett

The extra bacon at breakfast was a mistake. I can admit that now. The stress of hiding under the bed while my obsession's obsession pulls her heartstrings didn't exactly help matters.

"Bennett?" Maverick says, his eyes wide enough to give him the peripheral vision of Sid the Sloth. "Why the fuck are you under her bed? And why . . . ? Fuck, did you shit yourself?"

"No, asshole. That's how men fart. I'm sorry it doesn't smell like daisies and goddamn sunshine. Now pull me out from under here. My leg's asleep."

He turns to look at Cat, like he needs her permission to offer me any assistance. When she nods, he turns back to me with a puzzled look and reaches for my outstretched hand. Thank god the queen was feeling magnanimous today.

Once I'm out from beneath the bed, I flop back into my

spot on top of it. Because it *is* my spot, and I'll be damned if the pretty boy sits there ever again.

He looks between me and Cat, then licks his lips. "Would either of you like to explain what is happening right now? I mean"—he turns to Cat—"shouldn't you be clawing his eyes out for sneaking into your room?"

"I didn't sneak in. She left the door unlocked."

"Bennett!" Cat squeals. "What the fuck?"

I shrug. "The cat's out of the bag, sweetheart. Or should I say . . . *kitten?*"

Maverick wobbles on his feet. "I feel like I'm in an alternate dimension."

Cat grips his hand and leads him to the bed to sit, and I want to beat Maverick's face in for allowing her skin to touch his. I rein in my anger, though, and remind myself that I'm about to solidify her as mine.

"We're fucking," I say.

With a groan, Cat covers her reddening face.

Maverick blinks, then chokes on his spit. "Come again?"

"I mean, if you insist." I reach for my fly.

Before I can reveal myself, Cat rushes over in a flurry of waving hands. She smacks my fingers away from my zipper and glares down at me. "Can you fucking grow up for five seconds? Please? This is serious!"

"Everything okay in there?" a female voice calls from outside the door.

I open my mouth to say we're fine, but Cat slams her palm over my lips.

"Yep, everything is great!" she shouts.

The carpet outside the door rustles as the woman shifts her weight. "Are you sure? I heard a male voice. That asshole isn't in there bothering you, is he?"

"Oh! It's just Maverick!" Cat shouts, her hand still

clamped over my mouth. "He was just . . . coming to pick me up to take me bow hunting, but now I can't go because my cat's missing."

"Could I come in?" the woman asks. Kindra wouldn't ask to come in, and Rosie can't. The few other females aren't this familiar with Cat, so it has to be Eve.

"Um, just a minute!" Cat rips her hand from my mouth and looks around the room. "Bennett, you have to hide again," she whispers.

Rolling my eyes, I get off the bed and head into the bathroom.

"What if she has to pee?" Maverick whispers.

I keep walking. Not my fucking problem. If it were up to me, we'd just tell everyone and be done with it.

The door clicks shut behind me, followed by the sound of Cat opening the door to her room to let Eve inside. I hate that I can't see what's going on out there. Specifically, what Maverick's hands are doing. If he touches her, he'll have a few less fingers come tomorrow.

Cat goes into her spiel about how she can't practice with Maverick because her cat is missing, and Maverick backs her up, which surprises me. I never pegged him as the type to go along with shenanigans. Well, not right off the bat, anyway. With enough coercion, I suppose anyone could be convinced to do anything.

"Your cat is missing?" Eve asks. After a pause, she continues. "Did anyone else bring a cat? Because I swore I heard some yowling coming from the room next to yours."

"You don't say . . ." Cat says, and I don't need to see her face to know she's pissed. I'll have to make this up to her. "Well, with the mystery of the missing cat solved, I guess I can go after all, Maverick. Why don't you go down and get the sleigh set up for us?"

"Oh, uh . . . I already pulled out the snowmobile," Maverick says.

Cat sighs. "But don't you think the sleigh would be a touch more romantic?"

I grip my jeans in tightening fists to stop myself from flinging the door open. *She's pissed about the cat*, I tell myself. *She's just doing this to tick me off.*

"Romantic, huh?" Eve says. "I take it you two have found your spark?"

"Something like that," Maverick says.

"Well, I won't keep you guys from your *date*. I just wanted to lay eyes on my girl and make sure she's safe. As long as you're around, I don't think we have to worry about Benson."

"Bennett," Maverick and Cat say in unison.

"Right. What's that guy's deal, anyway?" Eve says with a laugh. "I get that hot guys are notorious for being complete shitbags, but he takes the cake. At least you picked a winner with Maverick."

"Oh, well, we're just friends, so—"

"Honey, don't give me that," Eve says. "The man already knows you have hearts in your eyes, so there's no need to play coy."

If I squeeze my fists any tighter, I'll break my fucking fingers.

"Well, I'll get going," Eve finally says. "Remember to use protection."

Oh, they're gonna need protection, all right. Protection from my fucking rage if they think they're actually going through with this "date."

The door to Cat's room opens and closes.

"Coast is clear," Maverick calls from the bedroom.

I open the bathroom door. "There is no way in hell you're taking her out," I say as I step into Maverick.

"I don't have a fucking choice now," he says as he takes a step back. "Don't get pissed at me. None of this was my idea, remember?"

"Then make it a fucking choice. Either she goes bow hunting with me, or she doesn't go at all."

Cat clears her throat and steps between us. "Excuse the fiddling *fuck* out of me, but I'm capable of making my own decisions, or have you both forgotten?"

We turn to look at her, both our mouths opening with a rebuttal, but she holds up a hand.

"Shut up. Just shut the fuck up, both of you." She pins me in place with a glare. "Where is my fucking cat?"

"He's in my room." I look down at the carpet. I've only felt this sort of shame once before, and it was when my mom caught me beating off to the Food Network.

Look, in my defense, food porn is a thing.

"It's common knowledge that I had a crush on you," Cat says to Maverick. "I want to apologize if I made you uncomfortable. But if you ever offer yourself to a woman as a pity date again, I will cut off the entirety of your manhood and let Chef Maurice do something incredible with it."

Maverick swallows hard, and his throat clicks. "Uh, got it."

"Now, I'm going to get my poor cat from Bennett's room, and then I'm going to go bow hunting with Bennett. Are we all clear?"

Feeling triumphant, I smile, but Maverick quickly wipes the grin off my face.

"There's just one problem with that plan," he says. He mentions the cameras down at the shooting range and explains that someone is always monitoring them.

And Kindra is currently holed up in the surveillance room with popcorn and wine.

"She really wanted this for you," Maverick adds.

Cat sighs and sits on the edge of the bed. "Why does this have to be so complicated?"

Maverick goes to sit beside her, but then he notices my clenching fists and opts to stand in front of her. "It doesn't have to be. Why don't you just tell everyone? Yeah, they'll be shocked at first, but—"

"Shocked? You think they'll be shocked? I wish that's all I could expect."

"She's scared everyone will give us hell," I say. "I thought she was being ridiculous at first, but you've seen the way everyone tries to keep us apart."

Maverick runs his hand through his hair. "Yeah, but you're a dick, dude. We all care about Cat, and we just don't want her to get hurt."

"Wait!" Cat shouts, and we turn to look at her. "I have an idea."

Chapter Thirty-Two

Cat

I grip the sleeve of Maverick's coat as I snuggle up in the back of the sleigh. It's late afternoon, not yet dinnertime, but it might as well be night. I sigh and drop my head against a strong shoulder.

The horses' hooves thud against hard-packed snow. Gnarled branches creak in the light breeze, and the tack jangles like tiny bells. Cold cuts through my face mask, so I raise my hand to ward off the icy wall. Despite the slight discomfort, this is the definition of romantic.

"Are you too cold?" Bennett asks, and I lift my gloved finger to my mouth to remind him to be quiet. He grunts and wraps his arm around me.

Well, he tries to wrap his arm around me. Maverick is a smidge taller and leaner, so Bennett had one hell of a time squeezing into his clothes. I didn't complain as I watched him stuff his rippling muscles into the jacket and pants, though.

What with all the cameras, I figured this was the best

plan. While Bennett pretends to be Maverick, the real Maverick is in my room with Shorty. Now Kindra can eat her heart out and believe her little plan worked while I get to spend more time with Bennett. Maybe I can even get some clarity.

The sleigh pulls up beside the shooting range, and I hand the coachman a walkie-talkie as Bennett gathers our supplies—and Cattle—from the rear.

"We'll call when we're almost done," I say to the coachman, a squat little man with a scar running over the bridge of his nose. "That should give you enough time to hook up the horses."

The man nods down at me, then jingle-jangles his way back through the forest as I stand and watch him disappear.

A few grunts come from behind me, and I turn to see Bennett struggling with one of the Cattle we brought. The man in the red jumpsuit thrashes against Bennett, throwing his weight to try to knock him off balance, but Bennett is too powerful for him. He sets the red jumpsuit on his feet and glares at him.

"Couldn't we have practiced with normal targets like normal people?" I ask.

Bennett swings on the bound man and catches him in the jaw with a solid right hook. The man drops into the snow with a muted thud. After shaking out his gloved hand, Bennett turns to face me.

"If you aren't ready for the big leagues, we don't have to swing for the fences, but it's better to be prepared than to be caught lacking." He kicks the man in the gut. "This one is yours. If you don't want to kill him, don't kill him."

With a grunt, he bends at the waist and hoists the man over his shoulder. The action proves too much for the strained snow gear covering his muscled frame, however, and some inner seam rips with audible power.

"I'll buy a new jacket for Maverick," Bennett says. He carries the man toward the hay-bale targets at the end of the range, then drops him in front of the last one. Another rip breaks the forest's silence.

"And some pants," I mutter, though he's too far away to hear me.

He repeats the process with the second target we brought along, carrying the man down to the end of the lane, then plopping him in front of a hay bale. He doesn't have to knock that one out. His Cattle just whimpers and shivers. He has no fight left.

Bennett returns to my side, and I hold out my hand for the crossbow in his grip. He looks down at me, a smug smile in his eyes, which is all I can see. I made him promise to wear a mask the entire time so that the cameras—and any prying eyes—can't see his face.

"Not so fast, kitten. Before you can use a weapon, you must first learn the proper—"

I snatch the crossbow from his hand, aim it down range, flick off the safety, and fire a bolt into a distant hay bale. It doesn't strike center, but it's close enough.

"I grew up on a farm, city boy. I know how to use a crossbow." I lower the weapon and slide my hands back into my gloves. "Fuck, why is it so cold?"

Bennett just stands there and blinks.

"Load another one," I say. "I'm too cold to do it."

Regaining his composure, he begins loading another bolt. "You grew up on a farm, huh?"

"Yeah. Chickens and horses. A few goats when I was younger. Daddy had dreams of being a rancher, but he never made it big."

"Did you guys ever eat the chickens you raised?"

"All the time," I say. "I had a really fun Carrie situation at school because of it, too. My mother never told me that raising our food would be seen as taboo by some people, so I didn't keep it a secret. Girls who I thought were my friends dumped a bottle of red finger paint over my head when we were dressing out for gym class. They called me a murderer."

He hands the loaded crossbow to me and steps behind me. "Kids are fucking cruel."

"Yeah, they are." I raise the bow and fire. The bolt flies wide this time, and I miss the hay bale completely.

Bennett takes the bow and loads it again. He steps behind me, wrapping his arms around my body and helping me hold the weapon steady.

"What are you thinking about when you shoot?" he asks. "You're shaking."

"I'm cold."

"You're angry."

I laugh and turn in his hold. "No I'm not. I'm pretty sure I'd know what my own emotions are."

But he doesn't laugh with me. There's no glint of humor in his blue eyes, and thanks to the stadium lighting surrounding the shooting lanes, I can see them quite clearly. Feeling mildly uncomfy, I struggle in his hold, but he doesn't release me. Instead, he spins me around and raises the bow in my hands.

Warm breath filters through my hood as he says, "Remember how you felt when those kids dumped that paint on your head? I want you to feel that right now. Then I want you to push all of that pain into the bolt and send it."

I roll my eyes. This is a stupid fucking exercise.

I pull back on the trigger, and the bolt shoots forward. Right into a distant tree.

Bennett takes the crossbow, loads it again, and shoves it back into my hands. "Feel it, don't fight it. When you were confident, you shot straight. Now you're shaken. You're trying to stuff down what you're feeling. Just let it happen."

With a sigh, I grit my teeth and raise the weapon again. But I can't do it. I don't want to go back to twelve-year-old me. I don't want to remember what it felt like to be laughed at and mocked.

I lower the crossbow. "Bennett, I—"

"If that doesn't work, channel something else. Channel some rage. I know it's in there."

"Maybe toward you," I grumble.

"Five women."

"What?"

"The guy I picked for you. He raped five women."

Taking a deep breath, I look down the lanes and find the crumpled figure wearing a red jumpsuit.

"He has a type, too," Bennett continues. "He likes them weak and old. He doesn't even kill them when he's done. After breaking their bones and—"

"I don't want to know."

"You need to hear it. Aim the bow at a target."

A tear slips past my eyelids as I raise the bow and take aim at a hay bale.

"His first victim was eighty years old at the time of the assault. Her name is Rhonda, and she'll never walk again."

I fire the bolt, and it strikes the bale this time.

Bennett grabs the crossbow, loads it again, then moves us to the next hay bale in line. "Your next shot is for Greta. A breast cancer survivor. After enduring so much, he put her through a hell no woman deserves."

The bolt flies, and this time, it's a perfect shot. Dead center.

As he loads another bolt and takes us one step closer to the lane with the Cattle, I realize what he's doing. He's leading me down the line, hoping I'll take the shot when we reach the end.

"I can't do this."

"Yes you can." He shoves the crossbow into my hands and leaves no room for argument. "Stop thinking in terms of can and can't and start thinking like us."

"Maybe that's the problem," I say. "I'm fascinated by what you do, but I'm an outsider looking in. I'm not truly one of you, and I think it's time I accept I never will be."

"Bullshit. You're just afraid of your potential."

"What potential? My potential to fail? Because that seems to be all I can manage lately."

"Because you haven't tried yet."

I push the bow back into his hands. "Because this isn't something I can't take back. It's a life, Bennett."

He pushes the bow into me. "Do you think he cared? Did he care about lives? Now do it. Shoot him."

"No."

"Shoot him, Cat."

"No!"

Without thinking, I turn and fire the weapon. The bolt finds a home in the Cattle's shoulder, but it's the wrong one. I shot the guy in the pink jumpsuit.

"Oh, shit," I say as the man lets a scream squeal through his nose. "Sorry!"

I rush forward and drop to my knees in front of the man. Pulling his shoulders forward, I reveal the target just behind him.

Bennett whistles. "Bullseye."

"This isn't a joke!" I say. "Help him! He's bleeding!"

A red puddle gathers beneath the man at an alarming rate . . . and it's my fault.

Bennett pulls a knife from his pocket and uses it to slash through the superglue holding the man's lips shut. Unfortunately, he snags the man's lower lip in the process. The yellowed strip of flesh wobbles and pours blood with each scream he releases.

"Jesus, you're making it worse!" I shout.

"Tell her what you did," Bennett says over the man's screams. "Tell her the truth, and I'll let you live."

The man's red-rimmed gaze shuffles between us before finally landing on me. "My niece," he blubbers. "I made her—"

"I don't want to know!" I push the crossbow bolt deeper, and he finishes his sentence with a scream.

Bennett presses the knife to the man's throat. "I said, *tell her.*"

The man screams, then focuses on me. "I forced my six-year-old niece to—"

I wrench the knife from Bennett's hand and drive it into the man's throat.

Chapter Thirty-Three

Bennett

A red fountain jets from the wound as Cat yanks the blade backward again, and a bewildered look flashes in her blue eyes. Shock is setting in because she finally did it. She's taken her first kill.

"Don't stop now," I whisper. "Ride it, kitten. Ride the wave and keep going. Feed your rage."

Her breath comes in quick, short bursts, but instead of rushing headlong into a frenzy, she drops the knife and faces me. "Holy shit," she says on an out breath. "Holy shit, holy shit, holy—"

I lower my mask, then her face covering, and press my lips to hers. Fuck the cameras. She's two seconds away from losing it, and I need to ground her again.

"Hey, look at me," I whisper as I pull away. "You were amazing. Perfect. He's gone, kitten, and *you* did it. You rid the world of a dark spot, but we aren't done yet."

With wide eyes and a gaping mouth, she turns her head and looks at her handiwork. She breathes a little faster.

Gripping her chin, I turn her head so that she faces me. "Slow down or you'll hyperventilate. Breathe with me." I place her hand on my chest, then take a deep breath in and a slow breath out, and she follows my lead. "He didn't suffer. You slashed with such precision that he bled out in less than a minute."

Cat turns her head the other way and vomits in the snow.

Guilt creeps up my spine as she shivers against me. I'm fairly certain she's crying, and it's my fault. I shouldn't have pushed her so hard, but I'm just so fucking sick of seeing her inability to realize her strengths. Maybe she's done enough for one day. Maybe she's done too much.

"Do you want me to call the sleigh?" I ask.

She shakes her head, steps away from me, and swipes her cheeks with her gloved fingers before raising her face covering again. "No, we aren't finished, remember?" Still crying, she bends and picks up the crossbow. "It gets easier the more I do it, right?"

I nod at her.

"Get behind me," she says. "I'm still not ready to do this on my own."

She stands at the head of the last lane. As I step behind her, the Cattle at the end begins to stir. His legs shuffle back and forth, and he blinks to clear the fog my fist cast over his brain. He hasn't noticed the Angel of Death with a crossbow aimed at his skull.

God, I am so fucking hard right now.

"You said five women, right?" she asks.

I place a kiss on top of her head. "That's right, kitten. Five women."

"Tell me their names."

I say each woman's name. Rhonda. Greta. Elizabeth.

Jane. Marianne. They matter. The piece of shit with a crossbow aimed at his brain doesn't.

Cat raises her chin and the crossbow in unison. Bracing her arm, she prepares to fire.

"This is for them," I say. "This is for all of them, plus the women he would have continued to hurt had he not been caught. You aren't killing a person. You're destroying a monster."

Cat adjusts her grip.

"You can do it. Just pull the trigger and end him." I firm my hold on her shoulders and will my strength into her.

She takes a deep breath, adjusts her stance, cocks her head to the side, and fires.

The man's head whips to the side, and a spray of vermillion streaks the hay bale behind him. His legs straighten and dance a jig in front of him, and he falls onto his side, where he squirms in the snow and paints it red.

Cat doesn't celebrate. She doesn't jump up and down and squeal or any of those things she normally does when she's accomplished something big. The gravity of what she's done and what she still has to do is enough to keep her grounded. With the air of a predator, she kneels in the snow, then loads another bolt into the crossbow.

"It wasn't a good shot," she says. "He's suffering."

"Then finish it, kitten. End his reign of terror by beginning yours."

With the weapon in hand, she stands and takes aim. I don't stand behind her this time. Like a proud teacher, I watch my pupil apply her lesson all on her own. I watch as calm settles over her face and the bloodlust overtakes her.

I watch as she pulls the trigger.

The bolt whizzes down the lane and lodges in his chest. The man gasps and thrashes his legs as Cat loads another death missile into her war machine. She's no longer shaking, and though she remains silent, I doubt her voice would tremble if she chose to speak.

"Whoops, I went a little wide on that one," she says as she stands.

Once more, she aims, takes a deep breath, and fires. This time, the bolt lands right between his legs and disappears. The glue rips as the man's lips tear apart, and he screams.

"Naughty, naughty kitten," I say. "You shouldn't play with your prey."

"Prop him up. Point his ass toward me."

She doesn't have to tell me twice. I rush to the end of the lane.

The man is in pretty bad shape, and I'm fairly certain he's already dead by the time I pile enough snow beneath his burgeoning gut to angle his ass toward her. That chest shot flooded his abdomen with blood, and he's a bit unwieldy.

Like a good girl, she waits until I'm back behind her before she raises the weapon and shoots again, sending the ammo right into his ass. He doesn't even flinch, unfortunately, which further solidifies my belief that we've sent him straight to hell.

Realizing her work is done, Cat flops down on her ass and flings the crossbow away from her. The adrenaline must be wearing off.

"I did it," she says. "I actually did it. I . . . I killed him."

I sit next to her and pull her into me. "Damn right you did. You killed the other guy too, don't forget."

"Oh shit, I did, didn't I?" Cat lowers her mask, licks her lips, and looks around. A slight giggle slips out of her, and she covers her mouth. "When he said his niece, I just snapped. And then thinking about those elderly women . . . It was too much. I just . . . acted."

"You were a little blue-eyed demon, that's what you were. How did the knife feel? Or did you prefer the crossbow?" I swipe the hair away from her face. I don't want to miss a moment of the way she looks right now. I'm hungry for each response. The need to know how it feels for her drives me wild.

She glances at the two victims—*her* victims. "The crossbow was better for me. I'll be honest and admit that I didn't miss any of the shots I took. I wanted him to hurt."

"I know." I place a kiss on her nose, the tip of which has turned too pink, then raise her mask again. "Are you ready for me to call the sleigh?"

"Yeah, go ahead and call, but let me see that knife."

"It's over by the first guy." I point toward his body with one hand and pull the walkie from my pocket with the other. "Actually, you better call the sleigh. Someone might recognize my voice."

"Oh, right."

She depresses the button on the side and lets the coachman know we're ready to leave. He must be incredibly annoyed, as we've been out here for less than a half hour and already want to head back. There's no point in hanging around, though. I've accomplished my mission, and now I want to get her back to the bedroom and warm her up.

Watching Cat morph into a murderer has done something inside me. I see her in a different light now. She isn't some meek little thing that needs protecting. She's come into her own, and now people will need to be protected from *her*.

Part of me hopes that Kindra watched all of this. If she realizes just how strong her friend truly is, maybe she'll back off when we finally tell her we're fucking. I don't plan to stop anytime soon, and Cat will be forced to come clean at some point. This might just supply the backbone she's needed.

Cat returns with the knife and squats in front of me. After passing the walkie-talkie back to me, she lowers the knife toward her crotch.

"Whoa!" I shout as I snatch the blade away from the best pussy I've ever had. "What the fuck are you doing?"

"I can't exactly strip down out here. I'll freeze to death."

"Strip down? Why would you . . . oh."

As she looks up at me with a familiar hunger in her eyes, my brain finally registers what's happening. Like many of us, this girl isn't wired quite right, and now she's turned on by justifiable homicide. It's a common side effect.

"Say less." I toss the knife at her feet, then unbutton and unzip and move things around until my cock is free, though still hidden from the cameras. I'm careful to keep my ass hidden beneath my pants as well, as I have a very distinctive pineapple tattoo on my left ass cheek.

I had to commemorate the Sinners Retreat somehow.

Cat manages to slice through her snow pants, but she struggles when she reaches her sweatpants, probably because she's afraid to cut a second slit between her legs. Revolted by the possibility of that outcome, I take the blade from her and hold her pants away from her skin before cutting an opening.

"Fuck, it feels like Jack Frost is licking my pussy lips," she says. "Warm me up!"

There's no time for foreplay. Even if there is, I'm too hungry for her. I toss the knife away from us and lay her on her back. Like a beast in rut, I pin her to the ground and enter her. Heat coils around my cock, and a whimper rips from her chest.

"Fuck, I forgot about the piercing," she says. "And the size."

"Then I guess it's a good thing you're so fucking wet."

With a groan, I grab her wrists and pin them above her head. The layers of fabric between us make things difficult, but I keep her in place as I drive deeper inside her.

Her walls clench around me, gripping and pulling, and a bolt of pleasure shoots up my spine. She rocks her hips and takes every inch with a moan that lights my scalp on fire.

I fuck her harder, until her eyes roll back and her soul nearly leaves her body. Her breath matches mine, and we create a light fog as we grind against each other, each of us racing to finish before the carriage arrives.

And that's the game, isn't it? That's why she wanted to call them. That's why she didn't want to fuck until they were on the way. Subconsciously, I think my little kitten wants to get caught.

"I'm so close, Bennett," she says on a breathy moan that causes my balls to tighten. "Make me come. Please."

In the distance, hoofbeats thump to the tempo of my thrusts. She hasn't heard them yet, but when she does, she may come to her senses and put an end to everything. I release her wrists and put my hands on either side of her head, like earmuffs. I play it off as if I needed more leverage, but I'm only trying to buy myself a few more minutes. She's close. A few minutes is all I need.

The angle helps, and I fuck her a bit harder, scooping my hips every few thrusts and teasing her clit with friction as I lean forward. Looking into my eyes, she rips off her glove and drives her hand into her pants. It's not enough for me, though. I want to see her face when she comes. I want to hear every sweet sound, not have it muffled by a face mask.

I reach up and rip down her mask. My momentary lapse allows her to hear the jangle of tack growing closer and closer.

"Bennett, we have to stop," she whispers, though her hips keep right on rocking against me. "They're almost here."

I lean down and nuzzle her cheek. "Then you'd better hurry up. I won't stop until you come on my cock."

"I-I can't!" she says.

Oh, I think she can.

I move my hands to her shoulders and grind against her at a steady rhythm. She pushes my chest with one hand, silently begging me to save her, but I won't. Not this time. This time, I'll ruin her.

"Who's going to come first?" I say. "The kitten or the sleigh?"

As one hand works her clit, her other grips my coat. But she isn't pushing me away now. She's pulling me closer.

"Fuck, I'm coming," she whispers. "Cover my mouth, cover my—"

I slam my palm over her parted lips, right as she lets out a scream. Her eyes widen and roll, and she sucks air through her nose as she releases cries of pleasure against my hand.

Meanwhile, I'm fighting a battle of my own. And I'm losing. Hearing, seeing, and feeling her come is too much, and I fill her. Even as the horses draw close enough that I can smell them, I push deep inside her and empty myself.

"You are so incredible, Cat. Pineapples don't have shit on you." I roll off of her and tuck myself away.

"Glad to know I have the fruit market cornered," she says. "Now help me look presentable before the sleigh gets here."

I sit up with a shit-eating grin and help her fix her hair. The sleigh pulls to a stop as we get to our feet.

"I take it you two had a nice evening?" the coachman says as I help Cat into the sleigh.

She gives me a sideways glance, then smirks. "You could say that."

The coachman whistles when he spots the two bodies. "I guess those two didn't."

Cat looks out at the carnage. "No, they did not." She looks at me and smiles. "But they had the evening they deserved."

I take my seat beside Cat, and the driver urges the horses forward. Now if we can just get back into the mansion without any interference, this will be a perfect evening.

Chapter Thirty-Four

Cat

As the sleigh bumps over the ground, I glance at Bennett. Over the past few days, I've seen a side of him that he hides from most everyone. He's been vulnerable. Kind. He's taken care of me, and he went above and beyond to help me overcome hurdles and make my first kill. Hell, he's asked if I'm warm enough three times since leaving the shooting range, and he even offered his coat. I had to remind him that the coat is his disguise.

That's when the hurt flashed in his eyes.

"Maybe I'd better get out when we reach the barn," he whispers in my ear. "If Kindra was watching the camera feeds, she's probably waiting at the mansion's front door."

I want to tell him no, that we've hidden this long enough and I'm ready to come clean. But I can't. The words stick in my chest, sawing and tearing through me as the dark horses break through the trees and the barn comes into view.

Bennett waits to see if I'll argue and tell him no, come to the mansion. When I don't, the hurt returns to his eyes. He leans forward. "Stop the sleigh here," he says. "I'll walk the rest of the way."

The coachman nods and brings the horses to a stop just outside the barn. Bennett checks his pockets to ensure he remembered his knife—we left everything else back at the shooting range—then slides past me to exit the sleigh.

I reach up and grip his hand as he passes. "Thank you for everything. Seriously, B-Maverick."

He winces, then hops down.

Why do I have to make everything worse?

As I settle back again, the coachman clucks at the horses, and the sleigh jerks forward. I glance behind me, expecting some wistfully romantic moment where Bennett is just standing there, watching as I ride away. Instead, what I see is just depressing as fuck. Trudging through the sleigh's deep tracks, he looks so alone.

"Stop the sleigh!" I shout, and the coachman slows the horses.

"Everything okay?" he asks.

I set my resolve and stand. "No, but it will be."

With the grace of a drunk man on ice skates, I tumble out of the sleigh and pull myself to my feet. Bennett stops a few yards away, studying me as I dust snow from my ensemble, which doesn't even match, since I'm wearing my decimated pink pants and Bennett's tan coat.

"What are you doing?" he asks. "We can't ride back together. That's a suicide mission."

"I know." I turn to the driver. "Take the horses back to the barn. It's cold, and they've done enough for today. We'll walk back."

A true coachman would have stood on ceremony and asked if I was sure, but this guy is a former criminal, and he's more than happy to get back where it's warm. Needing no further encouragement, he's started the horses moving again before I've even finished my directive.

Bennett steps toward me, and I wait. I wanted to see something, and I definitely see it now. His posture is completely different. When the sleigh pulled away with me inside, he looked so defeated, with his shoulders down and his eyes on the ground. Now, as he's walking toward me, his shoulders are braced back, and his eyes are up. On me.

I have affected him, just as he's affected me. The shift is undeniable, and I feel it within myself. We may be a flame and a powder keg, but these things aren't only bound for a path of destruction. If combined just right, we could be fireworks.

When he reaches me, he takes me into his arms and leans down. "You'll be cold, kitten. Why didn't you take the sleigh?"

"Maybe I wanted a few more minutes alone with you . . ." I stand on my tiptoes and lower his facemask so that I can kiss him. But a small peck isn't enough for Bennett. He pulls me closer and kisses me fully, sending sparks of pleasure between my legs.

Or maybe that's the draft, since I slashed my fucking snow pants to hell and back.

"A few minutes won't be enough," he says against my mouth. "I want to stay the night with you."

My heart hammers through all fifty layers of clothing, and I'm sure he feels each terrified thump. "The night? Like, the whole thing?"

He rolls his eyes. "No, just the dark part."

"It's always dark."

"Then I guess I'll just have to stay there forever."

I smack his chest and giggle as he smirks against my jaw

and peppers my neck with kisses, the fear of what he's asked forgotten. Surely he isn't serious. It's so risky.

Hand in hand, we start for the log mansion like two lovesick teens sneaking back from a midnight make-out session. My palms begin to sweat as porch lights come into view, and I'm thankful Bennett can't feel my fear through the gloves. We'll have to part ways, and he'll need to sneak inside before anyone gets too close. On a shitty CCTV monitor, he can pass as Maverick, but if anyone gets within ten feet of us, the differences are obvious.

A large light at the front of the mansion casts a circle of discovery, which we're careful to avoid. We stand just outside it, holding each other as snow begins to drift from the sky.

"I'm proud of you," he says after a stretch of silence. "You no longer have to feel like an outsider. You're one of us now, all the way."

I smile against his—technically *Maverick's*—coat. Maybe that's where this sudden feeling of peace has come from. Though that orgasm certainly helped.

But then, as is often the case for me, the peace doesn't last.

"You two lovebirds still at it?" Eve calls from the porch. "Come inside where it's warm!"

"Shit," I say under my breath. I look at Bennett. "You have to—"

"I know, kitten. I know." He sighs, shakes his head, places a kiss on my forehead, and retreats further into the shadows.

A pit forms in my stomach as I round the corner and step fully into the light. Not even Eve's beaming smile and waggling fingers can ease the hurt I felt when I saw his face.

Because of me. *I'm* hurting him.

All this time, everyone was afraid Bennett would break my heart, but I'm the true villain here.

Eve and Kindra surround me and lead me inside. They cloak me in rapid-fire questions and high praises until I'm suffocating. I don't even have a chance to respond to anything.

I hold up my hands as we enter the main hall. "Guys, I'm so grateful you're excited for me, but I'm kind of tired. Any chance we can gush about this tomorrow?"

Their lips snap shut, and a worried glance passes between them. Kindra lowers my face mask and presses the backs of her hands against my cheeks.

"You okay?" she asks. "I mean, you just knocked two major events off your bucket list, and you don't seem very excited about it."

A flash of yellow rushes past one of the windows by the door—Maverick's coat. Seconds later, Bennett's face pops up behind the glass. I backpedal, angling my body in a way that forces Eve and Kindra to give the front door their backs.

"Actually, I think I'm catching a second wind," I tell the girls. "Why don't we head to the kitchen and grab something to eat?"

"*Now?*" Kindra says. "After taking two kills and fucking your crush, you want to eat?"

"Damn, you're cold as fuck," Eve says with a hint of admiration in her voice. "I couldn't eat for a week after my first hit."

I force a smile because food is the last fucking thing on my mind. I just have to get them away from the front hall.

"Well, the world takes all kinds." I take a few steps backward. "You girls coming, or do I need to tell all the dirty details to a lump of mashed potatoes and a glass of something bubbly?"

"Bubbly? Shit, I'm in," Kindra says.

"Me too!" Eve takes my arm in hers, and we start toward the dining room.

I sneak one backward glance over my shoulder, but Bennett is no longer outside the window.

My mind is a blur as we shuffle down the hallway. My mouth runs on autopilot, offering appropriate responses at the right points in the conversation. Even as we accept a bowl of lukewarm soup from Chef Maurice and take a seat in the dining room, my brain and my mouth are operating separately from each other.

I can't stop worrying about Bennett and whether he made it back to his room without getting caught. But am I more worried for him or for myself?

This situation is turning me into someone I don't want to be, and I'm not talking about the fucking murders I committed. I've become selfish, only thinking about myself and my needs. Lies come easily for me now, even when talking to the people I trust. I don't recognize myself anymore.

"What was more exciting? The sex or the kill?" Eve asks as she enjoys a spoonful of soup. I think it's a minestrone, but I'm not entirely sure.

I sip some champagne and swirl my spoon through the bowl. "They were both exciting for different reasons, but sleeping with Bennett probably wins."

Spoons clatter, and Eve nearly knocks over her champagne flute. "Bennett?" the women say in unison.

"Maverick!" I mentally kick myself. "The sex with *Maverick* wins."

Eve raises her eyebrows and her glass. "I was about to say . . ."

"And I was about to run to the basement for a fucking straitjacket," Kindra says with a shake of her head. "The day you fuck Bennett is the day we are having you committed."

"Hear, hear. And I'll co-sign on that commitment." Eve sips her drink, then studies the soup again. "You said you outlawed human meat for this shindig, right?"

"Yeah," Kindra says. "Why?"

Eve tilts her spoon toward us, revealing the glint of a nose-ring stud.

"Oh, fucking sick," Kindra groans. "First Cat says she fucked Bennett, and now you're telling me that I've been tricked into cannibalism again. I'm not even trying to lose weight, but everyone is making it impossible to keep food down at this point."

The women push their soup bowls away and continue giggling, but I can't even bring myself to fake it. Because this is the moment I wanted to avoid. The ridicule. The little jokes that cut so much deeper than they realize.

Without a word, I push away from the table and rush out of the dining hall before they can see my tears.

Chapter Thirty-Five

Bennett

Getting back into my room and swapping places with Maverick was the easy part. Being unable to comfort Cat when I saw her race down the hall with tears in her eyes? That was one of the most difficult things I've ever experienced in my life.

But I kept my eyes on the carpet and continued walking. Kindra and Eve were hot on her heels, and they didn't miss the opportunity to shoot eyeball daggers at me. It seems I can't exist without offending them. They followed Cat into her room and closed the door behind them.

I'm too fucking nosy to let this go, even though my stomach is screaming for literally anything, so I ensure the coast is clear, then head back to my room. The bathroom has great acoustics, and chicks love to chat in the bathroom, so I head there first.

But I'm out of luck. No matter where I stand, no matter which surface I press my ear against, I can't hear them.

Like some gossip-driven demon, I fly around the room,

ramming my ear against every adjoining wall. The low hum of feminine voices penetrates the wood, but I can't make out a single word. In my desperation, I even try the old drinking-glass trick, but it only muffles their voices even more.

Just as I reach for the doorknob with the intent of lying on the floor outside her door and pressing my ear to the tiny crack beneath it, I realize the depths of my insanity. I have reached the bottom and grabbed a fucking shovel.

"Get a grip, man," I say as I shake my head and try to clear the fog Cat's cast over me.

I need a distraction.

Looking around the room, my gaze lands on the ceramic pineapple that slid under my dresser. Shorty must have swatted it around and knocked it to the center of the room. I pick it up and grin.

The kitchen is almost empty when I make my way downstairs. A lone worker stands over the sink, scrubbing a stack of bowls and champagne flutes in a sea of soapy water. On a long silver prep table, a row of metal pans holds the contents of tomorrow's meals. And maybe the day after, judging by the sheer amount of food.

"Are we planning to take in refugees or something?" I ask as I lift a lid and reveal an entire population of button quail. "Jesus, why not pick a bigger bird? I shit things larger than this."

"Americans don't understand portion sizes," Chef Maurice grumbles as he hurries into the room. He always looks like he's running late for something.

"What do you mean, *Americans*? Your real name is

Andrew, and you were born and raised in fucking Ohio," I say with a scoff. "These little baby birds won't fill anyone up."

Chef tosses a hand towel onto the counter, then turns to face me. "If it were up to me, we'd have finger sandwiches made with real fingers, roast kneecap soup, braised back-strap, and a sundae with skin-flake sprinkles, but our bene-factor has denied my use of human meat, so enjoy your game hens and shut the fuck up."

"Fair enough."

It wasn't Jim who abolished cannibalism at the winter retreat, though. That was all Kindra's doing, and frankly, I'm okay with it. Humans are too high in cholesterol.

Chef's lackey finishes up the dishes, then retreats into the back area that leads to the staff quarters. They don't have their own rooms—aside from Chef, of course—but none of them can really complain. Compared to some of the prisons they've come from, those packed bunks are luxury accommodations.

As Chef busies himself with one of the covered pans, I stroll around the kitchen and poke through the cabinets. I'll likely find what I want in the walk-in fridge, but I'd rather wait until Maurice finishes molesting the largest turkey I've ever seen.

"That's more like it," I say as he manipulates the massive bird.

Chef shakes a greasy finger at me. "No, she is not for tonight. Or tomorrow, for that matter. This is for the masquerade feast on the final night. I'm just injecting it with some flavor so that it can marinate."

His hands move over the carcass, massaging a blend of spices into the skin. Each time he applies pressure, a buttery mixture oozes from the meat.

Fuck, why am I getting hard?

Once he's certain he's massaged the bird for the correct amount of time, he pops the lid onto the pan and carries everything to the walk-in fridge. I've already exited the kitchen by the time he returns.

I can't exactly steal the turkey while he's in there, after all.

And I plan to steal that turkey.

All the shit that's been happening with Cat has distracted me from my real-world problems, but now I need a distraction from the distraction. I need something less complicated, and food is never complicated.

Back in the dining room, I tuck myself into a corner table and wait. When Chef leaves the kitchen, he won't see me unless he turns around, and I've known him long enough to be certain of his complete lack of situational awareness. He won't turn around.

Minutes later, as if I scripted the moment myself, Chef Maurice toddles out of the kitchen and makes his way through the dining room. My pulse picks up as he stops in the center of the room to dig in his ass crack, but then he sniffs his fingers and keeps moving. It's late enough in the evening that he won't come back down to the kitchen, not even if Jim demands it, so the coast is clear.

I rise from my seat and hurry back to the kitchen on silent feet. The prep table stands empty; the pans have been tucked away in a fridge or freezer. Most of the lights are off, and the only sounds are the occasional drip from the tap and the hum of the walk-ins.

It's so quiet in here that I worry the entire mansion will hear me when I open the massive metal door that leads into the fridge. But that's part of the fun. The fear of getting caught.

Well, except when your brother, his love interest, and your future love interest catch you fucking a pineapple and then they never let you live it down.

Gritting my teeth, I throw caution to the wind and wrench open the door. Icy air rushes toward me, but it's laughable. This fridge has nothing on Alaska.

The turkey sits on the back shelf. I know it's the turkey because a bit of the marinade sloshed over the side, and its scent calls to me like an alluring perfume. I step closer and pull the pan down from the shelf, then set it on the floor.

Removing the pan's lid is like removing a woman's undergarments. The moment that shield is torn away, I'm met with vulnerability. Soft, smooth . . . and cold vulnerability.

Cold.

It's odd that I've never really thought about the temperature before, but perhaps that plays a part in my fascination. Or maybe I'm only now realizing it and that's why it's turning me off.

"Fuck." I look down at the turkey and frown.

This is my *thing*! I love fucking food. Until I fucked Cat, I almost enjoyed fucking food more than fucking women.

Cat . . .

Is she the reason I'm struggling to rip this bird from the pan and spirit it away to my room for some lovemaking? Because I definitely want to. I just . . . It feels like cheating. It feels like fucking this turkey would betray whatever I have with Cat.

"It's a fucking turkey," I mutter. "Get a grip."

But goddamn it, I can't. No matter how badly I want to destroy this supple mound of bird flesh, something doesn't feel right about it. Never having been one to care if something felt wrong or right, I'm not sure what to do with this.

Something clangs in the kitchen, and I nearly jump out of my skin. I hurry to replace the top on the turkey before I'm discovered. I'll deal with my hesitation later.

As I step out of the walk-in, a smile springs onto my face when I spot the fluff of blonde hair wiggling just on the other side of the prep table. It's Cat, and she's digging around on the bottom shelf for something.

"Need any help?" I ask.

If I'd strapped a live wire to her asshole, I don't think she would have jumped higher. With a squeal, she plants her hand over her heart, then breathes a sigh of relief when she realizes it's me.

"Oh, thank God," she says, then dips down once more. "I was worried I'd have to keep playing make believe. Help me out, would you? I need a bowl."

I step over to the drying rack and pluck one from inside. "Like this?"

She looks over and nods, then rises to accept the bowl.

I hold it just out of reach, high above her head. "What do you need it for? Didn't you and the rest of the hens eat already?"

"I couldn't eat. They kept . . ." She drops down from her tiptoes and lowers her hand. "I just couldn't eat."

I slide the bowl into her fingers. It's only fun to tease her when she's annoyed, not when she's downtrodden. And something isn't quite right. Now that I'm closer, I can see the red, puffy skin around her eyes. She tried to cover it with makeup, but the color peeks through. The cloak of confidence she wraps so tightly around her shoulders has fallen a bit, too.

"Let's find something together," I say. "I haven't eaten

either. I had to fill Maverick in on everything that happened in case he's questioned, and then I figured it would be better to stay out of sight."

Wrapping my arm around her shoulder, I lead her to a massive fridge.

"That was smart," she says as she steps inside. "Now I just have to figure out how to break up with Maverick and end this charade."

"End it?"

"Yes, once and for all."

Panic blooms in my gut, and fear throws a right hook into my lower intestines. I grip the metal shelf and wait for the pain to pass. If she wants to end it, does she mean *every*thing, or just the Maverick portion? Does she just want to cool it for now . . . or forever?

Fuck, is this how women feel? All the questions and uncertainty . . . No wonder they seem so unhinged most of the time. Shit, I'd be unhinged too.

I'm coming unhinged as we speak.

"Not us, of course," she adds as she picks up a can of beans and spins it around to check the label.

"Oh?"

"Well, I mean, we'll have to stop while we're here if I plan to dump—"

"Then don't do it."

She looks at me and places the beans back on the shelf.

"Don't break up with him," I add. "Now that he's looped in, we could use this to our advantage."

"I don't follow."

I look around for a way to demonstrate my point—particularly, the point that will allow me to stay in her room tonight. I pluck a cantaloupe, an orange, and an apple from the shelves, then grab two empty pans.

"Are you going to fuck that and make me watch?" she asks. "Do you need me to provide accompaniment? I know a few sixties tunes."

"Ha. Ha."

I motion for her to turn around, and she rolls her eyes and obeys. I love her obedience, but it's the sass for me, honestly.

While her back is to me, I place the cantaloupe and apple in one pan, and the orange in another. After placing the lids on the pans, I tell her to face me once more. She does, and I shake the pans. The fruit rattles around inside.

"Now, tell me which pan has the orange in it," I say.

She points to the pan on the left, and I lift the lid to reveal . . . the orange. Fuck.

"Okay, that was a lucky guess, but you get my point." I replace the fruit and the pans. "If everyone thinks you're in your room banging Maverick, and if Maverick is in my room, how will they know?"

"I think I just demonstrated that."

"We'll be in a room, not a pan with a lid."

"And we'll be humans, not fruit." She shakes her head, refusing to look at me. "It won't work, Bennett."

"Can't you try?" I take her hand, and she finally meets my gaze. "Please?"

She's right on the verge of agreeing with me. She just needs a little push.

I lean down and place my lips on hers. So warm, so soft. Slipping my hand to the back of her neck, I deepen the kiss. Her muscles relax in my hold, and she sighs as our lips part.

"No, Bennett," she whispers with a smirk, and hey, at least she's smiling now. "Help me find something to eat. I'm genuinely hungry."

With a groan, I acquiesce and begin helping her pick

through the jars and packages until we land on something she's interested in: a bag of fucking grapes.

"Wait, why were you in here?" she asks as she pops a green grape into her mouth. She bites down, and her mouth purses. "Fuck, these are sour."

I glance at the pan holding the turkey I planned to have my way with. "Uh, same thing. I was . . . hungry."

"Let's make some sandwiches, then. We could both use some food, and at least we're safe in here." She grabs what we'll need from in here—mayo, mustard, cheese, ham, lettuce, and a tomato—and I follow her into the kitchen.

She tightens her ponytail and sets to work, slathering condiments and veggies on toasted slices of thick bread before layering ham and cheese on top. When she's finished, she puts the sandwiches on a plate and pushes one in front of me.

"Don't you want to sit at the table and eat?" I ask.

She lowers her sandwich. "I mean . . . what if—"

"Right."

I take a bite and chew, and while I'm grateful for the food, which is delicious, I'm also very uncomfortable. It's so quiet in here that I can hear my teeth shredding every particle of food. Breath saws in and out of me like a gale force wind. My stomach gurgles as it accepts its prize, and Cat lowers her sandwich with a giggle.

"Why are we making this weird?" she says.

"Because it is weird." I lean across the prep table and swipe a bit of mayo from her lip. "That's why people hate it so much. We're heralding the end times."

"What?"

"You know, in the Bible. It talks about the lion lying down with the lamb. That's us."

"Lying down with the lamb, jackass, not going to pound town on it."

I swallow and look around for a drink, but we didn't think that far ahead.

"Same difference," I say as I snag the champagne flutes. After a little more searching, I find a bottle of Jack in a cupboard and a couple of cans of warm Coke. I pour us each a glass. "My point is, you can't expect everyone to understand right away. It's going to take some time."

"I know, but it's time we don't have here. Can't you just let it go?"

Ouch.

I shrug. "Consider it dropped."

Maybe it's for the best.

Chapter Thirty-Six

Cat

What the fuck am I *doing?*

This is what my brain keeps screaming as I make my way up the stairs, because what I want to do and what I'm actually doing are two very different things. I want to be with Bennett. Instead, I'm heading to bed at nine p.m. like some pearl-clutching cat lady.

We mustn't fuck the hot guy downstairs. What will our friends think?

God, I hate myself right now.

Then I notice the glob of mustard on my white shirt, and the hatred only grows. What am I, five? Did I think my tits needed a little flavor? Not that anyone will be tasting them anytime soon.

With a groan, I turn around and head back down the stairs. I paid a lot for this fucking blouse, and I'm not about to let a yellow splotch ruin something that took nearly a quarter of my most recent paycheck. A little soda water from the bar in the dining room should set things right again.

Maybe Bennett won't be in there to tempt me. After we washed up the dishes we'd dirtied, he said he wanted to take a walk around the property. Well, a walk around the mansion's interior. It's too cold for an outdoor constitutional.

As I reach the foot of the stairs, a door opens and shuts somewhere on the second floor. Moments later, a smiling Maudlin Rose races down the hallway and bolts down the stairs wearing a necklace made of pink flowers.

That's it. Just the flowers.

Grim isn't far behind her. His sinewy legs piston beneath him, and with each spindly stride, it sounds as if he's clapping.

I don't want to look.

I don't want to look.

But fuck, I do it anyway.

When he runs, his cock and balls smack against each other—and anything else within reach—which creates the sound that will haunt my nightmares for many years to come.

As they tear down the stairs and race through the main hall, they don't notice me standing here, with my mouth wide open and my eyes wishing for a Helen Keller type miracle. I mean, seriously. The woman overcame so much, but she was also spared some visual horrors.

Rosie opens her mouth, and it takes me a moment to realize what she's doing. No sound comes from her throat, but her stomach contracts, and I've never seen a smile so wide. She's laughing. It's silent, but it's unmistakable now.

As she doubles over in a fit of silent giggles, Grim catches up to her and pulls her against him.

"Oh, *mein Schatzi*, I have caught you now," he growls against her ear, and now I'm uncomfy.

I shouldn't witness such a private moment, but I don't know how to escape. If I move, they'll see me, but if I don't, they won't. And I don't know which outcome is worse.

I clear my throat and turn toward the dining room, hoping against hope that they'll just ignore me and carry on. I am not that lucky, however.

"Oh, Catarina!" Grim says. "Rosie would like to speak with you, if you have a moment."

I turn and blink at them. What do I do with my eyes? I don't know where to look. "N-now? You guys seem a bit . . . busy?"

The floor. I'll look at the floor.

"Nonsense, nonsense. It will not take up much of your time. She is a woman of very few words." He lets out a soft chuckle at his little joke. "Come closer so you can hear her more clearly."

Do I have to?

Seeing no way out of this, I swallow and walk toward them. As I draw nearer, however, looking at the floor is no longer an option. If I look any lower than Rose's navel, my left eye fills with an oddly large set of testicles, and my right eye is obscured by a bush the size of Rhode Island.

I'm not against women having pubic hair, but when the woman is as tiny as Rosie, the pussy ends up looking like a literal beaver dam. It's a lot of fucking hair.

"She said you need to listen to your heart," Grim said, and I pull myself out of the mental vortex their genitals have sent me into.

"Pardon?" I look at Rose.

She smiles at me—something that doesn't happen very often—and takes my hand in hers. As her soft skin brushes over mine, I'm reminded of my mother. The ass and titties being out, not so much, but that gentle touch is reminiscent of home.

Maudlin Rose takes my hand and places it over my heart, then nods at me.

"See?" Grim says. "She wants you to listen to what you want. Cut out the noise. We are not on this planet for very long, so why are you wasting time on your unhappiness? You give it more attention and consideration than what brings you joy. Do not waste another day, she says. Live."

"She said . . . all of that?" I look at Rosie, and her eyes glisten with tears as she nods again.

Rose turns to Grim, grabs his hand, and does something to his palm. Her countenance shifts from joyful to serious, and Grim nods at her before turning to me.

"She says . . ." He looks at her again, seemingly unsure about the message she wants him to relay, but she communicates her point again, once more using his palm. "She says that only a fool would run from love, and if you do not take the correct path, you will be dead to her."

I shift my focus to Rose, who smiles and blinks at me. "Um, okay," I say. "Thanks, I think? I'm just gonna go now. You two, uh, be safe."

Grim takes Rose's hand in his and gives it a pat. "Of course. But we will be busy for the rest of the evening, so please do not interrupt us again."

Rude, but he'll get no complaints from me.

Backing away seems like the right move, but I'd rather not gawk at their junk as I make my exit, so I turn and head toward the kitchen once more. As I hurry toward the bar at the back of the dining room, Rosie's words circle my brain.

Specifically, one word.

Love.

The rest of her message was simple enough to decode. Go for Bennett and stop worrying about what other people think. That part made sense, even if I can't take her advice, despite the threat of excommunication. Also, how hypocritical of her to threaten me with the loss of friendship if I don't follow my heart when that is exactly what I fear will happen if I do.

Kindra wouldn't go so far as to completely ditch our friendship, but she would no longer respect me. Somehow, that's worse. I admire her. She was an idol before I even knew her name or what she looked like. The woman stands for everything I believe in, and after getting to know her, my admiration has only grown. I don't ever hope to have her feel the same about me—I'm her opposite in every way—but to lose what respect I've gained would destroy me.

So it's not as simple as Maudlin Rose presents it to be. It's just not.

But love? Psh, not even close. I've never been in love, aside from the occasional high-school obsession, but I imagine it differs from whatever this is. I should feel like I can't get air when he's not around, and I'm breathing just fine. The thought of being without him should crush the delicate things inside me, yet I feel as sturdy as I ever have. Sure, there's a nagging itch to be near him, but I don't feel as if I need to claw my skin away if I can't get a fix.

Reaching the bar, I grab the soda gun and aim it at my chest, but then I pull it away. This will be a lot easier if the shirt is on the counter. After glancing around to be sure the coast is clear, I rip off the blouse and lay it on the bar. Aiming the gun's nozzle at the bright-yellow splotch, I depress the trigger . . . but nothing happens.

Well, fuck. I guess I'll have to go back to the walk-in. I

spotted a few bottles of seltzer in there, and I'm sure they'll work just as well.

I snatch the shirt from the bar and scurry into the kitchen, which is just as dark and empty as Bennett and I left it. His scent still lingers here—bergamot, sandalwood, and a hint of vanilla—and I close my eyes and breathe it in.

Clink. Clink-clink-clink.

I open my eyes and turn toward the sound.

Clink-clink-clink.

I'm definitely not imagining it, and something about the rhythm sounds almost familiar. Leaving my shirt on the long silver table in the center of the room, I head toward the gentle metallic tapping.

The door to the walk-in fridge stands slightly ajar, which is odd, since we closed it. I remember because I double-checked the handle to ensure the food inside wouldn't spoil. These doors are stout, so it couldn't have opened on its own.

I take another step forward and freeze in place. Bennett is on his hands and knees on the walk-in's floor and he's . . . thrusting?

Jealousy heats my chest, and I scream at him before I realize what I'm doing. "You fucking cheater!"

He shouts something I can't understand, but I don't care what he has to say. I just want to know who he's fucking and—

Then, as Bennett scrambles to stand and fasten his pants, I see what he was fucking.

It wasn't a person.

It was a fucking *turkey.*

So why do I still feel betrayed?

"I thought you were going for a walk!" I shout.

"Shh!" Bennett rushes forward to put his hand over my

mouth, but the thought of raw poultry touching any part of my skin causes me to recoil instantly. "You'll get the entire mansion down here if you keep squawking. Keep it down."

"Is that why you're so attracted to me? Because I squawk? Like a fucking *bird*, Bennett?"

His cheeks blaze red. "No, no. It's not—" He shifts from damage-control mode to indignation. "Wait, why the fuck do you care? I thought you wanted to put the brakes on this. Do you just expect me to sit on my hands and wait around until you're good and ready to stop being ashamed of me?"

"I don't know what I expected, but it sure as fuck wasn't this!" I whisper-yell as I motion to the defiled carcass. "How are you even fucking it? Its body is just one empty cavity!"

"Are you genuinely asking?"

I wasn't, but now he's piqued my curiosity. I sigh. "Please explain."

He seems torn between embarrassment and pride as he raises a round fruit from inside the turkey's gaping cavity. "A few months ago, I was on a message board for people who enjoy . . . food. Anyway, this guy recommended I try fucking a cantaloupe, and I figured I'd give it a shot. This one was small enough to fit inside the turkey, so I just carved a hole right here."

"Okay, that's enough."

Bennett shrugs. "I thought he was full of shit. I mean, he kept bragging about how he banged his therapist, so I worried maybe he was delusional, but no, he was right. The consistency—"

"I said I'm good, thanks."

He closes his mouth.

I don't know what to do with any of this, so I shake my head and turn to leave.

"Hang on a minute." He grabs my arm and turns me to

face him. "If anyone here has a right to ask questions, it's me. Why are you prancing around the mansion with my property on full display?"

My mouth drops open, and I have to laugh. "Your property? Your fucking *property*? Even if you put a ring on my finger and force me to take your last name, I would never be your property."

"Fuck a ring. If I stick my dick in it, it's mine."

"First, gross. Second, if I want to prance through the mansion stark naked, I will."

"You really don't get it, do you."

He releases my arm, but I don't move. Because he's right. I don't get it.

"Cat, you never have to fear me. Do you understand?"

I shake my head.

"I will never hurt you. Never. But if you walk through this mansion naked, I will have to hurt every man who looks at your body. You are blameless, but if they see the parts of you that are meant only for me, you force my hand."

He steps into me, and I take a step back because this feels like a threat. My ass bumps into the wall, and I have nowhere to go.

"I will hunt them," he continues. "I will hold them down and pull their eyeballs from their heads with my bare hands. When they scream and ask why, I will tell them they have sinned and coveted what belongs to me. So no, maybe I don't *own* you, but you're still mine."

This is insanity. These are the men our mothers warn us about. There are entire television networks dedicated to dramatic retellings of what happens when a girl like me ends up with a guy like Bennett.

And I've never been more turned on in my life.

Wrapping my arms around his neck, I leap up, and he

catches me under my ass. I no longer care that he was just raw-dogging a turkey-cantaloupe hybrid. I want him to raw-dog *me*.

"I thought you wanted to wait until we were back in the contiguous US?" he says as I reach behind me to unfasten my bra.

"I do." I toss the bra to the floor. "But what I want and what I need are two very different things right now."

"Aren't you angry that I was fucking the food?"

"Yes, but now I'm horny. I'll be angry later." I reach for the hem of his shirt, and he raises his arms.

But as I pull the shirt away, he stops. "Would you try something with me?"

"Try something? Like what?"

He smirks and kisses me once more. "Meet me in your room."

Chapter Thirty-Seven

Cat

It's the turkey. I know this as a fact before he ever enters my room with the massive pan cradled against his chest. What I don't expect is for him to bring company with him.

"Maverick?" I shout as I scramble to cover my nearly naked body. Bennett's warning rings in my head, and I don't want the poor guy to lose his eyes. "What are you doing in here?"

He looks at Bennett. "He explained it to me, and I still don't understand."

Bennett places the pan on top of the dresser. The shining metal side bumps against a moose statue, sending it to the floor. Thankfully, it doesn't break, and he places it back where it goes.

"It's fucking simple," he says. "I want to spend the night with Cat. That means you have to spend the night in my room."

"Why does that mean I have to sleep in your room?

299

Why can't I stay in mine?" Maverick shifts his weight and tries not to look at me. Bennett must have issued the same warning to him. "Won't people just *assume* I'm in here if they hear the sounds of lovemaking?"

"Please don't call it that," I say.

"What's the pan for?" Maverick asks. "That's not part of the fucking, is it?"

"Please don't ask any more questions," I manage to squeak out. All of this embarrassment is doing a number on my vocal cords. "Can you just sleep in his room?"

Maverick blows out a breath and swipes his hand through his hair. "I guess so, but I'm fucking glad this thing is over after tomorrow night."

"Tomorrow night?" Bennett and I say in unison.

"The retreat is supposed to run for two more nights," I say, "with everyone departing for the airport on the last day."

"Oh, that's right. You guys weren't here earlier when they discussed it," Maverick says. "This snow we're getting tonight is just the start, and we're due for a whiteout on what was supposed to be the departure day. Jim didn't want us to be stranded, so he thought it would be best to end things a day early. Everyone agreed, and Ezra went into town to adjust everyone's flights. Everything has been taken care of."

"Well, thanks for the heads-up. You can get the fuck out now." Bennett starts pushing him toward the door, but he digs his heels into the carpet.

"Wait, what's the pan for?" he says as he's pushed across the threshold.

Bennett closes the door on him and turns to me.

"No, seriously," I say. "What's the pan for?"

He smiles at me, and a glimmer of mischief shines in his eyes.

"I'm not fucking a turkey, Bennett."

His shoulders droop. "Oh, don't be so fucking closed-minded."

"I'm not. I'm closed-legged. You aren't getting cold, slimy poultry skin anywhere near my pussy."

"I didn't plan on putting it in your pussy."

My asshole pulls inward. "Get out."

He takes a few steps toward me, and I grab a pillow and hold it up like a shield. If there's one thing I'm beginning to understand, it's that his touch does something to me. His kisses are an amnesia tonic, scrambling my brain and causing me to forget my self-respect.

If he works his magic on me, I'll cave and degrade myself.

"Kitten, don't be like that." He steps closer and sits on the bed. "Look, if you aren't comfortable, I'll drop it."

"No you won't!" I toss the pillow at his head. "You'll just kiss me and talk me into it with your tongue."

He leans closer, and his body heat batters my exposed skin. "If you don't want to do it, we won't do it." His hands snake beneath the blanket and caress my thighs.

Goosebumps rise on my skin, and he smirks. It's all the encouragement he needs to keep going. His fingers wander higher, skating across my stomach beneath the thin satin. As he touches me, he looks into my eyes.

"I'm not a good man. I will never be a good man. But for you, I will be without reproach." He leans down and kisses my stomach. "For you, I will muzzle myself and come to heel." His lips part, and he sucks my skin into his mouth. His tongue swirls until I'm certain I'll come right on the spot. "I will never be a good man, kitten, but I will be good to *you*."

A moan eases out of me as I allow my hands to wander over his shoulders. He stretches his legs behind him and moves the blanket so that he can kiss my thighs.

"If you say no, then the answer is no." His warm breath brushes over the trail of wet kisses, sending a cooling breeze up my nightie.

On his stomach, he inches closer, until his mouth is only a breath away from my pussy. My toes curl as I anticipate the heat of his tongue melding with my sensitive skin.

"If you don't want to play out my fantasy, what about one of yours?" He pulls my panties aside and runs his tongue through my lips. "God, I could eat you for every meal."

"That," I say. "That's my fantasy. A man who can't get enough of me."

"Mission accomplished, then."

He dives between my legs again, and I lean back. As he licks me and bathes my sensitive clit with attention, I should be lost to the pleasure. I mean, it feels fucking amazing. But my mind keeps wandering back to his suggestion.

What part of the turkey did he plan to put in my ass, exactly? And how did he plan to retrieve it? Are we talking a shit-on-my-chest scenario? Like . . . how far does this fantasy run?

"Bennett?"

"Hmm?" The sound vibrates against me, and my toes curl again.

"I have questions. About the . . . turkey."

He keeps eating me out, only turning his head to say, "Ask away."

"Okay, so I know the 'where' is my ass, but I'm still confused about the 'what' and the 'how.'"

He pushes two fingers inside me and gently massages my clit with his thumb. "The leg. It's a process."

"Explain."

He releases a deep sigh and sits up. "Do you want to get off or do you want to launch into the stratosphere and lose all bodily function for a solid thirty seconds? If it's the former, shut up and let me make you come. If it's the latter, give me your ass and a little bit of trust."

I bite my lip. This is a very difficult decision.

"Well?" he says.

"Don't rush me!"

Having an orgasm that gives me an out-of-body experience is tempting, but again, raw poultry.

"Does it have to be the turkey leg?" I say. "I have some anal beads in the drawer. If they aren't big enough, I have an actual butt plug in my bag. You know, the sex toy that was invented for this precise purpose?"

"It has to be the turkey leg."

"It's not safe for so many reasons. It doesn't even have a flared base. It's the opposite of flared. And what if the meat comes off? How the fuck do we get it out of me?"

"Ye of little faith," he says with a shake of his head. "I brought a condom to ensure nothing actually touches you and everything can be safely removed. As for the rest, you'll just have to trust me."

I glance at the pan on the dresser. While I didn't get a good look at the bird while Bennett was busy fucking it, I imagine it's a pretty large carcass, considering the size of the massive metal casket. I've shoved some pretty sizable objects into my ass, but I doubt anything that big.

But then I look at Bennett, and I can almost taste that orgasm.

"Don't make me regret this," I say as I get on all fours.

I expect him to rush for the turkey leg, but he rushes toward me instead. His hands caress my ass, brushing over my skin before slapping down with an audible crack. I whimper and drop my head to the pillows.

"Your ass is so perfect," he whispers before biting it. His teeth drive into my flesh, but it's more pleasure than pain. Even the momentary pinching sensation makes my pussy clench.

He slides my panties down my legs, then tosses them to the floor. I try not to laugh as Shorty zips from beneath the bed and swats them under the dresser.

But all humor disappears as Bennett positions himself behind me and spits on my asshole. "You have to relax," he says as his thumb brushes over this delicate part of me.

He moves off the bed, but I don't watch him as he prepares whatever he has in store for me. I don't want to know how big it is or how he plans to get it inside me. My focus remains on the promise of an orgasm the likes of which I've never experienced.

Plastic rustles, and seconds later, something cold presses against my asshole. It's not nearly as large as I feared, but it's much harder than I anticipated. I can only assume he's coming at me with the bony end, though I'm not sure if that's better or worse.

So I do the only thing I can. I brace myself and bite the pillow.

Chapter Thirty-Eight

Bennett

She's nowhere near ready for anything more than two fingers, but that's okay. I'll work her up to it. I drag the bone against her sensitive rosebud, reveling in the way she tenses and relaxes that ring of muscle.

"Don't be scared, kitten. If it hurts, you just say the word and I'll stop. I promise. You just have to talk to me. Tell me how it feels."

She grips the sheet as I press the bone against her asshole with more pressure. "I guess it's a flared base if you're coming at it from that end," she says into the pillow.

"Oh, the other end is the goal, but you aren't ready yet."

Her butthole puckers at the thought.

I grin and press the bone against her ass with gentle, rhythmic force, but I won't push it in. When her body is ready and her mind is willing, she will accept my offering with very little effort on my part.

"Spread your legs and raise your ass a little," I say, and she obeys without hesitation. I wind my hand through her blonde hair and crane her neck to kiss her. "Fuck, you are so obedient. Good girls get rewarded."

I smack her ass, then get on my back and slide underneath her so that her pussy is mere inches from my mouth. Realizing what I plan to do, she lets out a small moan.

"Now sit on my face," I command.

She drops her hips with a whimper, and my mouth meets with heaven. As I taste the sweet and salty pleasure dripping from her cunt, I nearly forget the end goal. With one hand, I reach between her ass cheeks and feel for the sweet spot, then place the turkey leg against it.

"Oh, fuck," she says through gritted teeth. "I'm already close."

Thankfully, I'm not. I'm surprised I can even get an erection after the number of times I've come today, but Cat is the living embodiment of the little blue pill. Just one look from her gets me hard.

I turn my head to the side. "Have you ever come multiple times with anyone else, kitten?"

She shakes her head.

"That's because you were meant for me." I drag my tongue through her lips, and her thighs begin to shake. "I'm your first, and I'll be your last."

"Yes, I want that. Only you," she breathes.

She's lost to the pleasure, speaking in tongues and spouting nonsense she doesn't mean or understand, but that affirmation wrecks me. It blasts through the walls surrounding my heart, somehow leaving me feeling safer for it. And I want it to be true.

"Come for me." I suck her clit and massage her asshole with the turkey leg. "Come on my face, kitten."

She grinds down, rocking her hips over my lips and tongue. The closer she gets, the more she relaxes and the more I rub to encourage her to open up. Literally. Her legs tighten around my head, and the bony end slips inside her ass. Her body tenses again, sucking the turkey leg further inside, but I keep my grip on the meaty end.

"Fuck, I'm coming!" she cries. She doesn't even attempt to muffle her pleasure.

I wrap my arm around her waist and hold her pussy flush against my lips as I work her through the orgasm. My other hand holds the turkey leg in place. I don't need to move it. The full feeling is all she needs right now, though it doesn't compare to what's in store for her.

As she comes down from the orgasm, she reaches behind her to pull out the turkey leg, but I'm not ready for the fun to end just yet.

I place my hand over hers. "You can take it out, but I want you to work it back in while I watch."

She pulls it out, then lies on her back. Keeping her legs together, she wraps one arm around the backs of her thighs and begins working the bony end into her ass.

"Ah-ah, kitten. The other end."

Panic flits through her eyes as she reverses the turkey leg and feels the wide, meaty head. It's not quite as large as the ham-hock sized legs they serve at fairs and theme parks, but it's still larger than the average dildo. It's a struggle that only a pro could accomplish, but I have faith in her.

"I don't know if I can," she says. Doubt flashes in her eyes, and the hint of insecurity crushes my soul.

Moving toward the head of the bed means depriving myself of a glorious view, but it's a sacrifice I must make to comfort her. I readjust and lie beside her, then move the hair away from her face.

"Take your time with it. There's no rush." I lean closer and kiss her neck before placing my mouth against the shell of her ear. "Relax your body, then fuck your tight little asshole for me when you're ready. I can be a very patient man with the right motivation, and your perfection is all the motivation I need. Even if you can't fit it inside you, you are such a good girl for trying."

She readjusts her grip on her legs, then lowers her feet to the bed. "I need your help." Her knees part, and she rocks her hips, raising her ass. "Get behind me and hold my legs back."

"With pleasure."

I move behind her, and from this angle, with her ankles behind her head and her asshole pointed toward the ceiling, I can see everything. Arousal glistens on her pussy, and I nearly groan as she rubs her fingers through it and lubes up the condom surrounding the meat missile.

"I can't believe I'm doing this," she says. "It feels so weird."

"It's fucking disgusting, and I love it. Don't stop now. I want to see how filthy you can be."

Her nipples harden and press against the silk negligee. I want to rip it off so that I can see her gorgeous tits, but I don't want to ruin the moment. Instead, I settle for the hint of those delicious curves and the unobscured view of her more private places.

A black shadow leaps onto the bed. It's that fucking cat, but Cat hasn't noticed him yet. Her eyes are closed, and her hands are busy working miracles. But if his blown pupils and wiggling nose are any indication, he's about to ruin this for both of us.

Because he smells the fucking turkey.

Gritting my teeth, I stretch my leg and try to swat him away with my foot, but he dodges my big toe and looks at it like it offended him. With a silent sidestep, he avoids me entirely and inches closer to the raw meat. In one more step, his whiskers will be close enough to tickle her fingers.

Even though this black demon has come straight from hell to ruin my good time, I don't want to hurt him, so punting him across the room is out of the question. I just want him to go away. Using my foot, I try once more to nudge him off the bed.

This time, I succeed, and Shorty begins to slide off the mattress. Unfortunately, he saves himself by sinking his claws into my leg and holding on for dear life. As he finally loses his grip and makes the two-foot drop to the floor, the sound of my ripping skin overpowers Cat's rasping breath.

"What was that?" she asks.

"Nothing," I grit out. "The cat fell off the bed, and he tried to catch himself on the way down."

"Did the comforter rip? Kindra is going to kill me!" She goes to sit up, but I push her chest down and press her shoulder blades against my painfully hard dick.

"It's fine. It didn't rip. I'll pay for it. Just please don't stop." The words fly out of my mouth in a string of incoherence and need.

Cat licks her lips, then relaxes again.

I peer over the side of the bed as Shorty stares up at me with his ears pinned to his head. *Don't even fucking try me,* I think, and the cat turns his attention to the pan atop the dresser. Fuck it. Not my problem.

My problems are miles away.

"Oh, shit," she breathes, and I look between her legs.

To my absolute shock, she's actually doing it. Through sheer determination, she's immobilized her insides and allowed the turkey leg to push past her natural defenses. But she isn't just pushing it in. No. She's moving it. She's *feeling* it.

And enjoying it.

It slips inside her, leaving only the bony end protruding from her ass. My stomach tenses. If I hadn't already gotten off twice before, I'd have embarrassed myself again just now.

"Goddamn, I've never been this full before," she moans. "Fuck, it's stretching me. I don't know how long I can stay like this."

And that's my fucking cue.

Chapter Thirty-Nine

Cat

He tells me to get on my hands and knees, but I don't think I can. I'm too afraid to remove my hand from the bone. I'll swallow the entire turkey leg, and not with my throat. As he moves out from behind me, I don't know what to do. Pull it out or trust him.

Trust him . . .

That's what he said I needed to do, so I relinquish my grip on the bone protruding from my ass as his hand covers mine.

"I won't let it slip inside you," he says. "Now get on all fours so I can fill you completely."

As I slowly roll onto my hands and knees, he keeps the turkey leg in place, and it's one hell of an odd sensation. The meat takes up so much space in my ass that it pushes toward and bears down on my vagina. If Bennett has plans to fuck me, I don't know how he'll get inside me. There's no fucking room.

His free hand caresses my ass before he stands and,

with one hand still firmly holding the impromptu butt plug, strips off his pants. I take the pillow between my teeth and bite down as his heat closes in behind me.

"Oh, kitten . . . you're breathtaking," he says, then angles the turkey leg downward, applying more pressure. "Let me know if I'm hurting you, because that isn't my goal. If I'm pleasing you, though?"

He drags his hand through my pleasure, and I moan.

"If I'm pleasing you, you won't have to say a word, because I'll already know."

I hear the smirk in his voice, and it makes my pussy clench. He settles behind me, one hand still firmly holding that turkey leg in place, and I bite the pillow fluff between my teeth with surprising force when his thick cock nudges my entrance.

Then I remember what he's said this entire time. I only have to say the word, and he'll stop. And fuck, I trust him. I truly do. Taking a deep breath, I relax and wait for his welcome intrusion. Seconds later, he pushes inside me.

I can't catch my breath as his piercing clicks past my opening. He goes slowly enough, but there's so much pressure. I feel things inside myself that I've never felt before. Amazing things. Wild, feral, unhinged things.

Clawing the sheets, I open my mouth and produce a sound that is two-parts scream and one-part guttural moan. It sounds very unsexy to my ears, but Bennett seems to enjoy it.

"Scream through it, kitten. That's it," he says as he eases in and out of me. "Get used to the feeling and let me know when you want to come."

My interior muscles grip the turkey leg and pull, but Bennett keeps traction on the bone, and it doesn't slip inside me. That's a fucking relief.

With one of my fears assuaged, I gain enough courage to push back against him. Because I want more. I want every inch of him, and he's only giving half at most. I rock back again, moaning as the cuffs of my ass finally meet his powerful thighs.

"Damn, look at you." He smacks my ass and grips my hip with his left hand. "Hungry little slut, aren't you? So fucking greedy for what I'm doing to you. Are you ready for me to fuck you?"

I moan and rock into him again.

"Say it," he growls. "Beg me for it."

"Please fuck me," I plead, and my desperation is wholly genuine.

He thrusts forward, meeting my ass with his thighs again, and sparks fly up my spine. Those pleasurable jolts glide through my veins, into my lungs, and straight to my brain. My back arches, and I nearly go limp with ecstasy.

The meat in my ass presses down on his cock, and I can't tell where one ends and the next begins. As far as I know, I've completely blown out my insides and will be removed from this bed by a coroner. I'm okay with that. If Bennett keeps fucking me like this, if I keep feeling this full, I'll die of pleasure anyway.

He leans back, giving me a new angle to experience, and I bite the pillow again. His cock piercing rakes against my insides. My nipples brush against the silk, and pain ricochets off my ass as Bennett smacks it. I'm lost in a dizzying rush of sensations, and I never want it to end.

"Fuck, I'm ready," I moan. "I want to come."

"Touch yourself. Play with your pussy." Bennett's grip firms on my hip. "I want you to come so hard that I have to fight to stay inside you."

Considering the intense pressure building in my lower abdomen, that's a very real possibility.

I push my hand between my legs and find my clit, which is still so sensitive from the orgasm I had only minutes ago. He wants me to come, and I want to come again, but now I feel pressure of a different kind.

The pressure to succeed.

Clearing my mind as best I can, I turn my focus to the sensations thrumming through my body. If I rub a little above that overly sensitive nub, the feeling isn't so intense. It's almost . . . nice. I grip the tail end of that feeling and try to hold on to it, but it slips away.

"What's wrong?" Bennett asks. "Do you need to stop? Are you uncomfortable?"

I rock back against him to shut him up. While I appreciate his concern, it won't help me get off any faster. But his cock might, so I need him to keep thrusting.

"Just fuck me," I say. "Don't stop. Please, don't stop."

He finds his rhythm again, and I return to the puzzle that is my body. I want to come again, and I can feel the orgasm with every thrust of his hips. It's right there, so close, but it's just out of reach.

"Get Emilio," I say as I motion toward the drawer. "He's the little guy that should be right on top."

Bennett pulls out of me without any hesitation, leaving me feeling almost empty. He then reaches toward the drawer and grabs my little silver bullet, all while gripping that bone and ensuring I don't end up at the ER with a very embarrassing story. He drops the tiny toy into my hand and wastes no time getting inside me again.

I flick through the settings until I find the gentlest one—just strong enough to hold my orgasm within reach without vibrating my poor clit to numbness. As I press it against me, his rocking motions move my hand as well. The jolts are so quick, his thrusts so incredibly deep, and suddenly, I'm accomplishing the impossible.

"Oh, good girl," he groans. "Fucking soak me, kitten."

It doesn't matter if I want to or not, because it's happening. The pressure builds to a painful crescendo. My legs shake. My pulse thumps in places I've never felt it thump before, and I'm fairly certain I've lost use of all senses besides whatever fuels this brain-breaking orgasm. Sharp pains spear the joints in my toes as they clench and unclench at a feverish pace. I have no control over it. I have no control over anything.

Warm liquid gushes out of me, and Bennett growls.

"God, you are *so* dirty." He punctuates every syllable with a thrust.

My legs can no longer support me. The bones in my body dissolve, and I melt into the mattress as Bennett continues to fuck me senseless. The worst part? I fell with the vibrator between my legs, and I'm still fucking coming.

"I can't, I can't," I say.

At least, that's what I *try* to say, but my throat is spasming, and I'm not sure he heard me.

But it doesn't matter anyway, because he grips my hips with both hands and buries himself inside me as he comes. As he holds me in place, I will my arm to move. My hand slithers beneath the weight of two bodies, rushing straight to that buzzing demon clutched between my swelling pussy lips. I toss it away before I have to endure another second of pleasure paralysis.

"What the fuck was that?" I croak out. "Seriously. What. The fuck. Was that?"

Bennett rolls onto his side and smiles at me. The small scar in his eyebrow has never looked so sexy, his smirk so sensual. Those feel-good hormones rush through me at a feverish pace, and I have to stop myself from telling him I love him and that I never want to be without him again.

God, he is so handsome.

He reaches up and holds my face in his hands. Only then do I realize he's no longer holding the massive drumstick in place.

The butthole pucker is immediate.

He makes the same realization and sits up. His hand goes for the bone, and I breathe a sigh of relief when he grabs hold of it.

"Now just relax and I'll ease it out of you," he says.

I hold up a hand, then reach behind me. "I'll take it from here. I have more experience with pulling things out of my ass than you do."

Needing no more encouragement, he flops back on the bed as I shuffle to the bathroom.

My feet slap on the cold tiles, and I spare one more look at Bennett before I close the door. Then I squat and try to relax. If I'm being honest, I'm a little nervous to just grab it and start yanking. The meat will come out in one piece, thanks to the condom, so I'm not worried about leaving anything behind. I'm more worried about pulling something outside that should stay inside.

Panic hasn't set in yet, but that anxiety-ridden bitch lingers in my peripherals.

"No need to stress," I whisper to myself. "It's just a turkey leg. In your butt. This could be so much worse."

Could it? Could it be worse? Because I've gathered the courage to give it a little tug, and that son of a bitch is firmly lodged.

I lie on my back as sweat begins to slick my forehead. This is worse than the time I went shopping with Kindra and got stuck in a cocktail dress. I had to rip the dress to make my escape, but I will be goddamned if I rip anything today.

Relaxing every muscle below my pubic area, I reach between my legs again. To my absolute horror, there's even less bone sticking out now. I can hardly get my fucking fingers around it!

I start to cry. I can't help it.

"Never use anything that doesn't have a flared fucking *base*." I moan into my arm as I drape it over my face and wish for death.

Seeing no other option, I do the only thing I can. I keep gripping that last remnant of hope sticking out of my butt, all while scooting closer to the door. When I'm near enough, I stick my lips to the small crack and open my mouth.

"Bennett, tell Kindra we need the car. I have to go to the ER."

Chapter Forty

Bennett

When I enter Cat's room with help in tow, she looks at me as if I've lost my mind. After she slams the bathroom door, of course. She's still in the bathroom in her very vulnerable state.

"Were the instructions that fucking difficult?" she screams through the door. "I said Kindra, not Grim and Rosie!"

"Hey, keep it down unless you want the entire mansion to come in here." I look back at the elderly couple and mouth, *Sorry*, then turn back to the closed bathroom door. "Rosie was a medic for a bit in some war or something, so I figured she could help you out."

"I guess it beats heading to the fucking hospital." Cat groans.

Rose tries to step around me, and I let her pass, but I step in front of Grim when he tries to follow her.

I place a light hand on the old man's frail shoulder.

"Hang on. There's no fucking way you're looking at her asshole. You have to stay out here."

"I have no desire to look at such things," he says with a disgusted scowl. "Rose needs a voice, however, so if I cannot go, she cannot go."

The bathroom door squeaks open just far enough to reveal Cat's head. "I would actually prefer that *no one* look at *any*thing on my body. Thanks. Can't she just tell me how to pull it out?"

I look at Maudlin Rose. She shakes her head and grabs Grim's hand, then does something with her finger on his palm.

"She says . . ." He looks at her for confirmation, and she repeats the motions on his hand. "She says no."

"Why?" Cat whines.

"Don't panic, kitten," I say. And then I kick myself for talking sweet in front of other people, especially when Grim looks like I just ejected a horde of bees from my cock. "Oh, fuck off. You make googly eyes at Rosie all the time."

His cheeks flush, and I try to brush back my own embarrassment. Then again, if I want Cat—if I really want her—this is something I'll have to get used to.

"As you two can see, we are . . ." I fumble for the words, but Cat saves the day.

"We're exploring a connection," she says.

Rose clutches her hands beneath her chin and smiles down at Cat. It's all very sweet, aside from the fact that Cat has a fairly large poultry appendage protruding from her ass. Well, not so much protruding as peeking, I guess.

"Can you help her or not?" I ask Rose.

The woman holds up a finger and goes to the bed. When she sees the massive wet spot, her eyebrows rise and she offers us a round of applause. Then she grips one of the pillows and pulls the white casing away. She lays that on the bed—careful to avoid the wet spots—and begins folding it until it's a long, thin strip. Satisfied, she returns to me and Grim.

After draping the cloth over his shoulder, she motions for his hand, and he provides it. From this angle, I can see her hands more clearly. She alternates between signs, touches, and eye movements to get her point across, and he hears her, loud and clear.

Grim nods at her and turns to me. "She will blindfold me so that I do not see your mistress, and she will communicate with the patient through me. Does this satisfy you?"

No, not really. Even the thought of Grim being in the same room as Cat when she's in a vulnerable position—

"Yep, that works," I say.

My clawing need to save her overrides my fierce need to possess her. Especially when I look down and see the way she's panicking on the inside. The girl is great at hiding it, but she can't hide it from me. Not now. And not ever again.

Once Rose secures the blindfold around Grim's narrow head, we all file into the bathroom, careful to step over the prone patient. Cat stares at the ceiling, probably dissociating.

I kneel beside her and take her hand in mine. "Hey, I'm really sorry," I whisper, but not low enough, apparently, because Grim's jaw falls open.

He hurries to close it, but I saw, and his shock doesn't surprise me. Pet names and apologies aren't in my wheelhouse, and this isn't a side of me most people see. Hell, I didn't even know it was in me in this capacity. It feels kind of gross, but then I look at her and it just feels kind of . . . good.

Fuck it.

I clear my throat and brush away the little strands of hair that always seem to fall across her perfect face. "I'm sorry. This is my fault, and if you never want to fuck me again, I completely understand."

"Can we do this after we close down the KFC joint between my fucking legs?" Cat asks.

Grim shifts on his feet. "KFC is not turkey. It is chicken." He must feel my glare, because he raises his hands and says, "Rosie speaks these things, not me."

I look at Rose, but she doesn't crack a smile. She just gets on her knees in front of Cat as if she's about to deliver a fucking baby. When Grim doesn't sit beside her, she gives his gray slacks a light tug, and he feels around until he finds her. He plunks down a little too close to Cat's leg, but I just grit my teeth.

Let her get some help, jackass.

"Ow, you're squeezing me," Cat says, and I realize she's correct. I'm squeezing the fuck out of her hand. When did that happen?

Rose pats Cat's knees and motions for her to spread her legs. Cat closes her eyes and pouts before doing exactly that. Rose purses her lips and blinks down at the disaster zone.

"What? Is it bad?" I ask.

She feels for Grim's hand and relays a message.

"It is certainly not *good*." He waits as she finishes her missive. "But this is not bad."

Cat and I breathe a collective sigh of relief.

"Where is the lubricant for your genitals?" Grim asks. "Rose believes she can ease it out with digital penetration and anterior—" Another pause. "No, I misheard her. *In*terior manipulation."

"Oh, fuck. I'm gonna pass out," Cat says.

I place my other hand over hers, sandwiching her tiny

palm. "Look at me, kitten. You aren't gonna pass out. You're one of us, remember? We don't pass out when shit gets hard."

"*We* also do not shove turkey parts up our bottoms, but here we are," Grim mumbles.

I let it slide.

"Grim, the genital lubricant is in the top drawer of the nightstand," I say without looking away from Cat's eyes. "White tube, blue writing."

"Not sure how I am supposed to find it when I have been forced to forego one of my senses, but I will manage." He stands and feels around for the door.

"I'll be right back," I whisper to Cat.

She nods up at me.

"Sit down, old man," I say as I pass Grim, and he toddles back to his spot beside Rose. "You need any gloves?" I call over my shoulder.

A beat passes, and Grim says, "She brought her own, thank you."

I fetch the lube and hand it to Rose, then sit beside Cat once more. She's handling this really well, all things considered. Meanwhile, I feel like a complete asshole. I asked her to trust me, and she did. Then I went and fucked it up. She's probably waiting until she can walk before she lays into me.

Once Rose slides her slender hands into a pair of sterile gloves—they came in their own little single-use baggie and everything—she holds her hands out so that Grim can apply the lube. Grim having no sight and Rose having no voice creates a bit of a barrier, so I snatch the tube away from him on his fifth try to find her hands.

She scowls at me, unable to use Grim's voice to tell me how she really feels as I dump some lube onto her gloved fingers. She's got the body language thing down, though, because her message is crystal.

How fucking dare you belittle Grim. That's what that look says.

"Um, what's she doing now?" Cat asks. "Whoa, that's uncomfy."

Rose sits back and looks at the ceiling, and I think I know why she's so frustrated.

"Try to talk to me," I say to Rose. "I know I don't understand you as well as he does, but I'm not a complete moron."

She tilts her head toward me with a deadpan stare.

"See!" I shout. "I know exactly what you're saying. You just said, 'Yeah fuckin' right.'"

Rose's eyebrows rise, and she gives me another look.

"Now you said, 'Hmm, pretty good.'"

With a sigh of defeat, Rose nods her head and looks at me. Then she begins to speak.

Her hands rise, and she clenches them in fists. At the same time, she tightens her jaw and pinches her lips together until they are a thin line. Her entire body is rigid. Then she shakes her head emphatically, then mimes blowing out a breath and—

"Relaxing," I say. I look down at Cat. "She wants you to relax."

Rose nods, sending her short gray curls into a hurricane around her head. After raising her hand in a thumbs-up, she moves between Cat's legs once more. Reaching down, she shakes her head.

"You have to stop tensing up, kitten," I say.

Cat scoffs. "That's easy for you to say. You aren't the one with a turkey leg the size of John Coffey shoved up your ass. You aren't the one who is about to give *birth* to birdzilla! You did this to me!"

One thing is for certain. I'm getting a fucking vasectomy after this trip.

Rose mimes the motions for relax again, but Cat is too far gone. A fresh droplet of sweat speeds down her temple, and her hands have gone clammy. There's only one thing left to try before we have to give up and admit we're beaten.

"Cat, do you remember that special drink I gave you on the island?"

Chapter Forty-One

Cat

I don't know how many hours pass before I finally swim out of the fog, but I wake up in Bennett's arms. My head rests on his chest, and my arm drapes over his warm waist.

A soft purring sound radiates from somewhere above my head. I blink back the sleep still clinging to my eyes and squint through the dim morning light. Shorty is fast asleep, right on top of Bennett's head.

Wait.

Shorty. Morning light. My room.

Bennett.

I move to sit up, and a deep ache radiates through my ass. The memories of last night's events flit through my mind, and I wince when I remember how it ended. With me on the floor, sedated to the point of delirium as Rosie gave me the most uncomfortable asshole tickle of my life. I'm just grateful I didn't end up at the hospital.

But now I have bigger concerns than an embarrassing

butt plug. Kindra made me promise I'd attend the hunt, and that's today. If she comes to my room before I can get Bennett back to his—

"Bennett," I whisper as I shove his shoulder. "Bennett, wake up."

His eyes pop open, and he looks around as if I've just shouted that the bed is on fire. "What's wrong? Are you okay? What do you need? I'll get it for you."

God, I want to wake up to that gravelly morning voice for the rest of my life.

Shorty runs to the end of the bed and looks back at Bennett, as if annoyed by the sudden movements. Not too annoyed, though, because he licks his lips, swallows, and settles at Bennett's feet.

"I'm fine," I say, "but you have to get out of my room before anyone comes looking for me. The hunt is this morning."

He sighs and closes his eyes. "Are we really still doing this?"

"What? Hiding, or going on the hunt?"

"Hiding."

"Yes, we are still hiding. And we will continue to hide until I grow the balls to come clean to Kindra."

"Maverick, Rose, Grim—three people already know, and they seemed to handle it pretty well."

I toss the covers away from my naked body, then slide off the bed. "Yeah, well, they aren't Kindra."

He turns onto his side, then props himself up with his elbow. "What is it you fear she'll do, exactly? If you don't want her to crack jokes, just tell her that. I mean, it never worked for me, but she *likes* you."

"It's not that simple, Bennett." I move around the room, gingerly bending at the waist to gather his clothes from the floor. "Today is the last day. We leave tomorrow. Can't we just hold it together for twenty-four hours?"

Bennett sighs and shakes his head. "Whatever you need, kitten."

There's that pained look in his eyes again. I toss his clothes at his head so that I don't have to see it anymore. If I look for too long, I'll break and tell him to stay, and I can't do that.

"So how do you expect today to work, exactly?" Bennett asks. "Kindra and Ezra will do whatever they can to keep us apart. They'll probably push you and Maverick together."

I rifle through the dresser, searching for my warmest and most comfortable undergarments. "That could work in our favor." I hop on one foot and step into an unflattering pair of granny panties in a pretty shade of light pink. "You and Maverick hunted as a team at the summer retreat. Just run that pairing again, and I'll tag along."

"God, I love it when you scheme," he says as he watches me dress.

"That's great, but hurry to your room before the rest of the cabin comes looking for us."

He grabs his clothes, slides off the bed, and gives me a kiss before exiting my room. I shove down the butterflies and remind myself to play it cool. If we can just make it through the next twenty-four hours, we're going to be just fine.

Kindra peers over her shoulder to be sure I've followed her into the makeshift armory at the base camp for the winter hunt. I'm grateful she had a spare set of snow pants for me to wear. I'd forgotten all about the hole I slashed into mine. Now my outfit is a regular hodgepodge of mismatched snow gear.

"Are you sure you don't want to team up against the guys?" Kindra asks. "I thought me, you, and Eve in a head-to-head against Ezra, Bennett, and Maverick would be fun. Plus, it would ensure you and your arch nemesis don't cross streams."

"Oh, I think I'll be okay." I step toward a table filled with weaponry of every shape, size, and caliber. My hand drifts toward the familiar crossbow, and I pluck it from the pile. "Where do they keep the ammo?"

Kindra smiles at me, and water brims in her dark eyes. "Oh, Cat. I've hoped for this day for you for so long. You've finally claimed your weapon." She pulls me into a hug, and I can't even hug her back because I'm so shocked. She leans back and places her hands on my shoulders. "I'll get the bolts for you. You stay right here."

She shuffles off to a side room and returns with a bag full of bolts. With a grunt, she hefts it onto the table.

"It's kind of heavy," she says. "You might need Maverick to carry it for you."

"No need," someone says behind me, and I turn to see Bennett.

My heart picks up speed in my chest, and not just because he looks so ruggedly handsome with all that stubble on his jaw. He's offering to do something nice for me, and that's certain to send up warning flares for Kindra.

Kindra pulls the bag closer to her. "No fucking way. You'll 'lose' them just so that Cat can't hunt today. Fuck no and fuck *you*."

Ezra enters the shed and hurries to get between his fiancée and his brother. "What's all the fuss, you two?

Today is supposed to be fun. Let's leave all the paltry bickering to children, shall we?"

"Paltry bickering?" Kindra says as she wheels around to face him. "He'll block her kills, and you know it! The only reason she even got her first kill was because Maverick was nice enough to give her the time and patience she needed. Bennett is incapable of that kind of care. He'll rush her, Ezra. Or worse, he'll keep kill-blocking her."

Bennett winces, and I want to comfort him as the hurt reaches a visible level. Because the praise belongs to him, yet he's denied it, and it's all my fault.

I have to do something.

"We came to a truce," I blurt.

The three of them face me, and each face displays a different expression. Kindra is offended, Ezra is shocked, and Bennett is panicking because there is no predetermined story and I'm about to wing it.

"Yes. We talked," I say. "Last night."

"You were with Maverick last night," Kindra says. "I'm pretty sure the entire mansion heard your screams of ecstasy."

Bennett cocks his head behind Kindra and Ezra. His eyes widen. *What the fuck are you doing?* that look says.

Shit.

I hold up a finger. "Right, but it was before that. I went to the kitchen to clean some mustard from my shirt, and Bennett was in there. That's when we talked."

Kindra's eyebrows pull together. "Mustard? Cat, we had soup for dinner."

Double shit.

"Maybe it was some turmeric. I don't fucking know." I sling the crossbow over my shoulder. "There was a stain on my shirt, and I went to clean it off, and that's when I saw

Bennett. That's when we talked and made a truce for the hunt. What is with the third degree?"

The pressure weighs on me until my skin heats to a painful temperature. Before she asks anything else and forces me to lie to her again, I rush out of the shed. Cold air caresses my face, soothing me the moment I'm outside. I suck in a deep breath and power walk to the other side of the building, where I can collapse in private. Lying is not my favorite thing to do in general, but lying to someone I care about? It fucking sucks.

Footsteps crunch in the snow behind me. I turn, expecting to see Bennett, but Eve strides up on long legs draped in designer snow gear.

"Hey, is everything okay?" she asks. "I saw you run back here, and I wanted to make sure you're good."

"I'm fine. I think I'm just nervous." I swipe my glove beneath my nose before the snot freezes in place, and then I turn to face her. "This cold is making my eyes water. I'm not crying."

Eve purses her lips and raises an eyebrow. "Honey, we don't do that here. I don't know when it became cool to stuff down your emotions, but we don't do that. Now let it out and tell me what's got you so worked up."

I look into her eyes and consider breaking the news to her as a trial run. She and I are on our way to becoming close friends, but we aren't Kindra-Cat level close. If she doesn't completely disown me, maybe Kindra wouldn't either.

"What if I told you I've done something . . . really weird? Something that might change how you think of me."

"What are we talking about here? Like, you're addicted to coffee enemas weird? Or you want to be the next Mary

Kay Letourneau kind of weird? Because one of those things I can look past, and the other, not so much."

"What? No. It's nothing like either of those things." I blow out a breath. "What if I had some . . . sexual preferences that you considered harmful?"

"I used to enjoy putting lightbulbs in my pussy and squeezing until they broke. Is it worse than that?"

I open and close my mouth. "I have so many questions."

She shrugs. "You put the bulb into a baggie so that it—"

"Actually, I'm good." I shake my head. Beating around the bush is getting me nowhere, so I just need to come out with it. But as I open my mouth to tell her everything, Kindra rounds the corner and comes toward us.

"Cat, I'm really sorry," she says. "You aren't leaving again, are you? I'll keep my mouth shut if you'll stay."

"Oh, fuck." I flop down on my ass and immediately regret it when pain makes me wince. "Kindra, I'm not going anywhere. Eve, I stuck something in my butt."

"Maverick's into *ass play*?" Eve whispers. "He seems so . . . vanilla."

"Or turmeric," Kindra says with a smirk. "Sorry, couldn't help myself."

I finally crack a smile. "It's okay. I actually shared a sandwich with Bennett when we talked, and I was too afraid to say so. That's how the mustard got on my shirt."

A question springs onto Kindra's tongue, but she closes her mouth and swallows it. I already know what she wanted to ask. When we were in the armory, I said the mustard on my shirt was there before talking to Bennett. That was the entire reason I went into the kitchen in the first place, per my lie. She wants to make sense of that, but now she's too scared to ask. Which works in my favor, even if it makes me feel like shit.

But I deserve to feel like shit, so again, it's fine.

Eve drops down beside me. She looks up at Kindra and motions for her to sit as well. "We might as well get comfortable. Jim isn't here yet, and if I've learned anything about these retreats, it's that we can't start without him."

"No, we certainly can't," Kindra says as she sits at my other side. "So . . . you really plan to hunt with Maverick and Bennett?"

"Bennett?" Eve's spine straightens. "Why is he part of the equation? Doesn't he have other friends he can follow around?" She places her hand to her chest and laughs. "Oh, wait. It's Bennett. Of course he doesn't."

Kindra and Eve burst into a rush of giggles, and I'm ashamed that I would have willingly joined them only a few days ago. But now their laughter stings. Eve is right. Bennett doesn't have a lot of friends, and he's partially to blame for that.

But only partially.

I pretend to laugh along with them to keep up the farce, but my smile drops when I look up and see Bennett standing near the edge of the shed. He's looking right at us.

And he heard everything.

Chapter Forty-Two

Bennett

Ezra looks up from the weapon table and lowers a tire iron as I reenter the armory. I drop the bag of crossbow bolts by the door and lean against the metal wall. Even though Cat was only playing along to keep her story intact, her laughter at their cruel jokes still got under my skin.

"Is something the matter?" Ezra asks. "You look a bit miffed."

I shake my head and fix my face into a more neutral expression. "Nope, all good."

"It'll get easier once you two tell everyone, you know."

The vertebrae in my neck crack as my head whips around to face him. "The fuck are you talking about?"

"Oh, Bennett, Bennett, Bennett." He clucks his tongue and steps closer. "When will you realize that you can't hide anything from me? We may have grown up oceans apart, but the same blood runs through our veins. Sometimes I think I know you better than you know yourself."

My jaw clenches and unclenches as my brain misfires. "How long have you known?"

"About the attraction? Or that it was mutual?"

I stare at him. "Both."

With a smirk, he steps beside me and joins me against the wall. "The attraction was instant. No, don't argue. I was there, or have you forgotten?"

I close my mouth.

"Had you just acted on it then, we might not be in such a mess now," he adds. "I haven't mentioned my suspicions to Kindra, but has Cat considered how this will affect her?"

"Affect who? Kindra?" I roll my eyes. "That's *all* Cat worries about. She thinks everyone will ostracize her if they find out, and that's why she's made me keep it a secret."

"Can you blame us?" Ezra pins me with a deadpan glare. "You're nearly as deplorable as our father when it comes to women. Would you really fault Kindra for wanting to look out for her friend?"

"That's the other part Cat's worried about. She thinks everyone will harass the fuck out of me and tell me not to hurt her."

"She's right. We absolutely will, myself included."

"I haven't hurt her the entire time we've been here. Hell, I've been saving her ass and helping her any chance I've had." I glance around to be sure we're still alone, then drop my voice to a whisper. "And I've liked it, Ezra. I've liked caring for her and pleasing—"

He holds up a hand. "I'm good on that score, old chap. Let's keep it to must-knows."

"I care about her. That's all I'm saying."

He puts his arm around my shoulder. "And that's the only answer you need provide. The rest will come with time. It might take some longer than others to wrap their minds around it, and acceptance might be hard won for Kindra, but it will come."

"Well, now that you know, can you try to keep Kindra out of the way?"

Ezra smiles at me. "Not a chance."

"Oh, come the fuck on. How soon you forget the part I played in your little *romance*."

"Yes, but I'll be sent to the doghouse when Kindra discovers I knew and didn't tell her. If I don't want to live there permanently, I must meddle in your affairs as little as possible. As a man in love, surely you understand."

I kick off the wall and go to the weapon table. "Who said anything about being in love? We're just fucking."

"And just *whom* is Bennett fucking?" Kindra says as she enters the shed. "Let me know so I can book her a stay at the nearest CDC."

Feminine giggles reach my ears, and I turn to see Cat and Eve behind Kindra. Cat's wide grin doesn't reach her eyes, and the laugh is fake as fuck.

So why does it poke a soft spot in my heart?

"No, seriously, who is fucking Bennett?" Cat asks as she stands behind her friend. "I want to know too." Her eyes narrow and the muscles in her jaw jump as she grits her teeth and glares at me.

Ezra better make room in that doghouse.

I look at Cat. "She's beautiful, intelligent, witty, and no woman can come close to her in bed. I'm not in love with her, but it's probably the closest I've come. The closest I'll ever come. She saw a man alone on an island, and she didn't pass him by. She joined him." I move my gaze to the other three in turn. "When she's ready to meet all of you, she will, and I only ask that you keep your shit-ass comments to yourselves. If you want to make fun of me, go for it, but leave her out of it. Are we clear?"

Cat's jaw relaxes. Ezra nods, and Eve and Kindra exchange glances.

"Now . . . is that enough for everyone, or do I need to draw you a fucking picture?" I turn back to the weapon table and grab the blow gun and some darts. "Let's get this show on the road."

With my tools in hand, I push past the group of stunned and silent onlookers and step outside. A blast of icy wind snakes into my hood, and I tighten it around my face.

The sleigh pulls into the clearing moments later. The dark horses come to a stop, then hang their heads and doze as Jim, Ice Pick, and Maverick climb down from the carriage. Jim and Ice Pick meander toward the armory, but I pull Maverick aside before he can follow them. Once we're far enough from the shed, tucked into a little copse of trees, I come to a stop. Gripping his yellow coat, I turn him to face me.

"Ezra knows," I say, keeping my voice low.

Maverick pulls off his gaudy Pit Vipers and gawks at me. "Me, Grim, Rose, and now *Ezra?* The secret will be out to everyone by the end of the hunt!"

"Keep it down." I glance around, but most everyone is inside the armory now. Only a few no-names mill around outside. "That's why I need your help. Me, you, and Cat are going to hunt as a team."

His face falls. "I kind of wanted to hunt solo." He looks at me and registers the rage in my eyes. "But this is fine too."

"Look, I know it's a pain in the ass, but it'll be you eventually. One day, you'll be the one to beg one of us to join some fucked-up scheme so you can win over some fucked-up chick. Right now, it's my turn, but when you're up, I'll have your back. Deal?"

"Somehow, that's doubtful," he mutters. "What do I have to do?"

I smile and clap my hand on his back. "Light work. When others are around, you play the part of Cat's doting boyfriend. Once we're alone, you play lookout while Cat and I hunt."

"Aw, fuck, I don't want to babysit."

"It's not babysitting."

"But what about the hunt?"

I tip my head back and groan. "Dude, just focus on the task at hand and we'll kill some shit along the way, okay? We'll run the same setup we had on the island. You dart them, and Cat will finish them off."

"Can we take turns?"

My fists clench, and I struggle to keep myself from punching him until he stops speaking. "Sure. We can take turns."

Cat emerges from the armory and looks around. Whatever she's hunting for, she doesn't see it, but then her eyes land on me. The smile is immediate.

She waves and hurries toward us, hitching her pants every few steps. It was sweet of Kindra to loan her a pair of pants, but they don't fit very well. She'll need a belt if she wants to tromp through the Alaskan brush.

I turn to Maverick. "Are you wearing a belt?"

He nods.

"Give it to me."

"What?"

"You heard me. Hurry up." I motion for him to move, and surprisingly, he does. He's just lowered his snow pants to his knees when Cat reaches us.

"I don't think he needs to strip upon seeing me to make people think we're together," she says, eyeing him up and down. She looks at me, and her smile softens. "Thanks for what you said, by the way. I forgive you for telling your fucking brother."

A bit of snow falls onto her lashes and clings there. I want to step forward and brush it away, but Kindra and Eve emerge from the armory and stay my hand.

Maverick pushes the belt against my palm, and I pass it to Cat.

"What's this for?" she asks. "I was gonna use the crossbow. I mean, I guess I could use the belt if you guys are going to—"

"For your pants, moron," I say.

Hurt blossoms in her eyes. "Excuse the fuck out of me."

I clear my throat and look past her, and she turns around and realizes why I was being a dick.

"I guess the truce is off?" Eve asks. She turns to Cat. "Do we need to remove him by force?"

Cat shakes her head and cinches the belt around her hips. "No, this is just our way, I think. The truce is just for kills. I won't get in his way, and he won't get in mine. We still plan to give each other shit, though. That will never change."

The mischievous glint in her eyes nearly gets me hard.

"We just came to check in a final time before the hunt," Kindra says. "Cat, are you sure this is what you want?"

Cat looks at me. "I'm positive."

Kindra sighs. "Okay, bitch. But no matter what, I'm here if you need me. You just say the word, and we'll charge in and run him off."

Maverick steps closer to Cat and puts his arm around her. I understand why he's doing it, and the rational part of my brain is grateful. But the rational part of my brain is also small and malformed. The irrational side is large, volatile, and incredibly pissed off at this sight, despite demanding it of Maverick.

"You ladies have nothing to fear as long as I'm around," he says. "I'll protect her body"—he looks down at her—"and her heart."

"Gross, but good for you," Kindra says with a grimace. She takes Cat's hand in hers and gives it a squeeze. "Good luck out there today. Make me proud."

"Thanks, Mom." Cat rolls her eyes, then pulls Kindra in for a hug.

I wish Kindra and Eve would move the fuck along so that Maverick can remove himself from Cat's personal space. His arm is practically super-glued to her shoulder, and if his fingertips dip much lower, they'll need dental records to identify his body.

Kindra and Cat part, and Cat gives the two women a little wave as they start toward Jim and Ezra, who stand just outside the armory. Ezra hands a hatchet to Kindra as she approaches, and she passes the weight between her hands, testing the heft. The little group begins to talk, but I can't hear what they say. They're too far away.

I look at Cat. "Here's how today is going to work," I begin, but she holds up a pink glove and shakes her head.

"I don't need any help. You two can kill who you want, and I'll kill who I want."

"Sounds good to me," Maverick says, and I swat his arm.

"No, that *doesn't* sound good. When I—" I stop and clear my throat. "When *you* took her out to the range, those targets were static. She's a good shot, but now she has to aim at a moving target that's weaving through trees and trying to escape." I point to the dart gun lying on the ground. "You and I will swap back and forth between tranqing and hunting. Cat is strictly hunting. If you don't like it, take it up with the manager. Now go find a weapon and meet us here when you're done."

"Shouldn't Cat come with me?" he asks. "You know, for believability."

I grab Cat's arm and pull her closer to me. "No. She can stay right here."

Cat glances at the growing group milling around outside the armory, then snatches her arm from my hand. "He might be right, Bennett. We've raised enough suspicion for one day. Four people know, and that's four too many."

"Suit yourself," I say with a shrug, "but if you go into that armory with Maverick, I might just have to make the number, oh, six? Seven?"

"Are you blackmailing me?"

Maverick holds up a finger. "Well, it wouldn't be extortion because he's not—"

"Shut up, Maverick!" Cat and I say in unison.

He raises his hands and takes a step back. "You two have fun. I'm gonna go do my own thing."

"Wait, no, we're sorry!" Cat says as she races after him. "Bennett, look what you did!"

She follows him into the armory, whispering pleas the entire way. I stay in the trees for as long as I can stand it before I finally trail after them. I'm almost to the doorway when Eve steps into my path.

"Where do you think you're going?" She raises one of her perfect eyebrows and looks me up and down. "Can't you let them have a single moment to themselves? What is your fucking damage, Benson?"

I run my tongue over my teeth and crack my neck to release the tension building there. "I don't know how you think it's any of your business. You've known her for what, four days? I've known her for months. If I want to glue myself to her fucking asshole and create the next iteration of the human centipede, I fucking will, and there is nothing you or your new little pal can do about it."

She smirks down at me. "We'll see about that."

Having heard our voices, Cat hurries out of the building to break up the brewing argument. I only begin to relax when I see that Maverick isn't following her.

Eve works fast—much faster than I can—and slides her arm through Cat's. "Do you mind if I join the three of you on the hunt? I figure maybe Kindra and Ezra could do with a little alone time."

Cat's blue eyes jump to mine. I mentally plead with her to say no, to come up with any excuse she can pull out of her brain, no matter how ridiculous. I will go along with whatever story she concocts as long as it ensures our privacy.

If I have to watch Maverick paw at her all day, I will implode.

Cat licks her lips, clears her throat, and smiles sweetly at Eve. "I don't see why not. Welcome aboard."

Fuck.

Chapter Forty-Three

Cat

Bennett and I linger behind Eve and Maverick as we wander through thick brush and mounds of snow that reach our knees in some places. It's still early enough in the day, so the sun does its best to break through the cloud cover and shine on us. The temperature is still miserably cold, though. At least the view makes it worth it.

I look over at Bennett. He makes the shitty parts of this trip worth it, too. Even if he's pissed right now.

He's annoyed that I let Eve come along with us. I can tell by the way he keeps his hands in his pockets and his eyes on anything but me. It wasn't as if I had a choice, and I did the best I could to smooth things over. When we started out, I told Eve I needed to speak with Bennett about our truce—privately. That's how we managed to get at least a few feet between us and them.

Bennett slows a bit more, so I match his pace. Maverick and Eve don't seem to notice, not even when he clears his throat and leans closer to me.

"When we get back to the mansion, I'm punishing you," he whispers. "I will tie you to the bed and whip you with that belt around your waist until you beg me to stop."

"What if I like it?" I bump against him with my shoulder.

He stops, glances at Eve and Maverick, then grips my arm and yanks me into the trees. Our boots crunch on snow and fallen branches as we stumble deeper into the woods.

"Bennett, they'll notice we're gone," I say, but he doesn't slow down. "Hey, stop!"

He finally does, but not because I told him to. His hands rise as he looks past me. When I turn, I see Eve, with a slender blade pointed right at his head.

"Let her go," Eve says. She steps a little closer and to the side, lining up a shot at him. "Everyone else might be afraid of you, but the only person I fear is my mother. Now, release her arm or I'll send this blade straight through one of your baby blues."

With a grunt, Bennett drops my arm and pushes me behind him. Maverick races up to us from the path. He nearly plows into a tree when his gaze falls on the blade in Eve's hand, which is still aimed for Bennett's head.

"Whoa!" Maverick shouts. "We have plenty of targets in the forest. No need to turn on each other."

"Tell that to your fucking friend." Eve lowers the blade, sliding it into a tool belt hidden beneath her coat. "When a woman says stop, she means stop. That isn't up for interpretation."

Bennett smirks, then folds his arms over his chest. "Oh, do we have a feminist in our midst?"

"No, *asshole*. Consent isn't feminist property. It's common human decency. No wonder you can't grasp the concept." Eve holds her hand toward me. "Come on, Cat. You can walk with me."

I open my mouth to respond, but Bennett cuts me off.

"Maybe she doesn't want to come with you. Ever thought about that? Ever thought about asking what *she* wants?" He rolls his eyes and scoffs. "Maybe you're the one who needs a lesson on consent."

She ignores him, looking past his head to stare straight into my soul. "Let's go, Cat."

I lick my lips and blink. My legs won't move, and I don't know what to do anymore. "I—"

"Eve, let's go back to the trail," Maverick says. "These two get into it all the time. It's their normal."

"But it's not normal!" Eve turns her fury toward Maverick. "Are you seriously pursuing this girl? It sure doesn't seem like it if you can't protect her."

Maverick's green eyes widen. "I can protect her!"

"Then why am I the one who keeps running in to save the fucking day?" Eve shouts. "It seems like every hour that passes, fewer people are doing what we agreed to do to keep her safe. At this point, it's just me and Kindra!"

"Yeah, I heard about your little meetings," Bennett says. "Nice try."

Eve launches toward Bennett with a banshee-like scream, but Maverick wraps his hands around her waist and holds her in place. To her credit, Bennett takes a step back, and I've never seen a threat produce that reaction from him.

"You've got to tell her, Cat," Maverick pleads as he tries to keep his grip on the twisting tornado in his arms.

Eve jerks in his hold and looks back at him. "Tell me what?"

Bennett looks back at me, his eyes asking the questions his mouth can't.

What do you want me to do? What do you need? How can I fix this? And the reality is . . . he can't. No one can fix this.

No one except me.

"I'm fucking Bennett," I say, my voice so low that not even Bennett hears me.

Eve continues struggling against Maverick, and now his full attention is on her. She drives backward with her foot and catches him in the shin, and he goes down. He keeps his grip on her, but when she lands a shot to his jaw, he's out cold.

"Holy shit," Bennett says through a laugh. "I've never seen Maverick get coldcocked like that. Ezra will never believe this shit."

But now Eve's focus has shifted, and she's coming right for Bennett. I don't even recognize her as she stalks toward him. Her usually brown eyes have gone black, the pupils devouring every ounce of her irises, and the firm set of her jaw looks so far removed from her femininity.

She's terrifying.

Even so, I step in front of Bennett. Everything that's happening right now is my fault. If I'd had the courage to be honest with everyone, Bennett wouldn't be the target of so many hate-filled glares, and he certainly wouldn't have this psychotic siren barreling toward him.

"Cat, honey, I need you to move," she says as she stands in front of me.

I shake my head. "I can't do that, Eve. You can't hurt him."

"Oh, I can, and I will. When I finish with him, he won't have the balls to fuck with you ever again. Literally."

"That would be terrible," I say, "because I enjoy it when

he fucks with me. And . . ." I take a deep breath. "And when he fucks me."

Eve pulls back her hood and shakes her head. "I'm sorry, I don't think I heard you right. You're *fucking* him? Willingly?"

She's too shocked to assault him now, so I take a risk and pull Bennett beside me. "Yes. We've been having sex since the night we were stranded in the cabin." Then, for good measure, I add, "Consensual sex."

Bennett raises his hand, and his fingers give her a little wave.

"Were you under duress?" she asks.

I shake my head.

"Play for pay?"

"No. I've been fucking him because . . . I want to. Because I like him."

Maverick groans on the ground, and only then do we remember that he's there.

"Shit." Eve hurries to his side, then glances up at me and mouths, *Does he know?*

"He was the first to find out," Bennett says. "That night when you hens were watching the surveillance cameras, you were watching me fuck her, not Maverick. He let me borrow his clothes so that no one would know."

Eve drops onto her ass. "I'm gonna need a minute to wrap my head around this." She looks up at me. "I thought you hated him. Hell, I thought *he* hated *you*."

"The hate was misplaced sexual tension," I say as I go to her side. I sit beside her and take her gloved hand in mine. "I'm sorry I lied to you, Eve, and I don't have a good reason for doing it. Despite how everyone views Bennett, he's not the scum of the earth. He's actually very—"

"Okay, that's enough," Bennett says. "I won't have you sullying my bad reputation with tales of my chivalry."

Eve looks at him, then back at me. "Willingly? Really?"

I smile at Bennett. "Yes, willingly."

"So when he was talking about the chick he's banging and how amazing she is, he was talking about you . . ." She shakes her head, and her braids brush against her coat. "What about Kindra? Does she know?"

"No, and she can't. Not yet." Bennett steps closer and helps Maverick to his feet. "Cat needs to tell her when it's right for her, and I don't want anyone to pressure her into it. Not even you."

"I feel like I'm in an alternate universe or something. He's actually being protective of you. Holy shit," Eve says.

Bennett whistles as he examines the bruise forming on Maverick's jaw, then turns to Eve. "You're damn right I'm protective of her, but if she's gonna have other people in her corner, I want you there. You've got an arm on you."

She gets to her feet and goes to Maverick. "Hey, sorry about that," she says. "You understand, though, right?"

"I understand," he says. "We all want what's best for the people we care for. But maybe don't go so hard when it's one of your own next time."

"Can you forgive me for hiding this?" I ask Eve as Bennett helps me to my feet. "I would have told you when I was ready. I just—"

"Honey, say no more." She pulls me into a hug and places a gentle kiss on my cheek. "If he makes you happy, then I'll keep my concerns to myself, but if he ever makes you cry, don't tell me unless you want his head on a platter by breakfast."

"Thanks, Eve," I say.

She shakes her head. "Still doesn't make sense that you

won't tell Kindra. She's nice enough to me, and I consider her a friend, but she only shares her warmth with a few people. I've seen it. And you're one of them. If you're worried about the jokes—"

"That's part of it, but that's not all of it," I say. "I just need some time."

"Suit yourself." Eve shrugs. "If you want it kept a secret, I'll keep it a secret."

I breathe a sigh of relief, but the feeling is short-lived when a red jumpsuit rushes through the trees in the distance. Bennett hoists the dart gun over his shoulder and looks back at me.

"You ready for your first hunt?" he asks.

I look into the distance, at the retreating figure who doesn't know we're on his trail, and I nod. "Let's do it."

Before we can start off, Eve grips my sleeve and turns me to face her. "Do you want to do this just the two of you?" she asks. "Maverick and I can run interference if needed."

I shake my head. "I want all of you there. I'll need the support."

"Then you'll have it," Maverick says. "Let's go catch this son of a bitch."

As a group, we turn toward the forest and head deeper.

Chapter Forty-Four

Bennett

The tracks were easy enough to follow . . . at first. Somewhere along the way, our prey realized we were tracking him, and he got a little smarter. His footprints eventually doubled back on themselves, and we lost him altogether. Now we're standing in the middle of the woods without a clue in sight.

Maverick recommended we head back, but Cat and Eve argued that we still have a few hours of daylight left. He argued that it was lunchtime and he was hungry. In the end, the girls won.

"Maybe we should backtrack and look at the treetops," Cat suggests. "He might have gone to higher ground. That's what I would do if someone were hunting me."

"I don't think we'll need to backtrack," Eve says as she looks up.

We follow her gaze, and there, ten feet above our heads and roughly the same distance to our left, our target clings to a thin pine trunk and stares at us. His mouth opens, and he yells something, but we can't understand him.

Four sets of boots cut a path through the snow as we race to the bottom of that tree. The Cattle tries to climb higher, but he's losing his battle with gravity and physics.

I pull the dart gun from my shoulder, then ready a tranq dart. "He might die from the fall," I say to the group. "Are we in agreement that if that happens, it's not a fucking kill-block?"

"Yes, Bennett," Eve says. "Now that I know what's up, a lot of strange things make sense. Like that day in the rec room. You were covering for her, weren't you?"

I don't respond. I just steady my hand as I aim at the quivering red buttocks now twenty feet above me.

Fwoop!

The dart flies out of the chamber, the red-feathered end fluttering in the breeze until the needle finds its mark. The Cattle reaches back with one hand and pulls the dart from his ass cheek, but the damage is already done. The tranquilizer entered his body at the moment of impact, and now we just have to wait.

We lower our weapons and take a seat at the bases of some of the nearby pines, making sure to leave enough space for the asshole to fall without crushing any of us. The man doesn't look terribly big, but any amount of weight could be painful when it falls from that height.

"Wait a minute," Eve says. "If Cat's weapon is a crossbow, why doesn't she just shoot him now? She doesn't need close combat."

"Cat is a special killer," I say. "She needs a little foreplay before she can commit the act."

"Are you two *sure* you don't want us to give you some privacy?" Maverick shifts uneasily.

"Not that kind of foreplay," Cat says. "I just need to know what they did. I have to get mad."

Eve peers skyward. "The color of his jumpsuit isn't enough?"

"No, I think I get it," I say. "We hear about their crimes so often that the blanket terms used to describe them don't carry the same weight. We're desensitized. Sexual assault is awful, but the term doesn't make you feel awful enough. Hearing about the crime, however? The victim's name? It makes it—"

A red blur barrels from the sky, heading toward the snowy earth and silencing my voice. The man doesn't even scream as he collides with the ground, but Cat, Eve, and Maverick do. Cat nearly leaps into my lap.

The figure on the ground coughs, then tries to roll to his side. His eyes nearly bulge from his head as realization dawns on him. "My legs! My legs! I can't feel anything below my chest!"

He's bent in half at the waist, and his feet rest near his head. It's probably good that he can't feel his legs. The unnatural angles they're twisted into can't feel great. Not even the heavy tranquilizers can cut through his panic.

"Tell us about your crimes, jackass," I say as I step near him. "What did you do?"

He licks his lips, covering them in blood. One side of his tongue is missing, likely bitten off on impact. "She asked for it, man. She wanted it. The bitch let me buy her five drinks, and she was hanging all over me. I didn't do anything wrong!"

Cat nudges me out of the way and steps closer. She squats down and looks into his face. "You're dying. If we leave you here, you'll suffer for hours, but you *will* die. I'm giving you a chance to confess your sins and receive a more merciful end."

"Confess . . . confess my sins? What the fuck are you? The Grim Reaper?" The man pushes his arms out to his sides to gain traction to pull away. That's when he discovers his mangled legs. "Oh, fuck! I'm dying. I'm going to die. I'm going to die. I'm going—"

I pull back my leg and send the steel toe of my boot into his jaw. His head rocks to the side, and he shuts up.

"You killed him," Eve says, but then the man groans again.

Cat turns his face toward hers, but his unfocused eyes are concerning. I didn't push him through death's doorway, but I brought him right to the threshold.

"He hurt women, kitten," I say. "Look at his neck. He has tattoos of flowers with very few petals. There's a meaning there, I'm sure."

"The bitches who accused me of rape," the man gargles through a mouthful of blood. He drops his head to the side and spits, but his words are still slurred. "They wanted it. All three of them. The first two juries got it right. They let me go."

"Cat, you have about three seconds before I take the kill myself," Eve grits out behind us.

Unfazed by Eve's warning, Cat grips the man's collar and stares into his unseeing eyes. "What were their names?"

"What does it matter? They aren't the victims. I am!" He spits into Cat's face, and I've had all I can stand.

I nudge Cat out of the way and grip the man's right arm. Maverick has the same idea, because he grabs the man's left arm, and together, we hoist him into what would have been a standing position if his legs didn't dangle below him as they do.

"Kitten, load that crossbow and nail him to the tree by his wrists."

Cat sets to work on her task, then sends a bolt straight through his lower wrist. He yowls and tries to jerk his arm free, which only intensifies the pain.

"Other side too," I tell her.

"No, no more!" the man squeals.

It's music to my fucking ears.

Maverick holds his wriggling arm in place as Cat fires another bolt and pins him to the tree. We all take a step back to admire our pseudo-crucifixion, and as the man screams and throws his head from side to side, two black birds join us. I don't know if they're ravens or crows, but either way, they're harbingers of death.

The bolder of the two birds hops closer, then flutters upward to perch on the man's head. It cocks its head and peers down at the blood around the man's mouth before lowering his beak and pecking his upper lip.

"Ow! Fuck!" the man screams, and the four of us laugh.

"Go on, little bird friend," Cat says to the more timid of the two. "We won't let the big asshole harm you. Get yourself a strip of flesh."

Eve chuckles. "You're like a Disney princess, only darker."

The little bird hops forward, then joins its friend. It clings to the red jumpsuit and pecks at the blood dribbling down the man's neck. After a few well-placed jabs, the bird tears off a bit of meat and tips back its head to swallow the chunk. All the while, the man keeps screaming.

"I think our work here is done," Cat says. "Let's allow the birds to finish him off. It's cold, and they're hungry."

I wrap my arm around her waist and pull her against my side. "If that's what you want, then that's what we'll do."

Maverick and Eve agree, and we set off again.

The four of us hunt until dark. Cat surprises all of us when she tags a woman in a pink jumpsuit, proving me wrong about her inability to hit a moving target weaving through trees. Eve finished her off with a blade. Maverick and I don't end up with a kill, but that's okay. We've had more than the girls probably ever will, considering we're contract killers.

Well, I *was* a contract killer. I don't know what I'll do when we get back from the trip.

"What's bugging you?" Cat whispers as we make our way back to the starting area. Maverick and Eve walk a few feet ahead of us, arguing over who gets to hold the compass.

I don't really want to talk to Cat about my employment woes. A man without a job isn't exactly sexy. I also don't want to give anyone ammo. Who could encourage their friend to date a man who can't even keep a roof over his sickly mother's head?

So I smile down at Cat and shake my head. "Nothing at all, kitten. I'm just thinking about the masquerade tonight."

"Oh, shit!" Eve says, and she and Maverick stop walking so that we can catch up. "I completely forgot that was tonight. How will you two manage this . . . whatever this is?"

"I have no idea," Cat says. She hooks her arm within Eve's, and Maverick matches my stride as we all keep walking. "I hadn't really thought about it. Maverick's almost a foot taller than Bennett, so there's no chance he can pull off a switcheroo with everyone that close."

"Kindra has something planned for tonight, too, but she won't tell me what," Eve says.

"Yeah, she mentioned something to me," Maverick adds. "She wanted to make sure Cat and I matched."

"Ow!" Cat snatches her hand from mine, and only then do I realize I was squeezing it.

"Sorry," I say as I take her hand in mine again. "I didn't mean to hurt you. It's just hard to stomach . . ."

Eve glances at me. "Wow, you really do have it bad."

Yeah, I do.

"Maybe we could break up," Cat says. "At the ball, I can dump Maverick and say we're better as friends. Then I can go to my room and hang out with Bennett."

"And miss the entire ball?" Eve asks.

"Yeah," Cat and I say in unison. After all the murder, we clearly have the same thing on our minds: a hot shower and hot sex.

"Not to be that guy," Maverick says, "but Kindra and Ezra put a lot of work into the ball. I think you guys should at least attend."

"I hate to admit it, but he's right. Ezra won't give a shit either way, but Kindra would want you there." I brush the hair away from her eyes so that she can see how serious I am. "I'll keep it together for you, and if seeing you and Maverick together gets to be too much, I'll head back to your room and hang out with your stupid cat until you're finished at the ball."

"Maybe it won't come to that," Eve says. "We mainly just need to keep Kindra occupied. I can handle that, and I'm sure Ezra—"

I shake my head. "Ezra wants no part in any scheming, and if you knew Kindra a little better, you wouldn't either."

"It wouldn't be the first time someone has been pissed at me." Eve shrugs. "But I don't think Kindra will react how everyone anticipates. Maverick, are you in?" She faces him.

"I'm flying straight to Texas from here, so it won't matter if Kindra is pissed at me," Maverick says.

"And Rosie will help too," Cat adds. "Grim does whatever she commands, so that puts two more people on our side."

When they all put it like that, maybe it is doable.

"Cat, I have an idea!" Eve says, but before she can explain, we enter the clearing at the start of the hunting grounds. She leans closer to Cat, whispers something in her ear, then runs over to Kindra and Ezra, who stand by the armory.

A smile spreads across Cat's face, and she looks up at me. "Pick me up at Eve's room an hour before the party. Don't be late."

Before I can ask any questions, she races off to greet her friend.

Chapter Forty-Five

Bennett

Standing outside Eve's door, I struggle to take a breath, and not just because of the black bowtie cinched around my throat. For the first time in my life, I have pre-date jitters.

I swipe my sweaty palms over my black suit pants, then glance in the mirror beside the door. My hair remains in place, thanks to the hairspray Ezra insisted I use. I turn back for the door and raise my fist to knock.

"Wait," Maverick whispers. "You're forgetting these."

He pushes a haphazard bouquet into my hands. We crafted it along the way, snatching random flowers from vases we passed on our way to Eve's room. I don't know that I would call it pretty, and it just smells like dying plant matter to me, but maybe Cat will appreciate the gesture.

With the wilting flowers clutched to my chest, I raise my hand again, then knock. Seconds later, the door swings open.

Eve stands before us in a dazzling silver gown that drags

the floor. Thin straps fall over her shoulders and crisscross her back as she turns to guide us into her room. "She's just applying the finishing touches in the bathroom," she says. "She'll be right out."

I crack my neck to relieve the tension ratcheting my spine into an unbending line. More sweat collects on my palms, and I pass the bouquet back to Maverick so that I can dry them once more.

"Oh my gosh, how sweet," Eve whispers. "This was your idea?"

I roll my eyes and take the bouquet from Maverick again. "Yes."

"Let me see that." She plucks the bundle from my hand and glides to the bedside table. After pulling out the top drawer, she digs around inside and lifts a few colored ribbons from the shadows. She places the flowers on the bed, then studies how the colors look against the blossoms.

"Pink is her favorite," I whisper.

Eve and Maverick slowly turn to look at me.

"What? She wears it all the time, so I noticed."

"You really *do* have it bad," Eve says with a smile as she pulls the pink ribbon from the group and fastens it around the stems. "I love that for Cat."

I grumble my thanks and snatch the flowers from her hand. That's when the bathroom door opens, and Cat steps into the room.

If anyone speaks, I don't hear it. I don't hear anything as Cat comes toward me in a pale-pink dress. The shimmering satin hugs her body. A slit runs up either side, revealing her gorgeous legs with every step she takes. Clear rhinestones glisten at her waist, catching the light and throwing a rainbow of blinding colors against the ceiling and floor.

"Goddamn," I whisper. "You have never looked more beautiful than you look right now."

I hold out my hand, and she slides her fingers across my palm. As I pull her into me, I don't care that we have an audience. Even if they throw my sweet words back at me later, I won't care. If I don't kiss this woman right here, right now, I'll implode. That's my greatest concern at the moment.

Leaning down, I press my lips to hers, reveling in the way she can't help but smile. My hands want to dive into her hair, but I keep them planted on her waist. There's no telling how much time she spent styling the curls to sit so perfectly on top of her head, and I don't want to ruin this moment.

I pull back and look into her eyes. "I don't know how I'll keep my hands off you, kitten."

"Hopefully, you won't have to," Eve says. "That's where we come in. Dinner starts at seven, and the ballroom opens at eight. We can't do shit about dinner, but the ball is a different story. If we all work in shifts, we can keep Kindra away from the topmost western corner, where you two can dance and fuck around in peace."

"What's in that corner?" I ask.

Cat giggles and looks up at me. "Let's just say that Eve and I did a little redecorating, with Kindra's permission, of course."

"Kindra's big surprise was crowning Cat and Maverick as king and queen of the ball. We talked her out of it, and I mentioned that it might be fun to set up a couple of private play areas for people who may need them. She loved the idea. That's where you guys will be, safely tucked away from everyone." Eve grins, clearly pleased with herself.

"What happens when Kindra wants to know where Cat is?" I ask.

Eve's smile drops. "You can't keep her in there the entire time, Bennett. Jesus Christ. She'll need to do a little mingling, but you two will have a place to go when you need to blow off steam."

This woman grossly underestimates just how much steam I have inside me.

"Where does that leave me?" Maverick asks.

"You can do whatever you want. If Kindra spots you without Cat, just say she went to the bathroom or had to run to her room for something." Eve flicks her hand through the air. "I don't know. Just think on your feet."

"Okay," he says, though I'm not convinced.

But it doesn't matter. None of it matters. I'm holding a goddamn goddess in my arms right now.

"So, are we ready to head to the dining hall?" I ask.

Eve holds up a finger. "Not quite yet. I had one more surprise in store, but we have to wait for the signal."

As if on cue, someone knocks on the door. Eve shuffles toward the sound, her long braids swishing behind her as she walks. Tiny gems sparkle on some of them, and one falls to the floor as she sticks her head through the gap between the door and the frame. She says something, then opens the door wide, revealing Grim and Rose on the other side.

"Everything is ready," Eve says with a broad smile. "Follow me."

A speaker crackles in the natatorium, and then Maverick's

voice comes through. "Can you—" Feedback squeals, and he lowers the microphone.

Eve balances on stiletto heels as she squats and fiddles with something beside the podium. When Maverick raises the mic once again, it doesn't make the horrible sound.

"Testing, testing." He pulls the mic away from his mouth, then clears his throat. "If everyone would turn their attention to the doors, I would like to announce our first couple. Everyone, put your hands together for Mister Bennett Carter and Miss Catarina Novak."

Grim, Rose, and Eve clap their hands and pop tiny confetti cannons as Cat and I walk through them. This is stupid, but when I look at Cat and see the smile on her face, I just smile back. If she's happy, I'm happy, even if I feel like an idiot.

"Now, everyone grab a partner for the first dance," Maverick says. He leans over and dims the lights as Eve hurries back to the sound system to start the song. Seconds later, a romantic melody drifts through the speakers.

Grim and Maudlin Rose cozy up together as Eve grabs Maverick and pulls him onto the thin strip of concrete between the pool and the wall. I place my hands on Cat's waist and hold her close, resting my cheek on top of her curls.

Cat doesn't know it, and I'll probably never tell her, but I don't dance. No matter the occasion, I prefer to stick to the punch bowl and keep pumping booze into everyone. But for Cat, I'll dance. Whenever she asks, the answer will be yes, because moving with her like this feels amazing.

As the song nears its end, Cat sniffles against my lapel. I reach between us and place my fingers under her chin. She tilts her head upward, and I see the tears in her eyes.

There's no need to ask why she's crying. I already know why.

She's crying because she feels bad that we have to keep this hidden. She's crying because her heart is too big, and she's worried that she's hurting me. But most of all, she's crying because we have some pretty amazing friends who went to a lot of trouble to give us a really special moment.

"This is enough for me," I say. "Not forever, but for right now, this is enough."

That makes her cry harder, and everyone is looking at us as the song ends. Maverick hurries to the light switch, and Eve comes toward us, her eyes trained on me.

"What did you do to her?" She blinks and shakes her head. "Sorry, old habits die hard. What I meant to say is, what's wrong with Cat?"

"I'm just . . ." She raises her head, and I bite my lip. She should have gone with the waterproof mascara. "I'm just so happy."

"Oh, honey, come here!" Eve pulls her against her chest, careful to keep the runaway mascara away from her expensive gown. She looks up at me. "Bennett, you take everyone down to the dining hall. I'm gonna get her cleaned up, and she and I will enter together."

I like this plan. It means I won't have to hear Cat's and Maverick's names announced like a couple.

With a nod, I motion for everyone to follow me. I just hope these are the only tears Cat sheds tonight.

Chapter Forty-Six

Cat

After Eve repaired my smeared makeup, we hurried to the dining room for dinner. Kindra saved us some seats beside her, right across from Maverick and Bennett. Eve did her best to complete a sneaky switch before sitting down, but Kindra was having none of it.

Dinner progressed without a hitch after that. We enjoyed light salads, followed by tasting trays of things I can't even pronounce. Now we just have to get through the main course and dessert before we're off to the ball.

"Bennett, stop trying to play footsie with me," Kindra says as she kicks him under the table.

I glare at him, knowing it was my foot he was searching for.

"Oh, all the flight plans have been settled," Ezra says. He's clearly trying to take some of the heat away from his brother, despite having told Bennett he would do no such thing. "The only catch was that two of us needed to sit in coach for the flight to New York, so I put Cat and Bennett there."

Kindra nearly chokes on a puff pastry. "Absolutely not." Crumbs fly from her mouth, and she grabs her wineglass to drown whatever remains in her throat. "I'll sit with Cat in coach, and you can sit with your brother. I'm not subjecting her to his torment for an entire flight."

"It's okay," I say, grateful that Ezra has done what little he can for us. The rest is up to me. "We had a truce for the hunt, and we learned how to tolerate each other, didn't we, Bennett?"

He smiles sweetly at Kindra. A little too sweetly. If he doesn't pull it back a bit, she'll see straight through him. "I can keep my rude comments to myself if she can do the same. Right, *kitten*?"

That taunting snark is back in the word, but it still travels straight to my pussy. I grip the sides of my armless chair. "Yep, I can keep my mouth shut."

But not my fucking legs. If she asks me to promise that, I won't be able to.

Kindra places the back of her hand to my forehead. "Are you feeling okay? Maybe we should have a doctor check you out before flying."

"Hey, I'm serious," I say. "We get along fine when we want to."

"Why would you want to?"

Before I'm forced to answer that question, the doors on the other side of the room fly open, and Chef Maurice enters. A silver trolley with a large cloche on top glides ahead of him. As he pulls the cart to a stop, he lifts the lid and reveals . . .

A massive turkey.

Not just any massive turkey, but *the* massive turkey. I

can tell because one of the legs has been affixed in place with a bit of butcher's twine.

I look at Bennett, but he's already looking at me, likely thinking the same thing. The turkey that he fucked, the turkey that has been inside my asshole, is about to be served to the entire group.

"I got dibs on that turkey leg right there," Bennett shouts as he stuffs his napkin into his dress shirt and points to the Frankensteined appendage.

"Suddenly, I am not very hungry," Grim grumbles from another table.

Rosie just shrugs and readies her plate.

With growing horror, I watch as Chef walks around the room, cutting off bits of turkey and laying the white meat on the outstretched plates. His servers shuffle behind him, dropping fluffy dollops of potatoes and skewers of grilled veggies beside the meat. People begin digging in, and I can only watch as I remember the things we've done to that carcass.

Chef reaches our table, and I tell myself that Bennett technically fucked the cantaloupe, not the turkey, as meat falls onto Kindra's plate. It's okay if I take this one to my grave, right?

Right?

And now it's too late, because she's chewing and swallowing.

Bennett feels no remorse at all, as is evidenced by the way he brings the turkey leg to his nose and sniffs it. "I dunno, Cat. It kind of smells like ass. What do you think?"

He holds the leg toward me, and I don't know whether to laugh or scream, so I just lean forward and sniff. "Maybe a little rubbery."

With a chuckle, he pulls the meat toward his mouth and

takes a bite. His eyes roll back in his head, and he smacks his lips.

A slight moan creeps up my throat, but I snatch up my wineglass and swallow that sucker before it ever sees the light of day. Still, the way he looks at me as he devours that turkey leg . . .

"Cat? Earth to fucking Cat?" Kindra nudges me out of my daydream. "What do you think of the turkey?"

"Oh, I haven't tried it yet."

"It's very *filling*," Bennett says. "Just open up and stuff yourself."

Kindra grimaces at him. "Don't be vulgar."

Meanwhile, I want him to keep going. Openly mentioning our inside sex jokes is such a turn on, especially when I know there's no way Kindra can make the connection. I mean, who just sits around and suspects their friend has shoved a turkey leg in their ass?

"Did you girls get your little sex cubicles set up?" Kindra directs the question toward me and Eve.

"Play area," I say, "and yes, we did. We even pulled down some fancy serving bowls and stuffed them with condoms."

"How very practical of you," Kindra says as she takes another bite of turkey. She lowers her voice and leans closer to me. "Are you sure you're okay with sitting beside Bennett for the entire flight? I can insist we take another if—"

I shake my head and place a hand on her thigh. "I appreciate the concern, but seriously, we're good. He's actually not that bad."

Kindra snatches her napkin from her lap, dabs her mouth, then grips my hand and rises. "We need to use the ladies' room. Please excuse us."

She pulls me out of my seat and drags me from the

dining room, and I'm useless to fight her off. She's in sensible flats, and I'm doing the best I can in heels. I stumble behind her and try to keep up.

We finally reach the massive bathroom, and she pushes me inside.

"He's actually not that bad?" she says. "*Not that bad?* Cat, listen to yourself. You're talking about the man who fucked a pineapple wedged inside a dresser drawer." She pauses to grit her teeth and shake her head. "Then he sucked it clean!"

Her words should disgust me, but now I'm just jealous of the pineapple. He hasn't sucked me clean.

Yet.

Kindra snaps her fingers in front of my face. "Are you listening to me?"

"Yes!" I swat her hand away. "So he has some weird sexual urges. So what?"

"He's mean. He views women as disposable objects. He isn't fit to lick the dirt from the bottom of your shoes, let alone lick your pussy. Do I really need to keep going?"

No, she doesn't, because her words are making me hate her, and I don't want that. I don't want to choose between the man I care for and my best friend.

"What if he's not any of those things?" I ask. "What if he's actually a nice guy?"

Kindra huffs and steps toward the sink, where she reaches into her clutch and pulls out a tube of lipstick. "If he's such a great guy, why haven't we seen any indication in the months we've known him?"

Because he's scared. Because vulnerability isn't easy for him. Because it's just not his way.

And none of the reasons will be enough for her.

I sigh. "I don't know, Kindra, but maybe he's not who

we think he is. I've seen a different side of him on this trip, and I—"

"No." She lowers the lipstick. "Absolutely not. Look, I get it. He's hot, muscular, tattooed—a total catch. But Bennett is like an apple. It might look shiny and delicious on the outside, but when you get to the core, it's rotten and infested with parasites."

I roll my eyes. "Bennett doesn't have worms."

"He might. You never know." She leans over the sink and applies a daring shade of burgundy that only she could pull off. "All I'm saying is that you need to steer clear of him. If he gets his filthy hooks into you, I'll never forgive myself."

Well, she'd best learn how, because his hooks—and his dick—have been buried deep inside me.

She slides the lipstick into her clutch and turns to face me again. "Is this because of me? Have you become friendly with the devil because I've been so busy with the retreat?"

Tears spring into her eyes, and I rush to comfort her before she fucks up her makeup.

"What? No! And stop with the waterworks." I snatch some tissue from the holder on the sink and dab her eyes. "I knew you wouldn't have time to babysit me on the retreat, and I still wanted to come. I've had an amazing time so far, much better than you even realize, and I've made other friends. I dare say Eve has weaseled her way into our inner circle."

Kindra smiles, sniffles, and takes the tissue from me. "That she has. But you're still my bestie, right?"

"Of course."

It's so unlike Kindra to display emotion this way, and it's all because she's so concerned with whatever has occurred between me and Bennett. I wanted to come clean to her tonight, but now . . . Now, I don't see how I can.

She'll never accept it.

"Christ, I don't know why I'm being so silly," she says. She dabs her eyes, checks her face in the mirror, then tosses the tissue into the wicker wastebasket. "It's not like you're fucking him or anything. No way would you be *that* stupid."

As she laughs, the sound drives tiny daggers into my heart.

"Well, we'd best get back to the dining room. It's almost time for the ball. Are you excited?"

I nod my head and force a small smile, but now I don't want to go to the dance at all. Locking myself in my room and crying into Shorty's fur as he growls at me sounds like a better time than sneaking around in front of her face.

As we near the stairs, I'm already preparing my excuse. I'll just say that my stomach hurts. Since Kindra has gut issues, she's less likely to argue. Yes, that will work, and it will spare her feelings.

But then Bennett rounds the corner, and I can only think of reasons to stay. This is where I want to be. With him.

"I was beginning to worry that you two had run off together," he says. "Or that you fell into the toilet. Lack of brain cells and all that."

I can see his words for what they are—playful teasing— but Kindra is blind to his banality. For her, this is an affront of the worst kind, a joke made with cruel intentions. A week ago, I was just like her.

My, how things have changed.

"I'm not surprised you found us," Kindra says. "Even if I look through Cat's hair and find a tracking device sewn to her fucking scalp, I won't be surprised. You're like a dog trained to find only one thing: Cat."

"Isn't that what a *dog* like me does? Chasing a cat is just in my nature." Bennett smirks, but the playful curve of his lips doesn't translate to the rest of his face, least of all his eyes.

"Well, you can sniff her out all you want at the ball, but you won't get anywhere near her," Kindra says, and I don't like the confidence behind her smile. "She'll be attached to my hip for the duration of the evening, and there isn't a damn thing you can do about it."

With that, Kindra turns on her heel and drags me toward the ballroom. I glance over my shoulder, searching for Bennett, but he's already gone.

I guess dessert is off the menu tonight.

And so is Bennett.

Chapter Forty-Seven

Bennett

The ball has been in full swing for an hour, and I haven't gotten within ten feet of Cat without Kindra running me off. She's taking her job as a professional cock-blocker very seriously. Whoever's paying her should give her a fucking raise.

Oh, that's right. She's doing this for free.

I grit my teeth and swirl the glass of amber liquid in my hand. Knowing she's in the room and that I can't touch her or talk to her is killing me. My skin is crawling. My clothes feel too tight.

To make matters so much worse, I've had to watch her dance with Maverick. Twice. Eve interrupted their moment and "stole" him away the second time, thank fuck. Probably because she saw the way I was gripping the second-floor banister as I watched from on high like some angry god.

Accurate, considering how much rage I have inside me right now.

There are a few murder stations scattered around, but

not even violence can calm the calamitous storm inside me. The only thing that can soothe me is just out of reach. If I could just hold Cat in my arms, smell her hair, kiss her lips, then I'd find inner peace once more.

Maverick approaches my dark corner of the room and takes a seat across from me in a navy chair covered in crushed velvet. He glances around, then leans forward, keeping his voice to a low growl that I can barely hear over the thump of a fast dance song.

"We're . . . so just . . ."

I shake my head and hold my hand to my ear.

"We're trying . . . just . . . patient!" he says, speaking a little louder this time.

Not wanting him to shout it again—and risk the wrath of Kindra—I nod my head and wave him off. I've gotten the gist of things. They're trying . . . something, and they want me to be patient.

Haven't I already been patient? Haven't I been sitting here or standing there, dying inside as Cat shines her light on everyone but me?

Eve appears on the dancefloor, her glistening gown anything but inconspicuous as she weaves through the crowd. I don't know how she's supposed to help me sneak around when she's shining like a fucking lighthouse.

When she reaches my little grove of misery, she sits next to me on the couch and leans in, placing her hand around my ear. "Go to the corner we talked about. As soon as you step inside, you'll have exactly thirty minutes. Set a timer on your watch, and don't overstay your welcome. Past thirty minutes, you're on your own. And take this." She slides something into my hand, and I look down.

It's Maverick's mask.

"Hang it on the door," she adds.

Realizing her plan—or part of it, at least—I nod my thanks and hurry to the cubicle in the western corner of the room. Before stepping inside, however, I look around for Cat. She's seated at a table beside Kindra. And there goes Eve, heading straight for them.

She catches my eye before stepping toward them. She plans to keep Kindra occupied while I tuck myself away from view. That has to be the scheme. The woman is a genius.

The moment Kindra's head turns toward Eve, I hang Maverick's mask from the cubicle door and slip inside.

When Cat and Eve said they were setting up little sex pens, they weren't kidding. In the center of the box is a deep couch, covered in the same crushed velvet as the chair on the opposite side of the room. My heart goes out to whoever has to clean our remnants from this fabric, because despite the big bowl of condoms on a small table, I plan to go in raw and make a mess.

The thought of making Cat squirt while surrounded by all of our friends does something to me. This feeling is vile, filthy, and demanding. I love it.

Muffled voices filter through the music, and I recognize one of them as Cat. Another is Eve, and the third sounds an awful lot like Kindra. I duck behind the couch as the door swings open.

"Eve, he isn't even in here," Kindra says. "I told you I saw him leave the fucking ballroom! This is probably some diabolical plot Bennett cooked up to hurt her feelings."

Her feet venture toward the couch. I see them as I peer through that thin strip of nothingness between the furniture's bottom and the floor. And they're getting a little too close for comfort. One more step—

"He probably went to the bathroom!" Eve's heels join Kindra's flats, and they move away from the couch together.

I breathe a sigh of relief.

"Let's just give Cat some privacy. If he hasn't shown up in a few minutes, we'll let her out of here." Eve's voice sounds further away. She must be pushing Kindra out of the cubicle. I'll have to remember to send her a Christmas card this year.

The door clicks shut, muting their voices and deadening the music a bit. I don't know what these little walls are made of, but they're surprisingly soundproof. It would make for a nice little portable torture chamber. You know, for killers on the go.

Cat's shimmering pink heels move closer to the couch, and the springs below the cushions squeak when she sits. Silently, I readjust my position so that I'm on my knees behind her.

I'm close enough that my breath disturbs the small hairs at the back of her neck. She raises her hand to pat them down as goosebumps race over her otherwise smooth skin. It's an instinctual reaction; her body knows the beast is close.

I raise my hand to her neck and allow my fingers to trail over her skin in a gentle, romantic gesture. In my head, I pictured her turning and seeing me, then smiling. Instead, she doesn't bother to turn and look for what has touched her. No. She goes straight to jumping three feet in the air and letting out a scream that could shatter glass.

As I try to stand to show her she has nothing to fear, my bowtie tangles in the ornate wooden carvings running along the top of the couch. I'm locked in place, unable to hide and save myself when the door flies open.

But as luck would have it, Kindra hasn't rushed in to save the day. It's . . . It's my brother.

"Ezra, oh thank god," Cat says as she rushes into his arms. "I came in here to wait for Be-Maverick, and—"

She turns, and that's when she finally sees me. I give her a sheepish wave.

"Oh, shit." She hurries to close the door behind Ezra. "Shit, shit, shit."

"Yeah, shit is about right," Ezra says. "Kindra wanted to come over here and make sure you were okay. I practically had to beat her away from the door as Eve tried to distract her. How many people are in on this now?"

Cat covers her face and groans.

"Damn near the entire retreat, at this point," I say. I motion toward my bowtie. "Little help?"

"She can help you." He points to Cat. "I'm off to forget I ever saw you in here. At this rate, I'll be divorced before I'm even married." With a shake of his head, he exits the booth.

Cat hurries over to begin the Rubik's cube that is my bowtie. After a few seconds, she groans and sits back. "You'll have to take it off. It'll be easier that way."

"We only have twenty-three minutes left. Maybe we should both strip and save ourselves the trouble."

"Why only twenty-three minutes?"

I raise my watch to my face. "Twenty-two now, and fuck if I know. Eve didn't exactly give me the rundown. She just said to start a timer for thirty minutes, then be out of here before it's up."

"She's come up with something, but what?" Her thumbnail goes into her mouth, and as she nibbles, I imagine pushing something else past her lips.

I grip the bowtie and pull at both sides until something

rips. Free of my chains, I stand and go to her. "What does it matter, kitten? For the next twenty minutes, you're mine."

Her worries melt away when my lips press against her neck. A soft moan slides out of her, and her hand moves toward my dick. She grips it through the dress pants.

"Did you already get started without me?" she asks.

The song fades, and each movement of my tongue sounds like a firework crackling in a silent sky. Why is it so fucking quiet?

"We had a special song request tonight," a voice says through the speakers, and I'm almost certain it's Ice Pick.

"No, not now," Cat whispers.

The song starts, and I know exactly what it is by the first note.

"This song goes out to Bennett, wherever he is," Ice Pick says. "From your friends Kindra, Ezra, and Cat."

As Ice Pick lowers the mic, Tom Jones' buttery vocals caress my brain as he reiterates how unusual this situation is not. It's such a good song that I'm not even mad at Kindra's little joke.

"I'm sorry, Bennett. She thought it would be funny," Cat says.

I pull down one of the slender straps holding her dress upright. Leaning down, I kiss her skin and revel in the bite of salt against my tongue. "No need to apologize. It is funny."

I lower the other strap and kiss her shoulder.

"Really?" she asks. "You aren't mad?"

"Not even a little bit."

I pull her closer, reach behind her to drag down the dainty zipper, then lower her dress to her hips. My mouth waters at the sight of her full breasts. She didn't bother with a bra, and her pale pink nipples beg for my mouth.

Unable to stop myself, I move her to the couch and get on my knees in front of her. She's delicious perfection, and I am *so* hungry. I raise her dress to her hips and kiss her inner thighs.

"Wait a second," Cat says. "You're always going down on me and making me come my brains out. Let me have a turn."

"Kitten, as much as I would love to feel your mouth on me, we don't have a lot of time."

"Bullshit. We don't have a lot of time right now, but when we get back home, you can eat me for every meal of the day for all I care. We'll have lots of time then."

I want to ask if she's serious, if I can live inside her for the rest of my life, but there will be time for talking later. Right now, I'm about to get my dick sucked.

Needing no further encouragement, I climb onto the couch and begin unfastening my pants. Cat swaps places with me, getting on her knees and taking my cock in her hands as soon as it's free.

She starts by stroking me to the beat of the song, which is pretty fucking fast-paced. I can only hope Tom Jones stops crooning before she puts her mouth on me. I won't last longer than the chorus at that speed.

But as the song gears up for its final thirty-second push, she lowers her mouth to my cock, and I grip the cushions for dear life. The woman is sucking the very soul from my body, and to top it off, she stays on beat. When her fingernails curve around the base of my cock and brush against the piercings running through my tightening balls, a pleasure-laced groan comes out of me like a growl.

The song ends, and another replaces it, but Cat keeps going. She matches the beat once more, and I'm thankful it's a slow R&B number. I was two eight-counts away from filling her throat.

With a final, long lick up my shaft, Cat looks at me. "How much time do we have left?"

I pull my watch around to my face and squint into the screen. "Seventeen minutes."

It's a lie. At this point, I'm just guessing about the time. When she was busy giving me the best sloppy toppy I've ever had, I must have bumped my watch. The timer stopped at eighteen minutes and some seconds, and I don't want to tell her. She'll probably panic for no reason and put an early end to our fun.

"Will I have time to put my dress on if we stop with five minutes to spare?" she asks.

"Better not risk it. Leave it on." I stand and raise her straps, covering her chest. As much as it pains me to do so, I'm simply trying to ensure she isn't placed in a compromising position if someone comes knocking.

Which they certainly will.

"Bend over the arm of the couch and raise your dress for me," I command.

"Wait," she says. "We've been doing what you want all this time, and now I have a fantasy I'd like to fulfill."

I glance at my watch. Another minute has passed.

"Tell me, but be quick," I say.

She smirks up at me with a devilish gleam in her eyes.

Chapter Forty-Eight

Cat

"The mask," I say. "I want you to wear it, and I'll wear mine."

"I don't have one," he says. "I thought it was fucking stupid, so I left it in the room. You have a mask kink?"

I grab my mask from the small table and fasten it over my head. Unlike the half-masks Kindra initially ordered, the homemade iterations cover our entire faces. She made a glittering black cat, just for me, and now I want to fuck Bennett while wearing it.

"Use Maverick's." I point to the door. "It's just on the other side. I saw it when I came in."

Bennett looks at his watch, then tiptoes to the door, which looks ridiculous. It's not like anyone could hear his footsteps over the music.

"You can walk, dumbass," I say. "They kind of expect that I'm in here with someone."

He rolls his eyes and opens the door just enough to

squeeze his arm through the crack. After flailing around for a few seconds, he pulls back and begins fastening the mask over his head. It covers his entire face, but the eye holes are so large that the tip of his eyebrow scar peeks through.

I hurry to the couch and get on my knees on the cushions. We don't have a lot of time, so I hike my dress and thank myself for deciding to go without underwear. One less thing to search for when we're finished.

Bennett comes behind me and squeezes my hips once before lowering his pants. I peer over my shoulder at that strange mask. It's supposed to be a lion, but it looks more like a tan gorilla having a bad hair day. The fantasy isn't about his mask, though.

It's about mine.

Bennett's fingers swipe through my pussy. Looking over my shoulder, I watch as he shoves them beneath the mask to taste me. His eyes close, and his head tips back.

"You always taste so incredible, kitten." He groans under his breath and sucks his fingers again. "Later tonight, I want to drink from the source."

Someone bumps against the cubicle, and the walls tilt before settling again. I brace for the moment of panic, for the door to fly open as everyone discovers my dirty secret.

Bennett leans over me, his hard dick pressing against my ass as he whispers, "Relax. It's just us, and we only have twelve minutes left."

I nod and grip the couch. He's right. We're safely hidden, and part of the thrill of our arrangement arises from the risk of discovery, and it certainly doesn't get much riskier than taking Bennett's dick in a room full of people. If I can just give myself to the moment and forget about my concerns, I might have the second-best orgasm of my life.

I fear the best will always belong to that damned turkey-leg butt plug.

Bennett doesn't seem bothered at all as he rubs my pleasure over his dick and prepares to enter me. He presses against my pussy, and I relax.

"Fuck, is there an angle you don't feel good from?" he asks. "Push against me when you're ready. But only when you're ready."

Ready for what?

But I don't have time to ask the question as he thrusts forward and fills me with his cock. With each slow pulse, he drags his thumb over my asshole, sending ripples of pleasure through my abdomen.

I don't know what he has planned, but I want to find out. I rock back against him, wincing as his piercing rakes against my insides.

"Ten minutes," he says. "Can you handle it for ten minutes?"

When I push back against him again, he has his answer.

Seconds later, I have mine.

His hands circle my waist, and I have never felt so small. He could twist his wrists and snap my spine if he wanted to. "Hold on tight, kitten."

In the next breath, he pulls me backward and slams my ass against his pelvis. Colors dance in front of my eyes as his dick pushes into my guts. Pleasure and pain spike in equal measure, and I don't have time to register either feeling before he forces me forward, then slams me onto his cock once more.

"Oh, fuck, I have wanted to use your body for so long. I've fantasized about holding you, just like this, and pumping you on my cock until I come."

"Fucking destroy me," I whimper, and where the fuck

did that come from? The mask is giving me more confidence than I bargained for.

I hear Bennett's smirk when he says, "With pleasure."

His hands move from my waist, and he taps my shoulders. Knowing what he wants, I push my arms behind me so that he can grab my wrists.

"God, you are so fucking obedient." He snatches my arms backward, raising my chest from the back of the couch. He says something else, but I can't hear him. His voice is lost to the music.

Opening my mouth, I cry out, unwilling to hold in that sound any longer. It hurts. With each thrust, he drives so deep that I don't think I can take it anymore. Each punishing rush of his hips is like being in a car crash. His raw power drives up my spine. It curls my toes and brings tears to my eyes. But at the tail end of every pulse of his hips is the promise of pleasure. It's there. I feel it.

"Brace yourself," he says before releasing one of my wrists, and I grip the back of the couch as he pulls out and motions for me to stand. "I want you to ride me. We have seven minutes, and I want you to come."

"But what about you?"

He shakes his head. "You've taken very good care of me on this trip. Tonight is about you. Use me. Fuck me like I fucked you."

As Bennett sits on the couch and looks up at me, I can't help but wonder if I'm the first woman to have this privilege. He isn't someone I consider very generous, but right now, he's offering himself to me, and I plan to make use of him.

I raise my skirt and straddle his waist. My hand goes between us and holds his cock steady as I hover above him.

"Six minutes. Make it count." He puts his hands on my

waist, but I grab them and place them on my chest as I sit on him. Gritting his teeth, he sucks air through the mask.

I lift my hips and push down again. My clit rubs against the fine hairs on his pelvis, and I grind against him, chasing that feeling. The piercing in the head of his cock rubs against my insides, coaxing my orgasm closer with every scoop of my hips.

For what may be the first time in my life, I don't think about what I look like. I don't worry about what the man beneath me will think. The mask guards me from reproach, and the confidence unlocks some hidden place inside me.

I grind on his lap, moving faster and faster as pleasure coils in my stomach. Bennett squeezes my breasts. I lean forward and grip the back of the couch for leverage so I can fuck him even faster. Even harder.

My orgasm is right there, and nothing will stop me now.

I close my eyes and lose myself as he pants against my chest. Sweat slides between my breasts, though I don't know whose. I don't even care. My thighs burn, my pussy aches, but nothing will stop me from enduring every second of this orgasm. Not even Bennett as he grips my hips and tries to stop me from moving.

"It's fine!" I shout. "Come inside me! Fucking fill me!"

But he isn't coming. In fact, I feel his dick deflating inside me, and it's kind of ruining my post-orgasm high. With his arms still wrapped around me, I finally realize what he's doing. He's trying to hide behind me.

That's when my entire world comes crashing down around me.

The music is off, the lights are no longer so dim, and the door to the cubicle hangs open. To make matters so much worse, filling the entire doorway is a flashy purple dress I helped pick out.

"Kindra!"

I fall off Bennett's lap, and he hurries to hide his dick. No wonder he went limp. I don't even have a dick, but if I did, it would be fucking flaccid too.

Looking back at Bennett, I remember the cover story. It might even work. Maybe I can get her out of here and convince her that it was Maverick beneath me. Bennett is sitting down, so the height difference isn't as noticeable, and the lights aren't at full strength, so yeah, this could work.

But that plan flies out the window when Maverick and Eve raise their hands in a terrified little wave over Kindra's shoulders. Their masks are off, which means . . . she knows I'm not with Maverick.

"Wait, I can explain," I say as I snatch off my mask and try to block her view. "I thought it was Maverick, but I must have pulled someone else in here by accident. Whoops! Silly me." I step forward, hoping she'll turn around and talk to me away from the scene of the crime, but she doesn't.

She takes a step forward and goes around me.

And as everyone watches, she bends down and rips off Bennett's mask.

The moment passes in slow motion. In a whisper of paper and glitter, the mask slides off his head and clatters on the marble floor. A river of sweat gathers along my back and makes a beeline for my ass crack. Bennett stares straight at me, holding my gaze like a man at the gallows.

I expect Kindra to scream. We all do, because as a group, we hold our breath. No one moves, not even Bennett, as Kindra stands over him, her chest heaving up and down. We can do nothing but witness the oncoming train wreck, and Bennett is lying directly on the tracks.

In a moment of desperation, I move to get between them, but Ezra is there to hold me back. Eve hurries to my other side, taking my arm and trying to pull me out of the cubicle. What is happening?

Then I see it so plainly. This isn't a train wreck. It's never been a train wreck. We have been heading for this moment from the beginning. It's a war, and Bennett is about to fall on his sword.

"It was all my idea," Bennett says with a smirk.

My stomach twists into a knot, and I can't breathe. He's so convincing in his lie that I would believe him if I didn't know the truth myself.

"I figured if I stole Maverick's mask, she'd think—"

Kindra pulls back her fist and punches him in the jaw. Bennett's head flies to the side, and the smirk is gone when he puts it right again.

What the fuck am I doing? Am I seriously willing to allow Kindra to think he essentially *raped* me? Bennett is capable of a lot of shit, but that isn't in his wheelhouse. It's not even in the same country as his wheelhouse.

And for what? So that she'll still like me?

I shake my head and take a centering breath. This has to stop, and I'm not talking about my relationship with Bennett or my friendship with Kindra. The lying has to stop. It's hurting too many people.

"Kindra, stop," I say.

Eve leans close to my ear. "Honey, what are you doing? This man is going to take the heat, so let him."

I shake my head and struggle out of their hold as Kindra rears back to let Bennett have it again, but before she can strike him, I dive between them. My gown rips as I land on my stomach in his lap, though I only hear it and can't see the damage. All I get is an eyeful of crushed velvet.

"Cat, what the fuck are you doing? Don't protect this piece of shit! Not after this!" Kindra wraps her arms around my waist and tries to haul me away, but I grip Bennett's thigh and hang on for dear life.

That's when I feel the draft and realize my splits have risen much higher.

I look back at Kindra. "Please don't do this."

"Let. Go. Of. Him." A forceful tug accompanies every word, and the dress slides away, leaving me naked.

"Everyone, turn around!" Kindra and Bennett shout.

Feet shuffle on the floor as the crowd obeys. I'm even tempted to turn around. They both sound so protective of me. So angry.

As the door to the cubicle squeaks shut, I hear Ezra commanding everyone to move away. I stand and hold the dress to my chest, covering what I can. I didn't plan to have this conversation while in the nude, but I guess I don't have a choice anymore.

I look at Kindra, then the couch. "You might want to sit down for this."

Chapter Forty-Nine

Cat

Kindra stopped me before I could explain anything. She couldn't even meet my eyes as she looked between me and Bennett and formed her own conclusions. After only a few seconds of uncomfortable silence, she stood, walked out of the cubicle, and left the ballroom.

The lights came on shortly after, and the music never returned. That brings us up to now, as Bennett and I sit on the couch in the small cubicle, staring at our hands.

He moves beside me, then drapes his suit jacket over my shoulders. I pull it snug and settle back with a sigh.

"This couldn't have gone any worse," I mutter.

Bennett takes my hand. "Why didn't you let me take the heat? I wanted to protect you."

I grit my teeth to fight back the tears, but I quickly give up and let them come. "I'm sick of being protected all the time. I'm tired of everyone believing I *need* the protection.

Maybe, for once in my life, I wanted to be the one to protect someone else."

"Kitten—"

"No, don't call me that." I push him away. "I don't want to be a kitten anymore. I want to be strong. Fearless. A tiger or a fucking bobcat or even a regular house cat, but not a kitten. I want to be proud of who I'm fucking instead of terrified to tell everyone! I want to be proud . . . of me."

Someone knocks on the cubicle, followed by Ezra saying, "Is now a bad time?"

"No, having your woman barge in and fuck up a wet dream was a bad time," Bennett mumbles.

"Come in," I say.

Ezra eases the door open, keeping his eyes on the shining floor as he speaks. "Kindra would like you to come to our room so that you two can talk."

I swipe the tears from under my eyes and nod, though he can't see me. "I'm on my way."

Ezra steps away, then leans through the doorway again. "Bennett, when Cat goes to speak to Kindra, I think it's best if you stay with me."

"No shit." Bennett rolls his eyes. "I'm not sure what we'd do without your guidance."

"Just trying to help."

The door closes.

"Yeah? Where was the help when she was charging toward the door like the fucking feds, Ezra?" Bennett shouts, but his brother doesn't respond.

"This isn't his fault." I stand and try to find some way to hold my dress together. The straps are no longer connected, and the material is in three pieces at this point. "It's not your fault, either. I'm the one who was too scared to own this."

Bennett stands and removes his belt. As he fastens the thick leather strap around my chest to hold up what's left of my dress, he looks into my eyes. "You aren't a kitten anymore, remember? Isn't that what you said?"

He pulls it tight, then smacks my ass.

"So go on, tiger." He pauses. "No, that sounds really gross. Like what I'd say to a kid or something. Maybe, go get 'em, you little lynx."

I scrunch up my nose.

"Okay, we'll figure it out, but I need to be serious for a second." He takes a deep breath, then kisses my cheek. "I don't really know what it's like to have a best friend, but I imagine it doesn't come along often. You know, having someone who cheers you on and just wants the best for you."

"What the fuck am I?" Ezra says from the other side of the door.

Bennett rolls his eyes and presses on. "If it comes down to it, if you have to choose between me or her . . . pick her. I'll probably find some way to fuck this up anyway."

I stand on my tiptoes and kiss him. "Bennett Carter, if she's any friend of mine, she won't make me choose."

"Then go tell her the truth." He places his forehead to mine. "I'll be waiting for you in my room when you're done."

"Can I bring Shorty for a spend-the-night party?"

"I'll be waiting for you in your room when you're done." He places a kiss on my nose and slips out of the booth.

I've been standing outside Kindra's door for a solid seven minutes, and I still can't bring myself to knock. After putting everyone through hell, it all came down to this moment that I've been desperately trying to avoid. There's nowhere left to hide, though, and it's time to do the scary thing.

My pulse beats in my cheeks as I raise my hand and knock.

"Come in," Kindra calls from inside, and I open the door.

She's seated on her bed, a brown brush in her hand as she combs through her curls. As I enter, she pulls her long, dark hair into a ponytail, then pats the mattress beside her. The gesture is familiar enough, but I'm not accustomed to seeing her eyes so puffy. Kindra isn't usually a crier.

"Ezra said you wanted to see me," I say. "I guess you have some questions."

Kindra pulls her legs up so that she's sitting tailor fashion, but she doesn't respond. She just looks at her nails and picks at the skin around her thumb.

I sit beside her and try to think of where to begin. But how can I do that when I don't even know where this started?

Kindra clears her throat. "The night . . . at the cabin . . ."

"It just happened."

"Did he force you?" Kindra finally looks at me, and her eyes are filled with tears. "If he did, I'll never . . . I'll kill him, Cat."

"Oh god, no!" I pull her against me, and she weeps on my shoulder. "Kindra, I know it's hard to believe, but everything that's happened between us has been completely consensual."

She sits back and plucks a wad of tissue from the

rumpled covers. After blowing her nose, she shakes her head. "It's not that hard to believe. Any woman with functional eyes can see he's attractive, but why did you feel you couldn't talk to me about this?" She blows her nose again. "You're my best friend, but I don't feel like I'm yours anymore."

"I didn't want to tell you because I knew you'd be disappointed in me. I've admired you for so long, and I couldn't bear the thought of you thinking less of me."

"Did you ever stop to think that I admire you too?"

My mouth opens and closes, but I don't know how to respond to that. I can only come up with questions. "Why would you admire me? The girl who can't do anything well. The girl who was bullied in school. The girl—"

"The girl who makes everyone smile, even when they don't want to. The girl who befriended the unwilling serial killer. The girl who is so beautiful and intelligent and too humble to see it for herself." Kindra shakes her head. "Cat, you are everything I'm not. There are parts of you that I admire to the point of jealousy. Who you choose to fuck has no bearing on any of that. I still admire you. I'm still your best friend."

"So you aren't upset that I'm sleeping with Bennett?"

She sighs and flops back on the bed. "I'm more upset that you didn't feel you could tell me."

"No offense, but you're kind of a judgmental bitch."

"Fair."

"But I wouldn't want you any other way, either." I lie on my side beside her. "Will we be okay?"

Kindra nods. "I still need some time to wrap my head around this, and Bennett is in for a fucking lecture, but yes, we'll be okay." She grabs my hand and gives it a squeeze. "If he hurts you, though . . ."

"The funny thing is, I don't think he will. The Bennett we know is the real Bennett, but there's another side to him. He can be kind, caring. Hell, he's even been vulnerable."

"Does he make you happy?"

I roll onto my back and look up at the ceiling. "Yeah, he does."

"Does this mean we have to stop picking on him?"

I bite my bottom lip and laugh. "Absolutely not."

Kindra laughs too, and the tension melts away.

"You know what this means, don't you?" Kindra says as she rolls to her side. "One day, we'll be sisters."

"Hang on. We're getting a little ahead of ourselves. I mean, we've only been fucking for a few days."

"That's a few days more than Bennett fucks anyone, so I'd say it's a done deal."

We both giggle at that.

"Thank you for being so understanding," I say.

"I'm not sure I completely understand, but I'm beginning to. Your insecurities run a lot deeper than I realized, yet you seem so confident on the surface. I'm sorry I didn't make you feel safe enough to talk to me." She winces. "All those jokes about Bennett probably didn't help."

Her words hurt my heart. All this time, I've been so concerned about what she'd think and never stopped to worry about what she'd feel.

"This wasn't a shortcoming on your part, Kindra. You're right. I have a lot of insecurities and anxieties that I keep buried, and that played a big part in the fear. Believe it or not, Bennett gives me confidence. He makes me feel stronger when he's behind me. I think that's why I was finally able to get a kill."

"Wait." Kindra sits up. "The night you got your first kill . . . Does Bennett know you fucked Maverick?"

I drape my arm over my eyes as a low groan rumbles out of my chest. "I have so much to catch you up on."

Kindra's bedroom door flies open, and we both jump. I hurry to tug Bennett's jacket over my chest as I sit up. Ezra steps into the room. His hair is a mess, and sweat covers his forehead. He's also out of breath.

"What's going on?" Kindra asks. "Is everyone okay?"

He nods and holds up a finger. "One . . . sec."

"Where's Bennett? Is he hurt?" I jump from the bed and race toward the door, but Ezra stops me.

Gripping my shoulders, he looks into my face and says, "He's gone."

Before he can say anything else, I push past him into the hallway and run for Bennett's room.

Chapter Fifty

Bennett

Warm air roars against my face in the back of the stretch limo as the long car slinks down a desolate road in the middle of Alaska. A green haze runs across the night sky, like some massive deity took a sequoia-sized brush and dragged luminescent paint across a navy canvas.

I wish Cat were here with me for so many reasons, but mostly so that I could see the sky through her eyes. The tears prevent me from seeing much of anything for myself right now.

Reaching into my coat pocket, I feel for the slip of paper. I need to remind myself why I'm leaving and why I couldn't ask Cat to come with me.

"You sure you've got a plane to catch?" the driver asks. "With that storm moving in, I don't think they're letting any private planes on the tarmac."

I don't answer him. I just look out the window and watch the trees flash by.

The jet will be there. Ezra arranged everything the moment he read the letter. He foolishly told the pilot he'd be rushing two passengers to the states to catch a ride to Florida, but I couldn't ask Cat to witness my weakest moment.

The plans I'd begun to formulate disintegrate and fall through my fingers.

My mother has taken a turn, though not in the way anyone expected. She experienced a mild stroke yesterday morning. Despite quick action on the part of her very expensive medical team, her symptoms only worsened, and a second stroke occurred. My mother isn't expected to recover. They don't even believe she'll wake up.

The letter says I'll be lucky to arrive before she expires.

Expires. What is she, a carton of fucking milk?

I crumple the paper and toss it to the floorboard as if I can make this someone else's problem. Maybe I can pretend this is anyone's life but mine.

The limo hits a patch of ice, and the car's tail wobbles to the left. I sit back as the driver regains control, but I buckle my seat belt. If we get in a wreck and I die, I won't have a chance to apologize to Cat for leaving without so much as a word her way. She has a heart of gold and won't hold any of this against me, but I still feel like an ass for taking off. But she's trying to work things out with her friend, and I didn't want to interrupt their important conversation.

I also didn't have time to wait around. For all I know, none of these worries even matter. Kindra is probably busy convincing her to end things with me, and Cat may not be someone I'm permitted to worry about much longer.

Even if that's the case, I'll still worry about her. I'll love her from a distance if I have to.

Love . . .

I lean forward, as far as the seat belt allows. "Hey, have you ever been in love?"

The driver looks at me in the rearview mirror, eyebrows raised to his hairline. "Love? Well, yeah. I'm married, ain't I?" He raises his left hand, revealing an aged gold band, scuffed with time.

"How did you know you loved her?"

The man shrugs. "Fuck, I dunno. She said she loved me. I said it back. We've been saying it for twenty years now."

"That doesn't tell me a fucking thing." I flop back.

"I don't know what you were expecting, buddy. I got no sage advice. You either love somebody or you don't." He shrugs again. "Why does it always gotta be some big production? You need fireworks? Explosions?"

He lets out a laugh that claws against my psyche.

But as I mull over his words, I'm forced to acknowledge how right he is. Maybe love isn't what romantics paint it to be. Maybe it's just a choice you make one day, and then you keep making that choice for every day after. Maybe it's really that simple.

And maybe I love Cat.

"Fuck." I slam my fist against the leather seat. "Turn the car around. I forgot something."

"Are you sure?"

"Yes."

"Because if you don't even know if you love the girl—"

"I'm sure. I love her. Now turn around or I'll slit your fucking throat!"

His eyes widen, his mouth closes, and he brings the limo to a stop before initiating a twenty-point turn.

If loving someone means choosing to love someone, then I choose to love her, but if I want that same love in return, I have to give her the choice. To love me, even when I'm not strong. To love me, even when I'm unemployed. To love me, even when I'm me.

And if I'm choosing to love her for the rest of my life, I want her to meet my mother at least once.

I check my watch. It's been over a half hour since Ezra slid that letter into my hand. Cat probably knows I've left by now, but she'll have to settle for an apology on the drive to the airport. We don't have time for anything else.

I lean forward once more to urge the driver to step on it. That's when a massive shadow steps onto the road, and everything goes dark.

Chapter Fifty-One

Cat

I clutch Kindra's waist as the snowmobile barrels down the side of the road. We chose this instead of the sleigh, figuring we could possibly catch them. The horses' hooves aren't meant for icy roads, but snowmobiles thrive on the snowy conditions. We don't drive on the road, though. Kindra sticks to the shoulder, where the snow is thick enough to support the vehicle's weight.

Twenty minutes into our speedrun, she slows the snowmobile as lights brighten the road ahead of us. I'm shocked that we've caught up to them so quickly, but then I peer around her shoulder and spot a massive moose lying in the middle of the road.

And to our right, with its back half wedged in a snowbank, is the limo.

"Bennett!" I scream.

I leap from the back of the snowmobile and rush toward the accident. A crumpled mess of mangled metal releases tendrils of steam at the front of the limo. Brown fur clings to the point of impact. Stepping closer, I see the driver.

His head lolls at an unnatural angle. Well, half of it does. He's either missing a chunk of his forehead or it's been pushed to the back of his brain. Peering through the shattered glass, I search for any sign of Bennett, but I don't see him.

"Help me dig!" I shout to Kindra.

She hurries over, and like two psychotic hounds, we begin shoveling fistfuls of snow away from the back doors. When we finally have enough clearance, I wrench the door open and look inside.

Bennett slumps in his seat. A large knot protrudes from the right side of his head. He must have been knocked unconscious. At least, I hope he's just unconscious.

"What do we do?" I plead with Kindra. "We aren't supposed to move him, right? But what if he's cold? What if he needs CPR?"

"Check for a pulse!"

I tear off my glove and lean into the car, but when I put my fingers to his neck, I feel nothing. My fingers are numb from bone-deep cold. I cram them into my mouth and suck, willing warmth into the tips, but it's taking too long. Closing my eyes, I swirl my tongue around and around until—

"Me next," Bennett croaks.

My eyes fly open, and I practically throw myself on top of him. "Oh god, I thought you were dead. Where do you hurt? How many fingers am I holding up?"

Bennett smiles and rights himself with a quick shake of his head. "Calm down, Florence Nightingale. I'll be fine. I've taken worse hits than this, but check on the driver."

His fingertips go to the knot on his head, and he winces as he pulls his hand away. I'm surprised he isn't bleeding.

Boots crunch beside the open door. "He's gone, Bennett," Kindra says.

"Damn." Bennett swipes his hand down his face and unfastens his seat belt. "This is my fucking fault. I should have just asked you to come with me."

"Yeah, you should have," I say. "Instead, you decided you wanted to live on the island alone again."

"Who's going to the island?" Kindra asks. "I thought your mom was sick. Why are we going to the island?"

"No one," I say. "I'll explain later."

Bennett moves to get out of the car, and Kindra and I try to stop him. He just looks at us and swats our hands away. I ease out of his way.

He pulls himself out of the wreckage and stands on shaking legs. "I still need to get to my mom. Nothing has changed. I'm not getting checked out by a doctor or any dumb shit like that. We have to get to the airport."

"We?" I say, shocked that he's willing to take me with him. I figured I'd have to sneak onto the plane, that he'd be too stubborn to let me remain by his side.

He doesn't respond to me, though. He walks to the front of the limo and hangs his head. "Well, we aren't going in this. Fuck!" His boot jets out and collides with the flattened front tire.

Kindra winces, then takes a cautious step toward him. "If you guys can wait here, I'll go back to the mansion for help. I can't call a car, but Ezra can."

Bennett shakes his head. "I don't have that kind of time."

"Then take the snowmobile."

Bennett and I turn to face Kindra.

"I'm serious," she says. "Take the snowmobile. I'll walk back."

"You'll get frostbite," Bennett says. "I get that it would go with your frigid persona, but I doubt my brother will want to suck your toes if they turn black."

Instead of getting angry, Kindra's eyes soften. "Thanks for the concern, but my socks are double insulated, and the mansion isn't that far off. I'll be okay. And besides, this is mostly my fault, so I need to make it right."

"No, it was my fault." I step over part of the front bumper and stand beside Kindra. "I was the one who was too afraid to be honest."

"Because of me," Kindra says. "I made it hard, and I wasn't a good friend. Let me fix it!"

"Freezing to death isn't going to fix it!" I yell. "And there is nothing to fix!"

A snowmobile engine rumbles in the distance, and the three of us turn to see two headlights buzzing toward us. When they pull to a stop beside us, we're shocked to see Ezra, with Maverick and Grim on the second machine.

"What are you doing out here?" Kindra shouts. "I told you I could handle it!"

Ezra climbs off the snowmobile and tightens his hood around his head. "I just wanted to be sure you were okay. I was worried about you, and aren't you glad? You three would have been in a sorry state had we not shown up."

Bennett motions toward Grim and Maverick. "And what about those two? Were they worried too?"

"Backup," Maverick says with a thumbs-up.

Grim just glares at the woods.

"Shit, what happened to the limo?" Ezra asks.

"We hit something . . . big. I don't fucking know," Bennett says, "but the driver is dead, and I still need to get to that jet."

Kindra turns to the two men on the snowmobile. "You

two, get the driver's body back to the mansion so that Jim can figure out how to handle this part." She faces Ezra. "You and I will ride ahead and ensure a clear path to the airport."

"On snowmobiles?" Ezra asks. "You can't be serious. These things aren't meant to run on asphalt."

"That's why we'll run along the side of the road and clear any debris ahead of them." Kindra takes Ezra's hands in hers and looks up at him. "Your brother needs to see his mom, and we need to help them get to that plane."

"Everyone has done enough," I say. "Bennett and I can make it to the airport. It's not that far, right?"

Ezra looks at Kindra. "They might make it."

"No!" Kindra stomps her foot, which is code for an upcoming explosion if Ezra isn't careful with what he says next.

His shoulders drop. "Guys, you heard her. Do what the boss says. And if we aren't back in an hour, send the sleigh."

"That is all we will have left," Grim says with a dry laugh.

As everyone moves to their stations, Bennett and I head for the snowmobile. Grim and Maverick walk toward the car, and I turn away. I don't want to see that man's face again.

Kindra and Ezra climb onto their snowmobile, and she looks back at me. "We're going. Give us a ten-minute head start, and don't go too fast. If there's trouble anywhere ahead, we'll need time to clear it before you plow into us."

I nod at her, and Bennett and I walk toward our machine as they speed away into the night, their lone head-light disappearing over the next hill. Minutes later, Grim and Maverick head in the opposite direction as the driver's body bounces behind them, leaving a gory trail.

"I hate that for the poor guy," Bennett says with a shake

of his head as he looks at his feet. "If I hadn't told him to turn around . . ."

"You were coming back for me," I whisper.

Still looking at his feet, Bennett nods. "Yeah. I wanted you to meet my mom before . . ."

He blows out a breath to keep himself from crying, and I step closer. His arms wrap around me, and he pulls me against his chest and allows himself to break. It's only a slight crack in his armor, but he's made of tough material. A slight crack for Bennett is like a crevasse for anyone else. The tears falling against my coat are his humanity, leaking out, unprotected.

I wind my arms around his waist and hold him closer. As cold nibbles the tip of my nose, I wait for him to speak. Several silent minutes pass this way, with two lost people finding themselves on a cold Alaskan night.

"Look up, kitten," he whispers. "Please look up and tell me what you see."

So I do. I tip back my head and peer into the night sky.

"Oh my gosh," I breathe.

In my panic to reach Bennett, I'd gone blind to Alaska's beauty, not once looking up on the short drive to reach him. Now that I'm in his arms, however, my eyes can focus, and the magnificence running across the stars can't be described with words.

Bennett pulls me against him until I can scarcely draw my next breath. He clings to me like a man lost in a storm. "Tell me what you see."

I lick my lips and rest my head on his chest. I stare upward, but I'm not looking at the lights. I'm looking at him.

"It's magnificent. Literally breathtaking. It's something I never imagined I'd experience in my lifetime, and now, here it is."

Bennett smirks down at me, with tears still brimming in his eyes. "I meant the Northern Lights, not me, dumbass."

"That's what I meant too," I say, then stick out my tongue.

He kisses the tip of my nose. "Better be careful about making ugly faces like that. It'll stick that way."

My tongue slides back into my mouth.

"Damn, too late," he says through a hoarse laugh.

I swat his arm and laugh with him. The time for feigned outrage is finally over.

"Kiss me, Bennett," I say.

He looks down and brushes the hair from my forehead. The gesture is becoming so familiar to me now, and I sometimes find myself wishing my hair would fall over my eyes, just so that I can feel that gentle touch.

"With pleasure," he whispers.

His hand supports the back of my head as he leans down and places his lips on mine. In the dark, under the Aurora Borealis, we tangle ourselves in each other's arms and find a moment of peace. Worries slip away. Fear evaporates, carried off by the icy wind.

"I don't want to do this alone anymore," he whispers as he pulls back. "That's why I came back for you. I want you by my side, Cat. Will you stay on my island with me?"

"Yes, as long as I'm the only one with a standing invitation."

He smirks and raises his scarred eyebrow. "You're receiving the first and last invitation, kitten. I can promise you that."

"What about Shorty? Can he come?"

Bennett grumbles under his breath, and I swat his shoulder again. A little harder this time.

"Yes, the stupid feline can come." He leans down and

kisses me once more. With a contented sigh, he pulls away and grabs my hand, leading me toward the snowmobile. "I think we've given them enough time, and I don't know how long my mother has. Let's not waste another moment."

I squeeze his hand. "We've done enough of that, haven't we?"

Bennett straddles the seat, then holds my hand as I climb on behind him. I fish a spare pair of goggles from the saddlebag and hand them to him. They aren't as nice as his personal set, but neither of us brought any luggage along, so we have to make do with what's available.

He slides them on, raises his hood, and looks back at me. "What about you? Do you have goggles?"

"I don't need any. I'll keep my eyes shut."

"You trust me?"

I smile and hug him tighter. "I do."

Bennett starts the engine, and the snowmobile jerks forward. With a deep breath, I close my eyes and hold on tight.

Chapter Fifty-Two

Bennett

The elevator dings, and the doors open on the third floor. Cat and I step into a silent hallway lined with dim lights, our shoes clacking along the glistening tiles. Aside from our footsteps and the intermittent beeps and whooshes of hospital equipment, the hallway is quiet.

Oddly quiet. Despite this being the hospital floor, we haven't seen a single member of staff since stepping out of the elevator.

"It looked like a mansion from the outside, not a hospital," Cat whispers. "Is this where your mother has been all this time?"

I nod and motion for her to step through the double doors just ahead of us. "Only the best for my mom. If she has to deteriorate slowly, I want her to be comfortable while she does it."

As we pass doors, I check the numbers. The rooms are large and spread out, but there aren't very many of them. I guess not everyone can afford for their parents to waste away in the lap of luxury.

Fuck, I can't afford it either, and I don't know how I'll cover the expenses accrued from this particular setback. But I can think about that later. Right now, I just want to see my mother.

We reach the last door on the left, and I step forward to open it.

Despite the daylight outside the walls, the room is shrouded in darkness. A strip of light from the hallway reaches toward my mother's hospital bed, and my eyebrows pull together.

"Cat, open the door a little wider," I say.

She steps back and opens the door, and the strip of light widens to a rectangle. My mother's hospital bed is empty.

"I didn't expect you'd have company," a familiar voice says from the corner of the room.

I spin on my heels and search for the light switch while ensuring I'm standing between Cat and the man waiting in the dark. My fingers land on a raised knob, and I flick it upward, filling the room with a bright light.

Doctor Whitlow rises from his chair, covering his eyes and squinting at me and Cat. I don't know what I expected to be in his hand—a gun, maybe—but it wasn't a manila folder.

"Where's my mother?" I take a step toward him. Just one.

Doc holds the folder to his chest and taps it with his index finger. "Your mother is downstairs in her bed, though it won't be her bed for much longer. Unless you pay in advance, as we discussed—"

I cross the room in three strides, pull back my fist, and send it into Doc Whitlow's weak-ass jaw. Something cracks, and he stumbles and falls into a chair, looking up at me with fear in his eyes.

Good. He should be afraid.

"You lied about my mother's condition to get me here to talk about payment? Are you truly this fucking stupid? You know what I do for a living."

Doc has the audacity to raise his finger and say, "What you *did* for a living. You are currently unemployed, Mr. Carter." He points to Cat. "Does she know she's crawled into bed with a penniless killer who can't scrape up a contract to save his mother's life?"

I reach forward and grip that pointed finger, then twist until something snaps. The doctor lets out a scream that sends a dangerous signal to my brain. If he isn't careful with what he says next, he'll learn why they call me the Chaos Killer.

"Bennett, could we take your mother home?" Cat's hand lands on my arm, and like a tranquilizer for my soul, she quiets the beast inside me. "I can help you care for her. She doesn't have to stay here."

"Listen to the girl," the doctor says through gritted teeth. "Take your mother back to your roach-infested hovel and let someone who can actually pay take her place."

Shame punches me in the chest. I never wanted Cat to know how I live. When I'm in New York, I keep up appearances, but this is my reality. Everything the asshole says is the truth.

"Better to live with the roaches than people like you." Cat steps closer. "You should be ashamed of yourself. Didn't you become a doctor because you want to help people?"

"I don't see how this is any of your concern." Doc Whitlow doesn't even look at her as he speaks. He's too busy fiddling with his finger, which slants at an unnatural angle. "You're just this man's flavor of the week, sweetie."

I've had all I can take. I look around the room for something to throttle this man to death with, but Cat rushes past in a blur of blonde hair and rage. A flash of silver glints in her hand as she leaps onto him and presses the object against his throat.

It's a pair of scissors, and one of the blades presses dangerously close to a thumping artery.

"Listen here, you piece of shit. I'm not a flavor of the week, month, or year. I'm not anything so pleasant as a flavor at all. And you have pissed me the fuck off. Tell me what you've done."

I rock back on my heels with a grin I can't suppress. "You've fucked up now," I say through a laugh.

"Get her off me," Doc Whitlow whines. "Your mother can stay. We can work out a payment plan."

"Fuck you!" Cat spits into his gaping mouth and presses more weight into the blade. "Not only will you let his mother stay here, but you'll also upgrade her to the highest level of care and luxury. She will be kept at this facility for the remainder of her life or until Bennett chooses to move her, and neither Bennett nor anyone else will ever owe a dime."

"I can't do that!" Doc Whitlow shouts. "I own the facility, but there are partners."

"Then *you'll* cover her bills. Don't piss me off, shit head." Cat drags the scissors at a downward angle, and a thin red ribbon of blood unfurls from his neck.

"You cut me!" He reaches toward the small wound, hardly larger than the width of a pinky nail. Pussy.

He's getting a little wiggly now, and I don't want Cat to get hurt, so I step closer. That's enough to settle him again.

Before Cat can continue negotiations, my phone buzzes in my pocket. As I pull it out, I see Jim's name flash across the screen. I answer the call.

"Bennett, my boy, how is your mother?" he asks. No pleasantries, just straight to the heart of the matter.

I look down at the doctor. "We were lied to," I say. "She's as good as she was before I left for the trip. Whitlow decided to bluff for payment."

Jim grunts on the other end of the line. "I never liked that man. Hand him the phone."

My eyebrows pull together as I hold the phone toward the doctor. I never knew they were acquainted.

"It's for you," I say with a smirk.

Doc Whitlow takes the phone and licks his lips, trying to wet them with his sandpaper tongue. "Hello?"

His eyes widen and his skin turns a ghostly gray as Jim says something to him, but his demeanor quickly shifts to something more joyful. He smiles and nods, offering yeses at every turn.

Cat keeps the scissors in place, ensuring he can't lash out at either of us, but she looks between me and the phone repeatedly. Questions haunt her eyes, but I know about as much as she does.

Is that Jim? she mouths.

I nod.

The color returns to Doc Whitlow's cheeks, and he hands the phone back to me. I press it to my ear.

"Turn him loose," Jim says. "I'm buying out his little hospital spa, and I'll replace any staff as you see fit. Your mother will never want for anything again, Bennett, I promise you that."

My shoulders droop. Owing a friend money is far worse

than owing money to an asshole. At least you don't have to feel guilty when you can't pay the asshole.

I shake my head. "I can't do that, Jim. You know my situation."

"Oh, about that. Once the deal is done and the hospital has transferred ownership, I want you to take on your first hit under me. After the appropriate amount of time has passed, you'll murder Doctor Whitlow so that I can recoup my money." He laughs on the other end of the phone, the devious joy palpable in that tittering sound.

But then his words register.

"First? You're . . ."

"Yes. I'm hiring you. Unlike your previous employer, I like your flair, boy. I didn't want to mention it at the retreat because I don't like to mix personal time and business, but now the retreat is over. I'm already at the airport, ready to head back to my island."

I stumble backward and sit on the hospital bed. "Are you serious?"

"As a heart attack."

That's a horrible choice of words, because I fear I'm about to have one now.

"Bennett, what's wrong?" Cat asks.

I motion for her to come to me, and after a moment's hesitation, she slides away from the doctor and sits beside me on the bed.

"What's wrong?" I say with a laugh. "Absolutely nothing now."

I lean down and kiss her.

Chapter Fifty-Three

Cat

Down on the first floor, Bennett leads me through a maze of hallways until we reach a glass wall overlooking a courtyard. Aside from a woman sitting at a small table near the hedges, the grounds are empty.

My body still hasn't adjusted to the difference in temperature. Each time we step outside, I brace myself for a frigid wind, and this time is no different. But the cold doesn't come, and we're bathed in Florida sunshine as we step toward the woman at the table.

Bennett warned me that he doesn't know what state of mind she's in. He said she may be a little confused. I don't have any experience with diseases of the mind, so I don't know what to expect.

As we draw near, she lowers her coffee cup and looks up at us. She gives Bennett a wave, but I see no recognition in her eyes. My heart breaks for him, but then I see the smile on his face.

"Hey, Miss Tierney. I've brought a friend to see you."

He places his hand on the small of my back and pushes me toward her. "Her name's Cat, and she made a very long trip to say hello."

His mother looks up at me, then fiddles with her hair. "Oh goodness, all this way for me? Are you here for more tests?"

"No, Miss Tierney. You just sounded like someone I'd like to be friends with." I take a seat across from her and hold out my hand.

She reaches across the table and slides her soft palm against mine. "We can all use more friends, can't we?" With a smile, she shakes my hand. "Please, call me Connie."

"It's very nice to meet you, Connie."

"Are you and this young man . . . ?" She motions between me and Bennett and raises her eyebrows.

"Oh, yes. We're . . ." I look back at Bennett, and he nods. "We're together."

The frail woman shakes her head. "No wonder my boy can't find a good girl. They're all taken."

"I'm sure he'll find someone. When he's ready," I say.

"Sir, would you be kind and fetch an orderly? I'd like to share a cup of tea with my new friend here." Connie reaches toward her cup, but her fingers fumble with the tiny vessel, and it falls into her lap.

Bennett steps toward her as she fumbles with the spilled drink in her lap. He places a napkin into her hand, and she wipes her pants. Her cheeks blaze pink, and she's clearly embarrassed.

"I'm such a butterfingers." She forces a smile. "I'm afraid I'll have to go up to the house to change, but I'll return shortly."

As she rises from the iron table, her chair totters behind her and falls over. Bennett rushes to her side to help her, righting her when she nearly falls. Her face changes. Fear and uncertainty cloud her features, and her eyes aren't as clear as they were moments ago.

"Miss Tierney—Connie, can I help you up to your room?" I say.

She shakes her head, sending her gray hair into a flurry around her head, but she doesn't speak.

I step beside Bennett and take her arm, easing him out of the way. "That's okay. If you don't want me to go with you, I don't have to. Would you like to sit down? I can bring you more tea."

Connie's fingers grip and release the hem of her shirt, but she finally settles and sits in her chair.

Bennett grips my arm and tries to guide me away, but my feet remain planted. My hands may be shaking, and this may be a little uncomfortable, but when you love someone, you do the scary thing. You do the uncomfortable thing. And I love Bennett.

"Sometimes a strong emotion is hard for her," he whispers in my ear. "It can cause her to sort of . . . You saw it."

I place my hand over his. "It's okay, Bennett."

His shoulders finally relax.

An orderly steps outside, and we explain that Connie needs to go to her room for a fresh change of clothes. He helps her to stand, then escorts her away. As she leaves, I hope it's not the last time I see her. In fact, she's just given me the last piece of the puzzle that I've been missing.

"I'm really sorry about this. I don't know what I expected." Bennett runs his hands through his hair. "I just wanted you to meet her, that's all."

"Don't you dare apologize." I round on him and fold my arms over my chest. "That's the woman who raised you, and I feel honored that you introduced us. Sure, I don't know much about her disease or how best to interact with her, but I want to learn."

Bennett blinks down at me. "Huh?"

"Just now, speaking with your mother . . . it reminded me of what it felt like to care for my brother. And it feels good, Bennett. It feels . . . right."

"What are you saying?"

I smile. I can't help it. I've never seen things so plainly before, never been filled with so much hope for my future. "Acting hasn't worked out because it's not what I'm meant to do. It's what I've wanted to do, but even if I'd succeeded, it wouldn't have left me fulfilled."

"So you're just going to give up on your dream? Just like that? What will you do?"

I shrug and shake my head. Uncertainty has never felt so good. "I have no idea. Go back to school, for a start. I can figure out where I go from there, but I think I'd like a career in nursing."

"You're serious?"

"Yes."

I wait for him to say something, but he just stares at me. The excitement dips, and I worry he's upset with my plan or that he thinks I'm being a stupid, silly girl or that—

"I am so fucking proud of you." He pulls me into his arms and kisses me. "Whatever you want to do, I'll support you. But what does this mean for the Confessor?"

"The Confessor?"

He pulls me closer, that devilish smirk playing on his face as he looks down at me. "Yeah. I mean, you found your tag line. *Tell me what you've done.* Tweak it a bit—*tell me your sins*—and bam, you've got your name. The Confessor."

"Hot damn, you're right!" If I smile much wider, my fucking cheeks will split. "Even if I become a nurse, I don't plan to give up my new hobby. I enjoy helping people, but I also enjoy ending people who deserve it. Can't I do both?"

"Kitten, with me by your side, you can do whatever you want."

And as he kisses me again, I know it's true.

Epilogue

Three Months Later

Bennett

A newspaper looks up at me from the kitchen table in my New York apartment. Well, the apartment Cat and I share. We have a second apartment in Florida so that we can visit my mom and check on Jim's newest business venture, and a third in Portland so we can visit her parents. Being under Jim's employ has done wonders for my bank account.

So much so that I've already paid for Cat's upcoming semester at a local community college.

Cat lies on the couch, stretched out with Shorty on her lap. She chews the tip of a pen as she studies a crossword puzzle. The cat jumps down and slinks under the couch as she sits up.

"What's a six-letter word for a weapon of mass destruction?"

Sounds of mass destruction burble underneath the couch as the cat begins using his claws to remove the underpinning.

"Shorty," I say.

"Ha. Ha." Cat lies back again. "I'm serious."

"So am I. That may not be a designer couch, but I worked hard to pay for it."

Cat rolls her eyes. "You shoved a bottle rocket into a man's ass and lit it on fire, then laughed as he bled out. I was there, remember? There wasn't very much hard work going on." Her eyes light up, and she presses the pen to the paper. "Rocket! That's the word!"

"Have you seen the paper?" I lift it from the table and go to the couch. Cat raises her legs, and I scoot beneath them. "Look at the front page."

She plucks the paper from my hand, reads the bold headline, and smiles. "The Confessor strikes again," she says. "I'll never get used to that."

Doctor Whitlow was her most recent kill. We finally made that fucker pay for the little stunt he pulled, and we also discovered that Cat wasn't so far off when she initially asked him what his sins were. As it turned out, he'd been abusing elderly men in his facility for years.

With him fully out of the picture, my mother's safety is assured. Her health has steadily declined, and the time I have left with her is limited, but with Cat planning to become a hospice nurse, we'll soon be able to bring her home.

My phone rings, and a woman's name flashes on the screen. I hurry to push my phone into my pocket before Cat notices.

"Hey, I gotta take this call."

She places the newspaper on the coffee table and resumes her crossword. "Who is it?"

I frown and shake my head. I hate lying to her, but she can't know about this. "Just work."

The phone stops ringing before I reach the bedroom, so I hurry and pull it from my pocket and return the call. The woman answers on the second ring.

"Hey, did you still want to meet today?" she asks.

I peer through the crack in the door to be sure Cat is still occupied. "Uh, yeah. Can we meet later tonight? I'm having friends over in a bit, and I didn't want you and I to feel rushed."

"Now would be better. My husband will be home around three, and he wants to know as little as possible about my little hobby. It pisses him off, but he says as long as he doesn't have to be around it, it's whatever."

Yeah, I get it. I wouldn't like it if this were Cat's hobby, either. My skin crawls at the thought.

"I can be there in twenty," I say. "Is the agreed amount the same?"

She confirms, and I end the call.

Back in the living room, Shorty has taken up his spot in her lap once more. He kneads her stomach, his eyes half closed as a beam of sunlight warms his stupid back.

"I'm heading to the store. Do you need anything?" I ask.

Cat nibbles the pen. "No, but don't forget that everyone's coming over around six. I called that wing place you like, but they don't deliver. You'll have to pick up the food."

I brush the hair from her face and lean down to kiss her forehead. "I'll get it taken care of."

Then I leave the apartment to do something I know I'll regret.

By the time everyone arrives, the apartment has never felt so small.

Maverick and Eve sit at the kitchen table. The two have become best friends since the winter retreat, and they're even discussing moving in together. That's if Eve stops setting him up on disaster dates with her straight friends.

Kindra, Ezra, and Jim crowd together on the tiny loveseat. Kindra and Ezra sat down first, and Jim just sort of did what Jim does and inserted himself into the situation. I've never seen Kindra look more uncomfortable.

Grim and Rose even showed up for a few minutes, but they made their excuses and left as abruptly as they arrived. No one knows where they're headed, but no one ever does.

And then there's Cat. She bustles around the apartment, refilling drinks and playing the part of hostess.

"Bennett, where are the wings? Didn't you pick them up?" Cat rushes around the kitchen in search of the food she won't find.

"Shit, sorry. I completely forgot."

She nibbles her lip and looks around the kitchen once more. "Didn't you go to the store this afternoon? Where's the cake?"

A gasp comes from the living room, followed by Kindra nearly shouting, "You bought a what?"

Everyone heads into the living room.

"Who bought what?" Eve says. "I'm a nosy bitch, and inquiring minds want to know."

"Jim bought a cruise ship," Ezra says.

We all turn to look at the man beaming up at us with childlike enthusiasm.

Jim stands, puffing his chest as he walks to the head of the room. "We had so much fun with our vacations, so I thought, why stop here? Why not expand and have something for us to do year-round?"

"Maybe because some of us have jobs," Kindra says.

"Or school," Cat adds. "Plus, I get seasick."

Maverick holds up his hands. "Hang on, let's not shit on this just yet. I mean, a cruise ship does sound like a pretty nice vacation."

"Murdering at sea could be fun," Eve adds. "I'm in."

Jim holds up a finger with a sparkle in his eye. "Oh, I can promise none of you will want to miss this. I have plans for certain . . . changes. It will be very interesting."

"Just so long as there are no secret passages that everyone refuses to tell me about," I say with a roll of my eyes. "I'm still pissed about that one in Alaska."

Ezra laughs and shakes his head. "Wait, you still don't know?"

"No, don't ruin it now!" Cat shouts.

"There was no secret passage in the winter mansion," Jim says. "Cat fabricated the entire story to vex you, and we all went with it."

Cat folds her arms over her chest. "Damn. That was a good joke, and now it's over."

"Hang on. Back up to the cruise again. What about the Texas trip?" I say. "What happened to planning that? Our sister is still in the wind, and we want to find her, don't we?"

Ezra shrugs. "We have no new leads, Bennett. We might have to accept that we will only ever have each other."

I open my mouth to argue, but a crash in the bedroom interrupts me. More specifically, a crash in the closet, where the proof of my lies currently hides.

"What was that?" Cat asks. She starts toward the bedroom, but I grab her hand and pull her back.

"It's probably just Shorty," I say, but then the big black fucker hears his name and pokes his head from beneath the couch. When he realizes we still have guests, he hides again.

Cat looks at me and cocks her head. "What are you hiding?"

Fuck.

I blow out a breath. I didn't want to do this right now, but I don't have a choice.

"Just . . . stay here," I say, not wanting the entirety of our friend group to enter our bedroom. I'm not sure we put away the sex swing last night.

Embarrassment colors my cheeks as I walk to the bedroom. An entire room full of people is about to witness a very dark moment for Bennett Carter, but I love Cat. I love her with every fiber of my being, even if it's to my detriment.

When I return to the group, I hold a box toward Cat. It's large enough that I have to wrap my arms around it to carry it, though what it holds isn't that large. Yet.

"What is this?" Cat takes the box from my arms and lowers it to the floor. Her fingers grip the fancy ribbon and pull it away, and she removes the top and looks inside.

"When I left to go to the store, I was really going to pick this up," I say. "That's why I left the room earlier. The lady called while you were working on your crossword puzzle."

Too stunned to speak, she reaches into the silk-lined box and lifts a fluffy silver ball of fur to her chest. A very expensive, extensively papered, and thoroughly adorable kitten, to be exact.

"Is that the one you wanted? Saharan?" I ask.

"Siberian," Cat cries into the kitten's fur. "Yes, this is the one. Oh my god, he's so perfect, Bennett."

Ezra steps closer to me, then speaks so that only I can

hear him as everyone else oohs and ahhs over the kitten. "I thought you hated the damned things. What possessed you to buy a second one?"

I shake my head and shrug my shoulders. "I don't fucking know."

He pats my shoulder and smirks. "Yeah, you do."

Cat looks up at me with tear-filled eyes, then struggles to stand with the adorable shit stain in her hands. But she manages. "I love you so much," she says.

And yeah, I know the reason why I did it. It's the reason we all make stupid decisions and do stupid things. It's one hell of a sleigh ride, winding through trees and often feeling like we're heading for a cliff, but we take it anyway.

I brush the hair from her forehead, not caring who's here to see. And with a smirk, I bend down and kiss the woman I love.

Check out *Ship Happens*, the third book in the Slaycation series: Books2read.com/ShipHappens

Want to read something other than a rom-com? Check out Lauren's dark-lite offerings.
Stranger Session: Books2read.com/StrangerSession
Her Fantasy: Books2read.com/HerFantasy
Last Mistake: Books2read.com/LastMistake
Protect Me: Books2read.com/ProtectMeNovella

If you're ready to dive into darker reads, check out Lauren's

hitchhiker romance standalones in her Ride or Die series. These can be read in any order.
Hitched: Books2read.com/Hitched
Along for the Ride: Books2read.com/MFMHitchhiker
Driving my Obsession: Books2read.com/DrivingmyObsession
Across State Lines: Books2read.com/AcrossStateLines
Don't Stop: Books2read.com/Dont-Stop

Connect with Lauren

Don't miss a thing from Lauren Biel! Check out all of her books, social media connections, and other important information at Campsite.bio/LaurenBielAuthor and LaurenBiel.com

Acknowledgments

To my VIP gals, Jessie, Nikita, Lexi, Grace, and Kim, I love you more than I can explain!

Thank you to my husband for dealing with millions of questions.

Brooke, my editor, you're the best and I couldn't have done this without you.

Thank you to my valued Patrons. Your contribution helped make this book happen!

Ashley S, Nikkie B, Rebecca C, Kaat, Monnah P, Emily S, Kimberly G, Chan, Amber F, Lilybeth S, A.Reads, Samantha O, Danielle M, Megan S, Danielle N, Sunshine_the_Bookie, Sara M, Harley B, Jenn C, Heather M, Bonnie F, Lauren S, Pyro, Iris, Marguerite, Courtney, PaigeeBear, Sarah S, Tiffany M, Tara H, Vikki S, Amanda T, _____ britneyxO, Suzy A, Andie J, Lisa W, Court's Bookshelf, Nicholetta88, Emily S, Sheena E, Queen Ilmaree, SerenaLorraine, Iesha E, AprilCoats, Jasmine K, Heather S, Lizzie Borden, Jennifer S, Just Jen Here, Mikasa_Kuchiki, Jada W, Briyanna M, Gini R, Shannan T, Heather C, Jesi D, Charmaine B, Michelle, Christy P, Melissa, Dani C, Sandie W, Kayla T, Arnica S, Cassi K, Gumdrop, Maxine T, Amanda C, Barrie, Alexandria R, Leeat S, DirtyPanda,

Leslie W, Jordyn J, Kayla M, Marisa K, Smitty, Brooke, Ashley P, Mandy G, Bailey A, Anna S, Shelby F, Tiannah B, Sharee S, Courtney P, Kristiana B, Vero A, Chelle, Sara S, Samantha R, Jessica G, Kimberly S, StjoReads, Tabitha F, JesStenger, Lindsey S, Laura T, Joanna, Nicole M, Nineette W, BoneDaddyAshe, Kimberly B

Also by Lauren Biel

To view Lauren Biel's complete list of books, visit: https://laurenbiel.com/laurenbielbooks/

About the Author

Lauren Biel is the author of many dark romance books, with several more titles in the works. When she's not working, she's writing. When she's not writing, she's spending time with her husband, her friends, or her pets. You might also find her on a horseback trail ride or sitting beside a waterfall in Upstate New York. When reading her work, expect the unexpected. To be the first to know about her upcoming titles, please visit www.LaurenBiel.com.